Veritas Series

CAT'S PAW
KILLING GAME
BROKEN DREAMS

CAT'S PAW

A Veritas Novel

Jana Oliver

 Nevermore Books

**Published by
MageSpell LLC
Coimbra, Portugal**

This work is a novel of fiction. Names, characters, places, and incidents are the product of the author's imagination and are not to be construed as real. Any resemblance to actual persons, living or dead, events or locales, businesses or organizations is entirely coincidental.

CAT'S PAW

A Veritas Novel

ISBN: 978-1-941527-31-3
2nd Edition

Cover Art courtesy of Belaurient Arts

Acknowledgments

An author can write a book, but it takes a village
to see it published.

Mollie Traver (www.MollieTraver.com) who supplied the
editorial and copy-editing expertise.

Lily Elliott, who served as my Russian translator.

Melanie Fletcher (https://melaniefletcher.com/belaurient-arts)
who created the cover design.

~ Jana Oliver
August 2025

In an effort to make your reading experience
as enjoyable as possible, we have chosen not to
right margin justify the typeset text,
although this is industry standard.

Studies have shown that people with reading
difficulties, including those with dyslexia, find
it easier to follow free-flowing text, with better
reading comprehension as a result.

"Every saint has a past, and every sinner has a future."

~ Oscar Wilde, A Woman of No Importance

Chapter One

His nerves on edge, Alexander Parkin carried his tray to the long dining table lined with other inmates, his final breakfast in prison. He'd eaten 1,825 of these in Angola. Maybe fewer, given the time he'd spent recovering in the infirmary.

Last day. Last chance to kill me.

Muted conversations flowed around him, some between men who had become his friends, some between his enemies. Alex had long ago accepted that some grudges wouldn't die until he did.

It wouldn't matter that he'd been marked "off limits" by Grigori Danshov, the nephew of New Orleans's notorious drug kingpin. Or that the Russian had recently reissued that warning, in case someone thought to settle scores before Alex's release. Even Mikhail, his cellmate, had remained close over the last week, a deadly deterrent.

The room fell into abnormal silence at his arrival, as if the others heard the same clock ticking down. When the attack finally came, Alex would be ready. In fact, he would welcome it.

He nodded at a couple of his fellow prisoners and set his tray on the table, his senses on overload. Everything was heightened now: the smell of the food, the heat, the funk of too many men in one place. Mikhail had just begun to ask him a question when Alex felt the air shift behind him. Before his friend could bark a warning, he was on the move.

Spinning, he grabbed the brown, muscled arm as the shank drove toward him. Leveraging his weight, Alex yanked the prisoner down, ramming his wrist against the edge of the table. The audible snap of bones filled the room, followed by a shriek as the shank tumbled free. He followed up with a knee to Jesus Martinez's nuts, which turned the shriek into a high-pitched scream.

The blood beast rose within Alex, the one that demanded this bastard die. Make him and his kind pay for the hell Alex had endured all these years. A quick stab in the chest, and it'd be over before the guards could interfere.

His hands shook now, eager to take the next step, to strike back. To prove he wasn't helpless. That he wasn't the man he'd once been.

"*Nyet!* Not worth it," Mikhail called out.

God, he's right.

Alex released his grip and the would-be assassin collapsed to the floor. *No way I'm taking the heat for this.* He made sure to nudge the shank close to Martinez's writhing body.

Breathing heavily, hyped up on adrenaline, he turned to find every eye on him. "Who's next?" he said.

There were laughs, a few frowns. The show over, those who'd risen resumed their seats. Martinez's pained cries abruptly cut off when one of the guards jammed a boot in his side.

"Can it, asshole. You started it," the man said. He scrutinized Alex now. "You hurt?"

"No."

What if they blamed him for this brawl?

"Had to know it'd be Martinez," the guard continued. "I wondered when he'd take a crack at you."

It hadn't surprised Alex either. The wiry gangbanger was a member of Los Impíos, and they hated him. When he'd been with the DEA, he had cost them some major bucks every time he'd confiscated one of their loads.

"I just lost twenty-five bucks," the guard added, shaking his head.

Mikhail had told Alex there was a betting pool as to his survivability.

"What are the odds now?" he asked, genuinely curious.

"Hundred to one that you wouldn't clear the front gate on your own two feet," the man responded matter-of-factly.

Better than Alex had expected. When he'd first arrived, it'd been a thousand to one. Martinez stifled a cry when he was hauled to his feet. He spat at Alex, outraged Spanish filling the room. Alex murmured an insult back and Martinez went crazy, trying to tear himself out of the guards' arms, his shouts following him out of the dining hall.

"What did you say to him?" the head guard asked.

"I told him his mother is very pretty."

The guard raised an eyebrow.

"Well, something like that."

The man laughed. "Good thing you're leaving today, Parkin."

"Can't be soon enough."

There had been times when Alex had believed today would never come. His "welcome" to Angola five years before had been brutal, a wake-up call. A trio of drug dealers he'd sent up during his time at the DEA had delivered that welcome. They'd made sure to crack four ribs, bruise his kidneys, rip open his neck, and break his left arm. Would have done worse if they hadn't been stopped as they'd pulled down his pants.

Never show fear.

It had become his mantra. It would remain so.

His other mantra? Find the son of a bitch who had framed him and make him pay. But first, his last meal here. Now that the action was over, the room quieted. Alex settled on the bench, pulling his plate closer, noting that his hands shook. Mikhail delivered a proud nod from across the table, then went back to eating his breakfast.

"I wondered if it'd be Jesus," Alex said quietly. "He's a hotheaded little prick."

"Soon to be a dead one," Mikhail replied, his accent heavy. "Grigori will not appreciate that his orders were ignored."

"That too."

Mikhail Yovanoff was a lifer, a contract killer who worked for Vladimir Buryshkin. Mikhail had been the best of Alex's cellies, and he would miss him. Over the years, they'd forged a friendship as the Russian had protected him, taught Alex his native language. Pretty decent for a stone-cold contract killer who had at least a dozen hits to his credit. He'd probably be the one to put Martinez in a shroud.

Mikhail took a sip of coffee, his fingers revealing multiple tattoos. "You handled that well, Sasha."

Sasha was the Russian diminutive for Alexander, and it'd taken a while for Alex to answer to the name. Now he rather liked it.

He nodded gratefully. "I learned from the best. Thank you, my friend."

Mikhail nodded back. His eyes rose to someone behind Alex, but this time they held no warning. Alex turned, then stood to shake Grigori's hand. Tall, thin, and blond, he cut a wide swath through the prison. Few would mess with him. Those who did ended up dead, or worse.

"I shall miss you," the young Russian said. "Not for long, though. I shall be free myself very soon, God willing."

"Hunt me up. I'll buy you a beer. Hell, I'll buy as many as you want."

Some would say that associating with members of the Russian mob when just out of prison probably wasn't the smartest move. Alex might not want to work for him or his uncle, but he could at least buy the man a drink.

He kept me alive.

"Make it Russian vodka and we have a deal."

"You're on. You finally going to tell me who framed me?"

Grigori shook his head. "Not today." He leaned over so only Alex could hear him. "'*Voda kamen tochet.*'" Even as Alex worked through the Russian, Grigori added, "'*Water wears away stone.*'"

He straightened up. "Be patient, Sasha. Your time will come."

It was classic Grigori. The man was an enigma, a scholarly Russian who had come to Alex's aid the night he'd nearly been raped. Grigori had arranged to have Mikhail be Alex's cellmate to keep him alive. But he was also Buryshkin favorite nephew, so he was deep inside the mobster's organization.

All this care meant one thing: The elder crime lord wanted Alex alive for some reason and the moment he exited the prison gates, that debt would become due.

"You got all that?" The balding paper pusher handling Alex's discharge sounded bored, but then, how many of the inmates had he set free only to have them roll right back through the doors down the line?

"Yeah, I got it." Alex had a portion of the money he'd brought with him to prison, plus some sent by a friend. He'd signed the appropriate discharge papers. At least he wasn't required to have regular visits with a parole officer.

"Hope you got good shoe leather. Your ride called. She isn't going to make it."

"What? Why?" Alex had made the arrangements with his sister a month ago, and now she'd bailed on him?

The man shrugged. He handed Alex a full bottle of water and grinned. "Go forth and sin no more."

The opportunity to sin was limited: There wasn't a bus from the prison to St. Francisville, nearly twenty-five miles away. Which meant he'd have to hitchhike.

Alex swore under his breath.

Ten minutes later, he stood outside the fortress that had been his home for so long. In one hand was a plastic bag with his belongings, all he possessed in this world after thirty-two years. In the other was the bottle of water.

His heart raced and he was sweating, not only because the morning was heating up. The day was clear, the weather as humid as you'd expect for mid-September in Louisiana, a thick blanket that seemed to press down on his body like a dead weight. Another day in the South and his first one outside the wire.

His disappointment was as oppressive as the humidity. This was supposed to be when he reunited with his sister. He'd actually dreamed of this moment. The *one* day he really wanted Miri to be there for him, and she wasn't. There would be no chance for them to spend a few hours catching up on their lives, starting over. This was her revenge, pure and simple. He'd fucked over her life, and now she was doing the same to him.

Alex glanced back at the guard towers, the concertina wire. He was free. *Free.* The word didn't feel right, at least not yet. Maybe someday.

Maybe never.

Chapter Two

As he dragged the back of his hand over his sweaty forehead, Alex judged that he was two hours into his hike, though he had no watch or phone to verify that estimate. If he was right, it should be about noon. His stomach concurred.

The heat rose off the road in unrelenting waves, baking him like a piece of overcooked meat. He slapped at another bug that had nailed him on the neck. They'd proven relentless.

Just another kind of hell.

The road signs posted near the prison, warning drivers not to pick up hitchhikers, had reduced his chances of a ride to zip. He couldn't argue with that wisdom, except when it came to him.

According to one of the more helpful guards, he had two ways to get to the town. He could stick to the main highway, which angled north before it cut back south, adding another hour to an already eight-hour hike. Or cut through the Tunica Hills, which would offer fewer chances to be picked up by a passing motorist. He'd opted for the latter, eager to get home.

It wasn't long before Alex had regretted that decision. He'd already stripped out of his shirt and stuffed it inside his bag. Right now, he'd commit armed robbery for another bottle of water. Hell, it didn't even have to be cold.

At this rate, he wouldn't make St. Francisville until five or six in the evening. Then, if he was lucky, he'd find someone headed for Baton Rouge, where he could catch a bus. At this rate, he wouldn't be at home in New Orleans until midnight.

Alex heard the sound of an approaching car and turned, casting a hopeful thumbs-up, though he knew it was a waste of time. As expected, the black sedan flew by him.

"Thanks for nothing," he muttered, dropping his thumb.

To his surprise, the car slowed and then stopped along the side of the road.

"All right!" he said, taking off at a jog. As he drew near, he realized it was a BMW with tan leather seats. A carjacker's wet dream.

The passenger window rolled down in a smooth motion. The driver wore tortoiseshell sunglasses, her mink brown hair up in a loose bun with a few tendrils floating down onto her slim neck. He guessed her to be in her early thirties. From what he could see, her body was lingerie-model worthy, with that toned "I will rock your world" vibe.

A light tan emphasized her subtle curves, from the sleeveless, blood-red silk top that clung to her ample breasts, to the molded pair of jeans. His instincts twitched. What the hell was she doing out in the middle of nowhere?

Bait. She had to be. Just the kind of thing Vladimir Buryshkin would use to get him on the team. What else would a hot and horny ex-con want?

The woman flipped up her sunglasses, revealing startling green eyes.

"Need a ride?" she asked, her voice low.

But no hint of a Russian accent. For some reason, that made him even more uneasy.

"Do you usually pick up hitchhikers?" he demanded.

"Depends."

"It's dangerous riding around with strangers," he said, as if that wasn't obvious.

"I promise to be on my *very* best behavior," she replied.

Alex frowned. He could easily become the victim here. This woman could claim he tried to rape her, and then he'd be back in a cell. Or working for Buryshkin to make those bogus charges magically vanish.

"I'll pass," he said, and set off again.

Rather than blowing down the highway, she coasted alongside him.

"Are you crazy?" she said. "It's hotter than hell out there. Besides, I have a proposition for you."

His instincts had been right. "I'm not interested. I have my own plans."

"We know. You want to find out who planted the coke in your house. We can help you with that."

He ignored her and kept walking.

"Come on, Parkin, don't be an idiot." At the mention of his name, Alex came to a halt, as did the car. "We have resources you can't even imagine. We can make this happen for you."

"Who are you?"

"Morgan Blake."

"Okay then, *Morgan Blake*. The answer is still no. Just stay the hell out of my life."

"You can't be serious."

"Go the fuck away!" he shouted. "Tell your boss the same."

His anger appeared to stun her. "It's your call. And your funeral."

The woman left him behind on a road that shimmered in the heat, shimmered with his anger.

All those years in Angola—having someone tell him when to sleep, when to eat, when to shower—had done a number on his head.

"This time I do it my own way. Nobody owns me now. *Nobody*."

An hour later Alex wasn't surprised to find the Beemer sitting on the side of the road, Ms. Blake leaning against the vehicle. She had a full bottle of water in hand. More bait.

"Not going there," he muttered.

Alex owed Grigori, not Grigori's uncle. Buryshkin could go screw himself. It was a fine line to walk, but Alex was good at that—or he wouldn't still be alive.

"Changed your mind yet?" she called out.

"No."

"God, you're a stubborn SOB."

He didn't bother to reply. As he walked by her, he grabbed the bottle out of her hand and kept going. And couldn't help but notice the line of sweat that had rolled down into her cleavage.

"You were a very special snowflake while you were in prison," she said. "You had Russians guarding you as if you were a rare Fabergé egg. If not for that, you'd be dead, or messed up so bad you'd have to drink your food through a straw."

"So?"

"So that means you're important to them. That intrigues us, Mr. Parkin."

Us? That hit home and he halted, turning back toward her. "You don't work for Buryshkin?"

"Hell no." She spat the words as if she'd gotten a taste of road kill.

As he thought this through, he unscrewed the cap and took a massive gulp of water to wet his throat.

It didn't matter who she worked for.

"Still not interested," he said.

"Not interested enough in knowing who put you in prison? Not interested in why you lost all those years of your life?"

She had his full attention now. "You know who it was?"

"People talk to us, and we pay attention to what they say. There were those who wanted you out of the way because you were causing trouble. You were too gung ho, and drug lords hate that sort of thing, especially if you're good at your job."

"What's the catch?"

"We want you to help us put Vladimir Buryshkin behind bars."

Well, hell. "Why me? Besides the fact that I'm a special snowflake, as you put it."

That got him a wry grin. "Because your cellmate was a Russian who excels in wet work, and you're best buds with Buryshkin's nephew. That gives you a leg up in their organization."

"And?"

"Since Grigori watched your back all these years, there's going to be a quid pro quo for that protection. We want you on our team when his uncle insists you join his organization. Because he will."

"You sound really sure of that."

"We are."

"So who the hell are you people?" he demanded.

"We're the people who are going to keep you and your sister Miri alive."

Miri. He hated hearing her name from anyone's lips, especially someone who had their own agenda.

"That isn't an answer," he said.

"I work for Veritas," she replied. "It's Latin for truth. You might have heard of us."

He *had* heard of them. They were a private shadow agency known for taking huge risks, the kind that law enforcement folks avoided. They'd put several big-name criminals out of circulation in ways that made the alphabet agencies envious as hell.

From what he'd heard, they were financed by a consortium of folks with incredibly deep pockets. Veritas was chummy with the kind of VIPs who could smooth things over when they colored outside the lines, which was most of the time.

Rumors said they had a friend in the Oval Office, one at 10 Downing Street, and others in rarefied offices across the globe, including the Vatican. But no matter their connections, they weren't part of any government and that made them even more dangerous.

"You work for us," she continued, "and we'll give you all we have once Buryshkin is in custody. Or dead."

It was a sure bet the drug lord would try to recruit him. Could he parlay that into a takedown and restore his reputation? Was it worth the risk? A sharp flash of hope ignited in his chest, then went out just as quickly. Even if the courts found he'd been set up, no one in the DEA would welcome him back. He was tainted goods.

No way.

It was suicide. If the Russians thought he was working for Veritas, they'd kill him. No matter what this woman said, he couldn't trust her or the people she worked for. If he did, he'd be putting his sister in danger, and nothing was worth that risk.

Alex drained the last of the water. He tossed the empty bottle at her and she caught it effortlessly. "No deal."

"Huh. I thought you were smart. You could have at least strung me along until I drove you to the next town."

He set off again, ignoring her.

"You will regret this," Morgan called out. "The Russians won't ask. If you turn them down, they'll go after your sister. We can keep her safe."

He caught the threat and spun around. "You go anywhere near Miri, I'll break you. You got that?"

"You won't get the chance, not once Buryshkin is done with you."

"Just stay the hell away from her."

Morgan got in her car, then caught up with him. The passenger window went down again.

"If you ever grow a pair, let us know. Maybe we'll still be interested."

A full bottle of water landed at his feet right before the Beemer zoomed away, kicking up dust. He resisted the urge to flip off the driver. As the car vanished from view, his gut told him he might have made a big mistake.

Chapter Three

"Stupid, stubborn prick!" Morgan said, barreling past the speed limit.

No wonder Parkin had made enemies at the DEA. That lone-warrior, "I'm smarter than anyone else" crap was what had gotten him hung out to dry. It still was.

She should have expected his reaction. She'd read everything she could about Alexander Michael Parkin: his psychiatric evaluations, his medical and college records. She expected him to have changed—you didn't do all that time in a maximum-security prison and not come out scarred. Now he was a powder keg waiting for an open flame.

"You're trouble," she muttered. The kind of trouble that ruined missions and that wasn't an option with this one. She wanted revenge. So did he. "Which is why we should be working together."

With another long string of swear words, Morgan let her foot off the gas, allowing the car to slow of its own accord. She didn't need a ticket.

I blew it.

She'd been so sure he'd want a chance to clear his name that she hadn't even considered it might be a hassle. Now, looking back, it would have been better to have had one of the others in her team serve as Parkin's contact. Someone male, maybe.

As she got within spitting distance of the speed limit, she knew it was time to report the bad news.

"Phone CW," Morgan said, and the car obediently connected to her boss.

"I'm guessing it's a no go if you're calling me," Crispin Wilder said, not bothering with a greeting. His accent was hard to place, a blend of British and European, with a dash of the Old South.

"It was a total wash. He wants nothing to do with us. He's on his own crusade."

"I gather the Russians haven't made their move yet."

"Not from what I can tell. I give it a week before Parkin's facedown in an alley with a bullet in the back of his head. They aren't going to allow for that kind of disrespect."

"We'll see. Knowing Buryshkin, he'll find a way to push the con's buttons. We may yet have a chance to bring him onto our team."

Not likely.

But then, Crispin was a strategist. In his forties, he spoke at least ten languages fluently and had logged serious time doing super-secret activities that he never spoke of. He had good instincts.

Morgan often envisioned him as a very savvy spider sitting in the middle of a massive global web. If a twitch at the far end of that web caught his notice, one of his people would check it out. Then he'd decide if the issue needed Veritas's intervention, or if it was something that could be safely ignored. Buryshkin and his organization were way past the "let's ignore this" stage.

"The Russians will make their move soon," Crispin added, bringing her thoughts back to the situation. "Please take precautions to ensure that his sister is not harmed."

"I already have."

"Excellent." He paused. "The people in London send their regards. Your work on their behalf has made them *very* happy. They've offered to help us in any way possible in the future."

"Good." The ache in her lower back eased a bit. At least the bullet wound had healed properly. "Is their daughter getting better?"

"That will take time, I fear."

It always did in kidnapping cases. Especially when the kidnappers buried their victim in a pit and left her to die.

"Keep me in the loop on Parkin," Crispin added. "If he doesn't go for our offer, we'll have to decide what to do next."

"How aggressive can I get?"

"As aggressive as you want. If my sources are correct, there's a power struggle about to erupt inside the Russian's organization, and if we don't get a handle on it, there may be open warfare."

"I'll let you know how it plays out."

"Thank you, Morgan."

As the miles rolled by, she found herself replaying the confrontation with Alex Parkin. At six-two or so, all muscles after his stint in prison, he was ruggedly handsome with dark hair, a deep tan, and flinty brown eyes that had seemed to pierce right through her skin. But that all-male package included a strong dose of arrogance, the kind that made her angry. Now she'd been forced to protect the fool from himself.

After two more phone calls to put her plan in motion, she synced up her smartphone with the radio. Carlos Jean's "Prisoners" filled the car.

Parkin's dark eyes occupied her thoughts again. For all his bravado, the man was hurt and angry and confused. It was like finding an injured puppy on the side of the road. You just couldn't drive by and leave him behind.

But she had done just that, and dammit, now she felt guilty.

Chapter Four

Alex's luck had finally turned on the main highway to St. Francisville. An older Black man in a truck picked him up. The man even let Alex use his phone. The first call on the outside was to his sister.

"Miri? It's Alex."

"You got my message, right?" His sister sounded upset, angry, all of the above.

"I got the message that you weren't picking me up. I know you're pissed at me, but stranding my ass—"

"I had a flat tire and no spare. I didn't have a way to get it fixed fast enough, so I couldn't come get you."

Oh. No doubt the prison office *had* gotten her message and just hadn't bothered to pass it on. One final way to screw him over. And he'd thought she had blown him off.

"Sorry, sis. I got a ride," he said.

"Where are you now?"

"Nearing St. Francisville. I'll try to catch a ride from there to Baton Rouge."

"Okay," his sister said. "I'll see you later."

She hung up on him. No "glad to hear you're out, bro." Nothing.

Hell. He knew it was going to be hard, but not this hard.

Year after year, he'd worried about a lot of things. Staying safe, avoiding anything that might lengthen his sentence, keeping on the right side of the right people so he didn't end up a corpse. Worrying about how his sister was surviving without him.

Alex had made a list of things he had to do once he was

out; get a job was number one on that list. It'd probably be working at a car wash or burger joint because of his criminal record, most likely at minimum wage. He'd tried to convince himself that anything would do at first. Maybe he could move up the ranks and . . . then what? Become a night manager at a convenience store or a Bourbon Street restaurant?

It was as if all his years with the DEA meant nothing; he was back to square one. Worse than that, because how many people wanted to hire a guy who'd been convicted of cocaine possession?

Fear wasn't his usual emotional setting, at least not until the last month or so. Was he ready for the real world? Six years was a long time—one year awaiting trial and five inside the country's largest maximum-security prison. He'd tried to stay current by reading news reports on the internet in the prison library, but that wasn't like really living out here. How much had changed?

"Everything okay?" the driver asked. He'd said that his name was Russ and he was retired. Alex noted that he hadn't said what he'd done for a living.

"Life's not great right now."

"You just get out?" the man asked, examining him with bloodshot eyes.

Alex gave him a long look. "Yeah. How'd you know?"

"The muscles. The tan. You get them from working on The Farm. You on parole?"

"Nope. 12/12." The full sentence.

"I did the same. That's why I picked you up. You looked like an ex-con. I can see it in your eyes."

"It's that noticeable?" Alex groaned.

"Only to those who've been there. You gonna do something stupid to get yourself back in there?"

"Hell no. I'm done with that."

"Good. I was the same. My life turned out okay. Maybe yours will too."

Like I believe that shit.

Once in St. Francisville, Russ took Alex to a convenience store, where he bought a pay-as-you-go phone, water, and protein bars. Then they were back on the road to Baton Rouge, because his driver refused to let him hitchhike any farther.

"The cops will check you out if you're hitching," Russ warned. "If they find out you're just out of Angola, it could get rough." That, he didn't doubt. "What were you in for?"

Alex told him the story.

"Well, shit. That sucks. I was in for armed robbery. I was good for it."

"I wasn't. It didn't matter either way."

"That's often the case," Russ replied, shaking his head.

Thirty minutes later, they were closing in on the Baton Rouge bus station.

Alex cleared his throat. "If you were me, would you want revenge on whoever fucked up your life?"

The older man sighed. "If I were your age, yes. My age? No. Wouldn't matter now."

"That's not really an answer."

"There isn't a right one. You gotta ask yourself how much this revenge is gonna cost you. What is the price you're willing to pay? You will have to decide whether that's a bill you're willing to cover."

When they pulled into the Baton Rouge bus station off Florida Boulevard, Alex thanked the man and offered to pay for gas.

"No. I won't accept it." Russ smiled. "Just do me a favor: Be sure you don't ruin your future to settle the past. The past isn't worth it. Only your future counts because that's all you've got left."

It was sound advice, which Alex knew he'd ignore.

After a quick trip to the restroom, he made his way to the ticket counter, skirting around various travelers. The noise in the station felt off, not the routine sounds he was accustomed to. He found himself becoming increasingly jittery. Prison routine had a purpose: It reminded the inmates they weren't in charge. Out here, he could go anywhere he wanted. Do anything he wanted. In many ways, that scared the hell out of him.

Alex was relieved to see he could easily afford a one-way ticket to New Orleans. The next bus left in fifteen minutes, so he bought a ticket and found himself a seat on the bus. One step closer to his sister.

He'd always been tight with his only sibling, from the moment Miri was born. That had been a given, since their mother was a drug addict and their father an over-the-road truck driver. It'd been up to eleven-year-old Alex to take care of the new baby, who probably wasn't even his dad's kid. He didn't care about that. All he knew was that Miri was the brightest light in his miserable life and he adored her.

For a time, his sister had felt the same about him, right up until he'd been arrested for possession of cocaine and her rampant hero worship had imploded. Miri grew to distrust most everyone.

Especially me.

He had to mend fences with her. Then, after he had a job, he'd figure out who had sent him to prison—and decide exactly how to take his revenge.

No matter what, there'd be blood and a lot of screaming. None of which would be his own.

Despite the uncomfortable position and the low murmuring of the other passengers, Alex didn't wake until the bus pulled into the station in New Orleans.

I'm home.

Or at least back where he'd started years earlier. As he trudged down the bus steps, he caught the smell of a city unlike any other, a blend of fish, river, people, and swamp. With a bit of jambalaya and evil thrown in to spice up the mix.

The place was busy, doubling as the city's Amtrak station.

Alex half expected to see the Blake woman waiting for him, tapping her foot, arms folded over her chest in annoyance. But there was no one to greet him except a panhandler outside the station. Alex dug into his pocket and dropped a few coins into the guy's paper cup.

"Thanks," he said, looking up with watery eyes.

"No sweat," Alex replied. He'd been at the bottom himself, what with the time in prison, but during all those years, they'd fed him and given him a place to sleep. This guy didn't even have that.

Not needing to claim any luggage, he walked outside the white stone building, his plastic bag over a shoulder. Looking up, Alex studied the hazy sky, then the buildings toward downtown. He paused for a moment, picturing where he was on a mental map, and then set off.

Miri's place was located in Central City, on the other side of the interstate. He still couldn't believe she'd be living in such a dangerous, run-down neighborhood, and that told him she was squeezing every dime she earned.

Not now. I can help her.

No one messed with him as he walked along. Prison had given him a hard look, and the people who could read that message respected it. A couple young gangbangers called out to him, but he kept moving and they made no attempt to follow.

Finally, he made the turn onto South Liberty and then paused. The street was a classic example of poor New Orleans—small one-story houses, sometimes two stories, with a few steps up from the street in case of flooding. Most had dilapidated fences shielding them from the street. Weeds grew in some of the yards, but not in others. He passed several houses that were boarded up, abandoned. A bird flew out of the broken second-story window of one.

Alex finally found Miri's rental house—not by the street number, but by the old car sitting in front of it with a flat rear tire. The house was small, and if it had been a person, it would have been drawing Social Security.

A dirty, uneven teal, it desperately pleaded for some

maintenance, starting with a coat of paint. Clearly, the landlord didn't give a damn, as the hurricane shutters were either damaged or missing, and Alex bet you could read a newspaper through the roof's pathetically thin shingles.

Jesus.

His baby sister lived here. Why the hell hadn't she told him it was this bad? Probably because there was nothing he could have done about it, not when he was earning a few cents an hour on prisoner's wages.

The place was divided into a duplex, the apartment door on the right sealed shut with warped plywood. Graffiti added a colorful touch to the dull and blackened wood. The neighbor's house to the right was even worse, with a sheet of plastic covering a broken window and a rickety porch leaning lazily to one side, seemingly unable to decide whether to collapse or keep fighting gravity. At least the place on the left was a little better, with intact windows and an old tricycle in the yard.

Gathering his courage, Alex fought the rusty gate, then walked toward his sister's front door, taking note of a few scraggly flowers growing in little plastic pots along the cracked sidewalk. Miri had always loved to garden.

He was on the porch and about to knock on the door when he felt his pride sting. If it'd been Miri coming home after so long, he'd have been watching out the window, waiting for her. But she wasn't watching for him, as if he'd just been gone for a few days. When he knocked, it took a while for the door to open, revealing a thick security chain.

His sister's brown eyes peered at him, a decade older than her twenty-one years. They looked like his—same color, same pain.

"Oh, it's you," she said. She removed the safety chain, and the worn door opened. He couldn't help but notice that she held a pistol down by her side.

When the hell had that happened?

"Always meet people at the door with a gun?" Alex asked, stepping inside and letting the flimsy door close behind him.

"Yeah. Lock it, will you?"

He did as she asked, then turned to study the house's interior. It was better than he had expected, the walls painted a pale blue and the curtains a bright white. A pale lime-green dining table—just big enough for two people—sat in a tiny kitchen.

The floors were warped wood and promised splinters to anyone adventurous enough to go barefoot. The living room furniture was likely scavenged from thrift shops and yard sales. Despite the fact that it screamed "No money here!" it felt like a home. Something he hadn't had in over six years.

A lump grew in Alex's throat as his eyes dampened. He blinked to clear them as he set the plastic bag on the lumpy black couch. Miri put the pistol in a kitchen drawer, then turned toward him. Her hair was lighter brown now, cut shoulder length, her features more filled out than he remembered. She was about four inches shorter than him, five-eight or so.

Of course she'd changed—he hadn't seen her in three years, not since her last visit to his private hell.

"Well? It's a dump, right? Just say it," she demanded.

He shook his head. "No. It looks good. I'm so damned proud of you."

He'd meant it as a compliment, but somehow that set her off.

"Well, I'm not proud of you, okay?" she shot back. "If you think you're staying here more than a couple days, you're wrong. Get a job, move on. I have my own life now."

She couldn't have hurt him more if she'd taken her gun and shot him in the heart.

"You're serious? You don't want me around?"

"No." Then she frowned. "Just . . . this isn't easy, Alex."

"Not for me either, Monkey."

"Don't call me that! I'm not some kid."

No matter what he said, it was wrong.

"Okay, whatever you want. I'll get a job and move on. But . . . " He swallowed hard. "If you need me, I'm here for you."

"You weren't for six years, why would you be now?"

"Don't you think I know that?" he said, his voice rising. "Every damned day. Every damned night, I thought of you, and—"

"Don't tell me how rough it was," she retorted, taking a step closer now. "You got three meals a day, no matter what. You didn't have to worry about someone breaking in, beating you, trying to—"

He was in front of her now, his heart thudding, wanting to hold her but not sure if she'd allow it. "God, tell me that didn't happen."

Miri shook her head. "I ran out the back door and hid a few streets over. The bastard took the TV and ripped up the place. It's why I have the gun now." She shrugged like it didn't matter, but he knew it did. "I didn't bother to get another television. They always steal them."

Tears rolled down his cheeks, shocking him. "Miri . . . Jesus, I never . . . "

She blinked at him as her own tears formed, and then they were in each other's arms, sobbing like they had when their dad had died in that truck accident. Like they had when their mom had taken that final overdose and left them orphans.

"If there is any way I can make this up to you, I will. I swear to God," he whispered.

She tugged out of his grasp, as if embarrassed to be crying. "Just don't go back to jail, you hear? No cocaine, no pills, no nothing."

"I didn't do any of that in the first place," he said, wiping away his tears. "That cocaine was *planted*, Miri. I've told you over and over."

No matter how many times he explained that he'd been framed, she wouldn't accept it. They were right back to where they'd been all those years earlier. It was why she had no longer come to visit him at Angola—because it'd always come down to this.

"Just admit it, Alex. You got caught and you did the time. Now use your head and don't do something that stupid again."

His anger roiled. "You know, you're right. I'll find a job

and get out of your life. Because if my own sister doesn't believe in my innocence, why the fuck bother at all?"

"It's not my fault," she said. "Never was."

"Not mine, either," he shot back.

Miri shook her head, like he was just being stubborn. "I have to leave for work in a bit. There's some food in the refrigerator. There's only one bed, so . . . "

"I'll sleep on the couch."

"No, you sleep on the floor. That's where I put my mattress. People like to shoot through the windows around here, so it's best you're not up high. If they find out you used to work for the DEA . . . "

Time to change the subject. "How are you getting to work?"

"A friend's picking me up. She'll bring me home, too. It'll be late. It's Shanita's birthday, so we're going for drinks after work."

Alex nodded his approval of that plan. He couldn't stand to have her walking around these streets alone.

Miri dropped a set of keys on the kitchen table. "If you could get my tire fixed, that'd be good. Shanita can't drive me tomorrow."

"I'll take care of it." At least he could do that much.

"Oh, and if you see Mr. Toes . . . " She paused. "He's my cat. If he shows up at the door, feed him. His food is under the sink."

"I can do that, too. What kind is he?"

Some of the frost fell away. "Calico," she said with a faint smile. "The males are kinda rare. I found him in an alley. He's got six toes and he's really cool. You'll like him."

Maybe the cat was the way into Miri's heart. He'd find out soon enough.

Alex parked himself next to his plastic bag on the couch, his legs feeling like they couldn't hold him up any longer. He remained there while his sister dressed for work. When she exited her bedroom in a pair of jeans and a T-shirt, he frowned.

"Don't you have to wear a uniform or something?"

"I change at work. It's easier that way," she said as she

dropped some money by the keys, probably for the tire.

He dug in the bag for his new phone, found the number in the package, and gave it to her. "You call me if you need a way home tonight, you hear?"

"You don't have a driver's license."

"Doesn't matter," he replied. "Keeping you safe does."

She looked at him as if seeing him for the first time. "I am glad you're home."

His heart beat double. That was exactly what he'd been dying to hear.

Miri had always looked like their mother, at least before their mom started doing drugs. His sister was blessed with fine features, dark eyes, and a lithe build. "You've turned out to be a really pretty girl," he said.

"Yeah, I hear that all the time when some guy is trying to grab my ass or my breasts."

"So how many have you shot so far?" he said, trying to lighten the moment.

It worked, as Miri grinned. "I'm tempted, but I need my job."

"I can teach you a couple self-defense moves to make those assholes back off."

"Really?" she asked, interested now.

"Yup. I learned a few in the joint. They're the kind that will bring serious pain, but not the kind that will likely get you fired."

Or thrown in solitary.

Miri cocked her head, then nodded as if his peace offering was appreciated. "Yeah, I'd like that."

A car honked outside. When she reached the door, Miri flipped the lock, then hesitated. She turned back to him and a weary smile came to her face, erasing a year or two. "Stay out of trouble, okay?"

"I will."

Alex locked the door behind her, plugged in his new phone to charge, and stretched out on the couch, ignoring her warning about sleeping on the floor. If he hadn't died in prison, he sure as hell wasn't going to die in the real world.

When Miri ducked inside the late-model Ford, her friend Shanita smiled at her. The twenty-five-year-old blonde was the tallest of the cocktail waitresses at the Down and Dirty Bar, topping out at six-one. Add three more inches for her heels and she was an Amazon.

Miri was shorter and a bit bustier, which played well with the horny tourists who visited the French Quarter watering hole. She'd never understood it, but something about coming to New Orleans meant they left their good sense and morals back home. The cheap booze did nothing to help the situation.

Still, the money Miri made in tips more than compensated for the grabby hands. Or at least she told herself that. She hadn't let Alex in on the fact that she wasn't at the restaurant anymore, because he'd just go Older Brother on her and insist she quit. She was too close to having enough money to move to give that up.

As if tapping into her thoughts, Shanita said, "This neighborhood sucks. Tell me you're going to move in with me . . . like, tomorrow."

"Soon. I've almost got the money together."

"You don't have to have all of it."

"I know, but I want to have enough that I don't have to worry."

"Okay, it's your thing. Let me know when moving day is, and make it soon." Shanita headed down the street and turned the corner. "Your bro get home?"

Miri usually didn't tell anyone that Alex was in prison, but she needed someone to talk to and Shanita wasn't judgmental. Not when her own father had served time.

"Yeah," she replied. "He just got home. He had to hitch a ride because of the tire thing." She sighed. "He looks old, Shanita. I mean, he's older than me anyway, but it's even more than that now."

"Hard time does that. My daddy came home looking bad."

"Well, Alex looks healthy, but it's what I see in his eyes." Miri shook her head. "Of course, I got in his face right off. Rather than hugging him and saying I was so scared I'd never see him again, I went total bitch."

Her friend sighed. "Love will do that to you. Tell him tonight. Don't let him think you don't care."

Miri blinked back tears. "I do love him, but he keeps insisting he had nothing to do with that cocaine. Why can't he just admit he screwed up?"

"Was he always on the right side before he was busted?"

Miri nodded. "Totally straight arrow."

"Then maybe he wasn't good for it."

"But if someone set him up, that means . . . who did it? His ex-wife? His partner at the DEA? Who? Because it sure as hell wasn't me."

Shanita quirked an eyebrow. "If your brother was really doing his job, not just phoning it in, he'd have a lot of people who'd want to take him down. What better way than planting coke and busting him for possession? Five years out of circulation, easy."

Today, when Miri had seen Alex's face, seen how prison had changed him, her certainty of his guilt had begun to develop cracks, like a piece of flood-damaged concrete. It'd been easy to lay all the guilt on him for the hell she'd faced while he was gone. Now, she wasn't sure if that was still possible.

"I'll wait and see," she said. "If he stays clean, then I know they screwed him over."

"And if he doesn't?"

Miri frowned. "Then he'd better be dead, because if not, I'll kill him myself."

Chapter Five

Alex stirred from the couch, too keyed up to sleep, and began to explore the dinky house. He wasn't surprised to find roach traps everywhere—a nod to the bugs he'd always thought large enough to be Louisiana's state bird. Given that the duplex next door was empty, he could well imagine there'd be a problem.

Miri hadn't been lying about having her mattress on the floor, and even then, she'd made up the bed covers. The bathroom was small and tidy. He put the toilet to use, pointedly reminding himself to put down the seat. Out of curiosity, he popped open the medicine cabinet and found the usual things: bandages, razors, makeup . . . and condoms.

He sighed. Once again the passage of time bitch-slapped him—his baby sister was now a young woman who had sex. At least she was being sensible about it. There was only one toothbrush, which meant if she had a boyfriend, he didn't do sleepovers. Not that he would while Alex was here. No guy—unless he was a goddamn saint—was good enough for Miri. Even a saint was going to find it rough sailing.

A stack of file boxes in one corner of the bedroom caught his interest because they had his name written on them in black marker. He pulled one down and opened it, discovering the contents of his desk at the DEA: pens, blank notepad, his Dallas Cowboys coffee cup, which now had a chip in it, and all his citations from the agency. It was as if someone had created a time capsule and dumped it in this box.

Alex sat on the floor and shuffled through it, acid brewing in his stomach. That last morning had gone well—he'd just delivered a report on his undercover work, and he'd gotten a big break that brought his investigation one step closer to busting Buryshkin's organization. Then Alicia had called, frantic. His partner Dennis was at their house, executing a search warrant. Even before Alex could leave for home, he'd been arrested for cocaine possession. A small bag of it had been found in his home office.

He would always remember the shock, the anger, the click of the handcuffs as they closed on his wrists. His outrage and embarrassment during the perp walk past his astonished coworkers on his way to jail.

That dark suspicion rose once again, the one he'd nursed over the years. The one that tore him apart every time he thought about it. Only a few people had access to his home office, to the locked desk drawer where the coke had been found. Had it been Alicia, or his former partner? The man he'd trusted, only to find out he'd been shagging Alicia all along. Had they worked together to land him in jail?

Or had it been someone else? Someone like the Russians.

After all these years he still didn't have the answer, but Veritas claimed it did. Was selling his soul to them worth the truth?

No.

Alex kept digging through the box, hoping to find something to counteract the agony of the past. Instead, he found the picture of him and Alicia, the one that had sat on his desk at work. He'd been so proud of it: their wedding photograph, taken that hot summer day in Austin at Horseshoe Falls Ranch. She was beautiful, always had been, a honey blonde with bright eyes and a quick smile. A woman whose rich daddy ran her life and who had cracked Alex's heart in two like a hammer blow to a walnut.

"Why did you do it?" he asked, as if the photograph could answer.

Why had she cheated on him with Dennis? That had been a bitter enough betrayal, and then, the instant it looked like Alex was headed for prison, she'd divorced him, all because her father had told her to. No "stand by your man" for that woman. Just to twist the knife, she hadn't even bothered to stay with ol' Dennis. It was as if his buddy had been a convenient escape route, a handy parachute out of the smoking airplane of a marriage.

Alex hurled the photo and its metal frame across the room, hearing the glass shatter. He swore his heart did the same.

"Why the hell would you do that to me?" He'd always been faithful to Alicia, even when undercover and presented with the opportunity to get a little on the side. Lord knows, there'd been plenty of offers.

Alex leaned his head back against the wall, heart pounding and fists clenched. God, he wanted revenge. Wanted it for all those lost years. There'd been so many times he'd fantasized about that, how easy it would be. One bullet in the forehead, one in the chest. First Dennis, then her. *Bang. Bang.*

Revenge would be so sweet, but he knew it would destroy what was left of his and Miri's lives. The lovers' deaths wouldn't make one damned difference. He'd get the death penalty and Miri would be alone. With all Alex had lost, he wasn't willing to sacrifice any more.

Old Russ had asked the right question: What was the price he'd be willing to pay? In prison, he would have said "anything." Now? Now it wasn't so cut and dried.

With a long sigh, Alex closed the box, rose, and set it by the bedroom door near the broken glass. There was nothing in there he wanted. That was the old Alex.

He moved the other boxes onto the floor, only to discover a door hidden behind them, which apparently led to the abandoned unit next door. He turned the knob, and found the lock busted. That gave him the creeps. The sooner he got his sister out of this house, the better.

Inside the other boxes he found clothes, books, and a few of his favorite CDs. Somehow his old life hadn't entirely vanished, and he had his sister to thank for that. It appeared that Miri's harsh words weren't equal to her actions; she could have easily ditched all this crap, and he never would have known. Instead she'd kept it for him.

"Love you, Monkey," he murmured. "Even if you think you're too old for me to call you that."

After restacking the remaining boxes, he swept up the broken glass, ripped up the wedding picture, and tossed it in the trash where it belonged. The wastebasket was nearly full, so he headed outside to find the garbage can where it sat near the back fence, battered and grimy. As he drew near, he could see the flies boiling out of the lid, which was ajar. The stench hit him ten feet away, and he stopped in his tracks.

That wasn't garbage. That was something dead.

He edged closer and shifted the lid, then dropped it, gagging. In the midst of the garbage was a calico cat, painted with flies. Mr. Toes.

Only when Alex covered his nose and mouth to step closer did he find the note, scrawled on a piece of lined notepaper.

NOWHERE TO HIDE

The Hotel St. Sebastian was in the French Quarter, one of those true New Orleans beauties that had survived hurricanes, floods, and decades of dirty politics. Morgan's boss sat in an overstuffed armchair near one of the windows, a position she thought was inviting trouble. Though Veritas's home office was in Chicago, whenever the boss was in town he stayed here, and his enemies knew it. The Russians would love to take this guy out, and yet he made no effort to conceal himself.

Doesn't he realize how important he is to us?

As if he'd heard her thoughts, Crispin Wilder's attention rose from the tablet in his lap, his distinctive dark-gray eyes troubled. At present, he was wearing a black T-shirt and a pair of jeans, totally at odds with the elegant room around them.

It was actually a suite of rooms named after a famous author, decorated with crown molding, still-life paintings, a glittering chandelier, and comforting sage-green walls. The floors were wood, highly polished, a thick rug denoting the center of the room. A white fireplace was built into the far wall, and in a nearby hallway, an orchid bloomed on a carved table. The space spoke of tranquility, a sanctuary in a city known for glittery excess.

Morgan shifted on the sofa. As she waited, she noted that Crispin's beard had been trimmed, closely cropped. It revealed a few gray hairs. His long, dark-brown hair was graying at the temples as well, not unusual for someone in his forties. Caught in a ponytail at the nape of his neck, it made him ruggedly handsome. Both of his hands had a series of small scars in no discernible pattern.

She'd heard a lot of rumors about how those scars had come to be, but no one knew the real story. At one time Crispin had not served the forces of good, but had been a ruthless gunrunner supplying weapons of war to greedy despots across the planet. The kind of weapons needed to decimate whole villages or countries, sometimes in the name of God, but most times in the name of the Almighty Dollar.

Something had happened along the way, something that had changed Crispin Wilder forever. No one really knew the whole tale, and the man wouldn't speak of it. All Morgan knew was that he'd abruptly quit the arms business and vanished, only to resurface a year later, the head of Veritas. His vast fortune helped fund their activities, cultivating those nefarious and legitimate contacts he'd made across the globe.

Except this time he was peddling justice, not arms.

When Morgan shifted on the sofa again, her boss noticed.

"I did ask you to come see me, and now I'm ignoring you. That's rude," Crispin said, closing the tablet.

"That's okay. This is about Parkin, isn't it?"

He nodded. "Had any second thoughts since you met him?"

She cut to the chase, now that she'd had time to reflect on the situation. "I think we can still get him on board, but you really need to send someone else after him. He's not listening to me."

Crispin nodded, leaning back and crossing his arms. A tattoo peeked out from the right sleeve of his T-shirt. Morgan couldn't make out what it was, and she wasn't going to ask.

Her superior was open about some matters and totally closed on others, and you never knew where a topic fell on that scale.

"Buryshkin's shipment arrived last night," he said. "Cocaine. Street value in the millions."

"God," she murmured. "It never ends."

"My source says they will start moving the coke in a few days, but he has no idea where they're storing it in the meantime. He's trying to discover that, but I urged him to use caution."

Morgan sighed in resignation. "I'm sorry. I let Parkin push every one of my buttons."

One of her boss's eyebrows rose. "I'm surprised. Usually *you're* the one who does the button pushing."

"I don't know what was wrong with me," she admitted.

"Maybe your timing was off. Our ex-DEA agent might be a lot more receptive later tonight or tomorrow. Make another run at him. If you find Parkin's still playing games, turn him over to Iceman. If Neil can't convince him, then we'll cut our losses. I have a couple of other options, but neither is as good as the ex-con. Revenge is a very powerful motivator."

Morgan felt her breathing falter. That was a little too close to home. Buryshkin had destroyed her life, killed her husband and her career. Revenge was all she had left.

"I'll give it another try."

Which meant that, once again, she'd have to look at that face, see those eyes and the history behind them. Though she'd never admit it to her boss, Alex Parkin unnerved her on too many levels.

Crispin pulled a sheet of paper from under the notebook and handed it to her. "Just so you're not duplicating efforts, here's a list of locations we've already cleared. The coke isn't at any of these. Work your contacts, see what you hear on the streets."

She scanned the addresses. "I've got a couple folks who might know something—with the proper monetary incentive."

"If you do find the dope, call our contact at the DEA and let them conduct the bust. Only deal with *her*, not anyone else, you understand?"

Morgan nodded. The majority of the agents were clean, but a few couldn't be trusted. They'd found the lure of the drug lord's money too tempting.

"When you talk to Parkin again, push his weak spot—his sister."

She grimaced. "He'll hate us if I go there."

"Better that he hates us than he or Ms. Parkin ending up dead."

Crispin had a point. Veritas played hardball when needed, but there were certain lines they never crossed. Hurting some guy's sister just to get him to work for them was one of those. The Russians wouldn't recognize a line if they tripped over one.

As Morgan left the suite, her boss placed a call on his cell phone and began speaking in Dutch. He did it effortlessly, switching from one language to another like it was as simple as taking a breath.

As she quietly closed the door behind her, for some reason Parkin's dark eyes came to mind. It was time to let him know just how bad it could get if he didn't pull his head out of his ass. Because no matter what, the Russians were either going to recruit him . . . or kill him.

Shaken by the discovery of his sister's pet, Alex retreated into the house. How was he going to tell Miri her cat's throat had been cut? She'd hate him for that. Was this a warning to him that Miri was next if he didn't fall in line?

He knew what she'd say: Life was fine until you came home. Which wasn't the truth, not when she owned a gun to keep punks from breaking into her house and hurting her. Still, she wouldn't see it that way. Once again, somebody was playing God with their lives. But who had done it? One of Buryshkin's people? Or the babe in the Beemer?

Maybe he and his sister should just bail, take off for Texas in the morning. Anywhere but New Orleans. They could start over where no one knew them.

But what if whoever had left the threat tracked them down, caught his sister alone . . .

Someone knocked on the front door, at first a light tap, then growing stronger. He flipped the locks and flung open the door to find Morgan Blake on the doorstep. Veritas's mouthpiece had no idea that her timing was perfect. It was time to start lighting fires under these people and see who screamed first.

"I got your message," he said, glaring. "And you can just fuck off."

"What message?" she replied, looking confused.

"You know what I'm talking about. Don't play stupid."

"No, I don't know what you're—"

"Let me show you, then." He grabbed her arm and towed her through the house, ignoring her protests.

"What are we doing?" she demanded as he marched her out the back door.

"Letting you admire your handiwork."

He let her go right before they reached the trash can. Whipping off the lid, he waited for her to admit this was her doing. Instead, the woman's face went pale. Her hand covered her mouth and she stepped away. He lowered the lid, then stepped back to escape the cloud of flies.

Ms. Blake swallowed hard as she took another step back. "Who did that?"

"Your people."

"What? No way," she said. "We don't do that kind of crap."

His resolve wavered. "Then who? The Russians?"

To his surprise, she shook her head. "No. That's not Buryshkin's style."

If it wasn't her or the Russians, there was another player in the game.

No, it has to be one of them.

"That was my sister's cat," he said. "There was a note with it. It said, 'Nowhere to hide.' "

"Was it a message for you . . . or for her?"

That, he didn't know.

The frown on the woman's face grew. "Admit it, you're in deep trouble, Parkin. You've got enemies who'd love to break you in half, and they don't care who they hurt in the process."

"My problem, not yours."

"It's your sister's problem too. They won't hesitate to use her as a way to put a ring in your nose. You piss them off, and you're both taking a one-way trip to the swamp."

"Is that any different from you guys?"

"Hell yes." A fly landed on her face and she swiped it off. "With us, you get a chance to make things right. A chance to get even. Don't you want revenge?"

"Of course I want revenge," he said, stepping closer to her now. "But I won't be a pawn for anyone. I'll take care of my sister on my own. That's my job now."

His visitor shook her head in dismay. "You're so out of your league." She dug a business card from her purse and offered it to him. "Call me if you change your mind."

"I won't."

She tossed the card in the grass at his feet. "Someday, you may not have a choice anymore."

He made no move to pick it up. "Not going there, lady. I'd rather kiss the devil's ass."

"Dial that number and maybe we'll still have time to pull *your* ass out of the fire. Because we're going to be the only ones who can do it."

As the woman marched around the side of the house through the weeds, he stared down at the business card, then picked it up. A mobile number was listed beneath her name. He crumpled the card, then threw it toward the trash can and the rotting corpse, where it belonged.

By the time Alex was back inside, the kitchen clock told him he needed to get a move on; Miri's tire needed fixing, if for no other reason than to get in her good graces. Especially when he would have to tell her Mr. Toes was dead.

Who the hell would do something like that? Clearly it was some sick bastard, and the fact that he'd been anywhere near his sister scared Alex senseless.

After making sure the back door was bolted, he collected the ring of keys and the money from the kitchen table. Locking the front door behind him, he paused and took a deep breath as the open space loomed around him, pressing down on him like it had its own weight. Some cons took time to adjust to the outside, and apparently he was one of them. He wondered if he would ever be normal again.

No routine.

That was what he was missing. Routine meant stability. Relative safety. Now he felt like he was completely adrift in a sea of unknowns. Other people would go to the cops, tell them about the cat, maybe get someone to investigate. But not Alex. Not with his record. He was on his own.

It took work to get the tire off the car as the lug nuts weren't cooperating. The heat didn't help; he was dripping sweat by the time the task was complete. Slowly, he ran his fingers over the tire and found a slice in the sidewall, not a nail hole. His first guess had been right—someone, probably Veritas, had slit the tire to allow Morgan time to lure him into their web.

Their plan had failed.

Hefting the tire, Alex set off down the street. If he was lucky, he'd find a neighbor kid who could point him toward the closest tire-repair place. Once it was fixed, he'd order some pizza and decide what to do next. Figure out how to fight back.

Mr. Toes had been an innocent victim. Alex was determined that he'd be the only one.

Morgan flipped the locks on her front door, then tapped in the code to disable her apartment alarm. She was still fuming at Parkin's stubbornness. How could he think they would kill his sister's cat? They weren't monsters. This wasn't like the Russian's goons, either. They wouldn't mess with some pet—they'd go right after Parkin or his sister.

As Morgan kicked off her tennis shoes, her cell phone began to play "Ride of the Valkyries." She checked the caller ID and smiled—it was Lars Ericson, who had been assigned the task of keeping an eye on Parkin. Lars was the son of a Scandinavian pharmaceutical executive and a British-Jamaican flight attendant. He was a whip-smart operative and a devastating handball player. Morgan had learned about the latter talent at great personal humiliation and expense, because there was always some money riding on each game.

"Hey Lars, what's new? Parkin get his ass shot yet?" she said, bending down to scoop up her shoes.

"Nope. He's currently carrying the flat tire down the street. I'm guessing he's off to an auto shop."

"Being the dutiful big brother, then." She caught Lars up on what their subject had found in his trash can.

"Ah, hell. What kind of sick SOB would do that to a cat?"

"I don't know. It doesn't feel like Buryshkin. Could it be an ex-boyfriend who wasn't happy to be left behind?"

"According to our research, the sister's last steady guy was over eight months ago and he lives in Detroit now."

"So maybe it's a stalker," Morgan grumbled.

"Always possible. I didn't see anyone around the house, but then, I didn't start surveillance until six this morning."

"There were no maggots on the corpse yet, so it probably died sometime last night. They take about twenty-four hours to hatch out."

A brief pause and a shuffling noise, perhaps Lars switching the phone to the other ear. "What happened between you and Parkin? I saw him haul you into the house. I figured you could handle him, so I held back."

"Parkin was blaming us for the cat. He's got a short fuse, and the fact that his sister's space has been invaded has made him even more volatile."

"You want me to keep watching him?"

"Yeah, at least for another couple days. The Russians will be in touch with him soon."

"Who's taking the night shift?" Lars asked.

"Bill."

A laugh came down the line. "No surprise there. I swear that man is a vampire. He's pale enough to be one."

"True." Which was one thing that Alex Parkin wasn't—his time in the prison fields had made sure of that.

"I gotta go. Our guy is turning the corner so I better catch up with him. I'll call you later with an update."

"Thanks, Lars."

"Later, Valkyrie."

Morgan ended the call and tossed the phone onto the bathroom counter. Eyeing the bathtub, she turned on the water and began to strip. Dropping in a scoop of sandalwood bath salts, she climbed in.

Morgan slid farther down into the water, hoping it would wash away some of her worries. She had good people—Lars, Neil, and Bill were top-notch operatives, and they'd keep an eye on Parkin and his sister.

"Come on, you idiot, work with us," she muttered.

God help her, she was willing to use his desire for revenge to fuel her own.

Chapter Six

It was close to two in the morning and Miri really wanted to go home, exhausted after a six-hour shift—though the tips had been really good. Nevertheless, she'd agreed to go out for a few drinks after work to celebrate Shanita's birthday, so she'd put on her happy face and sucked it up. Because that's what you did for your best friend.

They'd started the evening with a couple of Shanita's buddies at the Two Friends Bar, a gay watering hole on Dauphine Street. After spending an hour or so there, they'd migrated to a raucous daiquiri joint down the river from Jackson Square. That was when everyone else's drinking had gone into overdrive.

The only things keeping Miri in place were loyalty to her friend and the fact that her brother was at home, probably wondering where she was. She needed to demonstrate her independence or Alex would treat her like she was still a teenager. It had never been a contest of wills between them before, but she suspected that would be the case now. He'd be trying to make up for all the years she'd been on her own.

Day after day, year after year, she'd waited for that phone call to tell her that he'd died in prison, been knifed or beaten to death, because she knew that former law-enforcement officers didn't do well behind bars. Too many people had scores to settle. But somehow, he'd survived. She'd always known Alex was tough, but he'd managed to surprise her.

Miri had wanted to burst into tears, hug him, and tell him how relieved she was when he'd knocked on the door, but something had held her back. Something deep inside her that she didn't really understand. Something she wasn't proud of. It was as if she needed him to hurt as badly as she had. But that was stupid, because one look in his eyes had told her that he'd been there and suffered just as much, if not more.

Her eyes swept across the bar again, the third time in a few minutes. She'd had the feeling that someone was watching her all evening, but it was hard to determine just who with so many bodies in one place. It'd begun at work, then followed her to the first bar, and now here.

You're just being paranoid.

Mostly because she was a cocktail waitress, and that meant that a lot of guys—and a few girls—felt the need to hit on her. Most of them backed off, but every now and then there was one who just didn't understand "no."

She shook off the feeling and tried to refocus on the conversation between Shanita and her two friends. One was a realtor and the other a would-be fashion designer. All three were becoming drunker by the minute.

Miri's phone rang and the caller ID wasn't familiar, so she let it roll over to voicemail. It buzzed again a minute later, which meant it probably wasn't a wrong number. Then she remembered it might be her brother. Yet another new thing to adjust to. As she answered the call, Miri pushed her way toward the front door.

"Hello?" She stepped outside, where the noise level dropped by half, and moved farther down the street, leaning against a building to be out of the flow of foot traffic. She was careful to keep her small purse tucked between her and the brick wall. New Orleans bred thieves like it did tourists, and she had nearly a hundred fifty dollars of tips in there.

"Hey! This is your no-good ex-con brother, checking in to see how you're doing," Alex said, his voice straining to sound nonchalant.

She blinked in surprise, then frowned. "I'm fine. Did you get the tire fixed?"

"No. I—"

"Shanita can't drive me to work tomorrow. I *need* my car,

Alex." She'd given him one little job, and he'd let it slide.

"If you'd listen . . . I didn't get it fixed because it was too damaged. I bought a used one to replace it. I talked the guy down ten bucks, and it should last a long time."

Miri paused, realizing she'd been jonesing for a reason to argue with him. Which was dumb.

"Sorry. That's cool. Thanks."

"No sweat."

"Did you eat anything?"

"Yeah. I ordered a pizza. That was a novel experience. I'm not used to having to decide what I want to eat."

Just one of the many things she took for granted. "You find the beer in the refrigerator?"

"Yeah. I've had two, and it feels more like eight."

"Listen to you. You're a total wuss now."

"Tell me about it," he joked. "I'm about to go to bed, so . . . when should I start worrying if you're not home?"

She could tell Alex was lying—he was already worrying, and he sure as hell wasn't going to bed until she came through the front door.

"Actually, I'm really tired and Shanita's just getting started. I should be home in about an hour or so."

"You need a ride?"

"I'll catch the bus. Remember, you don't have a license? You don't need the cops nailing you for that."

A long sigh came down the line, telling her he'd forgotten again. "Where does the bus drop you off?"

"St. Charles and Josephine."

"Good. Then when you get on, call me, and I'll meet you at the stop. That way I won't freak out about you walking home alone in this craptastic neighborhood."

Rather than being angry at his interference, Miri smiled. Her brother could be a pain in the ass, but he always cared.

"Okay. You got it. You sure an old guy like you doesn't need his beauty sleep?"

"Smartass. You having fun?"

"Yeah," she said, though that wasn't as true as she made it

sound. "I'm just tired from work."

"I'll try not to snore tonight and keep you awake."

"You better not. Did you feed Mr. Toes?"

There was a long pause. "Ahh . . . no. Sorry."

She decided to let it go. Toes would be waiting for her when she got home, and she'd take care of him.

"I'll call you when I leave," she said, heading back toward the bar's entrance.

"Love you, sis."

Miri hung up without replying. *Why?* She didn't know. She loved him, but she wasn't good with the chaos he brought into her life. Her instincts told her it was just starting all over again.

Did she dare tell him what had really happened when he'd been in prison, the kind of hell their aunt and uncle had put her through? Would he understand why she'd kept running away, time after time?

Not yet. Maybe someday.

She found Shanita on her third daiquiri, doing Beyoncé imitations—which was goofy, since she was totally a white girl and her voice sucked. Miri still laughed at her attempts because it was *so* Shanita.

"Anything going on?" her friend asked.

"Just the bro checking in on me," Miri replied, sliding back into her seat. "You'd think I was like sixteen or something."

"Do you have a picture of him? I want to show him to my friends here."

It was an odd request, but Miri chalked it up to too much alcohol. She did have a photo in her wallet, but it was from before he went to prison. Alex *now* was different from Alex *then.* "Not really. I need to leave pretty soon."

"No! We should go until dawn!" Shanita protested.

"You can. I have to be at work at noon."

"Then let me buy you another beer. You guys want something?"

After collecting their orders, Shanita was off to the bar, leaving Miri to chat with the other two, both of whom she barely knew.

Awkward.

Yet another reason to drink her last beer and head for home.

As Morgan stepped inside the bar, she winced. It must be a sign of age, because all the noise and packed bodies didn't do a thing for her. Not that she was old at thirty-four, but the jumbled mix of spilled beer, sweat, and perfume made her head ache.

On top of all that, she'd had to leave her gun in the car, something she never liked to do. Since state law came down hard on folks who went armed into a Louisiana bar, that would violate one of Veritas's prime directives which was to avoid hassles with local law enforcement. With her luck, it would just get stolen out of her car and she'd still have to talk to the cops.

Since Bill had reported that all was quiet at the girl's home, Morgan texted her other contact, the one who'd been tailing Miri. Samuel Marsh was in his mid-thirties, a former Chicago homicide detective who now worked as a private investigator. Tonight he was serving as backup on the mission.

His return text served as her guide dog through the throng at the bar. With a slim build and a boyish face, he could pass for someone ten years younger, even a college student. That had worked to their advantage in the past.

He'd chosen a spot along the far wall, which made him look like he was scoping out the babes, not just one girl in particular. He had a beer in hand and was dressed in bar camouflage: jeans and a navy T-shirt. He worked out regularly, but his muscles weren't quite as defined as Parkin's. Morgan groaned to herself. Now she was comparing every guy to the ex-con. That wasn't a good sign.

"Sam," she said, leaning back against the wall next to him while keeping her focus on the milling crowd. "How's it going?"

"Good. Our lady is directly opposite us, with three friends."

Morgan's eyes skipped over the tables and settled on a

young woman. She'd seen surveillance photos of Miri Parkin, but she was even prettier in person, with an expressive face and a lighter version of her brother's thick brown hair. The way she held herself told Morgan she was exhausted and really wanted to be anywhere but here.

"How much has she been drinking?" Morgan asked.

"Not much. That's her third beer for the night. She's a smart one. She won't touch a bottle unless the cap is still on. Got a bottle opener in her purse."

Morgan found herself liking the girl already. "She works in a bar. Probably seen every roofie trick in the book. Thank God she's not a lush. Babysitting drunks is never fun."

Sam grunted his agreement. "We won't be babysitting much longer. She got a call from her brother. She told him she was going to be leaving soon."

"Good. I don't think my eardrums can handle this noise much longer."

"You get used to it after a while," he replied.

"Only after you go deaf."

Morgan pulled out her cell phone, acting as if she were just checking messages. Using it as a prop, she held it up in such a way that she could scope out the bar, noting certain faces, taking pictures of a few of them for reference. No one screamed "Russian," so she lowered the phone and looked back at Miri. The girl was doing the same thing—scanning faces—minus the phone. Had her brother warned her to keep an eye out for trouble? Or was it something else?

"Does she seem edgy to you?" Morgan asked.

"Yes, and I've been wondering why."

"I'll scope the place out, see if I find anyone who looks like they're working for Buryshkin. Let me know if anything changes."

"You got it."

Morgan made the rounds of the bar, wandering through the crowd of locals and tourists. Offers to buy her a drink came her way, but she politely turned them down. Finally, she grabbed a half-full beer bottle off an empty table and carried it with her to keep the come-ons to a minimum.

When she returned to Sam, she found that Miri was no longer with her friends. "Where is she?"

"Restroom. It's amazing how long you ladies can spend in a place like that."

Morgan's unease rose. "How long has she been gone?"

Sam shrugged. "Five minutes, maybe."

Except none of Miri's friends were with her, so there would be no reason to spend that much time hanging in the restroom.

"I'll check on her." She placed the beer decoy on a nearby table and headed through the crowd once more.

"Hey, honey!" a guy called out, but she kept moving.

The hallway to the restrooms had a series of classic New Orleans photographs on the walls, most of them of Mardi Gras, with lots of masks and beads and the occasional topless female.

Morgan pushed open the door to the ladies' room and found a lone occupant at the sinks. The girl had to be using a fake ID. Ms. Underage was busy adjusting her clothes for maximum exposure. Hiking her short skirt even farther up, flashing more thigh. Bending over and plumping her breasts to make them pop out from the low top.

Was I ever like that?

Unfortunately, the answer was "affirmative," at least when she'd been sixteen. Once the girl was gone, Morgan checked underneath the stalls. No Miri. Where was Parkin's sister?

When she pushed through the door to the hallway, Morgan had to step aside to allow an older woman in pink polyester pants and a "Do Whatcha Wanna" T-shirt to enter the restroom. Ignoring the Men's, she tried the two doors located closer to the bar. The first led to a deep storage closet, currently occupied by a pair of lovers who were not there to do an inventory of the paper towels. Not with the woman's legs wrapped around his waist and his jeans around his skinny ankles.

Once she'd determined the girl wasn't Miri, Morgan apologized and closed the door, slightly embarrassed. It wasn't as if she hadn't seen people having sex before, it was just that they were having such a good time at it.

Not once in her life had she gone into some storage closet and gotten it on. She'd always convinced herself it wasn't her thing. It certainly hadn't been her husband's. Now, as she grew older, Morgan wondered exactly what she'd been missing all these years. Besides the great sex.

She sighed and checked the other door, which led to a small, unoccupied office. That left one other possibility, one that she could not imagine Miri choosing on her own.

Morgan pushed open the heavy back door that led to the alley behind the establishment. It was like most New Orleans back alleys: smelly. A single security light offered a small patch of meager illumination. At the end of the alley to the right was a metal privacy fence, separating it from the main street. Along the adjacent building was a line of lidded trash cans, unfortunately reminding Morgan of the dead cat she'd seen today. That chilling image echoed the warnings her mind kept pushing at her. She was damned if Parkin's sister would get hurt on her watch, even if the ex-con insisted he didn't need Veritas's help.

To the left was another privacy fence, dividing that end of the alley in half. Its gate hung open on sagging hinges. Morgan stepped out of the light, moving toward the open gate. She'd just reached it when a sharp cry of "No!" and then the sound of a slap came from that direction. A low moan followed.

"Miri?" she called out. Another cry, this one quickly cut off.

Morgan's fingers hunted for the zipper to her purse. Then she remembered—no gun. She slung the strap across her body and edged through the gate. In the semi-darkness, she made out two figures, one large, over six feet tall, weighing at least 225. He was choking out the other, smaller figure, his massive arm around her neck as he dragged her down the alley toward a black sedan and its open trunk.

"Ah, hell."

To her credit, Miri fought the bastard, but it was plain that she didn't have the skills or the bulk to take on her attacker. She clawed at his thick arm, blood running down her face and onto her T-shirt from a cut on her scalp, her eyes panicked as she tried to breathe.

"Hey asshole, let her go!" Morgan called out as she advanced.

"Get lost, bitch," he snarled.

"Wrong answer," Morgan said, looking around for a weapon. None to be found, unless she wanted to throw a trash can at the guy. It wasn't going to be an even match because he had at least ninety pounds on her. But no way was this monster leaving with Parkin's sister.

He ignored Morgan as if she posed no threat. Instead, as he shifted his captive around to force her in the trunk, Miri took that opportunity to slam a fist into his face. A sickening crunch of cartilage and a roar of pain as the man reeled backward, holding his bleeding nose.

Morgan waded in, snapping a kick at his closest knee. He moved at the last minute, and it missed him, clipping his thigh instead. His fist shot out, but instead of targeting her as she'd expected, he hammered a blow into Miri's chest. She folded to the ground, curling into a fetal position, trying to catch her breath.

Exploding in fury, Morgan grabbed a beefy shoulder with both hands, and using all her leverage tried to ram his head into the open trunk lid. He swung a fist at her, catching her chin and snapping her neck around. She lurched backward, but the bastard just kept coming. He grabbed her throat with huge hands, digging his fingers into her flesh.

As black spots crowded her vision, Morgan swept her right arm down and broke the chokehold. Trapping his one arm against her, she elbowed his gut. When he bent over in pain, she brought her knee up, connecting with his chin. The man fell back, blood dripping down his face. Fumbling, he reached behind his back. When the gun came into sight, Morgan kicked it out of his hand.

When it skittered away, vanishing into the darkness, he staggered toward the front of the car, spraying blood with each step. Though Morgan really wanted to kick the hell out of this guy, a quick look back at Miri told her that the girl needed help, immediately. She lifted her up and began moving her toward the bar's back entrance.

They'd nearly reached it when the car fired to life and the reverse lights came on. Their attacker hadn't given up yet. As the tires squealed, Morgan dragged Miri into the narrow entrance. With a roar, the sedan ploughed backward through the fence, snapping off the metal pipes, which headed toward them like a line of sharpened stakes.

As the girl cried out in fear, Morgan wrapped herself around her, pressing her against the door. The metal spikes screeched against the asphalt, then cut along the bricks. The fence saved them as one of the stakes drove a hole into a rear tire and a loud pop echoed in the alley. Inside the vehicle, their assailant bellowed his fury, then put the car into drive and took off down the alley, the flat tire thumping with each turn. Shouts erupted as the sedan barreled out into the street, telling Morgan that he'd barely missed some pedestrians in his effort to escape.

"Jesus," she murmured, her knees no longer supporting her. She turned so her back was to the building, then slid down the bricks to the ground, cradling the injured woman to her chest.

Morgan's phone was trapped underneath them and as she tried to extract it, the back door opened and Sam stepped out. He took one look and swore. His phone was out of his pocket in an instant, dialing 911. Another face appeared in the doorway, one of the bouncers.

"Get a blanket, something to cover her. She's going into shock," Morgan called out. The man blinked, then nodded and vanished inside.

Miri murmured something, her head rising, eyes unfocused. At least her breathing had evened out. Maybe she didn't have a broken rib after all.

Morgan pushed back her bloody hair. "He's gone. The paramedics are coming. You're going to be okay. Just hang in there."

"He . . . he . . . "

"I know, honey. I know."

Morgan knew better than most that too many women ended up dead in shallow graves or in alleys, tossed away like garbage. She'd seen so many of them during her time at the FBI. Knew how close she'd come to the same fate.

"Why . . . me . . . ?" Miri asked, shivering in Morgan's arms now.

"Don't know. Some guys don't need a reason."

"Said I was . . . his . . . stalking me . . . " Then she shuddered. "My brother . . . he'll kill him . . . go back . . . to prison . . . "

"No, he won't. You have my word on that," Morgan said.

Because if I find that bastard first, I'm going to take him out before Parkin has a chance. And I'm going to smile when I do it.

Chapter Seven

By the time the cops and paramedics arrived, Miri had
stopped talking and fallen unconscious, which wasn't a good
sign. As the paramedics began their initial assessment of the
victim, a few of the bar patrons wandered out to check on the
commotion. The bouncer promptly earned his pay and herded
them back inside.

Still seated on the ground, Morgan leaned back against
the building. Her throat and shoulder ached in time with her
heartbeat.

"Ma'am?" a city cop asked, kneeling next to her. "You
hurt?"

"Nothing an ice pack and a stiff belt of whiskey won't
cure," she replied. Compared to the gunshot wound earlier in
the year, this was nothing.

"Can you tell me what happened?"

Morgan laid out the details of the assault step by step,
though some of it was pure fallacy. She could hardly talk
about the Russians and Alex Parkin, so she claimed to have
stepped outside to get some air when she found someone being
attacked. She noted that Sam was nearby, listening to every
word. He gave a short nod, indicating he'd spin his tale the
same way if asked. Fortunately, the cop seemed to buy her
story. It pissed her off that she'd only gotten a couple numbers
from the Dodge's license plate, but it was that or get flattened
like an armadillo on a state highway.

"Description of the guy?" the cop asked, taking notes.

"Closely cropped brown hair, cuts on his face, probably
from the victim's nails, and his left ear sticks out a bit more

than his right. He has a scarred face. And now he has a broken nose."

The cop cracked a smile. "That your doing?"

"Nope. The vic did the nose job," Morgan replied, wanting Miri to get the credit.

"Sweet. Sounds like the bastard deserved it."

"No argument there."

After giving the officer her contact info, she rose to her feet in slow motion, waving off his help. Sam was talking to another cop, and she knew he'd claim that they'd just been hanging together in the bar before the incident.

Morgan made her way over to Miri. Her eyes were closed, an oxygen cannula in her nose and an IV line in her right arm, pumping in fluid at a steady rate. The blood had dried on her face and clothes now, making her look like the victim of a multi-car pileup.

"How's she doing?" Morgan asked, kneeling next to her.

The lady paramedic looked at her. "Still unconscious. Vitals are pretty decent. We got the head wound to stop bleeding, so that will help. They'll check out her skull and the rest of her when we get to the ER."

"Which hospital?"

"Tulane Medical Center."

"Thanks."

"You need us to check you out?" the other paramedic asked.

"No, I'm good."

Morgan rose and stepped away, hitting a contact number on her phone. This was the kind of major screw-up you reported directly to the boss before he heard it from the cops. Because he would hear about it soon enough.

"How bad is she?" Crispin asked without saying hello.

How do you do that? "She got pretty badly beaten up."

"Russians?"

Morgan thought back to the man's voice, his speech pattern.

"I don't think so. She thinks he's some sort of stalker, and right now I'm inclined to agree. Especially with what happened to her cat this afternoon."

"Another complication," her boss said. "Give me your report."

Ensuring they had privacy, she brought him completely up to speed.

"I'll have Neil get with you for support," Crispin said. "You did good tonight, Morgan." Then he ended the call.

"Not from where I'm standing," she said, watching the paramedics and their patient.

If she'd been on the ball, Parkin's kid sister wouldn't be headed to the emergency room.

Neil's call came within a minute. "What do you need?" he asked.

That was Iceman's style: no fuss, no drama, just solid backup. It was what made him one of her favorite people at Veritas.

"Did Crispin give you the rundown?"

"Yes."

"Then tell Parkin what happened and bring him to Tulane's Medical's ER."

"You want your name mentioned?"

"Yeah, might as well get it all out there. He'll find out anyway. Be careful with him. This will set him off big time. We don't want him on a manhunt for this whack job."

"Understood. Send me a picture of her. That'll get him moving."

Then he was gone. Neil didn't let emotions rule him. He just did his job. Right now, that was exactly what Morgan needed most.

Alex hadn't meant to fall asleep, but the day had finally punched his ticket and he'd crashed shortly after talking to his sister. He woke up, groggy, thinking he'd heard a car door slam. He leveraged himself up on the lumpy couch and rubbed his eyes. When his vision finally cleared, he checked the clock above the stove.

3:09? Where the hell is she?

He was reaching for his cell phone on the floor when someone pounded on the front door. He sighed in relief. This was probably her. Still, she was supposed to call him . . .

Alex opened the door, ready to ream out his baby sister for being stupid, and found himself staring into the blue-gray eyes of a young man. He had a closely trimmed beard and moustache, and a flattened silver stud in his right ear. He was a big dude, obviously worked out regularly, and was about the same age as Alex. But what Alex noticed the most was the world-weary expression, the kind that said life had kicked this man in the balls more than once, and that he didn't expect that to change.

"Parkin—"

"Wrong house," Alex said, starting to close the door. A hand grabbed the door and shoved it open again.

"You need to come with me. It's about your sister."

The hair on the back of Alex's neck rose. "What happened to her? Who are you?"

"Name's Neil. I work for Veritas. Your sister got into some trouble at a bar tonight, and she's headed to the ER. I'll drive you there."

"How do I know you're not lying?" he demanded.

The guy pulled out a cell phone, scrolled through his messages, and handed it over. "Sorry to do it this way, but we figured you'd need proof."

Alex stared at the image of his sister being loaded into the back of an ambulance. There was blood on her face and clothes, a cervical collar around her neck.

"Oh my God."

His hand shook as he gave back the phone. His mind on autopilot, Alex sank onto the couch, fumbling for his shoes. "What the hell happened? How'd she get hurt?"

The man named Neil stepped inside the house. "Some guy beat her up. It didn't go any further than that. Valkyrie made sure of it."

Valkyrie?

Alex laced up the second shoe as he worked through the news: Miri was hurt, bad, or she wouldn't be going to a hospital and he'd been sleeping when it'd gone down.

Goddammit.

Grabbing the keys off the table, he jammed his phone in a pocket and headed out the door. Once he had it locked, they hurried across the lawn to where a black SUV sat at the curb, prime bait for this neighborhood. Surprisingly, no one was paying any attention to it, as if they knew it would only buy serious trouble.

He climbed into the vehicle, buckled up, and then they were headed down the street. Alex stared at nothing out the side window. "Who is Valkyrie?"

"Morgan. That's our nickname for her."

Alex glared at him. "What does she have to do with this? Why are you guys anywhere near my sister?"

The driver shot him a look, then turned back to watch the road. "Morgan was worried something might happen, so she was keeping an eye on her."

Alex's suspicions rose. "Sounds too noble. I'm thinking maybe you bastards set this whole thing up just to get me on your team."

The driver slammed on the brakes, rocking Alex forward until his seatbelt caught as they skidded to a stop. The driver grabbed the front of his T-shirt, yanking him forward so they were nose to nose.

"I'll say this once: Morgan Blake is the only reason your sister is alive and not some sick bastard's play toy. I don't give a goddamn if you work for us or not, but you better get your head out of your ass. This game just went into overtime."

Alex opened his mouth to argue, then snapped it shut, registering the seething anger in the man's eyes. Neil released him and went back to driving, jaw clenched.

As he straightened his shirt, he made a note not to piss off this guy again. There was a lot of barely repressed rage beneath that icy exterior, something far beyond tonight's attack.

"Was it the Russians?" Alex asked.

"Morgan doesn't think so. She thinks the guy was a sicko, a stalker maybe. Must have grabbed your sister when she came out of the restroom and hauled her into the alley before she could scream for help. By the time Morgan got there, the guy was trying to stuff your sister into his car trunk."

His blood chilled. "Did he—"

"You want to know any more, ask Morgan. I only got enough info to get your stubborn ass in the car."

Alex ground his teeth, but he didn't ask any more questions. He'd find out the details soon enough. Then it'd be his turn to rain hell on whoever had hurt his baby sister.

His father had called him Hurricane Alex when he was little because there wasn't much that could slow him down. It was the same now as he swept through the emergency room at top speed, nearly mowing down a nurse's aide in his haste. The instant he was inside the door, he remembered the place from when his former partner had been knifed during a drug bust. It was crowded, as usual, with people bleeding, vomiting, and moaning.

Tonight, his only goal was to find his sister.

A young, light-skinned Black man stepped in his way and gestured to him. "This way, Mr. Parkin."

"What?"

"Your sister's down this way. I'm Lars, one of Morgan's people," the man replied, hustling Alex past anyone who might have slowed them down.

Just how many *people* did this Morgan lady have?

They reached the door to the exam room, and suddenly Alex's feet locked up.

Lars seemed to understand. "She's still unconscious, but she's breathing okay. They stopped the bleeding. I'm sorry this happened. Honestly."

He swallowed hard, touched by the man's compassion. It sounded sincere. "Thank you."

"I'll be here if you need me," Lars said, and stepped aside.

Alex made himself move forward, fearing more than he could put into words. All he wanted to do was hold Miri and know she was going to be okay. He figured the ER staff would give him hell the instant he headed into the room, but instead a nurse looked up from a computer terminal. She was short and Black and looked like she knew what she was doing. Had probably been doing it for longer than his sister had been alive.

"I'm Miri Parkin's brother."

"Oh, good. Just know that she looks kinda rough."

The nurse waved him forward and pulled back the curtain.

Alex stepped closer and gasped. His sister lay on a bed, her neck and the upper portion of her chest covered in dried blood. A neck brace held her head immobile and oxygen flowed into her nose through a tube. Miri's eyes were closed, her chest rising slowly with each inhalation. Her skin seemed sculpted from wax, not the light tan he'd seen this afternoon. A heart monitor beeped steadily and there seemed to be a million IV lines.

"Oh dear God," he said.

The nurse patted his arm. "She's doing better, honey. Much better. The good Lord looked after her, that's for sure."

"Mr. Parkin?"

Alex turned to find a gentleman in a turban—Doctor Singh, according to the man's name badge.

"How bad is she?"

"She's stable. I've ordered a CAT scan to ensure there's nothing going on in her skull that we wouldn't like. Her pupils are equal and I'm not seeing any sign of an intracranial bleed, but we want to be sure. After that, we'll monitor her vitals and wait for her to regain consciousness. It all depends on what we learn from the tests."

Alex liked this guy. There was no "I am God" attitude. He just delivered the news in an honest and reassuring tone.

"Thank you for all you've done for her. She's . . . "

"Your sister," the nurse said, checking Miri's blood pressure. "Most of us got one. They're God's precious gift."

He looked at Miri, his eyes clouding with tears now.

"That's exactly what she is."

And I almost lost you.

After Lars had thrown an uncharacteristic fit and insisted that Morgan be checked out by a doctor, she had submitted to an exam and then found solace in an empty waiting room. Once she was settled, her friend brought her hot tea and an ice pack. She couldn't decide if the latter needed to be on her throat or her shoulder, so she kept shifting it around.

A nurse had been kind enough to give her a set of scrubs so the cops could take her bloody clothes. Maybe they'd get lucky and find DNA that would lead them to the attacker, if the fingerprints on the gun didn't turn up anything.

The cops didn't realize that Veritas had already turned its vast resources toward finding the bastard. Though she'd love to be the one to run him down, she suspected that honor would go to Neil. When Iceman was in hunter mode, nothing stopped him.

A text came through. As she picked up the phone, she noticed the blood embedded around her nails, and sighed. If she hadn't trusted her instincts, Miri Parkin would have been in that guy's trunk, headed for hell.

The text was from Lars: Parkin had arrived and word was that the X-rays and CAT scan were clear, though Miri still hadn't regained consciousness.

"At least that's something," Morgan murmured.

After another sip of tea, she lay down on the couch, pulling a blanket over her. She'd give Parkin a bit more time, then she'd go see him and his sister. After that, she was headed home, as dawn was only a few hours away.

Rest didn't come as easily as she'd hoped, not with all those questions firing through her head. Was this a random attack? Something the Russians had cooked up to sway Parkin to their camp? Or was this one of his old enemies hitting at his most vulnerable spot?

When her eyes finally drifted shut, all she could hear were Miri's desperate screams and the sound of screeching tires.

After the tests had revealed that nothing bad was going on, they'd moved Miri to a more private room. Her roommate was sound asleep, so Alex stood by the side of her bed, rubbing his fingers across the back of her hand. He used to do that when they were kids, even when she was a newborn.

His mom hadn't said much during the pregnancy, other than to complain about another mouth to feed. Her continued indifference had triggered something deep within Alex, and he took to watching over his sister from the moment she came home from the hospital. Because after all those years of being alone, he'd been given someone to love.

To his joy, that love had been mutual. He still remembered hurrying home from school, not bothering to take part in any after-school activities, always concerned about what had happened to Miri during the day. Once she'd learned to walk, she would meet him at the door, her tiny arms going around his neck. He blinked away tears even now.

Miri had never stinted on her love, at least until the day they marched him out of the courtroom in chains, the "guilty" verdict ringing in his ears. Barely sixteen, she hadn't cried, just stared at him as if he'd destroyed her whole world.

In some ways, he had. She'd been forced to move in with their maternal aunt and uncle in Belle Chasse, a solemnly religious pair who didn't have kids of their own. Suddenly having a teenager to raise, one who was hellfire on her best days, proved too much for them. They reacted with impossibly strict rules that no teenager could have handled. Miri rebelled. Repeatedly.

Alex had heard she'd run away twice during his first year

in prison. He remembered the rank fear he'd felt, knowing she was on the streets, alone. He knew what predators did with young girls, had seen the aftermath. Thank God nothing bad had happened to her. Or, if it had, she hadn't told anyone, not even him.

After the second time she'd run away and returned, he'd pleaded for her to stay with Aunt Karen and Uncle Mike. She had, though there were a few months when she didn't write or talk to him on the phone. Their aunt and uncle said she didn't want anything to do with him.

It came as no surprise that once she reached eighteen, she bailed out of their home to live on her own. Now she was under his care again, and he'd already failed to protect her the first night he'd been home.

Alex leaned against the bed railing, watching each breath. They'd removed the cervical collar and washed most of the blood off her face and neck, but there were still specks here and there. The ER nurse had Steri-Stripped the cut that reached into her hairline, but he knew Miri would be displeased when she realized they'd shaved the hair on either side of the wound.

"I'm so sorry, Monkey," he whispered, rubbing her hand again.

The door opened quietly behind him. He turned, expecting a nurse, but instead it was Morgan Blake who slowly entered the room. She was in scrubs, an ice pack lying over one shoulder, moving like every muscle was on fire. When she drew closer to the bed, he saw the start of a bruise on her jaw. The same on her throat.

Shit.

This woman had taken a beating to save his sister. Every spiteful word he'd intended to throw at her went back down like bitter medicine.

Morgan leaned on the bedrail next to him, looking down at the patient, her expression thoughtful. "How is she?"

"As good as can be expected. No fractures or bleeding in her head. We just have to wait for her to wake up."

Please God, let her wake up.

"She will. Your sister's strong. She nailed that bastard, hard."

He listened with increasing pride as Morgan explained how Miri, all of about one hundred twenty pounds, had splattered the guy's nose across his face.

"You're right, she is tough," he said. "Always has been stronger than me."

Morgan looked over at him, dark circles under her eyes. "I'm so very sorry, Parkin. I should have stuck to her, and I didn't. I let her out of my sight and—"

She's blaming herself for this?

"No, it wasn't your responsibility. This is *my* fault," he insisted. "I should have known someone would go after her to get to me. The cat should have been a wake-up call."

For a moment, the only sound was the beep of Miri's heart monitor echoing in the room.

Morgan turned to leave, and he caught her arm. His long, tanned fingers lightly curled around her, a dark contrast to her paler skin. The touch radiated heat, though the room was cool.

"Thank you. I won't ever forget what you did for her."

She nodded, the guilt still in her eyes, and left him alone to his fears. Not once had she spun a sales pitch about Veritas, how he should work with the good guys for a change. The Russians wouldn't have been so thoughtful. They would have used this situation to put the thumbscrews to him.

Because they all knew he had only one true weakness: the young woman lying on the bed in front of him.

Chapter Eight

September 18th
Tulane Medical Center

Alex opened his eyes as his neck complained about the hours spent in a chair. Not that he'd slept much. A glance at his phone told him it was approaching seven in the morning. Miri's heart monitor sped up, and he shot out of his chair. He looked down at her only to find two very confused eyes blinking back at him.

"Hey," he said, trying not to let her know he was only a step away from tears. "You're awake."

She kept blinking, but didn't reply. What if she didn't remember him?

"Miri? Talk to me. Let me know you're there. You're freaking me out."

She croaked, "Alex?"

Thank you, God.

"Need some water?" She nodded and he slowly raised the head of the bed and let her sip water through a straw. When she was done, Miri stared back at him.

"What . . . " Then she frowned as her hand migrated toward her head wound. He caught it before it reached its destination.

"Best not to touch that."

Now her eyes began to reflect panic.

"You have a concussion, but that's the worst of it. How much do you remember?" he asked gently.

Thank God he didn't have to tell her she'd been raped. That thought made his stomach pitch.

"Not much. I . . . went to work . . . " Her eyes widened.

"The alley . . . "

"You remember the guy?"

Miri gave a tentative nod, then winced in pain. "Yeah. He was big. He . . . " She reached up again, and this time he allowed her to gingerly touch the wound. She winced again. "How bad is it?"

"You look like a shaved poodle, but that's about it. It'll heal quickly. You're lucky."

She frowned, not appreciating his attempt at humor. "There was a woman. She went after that guy . . . kicked his ass."

"So did you. You broke his nose."

A half smile formed. "I wanted to do more than that."

You and me both, Sis.

"Your friend Shanita came by and stayed for a while. She's really worried about you."

"Oh, damn, it was her birthday. I totally messed that up."

"Don't worry, she said you guys can celebrate another night." He hesitated, then added, "She'll let your boss know you won't be in today. So how long have you been working at a bar?"

Miri grimaced, and he suspected it had nothing to do with the head wound. "I didn't mention that, did I?"

"Because you knew I wouldn't like it."

"Well, you weren't here, and I'm old enough to do what I want."

He had no way to argue that point. "So it appears. When did you change jobs?"

"Six months ago. I needed more money."

Something else he didn't know about his sister. "Is it possible someone followed you from work? Some creep?"

"Yeah, I've seen him before at the bar. He never talked to me, but he'd watch me all the time. Same thing tonight—I felt someone watching me. Might have been him."

Or it might have been Morgan and her people, and for once he was grateful for their interference. "You know this bastard's name?"

"No. He always paid cash for his drinks." She sighed

deeply. "I can't stay here. I don't have any insurance."

"I'll take care of it." Her frown grew. "I'll take care of it *legally*, okay? That's what big brothers do."

How the hell he'd pull that off, he had no idea, but right now the truth wasn't important. Alex took her hand, and her expression softened.

"The cops will want to talk to you. Tell them what you remember and maybe we can bag this SOB." She shivered. "It's okay to be scared, Miri. That's normal."

"But I can't get him out of my mind. I feel him touching me and breathing on me and . . . "

"That's as far as it went. Get some sleep. It'll help. It gets better in time."

She gazed up into his eyes as if he'd given something away.

"Things happened to you in prison, didn't they? Uncle Mike wouldn't tell me anything, just said it was the Lord's justice, but I knew it was bad."

Alex nodded. "It *was* bad, but I made it through. You'll do the same."

"I love you," she whispered. "I'm sorry I didn't tell you that last night, when you first got home."

Her eyes drifted closed again, and he tucked her arm under the sheets. Leaning over, he kissed her forehead, like he had every night when she was a kid.

"I love you, too," he whispered back.

Alex's stomach rumbled, reminding him that he hadn't eaten since the pizza the night before. Now that he knew his sister was going to be okay, he needed breakfast. He found the Neil dude leaning up against the wall just outside the door, arms crossed over his chest.

"She's awake," Alex reported, enjoying the euphoria those two words brought to his soul.

"That's good news," the man replied.

"Headed to get some food," Alex said. "I'll let the nurses know she's doing okay."

"I'll keep an eye on her for you."

Alex gave him a respectful nod. "Thanks."

Maybe having that intense of a guy watching over Miri wasn't a bad thing, just as long as he remained on the side of the angels.

The sound of ringing brought Morgan back to consciousness. As she shifted in bed, the pain in her neck brought her up short. She dragged a hand across the nightstand, finally locating the phone.

"Yeah?" she asked, blinking at the clock. It was just half past seven in the morning.

"Parkin's gone missing," Neil said.

She sat up, despite the discomfort. "What do you mean, missing?"

"He headed down to the cafeteria thirty minutes ago and never came back. I had Lars check on him, and according to the staff, he never made it down there."

"You get a tracker on his phone?"

"Affirmative. He was in the hospital for a short time, and then the tracker stopped working."

"You think he did a runner?"

"No way," Neil said. "His sister is awake now. He didn't strike me as the type to bail on her."

"The Russians?"

"That's my guess. They must have heard what went down last night and decided to nab him for a little chat. Probably something along the lines of, 'Nice sister you have there, pity if anything *else* happened to her.'"

"Which means Parkin could be anywhere." *Or dead.* Morgan groaned. "Okay, put the word out. Maybe someone will spot him."

"We need to move the girl to a safe house."

She blinked at his suggestion. "Since her brother's not on the team, we have no obligation to do that. At least not yet."

"Doesn't matter. This girl is in danger, and we need her out of the way so Parkin can make the right decision."

Morgan cranked an eyebrow. This wasn't Neil's usual

behavior. Did Miri Parkin remind him of his own sister, the one he hadn't been able to save?

"I'll talk to Crispin. Either way, if Parkin doesn't show back up, I have to let her know what's going on."

"Affirmative. I'll be here."

When the call ended, Morgan pulled herself out of bed and made slow progress toward the shower. After last night's battle, she felt eighty. Then she smirked at the thought of just how sore Miri's attacker was this morning, no doubt swimming in a world of hurt with that broken nose.

"Rot in hell, you bastard."

As the hot water hit the sore spots, her mind turned back to Parkin. He was a hothead, and if the Russians had picked him up, he might go ballistic, get in Buryshkin's face. If that happened, it was a good bet that Miri would never see her brother alive again.

The farther the car got from the hospital, the more pissed off Alex became. He'd been in the elevator, headed toward the cafeteria for an orgy of bacon, eggs, and biscuits to celebrate his sister waking up. He'd paid scant attention when a man had joined him one floor down. Then another guy had stepped into the elevator the floor below that and Alex's radar went off. One wore a black suit, the other brown, but the subtle bulges under their jackets spoke of armed thugs, not morticians.

Black Suit had informed Alex they were going for a drive and that if he thought to raise the alarm, someone—not him— would get shot. It wouldn't matter if it was a nurse, a doctor, or a visitor, that person would pay for his lack of cooperation. Given the heavy Russian accent, Alex knew these guys meant business. They'd waited for the perfect time to corral him, and they clearly knew which buttons to push. Though furious, he had to appreciate expertise when he saw it.

The instant they'd gotten into the car, Black Suit had demanded Alex's phone. His tone said that refusing would not be a good idea. Alex sighed and handed it to the man in the front seat. The Russian popped the back off, fiddled with it, then shook his head. He pulled something out and reassembled the phone.

"There is bug on the phone." The tracker in question went flying out a side window.

Veritas.

There'd been a moment during the night when Alex had gone to talk to his sister's nurse and had left his el cheapo phone in Miri's room. Apparently old buddy Neil had tapped it while he was gone. He made a mental note to check it over once this meeting ended, because it was a good bet the Russian had stealthily inserted one of his own, if they meant to keep him alive. A moment later the cell phone came back his way, the battery removed, no doubt to keep his location from being monitored by the cell towers. He shoved both into his back pocket.

After driving through a Starbucks to pick up coffee, a move that made no sense to Alex, they drove a short distance to park in Lafayette Cemetery No. 1, near one of the large mausoleums. A short time later, a car identical to theirs pulled up behind them.

The door locks clicked open and a man joined Alex in the back of the sedan. He was probably about fifty, with short graying hair and a blackwork tattoo of a skull peeking above the collar of his starched white shirt.

Mikhail had told Alex that tattoos were a Russian gangster's résumé, a skin-deep representation of his crimes. The skull meant the man had committed murder. There were more tattoos on his hands and fingers, along with letters in the Cyrillic alphabet, revealing that he'd been in and out of jail repeatedly. Buryshkin had not sent a low-level flunky to this meeting.

"Good morning, Sasha Parkin," the man said, his accent heavy. "I am Vasily. I am here on behalf of certain interested parties."

"What a surprise," Alex said, then took another sip of his

coffee. He calculated the odds of launching the hot drink in this newcomer's face, then getting out of the car before someone put a bullet in his skull.

"I see you working out an escape strategy. Don't. These two gentlemen are highly trained and will not allow you to harm me. Because if you did, they die."

"Now there's an incentive," Alex replied. "Let's get something straight right now. If you bastards had anything to do with my sister getting hurt last night, you are fucking dead. You got it?"

"We had nothing to do with that."

I almost believe you.

"Okay, so what's your spiel?" Alex already suspected what it would be; he just didn't know how hard they were going to play ball.

"You have two options," Vasily explained. "You agree to work for us, and in exchange, you and your sister will be offered our protection."

"And option number two?"

"You turn us down, and we will take you to the bayou and feed you to the alligators. While you are still alive. Your poor *defenseless* sister will never know what happened to you."

The coffee in Alex's stomach turned to corrosive acid even as his anger built. Right now, kicking some Russian gangster ass would feel so good. But it wasn't going to happen when it was three against one, not with them using Miri as leverage.

The old Alex would have taken them on, despite the bad odds. The new one was more patient, more willing to wait until the perfect moment to exact punishment.

He made sure to keep his voice free of the rage careening around inside of him. "With choices like that, you guys must be batting a thousand when it comes to recruitment."

Vasily smiled, revealing tobacco-stained teeth. "We take care of our own. As a show of good will, we will determine who hurt your sister and bring him to you. Then we will discard the body once you are finished with him, no questions asked."

Damn, that was tempting. If nothing more, these guys knew how to make corpses disappear.

Alex finished his coffee and set the empty container in the cup holder. "Why am I so damned important?"

"That is not for me to say. So what will it be? A new life, or a very brutal death?"

Alex knew this wasn't a bluff. He'd just disappear and there would be no one to take care of Miri. Veritas certainly wasn't going to watch over her once he was out of the picture.

As long as he was alive, he was the prize that made everyone sit up and take notice. He might even have an option to try to turn things in his favor. And now, given what they'd just threatened, a chance to go after Buryshkin himself. It wasn't what he'd planned as he'd walked out of prison, but these people had set the game in motion.

It was time to do some negotiating of his own. "I don't kill law enforcement officers, and I don't peddle dope."

"You will if we ask it of you."

Alex ground his teeth. "No, I won't. And don't tell me you're going to chop me into gator bait over those stipulations, because you want me on your team too badly."

No response.

"I want to know who set me up. Sent me to prison. Those are my terms."

The man cocked his head. "I would have figured you'd be willing to do anything to keep your sister safe."

"I am. Including killing *all* of you," Alex said, holding the man's gaze. "Slowly, painfully, and with great malice."

Vasily broke out in laughter, slapping his thigh. "*Grigori byl prav. Etot chelovek imeyet nabor zheleza sharov,*" he said to the others, and they laughed as well.

The senior Russian had said something about Grigori being right, that Alex had a set of iron balls. He kept his expression neutral, as if he didn't know the language that well.

"You are more than I anticipated, Parkin," Vasily said.

"I aim to please. If I join up with you, what do you want me to do?"

"We want you to accept Veritas's offer. Get close to them. Make them trust you. We will ask more of you at a later time, of course."

"Let me guess, you want me in position to conduct an assassination? The target would be Crispin Wilder, right?"

The Russian's bushy eyebrow rose. "Perhaps yes. Perhaps no."

That's what I thought.

They wanted to use him to take down Wilder in the optimistic hope that the rest of the organization would collapse without its leader. It was unlikely he'd get anywhere near Veritas's leader, but he'd cross that bridge when the time came.

"We have a deal?" the Russian said.

Alex nodded, knowing he'd just made a pact with the devil himself. Or at least the devil's head minion.

He held out his hand and they shook. "Deal."

His new business partners dropped Alex a block from the hospital. Knowing it would be suspicious if he didn't eat, and still starving, he popped into the cafeteria and wolfed down his breakfast. When he returned to his sister's room, he found Neil on guard duty. Didn't the guy ever have to go to the can?

"Where have you been?" the watchdog demanded.

"Went for a walk, then got some breakfast. My sister okay?"

Neil nodded, his expression telling Alex he didn't believe him. "That was some walk."

"Yeah, it was."

There was a stare-off for a second or two. "Doctor was in, and he's cutting her loose," he reported. "The detectives interviewed her right after that. She's eating breakfast and complaining about it."

"You know, I consider all that good news." Alex took a deep breath, feeling his future shift onto a razor's edge. It was time to bite the bullet. "Tell Morgan I'm in, if you guys will provide protection for Miri."

A nod returned. "Better warn your sister what's about to come down, because she'll be headed to a safe house."

Alex wasn't exactly thrilled with that, but it would get her out of harm's way if the Russians decided to come after her. At this point he had to trust someone, though that made his gut twist. "I'll let her know."

He stepped inside the room to find Miri picking dubiously at a poached egg like it contained live spiders.

"Hey, look at you," he said. No IV, no oxygen. She'd definitely made progress while he'd been getting the recruitment speech from the mob.

Miri frowned up at him and pointed at the egg with a fork. "This food sucks."

"It's supposed to. It's what gets you out of the hospital quicker."

She pushed the tray away. "Yeah, well, the doctor said I can go home in a couple hours. I don't know why they're stalling."

Alex suspect it was because Veritas needed time to get their plans in motion.

"That's great news, but there's something we need to talk about," he replied.

Miri cocked her head, giving him the once-over. "What's up, brother?"

He stalled for time. "You talked to the cops?" he asked, even though he already knew the answer.

"Yeah. They asked if I'd been drinking, why I went in the alley, and did I know the creeper. They said they'd run the fingerprints off the gun, see if it matched anyone in their database."

He shared her frustration. "They'll find him if he has a record."

"Maybe." She frowned at him. "Promise you won't go after this bastard."

"I won't make that promise."

She frowned. "Dammit, Alex, I can't handle it if you go back to prison because of me."

"What happens, happens," he insisted. "I don't think you should go back home just yet. I . . . have some people who will watch over you, but that means you'll have to go with them to a safe house."

"No, that's ridiculous," Miri said. "I'm going home."

"No, you're not. It's too dangerous. I have some stuff to get straightened out, and—"

"Stuff?" She glowered at him. "What the hell have you gotten yourself into now?"

He had no choice but to tell her some of the truth, though he knew it would only make her angrier. "The woman from last night? Morgan? She's part of a private security agency."

"So?"

He lowered his voice. "I'm going to be working with them to bring down a Russian drug lord. That way, I can prove that I was innocent. Get my record cleared."

Or at least that was the carrot Veritas had dangled in front of him. It could all be a lie, but now he had no choice.

She stared at him. "That's all that's important to you, isn't it? That the world knows you're innocent?"

Alex shook his head, growing angry as well. "No. The most important thing in my life is *you*. Nothing else. If anything happened . . . " His voice caught as he trailed off. He cleared his throat. "I need you someplace safe. I can't do my job worrying about you all the time."

"Why can't we just leave? Go somewhere else? Start over?"

"I'd love to, Monkey, but the Russians will find us."

"Why do they care about you? I mean, you're just an ex-con."

That was brutally honest and hurt more than it should.

"They say I owe them because they kept me alive in the joint. Kept me from being . . . " No, he couldn't tell her that.

Miri's eyes widened, indicating that she'd filled in the missing word. "That really happens in there?"

"Yes. Men get . . . raped, too."

"You?"

"No, but it got damned close."

"Oh God." She looked away, her eyes growing moist. "There's no other way?"

"No, I'm sorry, there isn't."

She wiped away a lone tear. "So is the Morgan lady going to be my babysitter?"

"No, it's a guy named Neil. Morgan says he's the best."

"You're ditching me with some dude you don't know?" she said, her eyes narrowing. "He could be a pervert or something."

"I've been called many things, but never a perv," the man said as he entered the room.

Miri sized up the newcomer. "You're the bullet catcher?"

"I prefer the term bodyguard," he replied. "We have a safe place to hide you until your brother finishes his business with us."

"What if I refuse to go there with you?"

"Then whoever worked you over last night will get another shot at you. Next time he'll do a helluva lot more than try to stash your body next to his spare tire."

Miri's eyes widened.

"These people are trying to help both of us," Alex added. "We're in over our heads now, and it's not because of anything either of us have done."

"I don't want anyone watching over me. Why can't I just go home? I'll stay there. I won't answer the door."

Neil moved closer now, arms crossed over his chest. "I can get into your house in under ten seconds, no matter how many locks you have in place. If I'm a pervert, I will do whatever I want to you and nobody will hear you scream. If I'm a Russian assassin, all it takes is one shot to the head. Or I could cut your throat if I'm really into sending a brutal message to your brother. Either way, you're dead, or worse than dead. It's just that simple."

Miri paled even more, sucking in a tight breath.

Alex held his own breath, hating this asshole for being so graphic, but maybe the man's instincts were right. She had to agree to this on her own.

Then that flare of defiance flashed in his sister's eyes, the one he remembered so well. "I got it. I'm a victim and only you big, strong males can save me. Well, that's bullshit."

"Miri—" Alex began.

"No. I am going to *my* house." She pointed at Neil. "If *you* want to keep me alive, then you're there with me. If not, *adios*, buddy."

The man's rock-hard expression cracked a bit. "It's not safe at your place."

"I understand that, but right now it's all I've got. So are you in or out?"

Alex and Neil traded looks.

"I'm in," Neil said. "With a fuckton of protest."

"Got that. I have a few tricks up my sleeve too, at least once my head stops pounding," Miri said, the defiance draining away now. She looked at Alex. "This is all legal, right?"

"Totally."

Her eyes moved back to Neil, still guarded. "You any good, Bullet Catcher?"

"I've been told I am," he replied evenly.

"So you have a black belt or something?"

"Krav Maga."

Miri shot Alex a questioning look.

"It's a form of defense taught by the Israeli military. It means he's seriously badass."

She raised an eyebrow, skeptical. "How long do I have to hide out with this seriously badass dude?"

"Until it's done," Alex said. *Or I'm dead.*

"What if something happens to you?" she asked, quieter now, almost as if she'd heard his thoughts.

"I'll be very careful," he said.

"He'll be working with Morgan, the woman from last night at the bar. If I had to have someone watch my back, it'd be her," Neil said.

Apparently that did the trick, as Miri gave a stiff nod of agreement. "Okay, you got me for one week. Get it sorted out, bro, because I'm gone if you don't."

"I'll set everything in motion," Neil said, then left the room, closing the door behind him.

"He's got a big rod up his ass," Miri said.

"Yeah, but he'll keep you safe. When this is done, we'll move on. Go someplace new and start over."

"Promise?"

Alex nodded. "There's one other thing you need to know. Your cat . . . is dead."

"What?" she blurted. "How?"

"Someone killed him. I found him in the trash can. I think it might have been the guy from last night." *Or a message to me.* "I'm so sorry, Miri."

"No, Mr. Toes . . . " she murmured. She reached for Alex and they hugged for a long time, her tears wetting his collar. He fought not to add some of his own, not just for the death of a pet, but the near loss of the only person he loved.

"You really didn't steal the drugs, did you?" she whispered into his ear.

"No, I didn't. I would never have done something like that to you."

She let him go. "So who did? That evil ex-wife of yours?"

"I don't know. But I'll find out soon enough."

Miri took a long breath and released it slowly. "Then go do what you have to do, but I swear, if you die on me I'll hate you forever."

Alex smiled. "You stay smart and stay safe. I don't trust most people, but I think this Neil guy will be there for you."

"He damned well better," she said firmly.

Alex found the taciturn man standing guard just outside the door.

"Morgan is waiting for you downstairs in the parking lot."

Alex took one last glance toward his sister's room.

"Don't worry, she'll be safe with me," Neil added more quietly.

Alex studied the man who held Miri's life in his hands. "I told her I trusted you, but if you're just blowing smoke up my ass and anything happens to her—"

A steel-cold look speared him now. "I don't blow smoke, Parkin, not about this kind of thing. I had a sister once, and I wasn't there to keep her alive. I know what that fear is like."

Shit. "Got it. And I'm sorry she died."

Neil's eyes remained frosty. "Believe me, so are the bastards who killed her."

Chapter Nine

"You made the right decision, Parkin," Morgan Blake said.

"Jury's still out on that," he replied.

No matter how he looked at it, he was hosed. Without trying, he'd put himself between two powerful organizations, either of which would be happy to roll right over him in pursuit of their goals. In the Russians' case, he'd be screaming gator bait.

Despite their reputation, he didn't completely trust Veritas, either. They were just a little too good to be true. Still, Morgan had protected his sister, and that had earned her a few points, at least until she did something that erased them. Which he knew would come soon enough.

Her phone rang just as she pulled out of the hospital parking lot.

"Yeah?" She paused. "Oh hell. When?" She looked at Alex and then back to the road. "Okay. Is Odin up to working today?" She listened for a time. "Okay, then we'll do a search on our own. What?" More words, then, "Yeah, that'll work. Bring him to Parkin's sister's house ASAP. Thanks, Sam." Morgan ended the call.

"What's up?" Alex asked, his nerves on edge.

"We have a contact in the DEA who says cops are going to drop by Miri's house and do a search to see if they can scare up some drugs."

"Jesus. Not again."

"Don't worry. If there is any stuff, we'll get rid of it."

"How?"

"Watch and learn, Parkin. Watch and learn."

When he entered his sister's house, he half-expected cops to come bursting out of the walls. Instead, it looked exactly as he'd left it the night before. Morgan walked to the back door, unlocked it, and stepped outside. Words were traded with someone and then she returned with a fawn and black Malanois, a Belgian Shepherd. Apparently whoever had delivered the dog had departed.

"Odin, meet Alex Parkin. Don't eat him. He can't help that he's a mouthy jerk sometimes."

Alex gave her a frown. "So what's with the canine?"

Morgan chuckled, then ruffled the dog's fur. "Odin has something in common with you: He's ex-DEA. He was at the top of his game until a dealer shot him and sidelined him from active duty. He's retired now, along with his handler. They work for us every now and then. Odin's job today is to keep your ass out of jail."

The penny dropped. "He's a drug-sniffing dog."

"Yup." She dialed her phone. "Hey, you feeling better? Good. The flu can be a bitch. Yeah, Odin's in place." She held the phone out toward the dog and a voice gave an order in what sounded like Dutch.

The dog began nosing his way through the living room, then to the kitchen. It wasn't the first time Alex had seen a drug dog working a scene, but this time it was his home, or Miri's at least, and the stakes were massive.

"He damned well better not find anything," he said, both aggravated and more afraid than he'd been in a long time. "Miri isn't a druggie. No way."

"I know. I read your bio. Your mom was an addict, so neither of you guys are into that kind of stuff."

"Bio?"

"We do a full background check on anyone we work with," she replied, following the hound as he made his way into Miri's bedroom. A moment later Odin whined, then sat down.

"That's his alert," Morgan said. The shepherd seemed

particularly interested in the stack of file boxes.

"There can't be anything in those," Alex said. "I just went through them yesterday. It's all old clothes and crap."

Morgan ignored him, pulling down one box at a time, revealing the door behind them. She gave that a frown, then kept working through the boxes until she'd reached the one that Odin had found of interest. She flipped open the lid and fished through the pile of clothes.

Alex moved closer, wondering if this was all just street theater to make him feel more grateful to Veritas.

"Hell . . . oo," Morgan muttered, pulling out a quart baggie full of white powder. Cocaine. "This has gotta be delivery weight. You're looking at thirty years for this. And what do we have here?" She used a piece of his old clothing to retrieve a Glock. She sniffed the barrel. "Been fired recently. Any chance this is your sister's?"

"No. She has a Taurus." He stared at the firearm and the coke, growing lightheaded. "I can't go back. I won't go back."

I'll die this time.

Morgan dug further into the box but didn't find anything else of interest. When she looked over, Alex had slid down the wall until his butt hit the floor, his head in his hands. It was as if he'd lost the will to remain upright. Odin sat nearby, watching him closely.

"Parkin, you okay?" No reply. "Hey! Talk to me," she said, growing concerned.

He let his hands fall away, his face ashen. "It isn't just me they're after. This might send my sister to prison, too."

"Yes, it might. Frankly, I'm not surprised. You put some heavyweight dealers away, and that means you have a lot of enemies." She weighed the bag in her hand. "Don't worry, I'll take care of it. Oh, and I'll need two clean trash bags."

A grunt was the reply as Morgan headed to the bathroom, Odin trotting along behind her. She flushed the coke, then set the plastic bag in the sink. then spoke to his handler on the phone. He sent the dog off again with another command.

Digging around under the bathroom sink, Morgan located the toilet-bowl cleaner and pulled it out.

Alex returned, watching her from the doorway. His color was better, and she knew it was only a matter of time before his temper took over.

"Has the hound's nose found anything else?" she asked as she took one of the bags.

"No, I think that's it. As if that isn't enough." He shook himself. "If you didn't have contacts in the DEA—"

"That's my job, outthinking bad guys. Sometimes I'm really good at it. Other times . . . "

"Like at the bar last night?" he asked.

She nodded. "I was looking for Russians, not stalkers. That's my fault. I'm sorry."

"You were there. I sure as hell wasn't."

It appeared they were both wearing hair shirts. She knew she'd never forget Miri's face covered in blood.

Morgan dropped the cocaine bag inside a trash bag and set it aside. Then she swished the bright-blue cleaner around the toilet bowl, flushed, repeated the process, took a few tissues and wiped down the outside of the tank, then flushed those. After cleaning her hands, she scrubbed down the sink.

When she returned to the bedroom, the one bag in hand, she stared at the gun lying on the bed. "Did you touch it?"

"No way. But with my luck, whoever put it there would have found a way to get my prints on it. Or my sister's," Alex said. "And there's more bad news: Miri's gun is missing from the kitchen drawer."

"Of course it is."

Morgan put the empty trash bag over her hand, then picked up the gun, reversing the bag over it to try to preserve any fingerprints. With both trash bags in hand she headed for the door. "I'll be right back after I hand these off. If the cops show up, don't let them in unless they have a warrant. Oh, and could you get Odin some water?"

"Sure," he replied, but she could tell he was only half paying attention. No doubt his head was already back in prison, hearing the cell doors close behind him.

Not this time.

Morgan slipped out the back door into the late morning heat. A quick walk through the neighbor's yard got her to the next street. Sam waited in a car at the curb.

He looked up as she approached, seeing something in her hand. "You found something."

"Yeah, we did. Have Crispin thank our contact at the DEA. I took care of the coke, but I need you to take the garbage out for me," she said, handing over the bags. "One is trash, the other can you run the serial number and see if you can get prints off of it. I want to know this gun's history before it was dropped into Parkin's life. Oh, and his sister's weapon is missing. She'll need to file a police report for that."

"I'll let Neil know." Sam placed the plastic bags on the passenger seat. "Who do you think planted the dope?"

"Parkin had an impressive string of busts against some seriously nasty people. Any one of them could have left these little 'welcome home' presents."

"They'd have to know he was out of the house. You think the assault on the sister was planned ahead of time?"

"That's a possibility. I'll take him to the safe house. Lars can pick Odin up there and get him back to his handler. He deserves a juicy steak."

"You regret taking lead on this mission now?" Sam asked.

"Not yet, but it's getting close," she said, then headed back toward the house.

The sound of slamming car doors had Alex up and at the window. His gut twisted when he saw four uniformed cops headed toward the front of the house, one with a battering ram. In front of them was the man he hated most in the world: his ex-partner, Dennis Simms.

Simms had packed on the pounds over the last six years and was going bald. It was petty, but Alex was pleased to see that time hadn't been good to him. He could never understand what his wife had seen in the guy.

No wonder she dumped your sorry ass.

Morgan entered through the back door. He shot a look at her. "They're here."

"Keep your cool. If you throw a punch, you're back in jail and the mission goes south."

Alex hesitated, his hand on the doorknob now. It felt molten in his fingers, he was clenching it so hard.

"He was screwing my wife. He executed the search warrant on my house. How do I know he didn't plant the dope then . . . and now?"

"You don't. But you have to trust me."

He glared at her, his jaw muscles tightening. "Last time I trusted someone, I got fucked over."

"This time you won't. Are you on board here?"

Alex took several deep breaths. "I have no other choice, do I?"

"No, you don't. I'm an attorney licensed to practice in the state of Louisiana. So as of now I'm *your* legal representative, so just look innocent and keep that anger to yourself. If you act like some juvenile dickhead, we're all screwed."

As she moved to open the door, Alex caught her arm. "You can be a pain in the ass, you know that?"

To his surprise, she winked. "Yeah, but right now this pain in the ass is in *your* corner, so let's get this done."

When Morgan opened the front door he took a long look at the man he'd once considered a friend. All Alex wanted to do was bury his fists in the bastard's face.

"Don't do it," she whispered. "It's not worth it at this point."

"Alex," Special Agent Simms said, pausing about seven feet out. He tapped a foot, his "tell" that he was nervous.

"Dennis," Alex said, trying to strangle his rage.

Better if I strangle him. Let him die slow.

Simms shot a look at Morgan and then back at Alex. "We need to search your house. I'm sure you'll want to cooperate and not create any hassles for us."

"Got a warrant?" Morgan cut in before Alex could tell him

to go fuck himself.

"Got one coming. Now just step out all nice and—"

"Wait a minute," one of the cops said. "You said you had a warrant."

"Dennis is known to lie," Alex said, boring his eyes into the man. "Especially on the witness stand."

Simms's eyes narrowed. "Come on, Alex, make it easy on yourself. You got nothing to hide, right?"

"Why are you here?" Morgan asked.

"Got a tip that someone was dealing drugs out of this location."

"Why you, specifically?"

Simms frowned. "I knew my old buddy was getting out yesterday, and I made sure that any tips about him or his sister were flagged to my attention."

Odin huffed.

Simms looked down at the dog who sat at Morgan's feet, then frowned again. "Look, just let us do the search, and then your . . . chick and the pooch won't get hurt."

Morgan laughed. "Wow, I haven't been called a chick in ages. I bet that charm gets you laid once every . . . decade?"

One of the cops snorted, failing to hide his smile, which said these locals didn't like Dennis any more than he did.

"Here's the deal, Special Agent Simms: I'm Mr. Parkin's attorney, so no warrant, no search," Morgan said. "And don't bother having these guys kick in the back door."

She stepped into his personal space. "Because if you try that bullshit, I'll be talking to your boss. And your *boss's* bosses," she said, the power rising in her voice. "By the time I am done, your next gig will be patting down incontinent little old ladies coming off cruise ships in Alaska. You got it?"

"Look, bitch—"

"Hey, watch your mouth," Alex cut in. "Treat the lady with respect."

"If you don't have a warrant, you're done," she said. "Come back with one and then we'll talk."

"So you have time to ditch the drugs?"

When Simms took a step forward, Odin sat and whined, his alert signal. Morgan looked down at the dog, then back up at the DEA agent.

"If you happen to have any drugs in your pocket, ditch them before you come back. Because if you think you're going to plant them on my client so you can arrest him, again, you're wrong."

Dennis blinked in surprise, his face growing red.

The lead cop swore under his breath, aggravated. "Look, I don't know what kind of pissing match is going on here, but we're out of it." He glared at Simms. "Next time, get a damned warrant."

The cops marched to their cars and drove off, leaving just the three of them and one panting dog.

Simms glowered. "You just bought yourself a shitload of hurt, Parkin."

Curiously, Alex felt his temper holding steady, and that wasn't what he'd expected. He should have killed this prick twice over by now. Maybe it was because, this time, he had someone solid watching his back. But when had he started thinking of Morgan as an ally, rather than an enemy waiting to throw him under the bus?

"Thanks for stopping by, Dennis," he said, putting on the false charm. "Say hi to my ex-wife, will you? Oh wait, she tossed you to the curb, didn't she? Sorry about that. We both got shafted."

He waited until Morgan walked inside, then closed the door in his ex-partner's face. His hands shook and his heart pounded. A short time later, a car engine gunned as Simms peeled out of the neighborhood.

Odin was back at the water bowl, slurping noisily, his job done.

"You okay?" Morgan asked.

She'd been impressive. Ballsy, even. Because of her, he wasn't headed back to jail.

"Thank you," he said, and meant it.

"Happy to help out. I'm just glad we caught it in time."

"He'll be back," Alex said, sobering. "The next time, we might not find the stuff, and—"

"There won't be a next time. We're about to move somewhere a *lot* more secure. I'll have someone keep an eye on the house until your sister and Neil get here, so her stuff doesn't get ripped off and nothing illegal is left behind."

Alex frowned, not liking the fact that he had no input in this plan. "I'm still not sure I can trust you, even after what just went down. You have to know that."

"Good. That's exactly where you should be, Parkin. Trust *no one* but your sister."

He blinked in surprise. That was the last thing he'd expected to hear.

"The biggest badass is going to walk away from this alive. Make sure it's you," she advised.

"What about you, Ms. Blake?"

"I just want to see Buryshkin fall. That's all that matters to me."

Which meant that everyone involved in this mission was expendable.

Even me.

Chapter Ten

Miri quickly realized that being under someone's protection meant losing almost all personal control. Once they'd reached her home, which had involved a circuitous route to ensure they weren't being followed, Neil, aka "Iceman", had dictated when and how she got out of his SUV. He'd insisted on doing a security sweep, then proceeded to give her a comprehensive set of rules that made her aching head reel.

Angry and frustrated, she slumped on the couch, trying to ignore him. Like that was possible.

"Did you hear what I said?" her bodyguard asked.

He'd positioned himself in the middle of the living room, hands on his hips, looking like a statue of some ancient warrior come to life. All he needed was a cape and he could double as a superhero.

Miri sighed, trying to comprehend how such a hottie could be such a dictatorial jerk.

"Did you hear me?" Neil asked, his voice tighter now, the only indication of his rising tension.

"Yeah, I heard you."

"Then repeat my instructions back to me," he insisted.

That pissed her off. She wasn't five.

"Let's see: This place is a damned death trap, I'm a complete moron for wanting to live in *my own home*, and because I've got two X chromosomes, you're the only reason I'll live to see next week. If I'm lucky."

He blinked. "I don't remember saying that last part."

"You thought it." And he didn't deny it either.

"Did you *understand* my instructions?" he demanded.

"Yeah. Don't go near the windows, don't answer the door, and follow your every command as if you're God Almighty."

A tiny quirk at the side of his mouth now. "That works."

Miri shook her head. She couldn't tell if that arrogance came from years in the military, or if it was just in her bullet catcher's DNA. No matter how Iceman got that way, she knew that he was going to drive her freaking crazy.

So damned unfair. The cutest guy I've seen in forever, and he's an asshole. And what is it with that earring anyway?

She'd come close to asking him a couple times, then backed off. Something told her that wouldn't be smart.

Her headache and the ache of her scalp wound said it was time to crash. She rose from the couch, more unsteadily than she preferred. "I'm going to get some sleep."

"Remember, stay away from the—" he began.

"I got it all the first time. You do your damned job, and I'll do mine."

As she entered her bedroom, she heard him muttering under his breath. Every fourth word started with "f".

Same to you, buddy.

By the time Miri was in bed, her anger was gone. Instead, tears formed as the last twenty-four hours caught up with her. Everything sucked. Alex was out of prison, but he was in deep trouble. Some sick creep had tried to kidnap her and beaten the hell out of her. Mr. Toes was dead. The sob came before she could stop it.

"You okay?" her guardian asked quietly from the doorway.

Wiping away a tear, Miri nodded. "Yeah. Getting there," she lied.

"Don't worry, I'll keep you safe," he replied, and then he vanished back into the living room, armed and lethal.

Damn you, Alex. What have you gotten us into?

Alex trailed alongside Morgan and the dog as they made their way through the French Quarter. They kept the pace slow in deference to Odin's limp, which had grown more noticeable now. Morgan had been right: Alex was like the dog. He was damaged, and no longer of value to his old employers. Put out to pasture. Except this pasture had wolves keen to rip out his throat.

His paranoia had gone full tilt, and that made him dismantle his phone, checking for bugs before they even left his sister's house. There hadn't been one. Apparently the Russians knew they could yank on his chain anytime they wanted. If not his, then Miri's, provided they could get to her.

Alex shifted his attention back to this part of New Orleans. His memories of the area had dimmed over time, both with the years in Angola and the fact that he'd spent most of the last six months of his pre-prison life working undercover in Baton Rouge.

The shops were all open, clueless tourists wandering around with beers or Hurricanes in their hands. The neon lights were gaudy, the music was in your face, and the sex for sale wasn't exactly subtle. "Hasn't changed much," he said, looking around.

"Never does," Morgan said.

"Where are we headed?"

"To do a little magic," she replied as she cut down a side street and led Odin up three short stairs into a business.

Alex paused and stared up at the sign. It was a Voodoo shop. "What the hell?"

The shop was painted a blue-green color, with mullioned windows and a gas lamp near the doorway. When he reached the entrance, he looked down to find a semicircle of white chalk markings just inside the door. The figures inscribed inside the arc made no sense to him.

As he debated whether or not he wanted to cross whatever the hell that thing was, a couple left the shop, chatting happily about something they'd bought. They didn't even seem to notice the symbols.

"Come on in. Adah won't bite," Morgan said, waving him in from her position by the cash register. At present, it was just her, Odin, and a shopkeeper inside. The moment Alex stepped over the threshold, a sneeze overtook him. Then another.

"Damned incense," he muttered. Then he realized the shop's clerk had heard him. Or was she the owner?

"We got ourselves a live one here, don't we?" the lady asked, smiling.

"We certainly do," Morgan replied.

Adah was about forty, with smooth mocha skin and dark eyes, probably a mixed-race Creole, descended from some of Louisiana's early colonial settlers. She was strikingly pretty, an earthy contrast to Morgan's more sophisticated beauty.

Alex tried not to stare at her or all the stuff in the shop. It proved impossible. Anything related to Voodoo had always spooked him. Some of the drug dealers swore they'd never get busted because they had a *loa,* or god, watching over them. Alex had proven a couple of them wrong. He wondered just how much that had pissed off their deities.

Why are we here?

He was about to ask that question when Morgan handed Odin's leash off to the woman.

"Lars will pick him up in about fifteen minutes and get him back to his handler. Figured you might like that."

"Surely," Adah replied, grinning now. "I wouldn't mind admirin' that fine young man again. Lars has got quite a smile on him."

"He's also a player, so watch out." After Morgan knelt to pet Odin, he settled his chin on his paws behind the counter and gave a long doggie sigh.

As Alex followed Morgan toward the back of the shop, he mouthed to the dog, "Thanks, buddy. I owe you one." Odin's tail wagged as if he'd actually understood him.

To his surprise, the woman reached out and touched Alex's arm. "Don't give up. Your time will come. But ya gotta believe it will."

He mumbled a thank-you and hurried to catch up with Morgan.

Your time will come. He barely suppressed the shiver that

rode up his spine. That was exactly what Grigori had said.

He found Morgan in a small room at the rear of the shop, a tiny space where Adah apparently did some sort of fortune telling. A whole bank of candles flickered on one side of the room, some graced with small offerings of coins or flowers or food. On the other side was a bookcase, filled with various tomes on the subject of Louisiana Voodoo.

Alex's skin twitched. He couldn't have been more ill at ease if he'd been in the middle of a gang shootout. He had zero desire to see into the future. His present was bad enough, so why find out what kind of hell awaited him down the line?

"I'm not really into all this Voodoo stuff."

Morgan eyed him. "Then you'll never really understand New Orleans, will you?"

"No need to. I'm from Texas."

"Ah, yes, Texas. The center of the universe. I once thought the same about New York City," she said. "Close the door, will you?"

He did as she asked, grumbling under his breath. When he turned back, Morgan stood in front of the bookcase. She tipped up onto her toes, clicked something on the top bookshelf, and the whole thing promptly swung open, revealing a heavy metal door. A series of numbers on an electronic keypad generated another click, which allowed her to push open the portal. It led into a hallway. She waved him through, clicked the bookcase back in place, and closed the door.

"You guys are really into cloak and dagger, aren't you?" he asked.

"Yeah, you could say that."

He followed her down the hallway. "Are all your safe houses like this?"

"No. Just depends on the location," she replied, heading up a wooden staircase. The stairs squeaked as she climbed.

"Maybe you should get these fixed or something."

"And ruin our early warning system?" she called down, grinning. "Not everything is high tech, you know."

She had to be messing with him, right? Or maybe not.

He admired the view as she continued up the staircase, and sighed. Nothing about this woman was low rent. Her butt was firm and round, her legs long and lithe.

I really do need to get laid. But first, he had to stay alive long enough to make that happen.

As she led him on, they passed through two more white steel doors, both requiring passcodes. Finally, they entered an apartment. The instant Morgan shut the door behind him, she set the alarm.

Alex walked farther into the living room, checking it out, and he had to admit that it was a nice place: warm beige walls, a big TV, black couch, and a couple chairs. The floors were wood and the lighting recessed.

If anything, it looked like one of those extended-stay executive apartments. It sure beat the hell out of a prison cell. When he went to one of the windows and carefully pushed back the curtain, he found that it overlooked a courtyard. No balcony. One less way for their enemies to get inside. He stared at the window and realized it had a special covering, most likely to keep someone from seeing inside the apartment.

Turning back, he found Morgan standing in front of the TV, which now displayed nine different security-camera feeds.

"Talk about being paranoid," he said.

"Better than being dead," she said.

"Okay, I'll bite. What if all this fancy security fails and the person you're babysitting dies?" he asked, just to see if he could get a rise out of her.

"We've got a great maid service. They're really good at sweeping up stray body parts and getting stains out of the furniture."

He found himself smiling.

"You want to eat first, or sleep?" she asked.

It was as if the S-word magically conjured up a yawn, one that hit him hard, no matter how he tried to stifle it. He raised his hand to cover his mouth.

"Sleep. I'm wasted," he mumbled around the yawn. He was barely able to move as it was.

"The bedroom on the right is yours. Keep the curtains drawn. You'll find clean clothes in the drawers and closet, and appropriate boy stuff in the medicine cabinet."

"Boy stuff?"

"It's like girl stuff, only different," Morgan said, deadpan. "Now, if the girl stuff is more your style . . . "

Alex cocked an eyebrow.

"Hey, whatever your kink is, it's all good," she said.

Before he knew what he was doing, he moved closer, pushing the space between them. So much had happened so quickly, and this woman had been in the heart of it. Saying "thank you" just didn't seem to cut it.

Something changed in her eyes, something about him being too close to her. Morgan immediately stepped back.

"Go! When you have a brain, we'll plan our strategy. Right now, you're too damn tired to be useful."

She was right.

The wood flooring creaked under Alex's feet as he entered the bedroom. The beige walls continued here, with heavy white curtains at the windows and a black, lightweight comforter on the bed. He kicked off his shoes, then made for the bathroom. Here, apricot walls greeted him—not his favorite color—and some sort of seashell shadowbox display on the wall beside the sink. It was too fussy for him.

He washed his face and arms, then toweled dry. Looking in the mirror told him that the dark circles under his eyes weren't going away without sleep. Lots of it.

Hearkening back to Morgan's comment, he pulled open the medicine cabinet and found the "boy stuff": razor, shaving cream, a comb, deodorant, a new toothbrush wrapped in plastic, and a tiny tube of toothpaste. He laid all of them on the counter near the sink. Then his eyes returned to the ribbed condoms stacked neatly in one corner of the cabinet. The grin came unbidden.

They gave a completely new meaning to the words "safe house."

His mind turned to his bodyguard and how her bruises were

barely hidden by her makeup. How she'd earned those bruises. For just a moment, he thought about what it would be like to take her to bed. Let that horizontal exercise clear his mind. Get his big head back in the game.

Another yawn stopped him mid-sexual-fantasy, so he stripped down to his underwear and crawled into a bed that was far too soft. He was so accustomed to sleeping on a hard surface, and Miri's couch hadn't been much better. This luxury felt surreal. How long would it take for that to change?

Alex tugged the blankets up against his nose, inhaling the floral scent of dryer sheets. The room was quiet. Too quiet. He blinked up at the ceiling, finding the glow of the small, red dot on the smoke detector distracting. It felt weird not to have a bunk above him.

This was how real people lived.

To try to lull himself to sleep, Alex closed his eyes and replayed the sounds of prison. He imagined the noises of the other men snoring, coughing, or talking in their sleep. The measured pace of the guards. The clang of doors. Perversely, the memories reassured him. Because, no matter how he looked at it, this new life scared the hell out of him.

"Parkin and I are at the safe house and he's crashed," Morgan said into her cell phone, cradling it against her shoulder as she moved around the kitchen. "I'm amazed he didn't fall asleep on the way over here," she added. "He was wiped."

"Not surprising, given all that's happened in the last day or so," Crispin replied. "Neil has his sister safely tucked away at her house. He reports that she's not a happy camper, and he hates the lack of security at the place. He called it a 'death trap.'"

"Good. Why should I have all the fun?"

"We're running down leads on the girl's assailant. I wonder if the attacker was a lone wolf, not part of the Russian deal."

"I'm inclined to agree, but the timing is suspicious as all

hell," Morgan replied. "Especially with planting the drugs and the gun in Miri's house."

Crispin spoke with someone on his end, then returned. "Sorry. What's your plan for tonight?"

"Once Parkin has slept, we're going to contact one of my confidential informants, see if he's heard anything about the new shipment. I'll find out if Parkin has any CI's we can tap as well. Between us, we'll try to locate where Buryshkin is hiding his dope."

"Good. Let me know how it goes. By the way, that gun you found was used in the murder of a local drug dealer named Juan Pablo Gutierrez. Fortunately, at least for Parkin, the gang banger died during the time our ex-con was in the ER with his sister."

"Damn, they really are trying to set this guy up." She looked toward the closed bedroom door and lowered her voice. "He won't go back. He'll die before that happens."

"I know. Keep an eye on him."

"I'll do my best."

"Remember, it's not always about winning," Crispin added.

"Riiight, boss."

Alex's dream was hardcore: just him and Morgan and a bed. She was naked, her long, tanned legs wrapped around him, her fingernails clawing his back as he drove himself into her, over and over. He felt her shuddering around him, and as she screamed his name . . .

His eyes snapped open and he groaned. It took a moment for his fog to clear. *Safe house.* With the woman he'd just been screwing in his dreams. The physical evidence of that X-rated dream eagerly tented the sheet in front of him. Alex groaned again. Maybe when he was in the shower he should just resolve that problem.

Or maybe once they'd dealt with Buryshkin, he would pop out to a local bar, pick up a girl, and get the relief he needed.

Any old port in a storm, as his father used to say. Most of the time, when he hit on a woman, the answer was a resounding "yes."

Or . . . maybe once this was all over, he and the lady in the other room could celebrate the old-fashioned way. He bet any woman with that kind of fire in her eyes would be scorching in bed.

Alex groaned again as he sat up, trying to tame the part of his body that was far more awake than the rest of him. His nose picked up the smell of roasting meat and his stomach growled eagerly. Which first, food or shower?

Shower. He'd make it colder than normal. He refused to let Morgan see that she was getting to him.

To his relief, the soothing routine of a shower and shave pulled Alex back to life, though it was odd not having an audience. He'd forgotten what it was like to be alone, even for activities most people conducted in private. No need to be on guard in case one of the inmates decided he needed a beat down. Or worse.

I could get used to this.

Remembering Morgan's comment about clean clothes, he dug around in the chest of drawers and found himself new underwear and a pair of black socks. It appeared that, no matter his size, there were briefs and undershirts to fit, ranging from skinny on up. The closet rewarded him with a pair of stonewashed jeans and a T-shirt from a local fish joint. He laced on his own shoes.

Pausing in the bedroom door, he checked out the view in the kitchen: Morgan bent over, checking something in the oven, her jeans tight across her rounded butt. Alex sighed as his mouth went dry and parts of him that he'd just tamed kicked back to life.

Morgan removed a roasting pan from the oven and set it on the cooktop. Then, as if sensing his scrutiny, she turned toward him.

"The dead have arisen," she said. "Four hours later."

"Yeah. You heard from Miri yet?" he asked, rubbing his

face.

"Crispin says your sister is doing well. Neil has her stashed away at her place. He's bitching about how he'd rather have her at a safe house."

"She's being stubborn. Runs in the family."

"I had no clue," Morgan said innocently.

"I want to talk to her."

"Honestly, she's fine."

"Now," he said, sterner.

From his tone, Morgan could tell this was non-negotiable, so she hit a number on her cell phone. Neil answered immediately.

"Hey, I got a concerned brother here. Can you put the sister on the phone?" She listened, then looked up at Alex. "He says she's asleep."

"Then wake her the hell up," Alex snapped. Part of it was worry, the other part a simple test. If they refused to let him talk to his sister, he was out of here.

Neil must have heard his order.

Morgan held the phone out to him, and he paced until his sister came on the line. "Hey, Monkey," he said.

"What is it with you? I was asleep. It couldn't have waited, or are you just being a selfish asshole?"

He whistled under his breath. "I was just worried about you."

"I'm fine. Mr. My-Way-or-the-Highway has got us barricaded in here like zombies are trying to raid the place. Now let me go back to sleep so my head doesn't hurt. And next time, I'll call you."

"Understood. Stay safe, you hear?"

"You too," she said, less upset now. "Bye, bro." Then the call ended.

Mission accomplished: Veritas had no issues with him talking directly to Miri, which meant they were keeping their part of the bargain.

"Happy?" Morgan asked.

"Yes. Thank you."

Placing the phone on the table, he sank into a kitchen chair, watching as Morgan opened a bag of pre-made salad and rinsed the contents under the faucet.

"My sis said I was a selfish asshole to wake her up."

"No, you're a brother. That comes with the territory."

He nodded. "She doesn't get that. Too many years of living on her own, I guess. I can't back off, no matter what she says."

"My brother's the same way."

It was an opening he hadn't expected, especially since he knew almost nothing about this woman. "Older or younger?"

"Older. He was always in my face when I was in high school and college. He's better now."

"How did you come to work for Crispin Wilder?" he asked.

Morgan froze for a moment, then brought two bowls of salad to the table. "I was with the FBI. I . . . joined Veritas three years ago."

"Any reason you're not still with the feds?"

"They can't always get the job done," she replied.

It was plain she wasn't going to tell him more than that, at least not at this point, so he switched subjects. "What's for supper? It smells incredible."

"Roast beef, potatoes, carrots, salad, and biscuits."

His stomach rumbled again. He watched with anticipation as she loaded up a plate.

"Usually we just do frozen dinners around here," she added, "but you rate."

Alex eyed the feast as she set it in front of him, swearing he'd died and gone to heaven. "Why am I so special?" he asked, genuinely curious.

Morgan didn't answer right off, placing her own plate and the basket of freshly baked biscuits on the table first. "Because you haven't had a real meal in a while."

"You cooked this for me?" he asked, picking up a fork. He wasn't entirely sure where he should start. Maybe the potatoes. Or the meat . . .

"I'm only good with making popcorn and scrambled eggs and roasts. Other than that, I'm a disaster."

The first taste of meat made him sigh in joy.

"Good?" she asked.

"Excellent," he said, trying not to talk around the food and failing. Though he had dozens of questions, he found himself eating far too fast. But he couldn't stop. Didn't want to stop.

Morgan ate just as heartily as he did. No picking at a lettuce leaf and calling it good for this woman—unlike his ex-wife, who had always been on a diet, even though she'd needed to gain a few pounds, at least in his opinion.

Which made him wonder if Morgan's appetites for other things were just as hearty. When Alex finally slowed down, he found himself watching his companion eat. How her mouth curled around one of the carrots. It also made him think of other uses for those full lips of hers.

Put it in neutral, will you?

"You married?" he asked, figuring he might as well just ask rather than wondering. No ring, but who knew nowadays.

"I'm a widow."

"Oh, sorry," he said.

"It was more than four years ago. I'm still getting over it."

"Have you dated since then?"

Her eyes rose from her plate, chillier now. "No."

"So if I were to hit on you, you'd just shoot me down?" he asked, partly jesting.

"I don't mix work and pleasure."

"What about once this job is done? What then?" he asked, pushing her just to see when she'd snap. For some reason, he enjoyed keeping her off guard.

"Once the mission is over, you go do whatever it is you do, and I go my own way."

"Before or after we have sex?"

The chill grew.

"Understood." He leaned back in his chair, watching her push her food around her plate now. He'd ruffled her feathers. "You did your homework on me so you know my sad story."

"You were married and now divorced."

"Yeah, a marriage that imploded when Alicia decided I just

had to be guilty. She bailed long before I went to trial," he said, the bitterness threatening to ruin the great meal.

"That had to hurt," Morgan replied, softer now.

"More than you can imagine."

Their eyes met, but she quickly broke contact and shoved aside her plate. "Feel free to have seconds. There's plenty."

She rose, collecting a large manila envelope from the counter and setting it near his plate. "Stuff you're going to need. There's a wallet, driver's license, passport, credit card, debit card, and five hundred in cash. Oh, and a new phone. That should get you started."

Alex opened the clasp and let the items fall out onto the table between them. After pushing the contents around with his finger, he looked up at her, stunned.

"You do realize that you just gave me the means to blow this town. I could fly out to wherever, tomorrow."

"You could, but you won't," she said. "You're not going anywhere until you can take your sister with you, and she doesn't have a passport."

Alex stared at her. "You people are spooking the hell out of me." He filled the wallet with the cards and cash. "How can you do all this?"

"We have connections. Don't worry, they're legit, at least for the most part."

"Is this phone bugged?" He knew had to be, but he wanted to know if she'd lie to him.

Morgan nodded. "Because when things go bad, sometimes the only way you stay alive is if our team can find you."

Alex gritted his teeth at that. "So what am I doing to help earn all this?" he asked, gesturing toward the items. Because there was always a quid pro quo.

"In the last couple days, our favorite Russian has received a shipment of prime cocaine. We're hearing rumors that the street value is off the charts. You came the closest to busting Buryshkin six years ago, and his tactics haven't changed that much. I need you to help me work our contacts and find the dope, and then we can take the bastard down."

"My snitches are probably long dead."

"There have to be a few left."

"And if we find the coke?"

"Then you're going to lure Buryshkin to the site so we can bust him instead of another one of his low-level flunkies." Morgan winced. "Sorry. I don't think of you like that."

"More like a stooge," Alex replied, unfazed. "So what're our chances of getting the Russian near the dope?"

"Decent. He likes to inspect the shipments personally now that Grigori is in prison."

"How do you know that?"

She didn't reply.

"You have someone in the organization." He hadn't framed it as a question.

She frowned, then nodded. "We have our sources."

"Another flunky?"

Morgan rose and took her plate to the dishwasher, not supplying an answer. It was clear she didn't entirely trust him. He pushed his plate aside and leaned back in the chair, thinking all this through. There was more here than she was saying.

She turned back toward him now. "My guess is that they offered you a job this morning. Did you accept it?"

Lie, or come clean?

"Yeah, I did. It was that or take a one-way trip into the swamp."

"Then it's all good. That's exactly what we hoped would happen."

He frowned. "That doesn't make sense. How can you trust me if I'm working for your enemy?"

"Call us optimists. You're not a bastard, Parkin. You'll do what's right, no matter what."

"That's a helluva risk you're taking."

"Same for you. You screw us over, and we can be as unforgiving as the Russians."

"That was a threat."

"That was a warning, nothing more," she said. "I promise we won't do anything to hurt your sister, which is more than I can say about Buryshkin." She dropped the dish towel on the counter. "There's apple pie in the oven for dessert. It's about done. I'll be back in a bit. I need a shower."

His eyes tracked her across the room, and he tried to understand the enigma that was Morgan Blake. Sultry, smart, and with a heart that could go from caring to brutally cold in a fraction of a second. Her nickname fit her; she was a valkyrie.

The bedroom door closed behind her and he heard the lock click. That made him smile. He was getting to her, whether it was in his best interests or not. As he made his way to the couch, he paused, looking around the apartment again. No bars. No guards. Just him and Morgan.

Maslow's hierarchy of needs claimed that food and shelter came first. Getting laid was third, but as time passed and the first two needs were being fulfilled, the third would take over his thoughts. Already was.

Part of him knew that wasn't smart. Just about the time he started thinking with his dick was when someone would put a bullet in his head. It was possible that someone might be the stone fox in the next room.

Chapter Eleven

To Morgan it was a usual night on Bourbon Street, a dirty thoroughfare populated by wide-eyed tourists and a few locals who came here only because they were insane, or after something. Usually a little of both. She'd brought Parkin down here to connect with one of her best snitches, provided the man was willing to meet with her.

Bar music blared out of open doors, along with the thick smell of sweat and beer that hung heavy in the humid air. She tried to imagine what it looked like to Alex: the press of bodies, the blare of voices, the *clip-clop* of a mule pulling a carriage along a side street. It had to be as foreign as if someone had dropped him in the middle of Bangkok or Red Square.

For some reason it felt important to understand what was going on inside Parkin's mind. Morgan told herself it mattered to the case, not because she cared. He was only a means to an end. A convenient weapon. A handsome one, but still, only a weapon.

Just keep repeating that. Maybe it'll stick.

Initially he'd come off as an asshat, but now that she'd spent time with him she'd learned that Alex had a dry sense of humor and didn't appear to be a chauvinistic jerk. He was someone who would do anything to keep his sister safe. That she could work with, at least on this mission.

Now, as they wandered through the crowd, he was jumpy, probably because of all the people around them. When she asked him a question, he was slow at responding, like he was thinking through each answer multiple times, unable to deal with the sensory overload.

Morgan gave it another try. "What's this like for you? I mean, after all those years inside?"

"You wouldn't understand," he said, his eyes scanning the crowd as if he expected a threat to materialize out of nowhere.

"Try me."

Alex ran a hand through his hair, agitated, causing it to stick up in front. It did nothing to ruin his bad-boy image. "When you're inside, your world is . . . confined."

"Well, yeah, that's the whole point. The system keeps the bad guys locked up so they don't hurt the rest of us poor souls. Present company excluded."

"No, it's not just in terms of security." Alex stepped into a doorway to avoid a rowdy group of drunks whose T-shirts proclaimed they were Hoosiers.

"You okay?" she asked, her worry increasing.

He shrugged, sweat on his brow. "It's hard to be out here. It's overwhelming."

"Then let's go somewhere else," she replied, tugging him toward a side street. Once they were off Bourbon Street, the noise level dropped precipitously. Still, the frown on his face didn't diminish.

"Better?"

He took a deep breath and let it out slowly. "A little. Thank you."

How could he explain this so she'd understand?

"Inside, it's all about control and the fact that you have none. What you can and cannot do. *When* and *how* you do certain things. You give up your autonomy the day you go inside. You eat what they feed you, or you starve. You line up when they tell you; you go to bed and get up when they tell you. They have absolute control over every part of your life." He gulped air and realized his hands were shaking, which pissed him off. He jammed them into his jeans pockets, hoping she wouldn't notice.

"If I'd been guilty, then maybe I could have dealt with it better. The fact that someone set me up made it harder to handle."

"Because you lost that control to someone else?"

He nodded. "When I was in prison, I found myself thinking through every action I took, because the last thing I needed was to get into trouble."

"With the guards?"

"With anyone. I didn't want to end up in solitary every time I beat someone down who got into my face."

"Somehow, I doubt many people would mess with you, Parkin."

Alex's expression tightened. "They did mess with me. You said you did a background check. I bet that means you read my prison record."

"Yes. I know what almost happened. The report also told me that you put up one helluva fight."

Sometimes, right before he went to sleep, he could still feel the punches, hear the shouts, his own screams. Taste the rank fear that had never completely left him since that night.

"But Gregori Danshov ran interference for you after that, right?"

"Yeah. It helped." He looked at her with a challenge in his eyes. "You got a problem with that?"

"No. We all do what it takes to survive."

Her tone of voice told him she knew that better than most.

"See the irony?" he asked. "You people want me to destroy the organization that kept me alive while I was inside."

Morgan jerked to a stop. "Then why did you sign up with us?"

"Because . . . I figured you'd be less likely to fuck me over than those Russian wolves."

She huffed. "Some endorsement."

"Well, live with it. That's where my head is."

"I think there's more to it than that," she said, not letting him take the easy way out.

Dammit. The woman was too perceptive. "I won't truly be free until I know I will never be sent back to that place," he admitted. "Right now, I'm just waiting for a cop to grab me, slip a dime bag in my pocket, and start the whole process all over again. Except this time, I won't survive."

"That's what gets you the most. You did everything right, and you still got screwed. Being a good guy didn't save you, it just made you a target," Morgan said, looking away now.

She does understand.

Not even his sister had made that connection.

They walked on for a time, and then she asked, "What's going on in your head right now, Alex?"

Morgan's use of his first name brought him to a halt. He looked at her, saw she wasn't baiting him. She genuinely wanted to know.

"I'm confused," he said. "Confused and bitter and tired."

"Scared it'll happen again," she said quietly, touching his arm. "I'll do everything I can to make sure that doesn't happen. I promise."

He nodded and looked away, unsure if he could promise anything in return. Then he knew that he could.

"I may be working for the Russians, but I'll do everything I can to take Buryshkin down. I promise that."

"That's good enough for me."

To distract himself, Alex homed in on a pair of young girls walking toward them, their skimpy summer dresses barely covering their butts. As the girls drew near, the blond one winked at him and smiled.

"Everything good, Candy?" Morgan asked.

"*Da*, it's good. Better than I hope," the girl replied, her accent hailing from somewhere within the former Soviet Union.

"They arrived in town about a month ago," Morgan explained as pair walked on. "Tanya is barely sixteen and Candy claims she's seventeen, but she's probably fifteen. Alexi Krupin is their pimp. He's not a complete bastard." She hesitated. "When the girls can no longer pull their weight, he pensions them off. Gives them a bit of money and a bus ticket to wherever they want to go."

"As compared to?"

Morgan's expression darkened. "Some of the Russian pimps have a more permanent retirement program that involves a boat trip into international waters, a heavy set of chains, and a swift drop overboard. If the girl has really pissed off her pimp, she's still alive when she hits the water."

"Jesus," Alex said. He'd heard rumors of that kind of thing but had hoped to God it was an urban myth. "What about Buryshkin?"

"He's a one-way-trip kind of dude. Or at least the pimps running his prostitutes are, and he tells them what to do. Thank God Krupin doesn't work for him." She shifted her gaze in Alex's direction. "Now you know why I want Buryshkin gone. I wouldn't hesitate to wind him up in his own chains, throw him overboard, and watch the bastard sink."

Alex couldn't help but stare. The Morgan he thought he knew had vanished. This one had a voice that spoke of raw, bleeding anger; a wound that had sliced so deep into her soul, she had no way to heal it.

"That sounds personal."

"It is," she admitted. "When I was at the FBI, I worked on child trafficking cases."

He blew out a sharp breath, his respect for her rising. "Ugly job."

"Yeah. But then yours at the DEA wasn't any better."

Morgan's cell phone pulled them out of their dark thoughts with a ping announcing an incoming text. She scanned it. "Okay, I have a CI with some info to trade. He's usually pretty reliable."

Confidential informants were the lifeblood of any investigation. Especially if you were trying to locate a shipment of drugs.

"I'll see if I can track down some of mine, if yours doesn't pan out," he said.

"Hopefully you won't have to do that."

Morgan headed them in a new direction, cutting down an alley, then halting, her attention focused on the way they'd just come. Checking to see if anyone was following them.

"Looks good," she said, then gave him a nod of approval. "It's nice to work with someone who knows what I'm doing without having to explain it."

"Is that a compliment? Damn, I'm on fire tonight."

She ignored that. "My snitch's name is TipTop. He's usually got a good nose for things. Just don't mention his hair, okay?"

"Why?"

"Ever seen a picture of Tiny Tim, the singer from the sixties?" Alex nodded. "TipTop could be his twin, except his hair is carrot orange."

"Only in New Orleans."

They ended up in a dive bar, the kind with sticky floors, surly servers, and watered-down booze. Morgan sat at a rickety table on the sidewalk, taking the seat closest to the building, which left him with his back to the street. He promptly adjusted his chair so it was next to hers, giving him a better view of any threat.

"Thinking someone is going to stab you in the back?" she chided.

"Old habits die hard."

A girl came to the table, probably in her early twenties and clearly wishing for any other job than the one she had.

"Whaddya want?" she asked, her eyes on Alex the entire time.

"Coke," Morgan replied.

"A bottled beer," Alex said.

"What kind?" the server asked.

"Does it matter?"

She shook her head. "It all sucks here."

"Your honesty just got you a bigger tip."

The server grinned and headed for the bar, while Alex checked out the clientele. Some old. Some young. All seen better days. "You sure know how to show a guy a good time."

"Nothing but the best for you, Parkin."

He looked at her. "I think all this attitude you're giving me is because you can't decide if you want to sleep with me or shoot me. Or both."

Morgan gave him a sidelong glance. "If you keep running that mouth of yours, I'll be fonder of the second option."

He laughed. "I like you, Blake. You don't pull your punches."

"Comes with the territory," she said. "Like me all you want, but you're still not getting laid. At least by me."

The drinks arrived and Alex insisted on paying the bill, even if it was Veritas's money. It felt right. Normal, even. Easing back into the real world, one step at a time. Deep in his gut, he suspected he was kidding himself.

As Alex checked out the bar, he wondered if this was the kind of place where Miri worked. God, he hoped not. He could ask Morgan—she'd probably know everything about his sister's place of employment—but then he wouldn't be keeping up his older brother street cred. Once this thing with the Russians was settled, he'd make sure wherever Miri worked was a good place. One that would watch her back when he wasn't around.

Alex took a swig from his bottle. The beer tasted okay to him, but then, he was hardly a keen judge of good brew anymore. He watched as Morgan pulled a small strip of paper out of her purse, set it on the table, and used her straw to drop some soda on it. It dawned on him what he was witnessing— she was testing the drink to see if it had been doctored with a date-rape drug.

"And I thought I was paranoid," he said.

Morgan studied the strip, nodded her approval of the results, then took a big sip of the liquid. "Once was enough. It was close, but he didn't get what he was after. I swear, next time I'm going to gut any SOB who tries it."

He blinked, realizing what she'd just revealed. "How old were you?"

"Twenty. I was in college and I was naïve."

Not anymore. "Well, God forbid it ever happens again, but if it does, let me know. I'll hold the perv down for you so you can gut him properly."

Morgan smiled. "You keep it up and I might just start liking you, Parkin."

"All part of my plan."

She returned to watching the street, but her eyes had grown haunted. Old memories were hard to shake. He had a few of those himself.

"So when is your snitch going to show up?"

"Whenever he feels like it. If he doesn't have anything tangible for us, we'll go to another watering hole. Maybe I'll see someone there who will talk to us."

"Please tell me the next place is at least a two-star establishment. We ex-cons have our standards, you know."

She smiled at him, and he found he liked that. It erased some of the sadness in her eyes. Her attention moved back to the entrance.

What will it take to get you in bed? He shook his head at the thought. *Next subject, Parkin.*

"Why are we sitting out here instead of inside? Is it because of your snitch?"

"Partly. Also because I'm packing. Guns are a no-no inside bars."

He'd forgotten that. "Hairsplitting, aren't you? You're still *at* a bar."

"I'm a lawyer. We can always find a way to skate around the edge of the law."

He sighed. "Did you notice the guy on the other side of the street, the one with crazy hair?"

She nodded. "He's my contact. He's sizing you up because I don't usually have someone with me. Well, except Iceman."

"Iceman?"

"Neil. That's our nickname for him."

"Tell me about him. Neil, I mean. Do you think he'll hit on my sister?"

Morgan frowned. "No. That's not like him. He's all business."

"He better be. If he thinks he's sleeping with Miri, he and his balls will be parting company. I will make sure of it."

"Your sister is an adult. And please don't even think about challenging him. Neil is . . . lethal. He promised to keep her safe, and he'll die doing it."

"Yeah, Krav Maga and all that shit. He said something about losing his own sister."

"I'm surprised he mentioned that. It's usually a taboo subject."

"Did it go down bad?"

"Very bad."

No wonder Iceman was so intense.

Morgan's phone chimed and she looked down at the text message. "We're on. I'll text you if he's okay with you being at the meeting. If anything gets weird, take off. You've got the code to get back into the safe house. I'll meet you there."

Like hell. No way was he bailing on her if this meeting went south. They'd take away his man card if he pulled a weenie stunt like that.

"How can I get in touch with you?" he asked.

"I saved my number in your phone. It's under 'Valkyrie.'"

Of course you did.

Alex watched as she made her way across the street, her jeans hugging her butt. He chugged his beer, trying to cool his libido. And failing.

"Another one?" the server asked.

"No, thanks," he said. The girl was attractive, but Morgan had something else going on, something hard to define. Whatever it was, he was beginning to see her as the ultimate challenge.

Though he'd been told to stay put, Alex set off to keep an eye on his partner. To his amusement, he managed to tail Morgan without her seeing him. Then she merged into a tour group and disappeared from sight. He held his position in front of a souvenir shop, acting as if he really cared to own a stuffed alligator with sparkly gold eyes.

"Come on, where are you?" he muttered, his anxiety rising. His phone pinged and the text indicated he was to head north and meet her in the third alley on the right.

With a sigh, Alex walked down the street, counting alleys as he went. When he reached number three, he slowed, then stopped, pausing to look around. As best as he could tell, no one was following, but in the Big Easy it was often hard to tell.

He swung into the alley and joined up with Morgan about halfway down the gloomy passageway, which was far too dark for his liking. To his right were the inevitable garbage cans. He hated the things, and not just because of their smell. Druggies ditched their stashes in these, and it used to be Alex's job to root around inside to find the dope. He'd pawed through his share of rotten food and baby diapers when he was a junior agent. A rite of passage, the older guys had claimed.

A quick glance upward showed there were no galleries above them, just a few windows. At the end of the alley was a chain-link fence, probably installed during Kennedy's stint in the White House. The alley beyond the fence was equally dark and uninviting.

If Alex was designing a trap, this place would be it. As he approached, he noted that Morgan stood with her feet apart, weight carefully balanced, her hand inside her purse as if she expected something to go wrong.

I'm not the only one who's twitchy.

"So where is he?" Alex asked.

"He'll be here in a minute."

"I'm not liking this place."

"I'm right there with you," she replied.

Alex tensed when a man stepped off the street and walked toward them. As Morgan had claimed, he was one of a kind, from his carroty hair to his long nose. TipTop appeared equally ill at ease, his eyes darting around.

"This is the new guy," she said, gesturing toward Alex. "This is TipTop."

"Heard of you," the man replied, eyeing him. "Heard you were dealing and the feds sent you upstate for it."

"Everybody has a theory on that," Alex replied.

The dude nodded like he wasn't surprised. "Richie told me about you."

One of Alex's snitches. "He still alive?"

TipTop shook his head. "Got gunned down a year ago. Funny thing—it wasn't one of the dealers who did him in. It was his old lady."

"He didn't put the toilet seat down or something?"

The snitch laughed. "Something like that."

"So what have you got for me?" Morgan asked, impatience edging her tone.

"Three possible places, all in the Warehouse District. I've got the addresses for you." He stepped closer to them now, holding out a small piece of paper. "Your best bet is—"

There was a sharp pop, and TipTop took a stunned step forward, his eyes wide with incomprehension. Bright blood bubbled out of his open mouth.

"Get down!" Morgan commanded.

As the snitch crumpled to the ground, she and Alex dove behind the trash cans, startling a rat in the process. Bullets impacted the cans, chipping bricks on the building. A piece hit Alex's forearm and it stung, as screams echoed from the street.

"Can you see the shooter?" she asked, her gun in hand.

"He's at the entrance to the alley. There're civilians behind him. You don't have a clean shot."

The shooter kept firing at them, growing closer to their hiding place.

"What about TipTop?" Morgan asked, out of position to see her informant.

Alex inched out from behind the can to get a look, then jerked back after ascertaining that the snitch's eyes were vacant, staring at nothing.

"History. One shot, through the back of the skull." It had to have been a hollow-point bullet, or they would have been wearing TipTop's blood and brains.

"Dammit!" she said.

In the distance, sirens kicked in. Alex took another cautious look.

"The shooter's legging it."

"You sure? He could be waiting for you to stick your stupid

head up so he can blow it off," Morgan grumbled. There was more to her tone than anger. He heard fear. But for sheer luck, either one of them could be dead instead of the snitch.

"No, he's gone. He just blew through a group of tourists like a rocket."

Stepping forward, Morgan tugged the piece of paper from TipTop's fingers and tucked it into her jeans pocket. As she straightened, she knew what had to happen. Money easily changed hands in this city. With just the right number of zeroes, an officer could claim he saw a gun, even if hers was in her purse. Shots might be fired, and then there would be three corpses in this alley, rather than just one. A quick whitewash of the official reports, and Veritas would have no way to dispute the "facts."

The sirens were closer now. Morgan took one last look at the dead snitch. "Sorry, TipTop." She waved at Alex. "Let's book it. You can't be here when the cops arrive."

"Amen," he said.

They sprinted down the alley, away from the street. She groaned when she saw the condition of the fence—the metal barrier appeared to be a thriving home to tetanus and a hundred other lethal diseases. Once he realized what she was about to do, Alex caught her right arm.

"Hold on," he said. After pulling off his T-shirt, he rested it over the sharp, rusty metal spikes, then helped her over. When he landed on the other side, he pulled down the shirt, now featuring a few jagged holes.

As he shook it out and pulled it back on, Morgan couldn't help but notice his chiseled abs, each one blessedly defined. She turned away from him, muttering under her breath about how she really needed to be a nun right now. Alex Parkin was a means to an end, nothing more. As long as she kept reminding herself of that fact, she'd be okay.

Noting her scrutiny, he grinned knowingly. Morgan opened her mouth to give him hell, then realized that would be playing right into his hands. Instead, she whirled and took off at a brisk pace.

Why are you doing this? Why can't you leave me alone?

There was a resigned sigh as Alex caught up with her. A shortcut down another street took them far enough away from the crime scene that her worry dropped a notch or two. They paused in a dark doorway as two cop cars passed by at the end of the street, lights flashing, letting the world know they meant business.

Morgan's gut roiled at how close it had been, and she closed her eyes to steady herself. Which was a mistake, as the image of TipTop's astonished expression popped into her head. He was dead because of her.

"You okay?" Alex asked, touching her arm.

The gesture caught her off guard. "This sucks," she said, not answering his question.

Pushing the Veritas operations number, she was relieved when Sanjay answered on the second ring. As the focus point for all those out on various stateside missions, he was the lifeline when things went wrong. Like now.

"Hello to my favorite lady," he said, his rich East Indian accent pouring down the line like spicy masala.

"We've got trouble. My snitch was just gunned down in front of us, and the cops are coming out of the woodwork."

Sanjay switched to work mode in an instant. "You still at the scene?"

"No. We took off. God knows what they'd do to Parkin if they found him there."

Her eyes met Alex's at this point, and he nodded in agreement.

"I'll let Crispin know what's up. Your leaving may complicate matters if anyone saw you."

Morgan winced. She prided herself on ensuring that her ops went smoothly and with little fuss. Clearly this one wasn't going to be like the norm.

No big surprise there, not if it has anything to do with that damned Russian.

"I'll monitor the police frequencies," Sanjay continued.

"If anyone comes up with a description of you two, I'll let you know so you can take precautions."

"Thanks. Maybe we'll get lucky. Someone knew where we were headed, who I was meeting. They had to have time to set up that hit."

"Was your snitch trustworthy?" Sanjay asked.

Alex must have overheard the question, because one of his eyebrows rose.

Had TipTop been tasked with luring her and Alex to that alley so someone could take them out, and somehow the assassin had missed? Or had her informant been betrayed, and this was nothing more than a way to get Parkin back in jail?

"I thought he was reliable," she replied. *Until tonight.*

"Anything else you need?" Sanjay asked.

"No. We have to . . . regroup," she replied. "I'll be in touch."

The moment after Morgan shoved her phone into her purse, her hands tightened into fists.

"I'm sorry for your friend," he said.

It was the right thing to say, and tears sprang to her eyes. "He wasn't a friend. He was just . . . "

"A one-of-a-kind guy," Alex finished.

She nodded numbly, struck by how TipTop's death had been so senseless.

"It wasn't your fault," Alex said, moving closer.

"But he's just as dead."

"Yes, but we aren't, and that matters." He touched her cheek with a calloused finger. "We'll find out who did this and make them pay."

Blinking against tears, she frowned at him. "You mean that?"

He nodded. "Yes. There are two situations where I always bring my A game to the table; one is when I'm taking down bad guys."

"And the other?"

The smile that came her way was pure seduction, which gave her the answer.

Morgan sucked in a breath. The night suddenly felt ten degrees hotter, and something deep inside her responded, a spark, a need that had been in hibernation since her husband died. The kind of primal urge that said having sex with this man would be worth the gamble, if for nothing more than a lifetime of memories.

She shook herself, pushing away the erotic images of what it would be like to be tangled up with Alex, moving together as one. Morgan chilled her voice on purpose, and not just for his benefit. "These bastards have been ahead of us all along. How do they know what we're doing?"

"I have no idea," Alex said, stepping back. For a second, she wished he hadn't.

"It's like someone is telling the Russian exactly what we're up to." Her eyes were on him now.

"It's not me. You know that could have been my brains on the pavement instead of your snitch's."

That thought made her gut clench.

Morgan wiped the tears out of her eyes, upset that she'd broken down in front of him. It wasn't like her, and it made her feel too vulnerable. She was starting to care too much about this man. She'd made that mistake once before.

Never again.

Chapter Twelve

After they'd secured a New Orleans map from a convenience store, they retreated to an all-night diner. Morgan ordered a burger and fries, as did Alex. It was another indication that this woman had earned her stripes at the FBI. Newbies couldn't eat after finding a body or watching a CI being gunned down in front of them. Seasoned veterans knew to eat when the chance came along, as there might not be another for a long time.

The piece of paper TipTop had given her was bloodstained now, torn from a larger sheet of paper. It listed three addresses in a barely legible scrawl. After Morgan marked the locations on the map, she phoned in the details so someone at Veritas could run a check on the property records.

"Probably going to be a waste of time. Buryshkin always had his buildings owned by shell corporations," Alex said. "I doubt if that's changed."

"At least it's a place to start."

There were faint blue-black circles under Morgan's eyes, and she was rubbing her temples like she had a headache. It was clear TipTop's death had hit her hard. Alex had lost a few confidential informants in his day, and he still remembered the names and faces of every one of them.

"We'll have to check the buildings ourselves," he said, dragging a French fry through a mound of ketchup.

"You're not thinking of adding breaking and entering to your criminal résumé, are you?"

"Not unless we have to. We'll eyeball the places. Maybe that'll give us an idea of which one TipTop thought was the best candidate."

Her phone lit up, and she spent a couple minutes talking to someone named Linda. When the call ended, he guessed the results by her sour expression.

"No joy," Morgan said. "Buryshkin's good at running under the radar."

"Part of the reason he's not doing life in Angola," Alex remarked. "Maybe we can change that."

Once they were done eating, Morgan's quick trip to the restaurant's restroom resolved one potential problem: TipTop's blood-splattered list was flushed. One less piece of damning evidence if the cops did pick them up for questioning.

Rather than use her car, they had a cab drop them two blocks away from the first address because Alex wanted to get a "feel" for the neighborhood. As they walked toward their destination on the darkened streets, Morgan seemed to perk up.

"What are we looking for?" she asked. "A big sign that says 'Drugs here! Come on down'?"

He snorted. "If only. What I'm looking for are guards at a place where you wouldn't expect them. Maybe security cameras, or too much in-and-out traffic for the location."

"How can you tell? If it's a legit business, they'd have customers."

"At this time of night?" he replied.

"This is New Orleans. You can buy anything at any time of the day, if you know where to go."

She had a point.

"Let me give you an example. A couple months before I did the perp walk, we raided a flower shop in Baton Rouge. Mom-and-pop kind of place, looked completely legit, but when we studied the foot traffic this place had in an hour, it didn't match the numbers of a similar shop in the same part of the city. Their state and federal tax returns claimed their sales were roughly identical to the other shop, but with twice the number of customers. Either they were giving the flowers away, or their main business was off the books. Which it was."

"How much did you seize?"

"Fifty thousand in coke, thirty thousand in pills. The

owners are doing hard time."

"Score one for the good guys."

Alex shook his head. "Their oldest son moved to Atlanta and set up shop. We warned our people over there, so hopefully they took him down. These bastards are just like roaches. You squash one and the others scatter."

That seemed to deflate Morgan's good mood.

"See anything around here that catches your eye?" she asked.

"Yup." Just to annoy her, he took hold of her left hand. For a second, he thought she was going to pull it away, but she left it in place.

"Just blending in," he reassured her, though that was only partly true. The longer he was near this woman, the more he wanted to touch her, wanted to know the feel of the skin on her face, her arms, and her full breasts. He wanted to bury his face in her hair and bathe in the intoxicating scent that was pure Morgan. Immerse himself in her and never come up for air.

What the hell?

That was bordering on obsession, something Alex had always avoided. He forced his libido in check, which proved difficult given all the blood eager to flow south of his belt buckle. He dragged himself back to the business at hand. The first building on TipTop's list was boarded up, clearly abandoned, and had been that way for some time. At this discovery, Morgan's temper grew shorter.

"Damn. Can't we catch a break for a change?" she grumbled.

"Relax, will you? We're just strolling around, enjoying the night air, two lovers taking a breather in between some rounds of seriously hot sex."

"Parkin . . . " she growled.

"Why do you shy away from talking about it? Had a bad experience?"

She pulled her hand away from his and put distance between them, ruining the whole strolling-lovers image.

"Come on, Morgan. Talk to me." Because for some reason,

it mattered.

"What do you think about that place next to the abandoned one? It looks dodgy."

He sighed, knowing that she wasn't going to open up. And he suspected that was because there was a lot of pain in her past, something that had made her distrust people, males in particular. Ahead of them, a car slowly turned the corner a block down. Under the streetlamps, he noted the row of top lights.

"Damn. It's the cops," he murmured. "Play it cool. Work with me here."

Alex cradled her face in his hands, then moved closer. The kiss was just for show, but the instant his lips touched hers, all his good intentions fell away. He finally had her in his arms, and he wasn't going to waste this chance. He feared it might be the only one he'd ever get.

Alex began the kiss like a proper Boy Scout—no tongue—but the longer it went, the more he put into it. She tasted of the strawberry milkshake she'd had earlier, and of Morgan. He felt her tension, but then she began to respond, her hands encircling his waist, pulling him tight against her body. He felt her breasts rise and fall with each breath, and his groin reacted with enthusiasm. A low moan came from her.

The car slowed. "Get a room!" one of the cops hollered, followed by laughter.

Alex still didn't break the kiss. Hell, even a police baton on the back of the head wouldn't have made him give up the sensuous heaven he'd found with Morgan Blake.

It was only when the police were around the next corner that Alex reluctantly stepped back, giving her space. She was either going to thank him or deck him, and he wasn't sure which. From her dazed expression and heavy breathing, it appeared she was having trouble deciding.

His kiss had caught her off guard. Initially she'd planned on protesting when he'd pulled her into his arms, but when she saw the cop car, she realized what he was doing. The playing along ended when she put her hand on his toned butt and pulled him against her, felt that solid column of manhood.

After that, his kiss had grown daring, and she found herself wanting more, as if it were an option to wrap her knees around him and let him have her right there on a city street.

Now her head buzzed and her cheeks flamed as embarrassment set in.

What the hell was I thinking?

As if he'd heard her, Alex murmured, "It was good for both of us. Just accept that, okay?"

She shook her head, trying to clear it. "That was your one big kiss, dude. Hope you enjoyed it."

A bad-boy smile came right back at her. "I sure as hell did. How about you?"

"How about we do our damned jobs?" she snapped.

His smile didn't fade, but grew wider, even more of a temptation now. He knew what he was doing to her.

No more kissing. *That way lies madness.*

Or the steamiest sex she'd ever have in her life.

"Third building's a charm," Alex said, as they reached the final address on the list.

"You're an optimist."

"No, this one is more what I was looking for."

"Why? It doesn't seem to have all that foot traffic you were talking about."

"Yes, but look how it's laid out," he said.

Ahead of them was an old concrete-block structure, situated behind a chain-link fence. Two overhead doors graced this side of the structure. They looked rusted shut, but there was also a side door, much newer, with an impressive lock.

As they knelt next to the fence, Alex pointed to the far right. "Doghouse. They probably had a guard dog at one time."

"But not now, or the thing would have been trying to rip our throats out."

"True. Which isn't good news. If there are no guards and no dog, there is no dope."

He's probably right.

"Let's scout it out anyway," he said. "Maybe we'll get lucky and find a map to every one of Buryshkin's other dope warehouses."

"You are delusional."

Alex waggled an eyebrow. "You say that now. Just wait. The old Parkin Luck should kick in any moment now."

"You mean the kind of luck that sent you to prison?"

Her companion's smile vanished.

The instant the words came out of her mouth, she knew she'd been a bitch. "God. I'm sorry, Alex. That was just mean. I don't know why I said it."

"Because it's the truth?" he asked, rising.

"No, it's not. You did time because people set you up."

"I was set up because I was too gung ho. If I'd been more laid back, taken bribes under the table, I would have been fine. I overachieved myself right into a prison cell."

She rose as well, looking deep into his eyes. "That wouldn't be you. You only do one hundred fifty percent or nothing. There's no half-assing in your world."

"How do you know that?"

"I read your prison psych report, remember?"

His brow furrowed. "What else did it say?"

"That you've got a firm grasp of right versus wrong, you don't trust easily, and that you have a temper that sometimes gets the better of you."

"So what's your verdict?" he asked.

Morgan cocked her head. "Bottom line? If I had to have someone watching my back, it'd be you. Because even if you hated me, you wouldn't let me die. You're too much of a white knight."

"I'll take that as a compliment."

"You should, Parkin. It's probably the only one you're going to get."

As if by mutual consent, conversation ceased as they

circumnavigated the perimeter of the building. Other than a noisy neighborhood dog a few streets away, there was no one around. They found another new door on the other side of the building, also with an impressive lock.

"I can probably get us inside. All it takes is a credit card."

"A skill you picked up in the pen?"

Alex frowned at her. "Among other things," he said, not really wanting Morgan to know what else he'd learned in Angola.

The fact that she'd had access to his psych reports unnerved him. What else had the shrink said about him? Had Morgan just chosen to reveal the sanitized version, or did she know that, for a time, he'd fantasized about what it would be like to kill his ex-partner and his ex-wife? That he had come up with at least a dozen ways to make those deaths as excruciating as his dark fantasies could imagine?

Not the time. Not the place.

Alex studied the fence, which wasn't electrified and was much less of a health hazard than the last one they'd scaled. Morgan followed right after him, and he resisted the desire to help her climb over. She wasn't just any woman, and he had a feeling being chivalrous wouldn't get him too far with her—in fact, it might even do the opposite.

Now, as they moved closer to the side door, he put on his game face, his heart picking up speed. God, he'd missed the adrenaline rush, the feeling that he was doing something that might make things better in this world.

Hell, she's right. I am a white knight.

Somehow, he didn't think that was a good thing. Wasn't it the knight who always got eaten by the dragon?

As he bent to examine the lock, Morgan snapped on a pair of plastic gloves that she'd pulled from her purse, then handed him a pair. He tugged them on. On a whim, he tested the doorknob. The door swung open.

"Oh boy," he muttered. "Can you spell t-r-a-p?"

Morgan pulled a small Maglite out of her purse and clicked it on, letting its brilliant beam dance around.

"You wouldn't happen to have a winning lottery ticket in there, would you?" he jested.

"Sorry. It's in my other purse," she said.

She stepped inside, then halted. "Oh, God. We got something dead. I sure hope it's a rat."

When he stepped inside, her fragrant sandalwood perfume was rapidly overwhelmed by the stench of mold, rot, and decomposition.

"Not likely. Too strong."

"Of course," she said. "Because our night hasn't been special enough."

"Keep an eye out for tripwires. They might be tied to a silent alarm system."

"Just what a girl wants to hear."

He grunted in reply. The flashlight's beam revealed the faint tremor of her hand now.

"Not rats," she said, shaking her head.

The bodies were near the back wall: two men, one in a black suit and the other in faded jeans and a long-sleeved shirt.

"Here," Morgan said. The Maglite illuminated something in her hand, a eucalyptus lozenge. It was an old trick to confuse the nose so the stomach wouldn't feel the need to purge itself at the stench.

"Thanks." He popped the lozenge into his mouth and let the pungent scent do its job as Morgan did the same.

There were no tripwires present as they made their way across the interior of the building. It was a big open space with a concrete floor and a series of metal pillars down the center. Alex squatted next to the bodies, ignoring the flies clustered on the faces and the sickly-sweet smell of decay.

"I don't see any blood," Morgan said, joining him now.

He leaned closer, then touched one of the corpse's arms.

"See how their muscles are all tightened up, the arching of their backs? They got some bad dope," he said. "Probably laced with strychnine, which totally screws up our guess of the time of death. The stuff hastens the onset of rigor mortis and makes it end quicker."

"You've seen this before?" she asked.

"Yeah. In Dallas. Some guy thought it'd be a great way to cut his stash of cocaine. Killed five people before we caught up with him. Trust me, it's a seriously bad way to die."

Alex leaned closer to the dead man in the suit, trying to breathe through his mouth. He waved away the flies. "I know this guy. He's Russian. He was in Angola a year or so back."

"So TipTop's intel was good."

"Looks like it."

Careful not to leave any trace of himself behind—which was nearly impossible—Alex stepped over to the other man and lifted his head. "Ledd Marston. Small-time dealer when I went in, but he must have gone up a few rungs on the food chain if he's handling Buryshkin's loads."

He shifted the dealer's hand. Underneath was a tiny mound of white powder.

"We'll get that tested," Morgan said. "See if it's tainted."

After rolling off one of the plastic gloves, she scooped up some of the powder and sealed it inside by tying off the top. Then she stashed the glove down her bra.

"That's not going to stop the cops if they strip search you," Alex said.

"They'll think twice about messing with me, since I'm a lawyer."

Which was probably true, though there was a certain kind of cop that felt lawyers deserved all the hell they received. Alex had been that way once. Still would be if he hadn't met Morgan.

She pushed up one of the dealer's sleeves, then the other, revealing bruised welts in the flesh. "Ligature marks."

Alex checked the dead Russian. "Same here. I'd say snorting this poison wasn't their idea."

"Clever way to execute someone." Morgan rose to her feet. "Why leave them here? Why not haul the stiffs out to the swamp and feed them to the gators? No bodies, no cops."

That was troubling him as well. Leaving corpses behind, which would eventually be found by the smell alone, was slipshod. Buryshkin was many things, but he was never sloppy.

"Maybe it's a message of some kind. If that whole new load of coke is tainted . . . "

"God, I hope not," she said, their eyes meeting.

"Yeah. Dallas all over again."

"It's time to get out of here."

Alex caught her arm right before she headed toward the door. "Let's not go out the same way we came in, just in case someone is waiting for us."

"Good call."

They hoofed it across the building to the other door. Alex unlocked it, then looked at his companion. "You ready?"

"Let's do it."

He twisted the knob, shoved the door open, and ran, Morgan hot on his heels, her gun out. He waited for the punch of pain in his chest or head, the fire burning through him as the bullet destroyed tissue and bone.

Mercifully, it didn't come.

They were two blocks away when Morgan phoned in what they'd found.

"I'll call our contact at the DEA," Sanjay said.

"Thanks. I got a sample of what looks to be cocaine. Can you arrange to have someone pick it up?"

"Sure. I'll have Ben get in contact with you."

"Thanks."

"When this is over, you must come to dinner," Sanjay said. "I'd like you to meet my girlfriend. She's amazing."

"What? I thought you were my guy," she teased.

"No. Sorry. You waited too long." He paused and added, "I'll let Crispin know what's going down."

"Thanks."

Morgan found her companion staring at something in his hand. His gloves were gone now, and she hoped he'd lost them somewhere along the way, some place the cops wouldn't be searching. Alex handed over a book of matches with a stark, red-and-yellow logo of a pitchfork and flames. "This was in the

Russian's coat pocket."

"Le Purgatoire," she said. "It's a bar near St. Ann Street."

"How's about we check it out? See if anyone knew the Russian suit and who he was running with before he got dead."

She looked down at her dirty clothes, which smelled too much like the warehouse. "We gotta change, or we'll never make it through the door."

"Then call us a cab, lady. We're going clubbing."

Chapter Thirteen

Morgan stepped out of her bedroom in the safe house to find Alex lounging on the couch, staring at nothing, seemingly lost in thought. He'd showered; his hair was slightly damp, but his five o'clock shadow was still in place. It moved him from handsome to serious hunk. He'd chosen a pale-blue shirt and black slacks, and she knew that once he hit the bar, the women would be all over him. Maybe one of those women would know the dead Russian.

Alex glanced up at her, then smiled, scanning her head to toe, taking in her little black dress. The smolder in his eyes made heat rise in her cheeks. "Hot damn."

Morgan couldn't stop the smile. "Thank you. The black hides bloodstains really well."

"Smokin' hot and practical. My kind of woman," he said, executing a double thumbs-up.

She'd opted to wear black flats, because running around in heels on New Orleans's uneven sidewalks was crazy, something tourists often learned the hard way, one twisted or broken ankle at a time. Her small, shiny, black purse was filled with the necessities: lipstick, money, ID, and cell phone. But no gun.

Alex rose from the couch and moved closer to her. He smelled of soap and clean male. The scar on his neck was more noticeable now, and she tried hard not to stare at it.

"I like your hair this way," he said, reaching out to touch the rhinestone clip that held it suspended above her right ear. "Makes you look . . . exotic."

Exotic. No one had called her that before. Suddenly, her

skin felt on fire. She needed to divert him before he tried to kiss her.

"Don't you ever shave?"

"Sometimes." Alex ran a finger down her cheek, leaving a trail of sensation behind it. "Sometimes not."

"Focus, Parkin."

"You know, I'd be able to if you weren't so damned hot." A sexy smile twitched the corners of his mouth. "Maybe"—his voice pitched lower—"you could help me work on my . . . focus. What do you think?"

Morgan stepped back just as he moved in for the kiss. "No. Nice try. Time for you to get your mind back in the game, okay?"

"I'm trying," he replied. "But that dress . . . "

"It's amazing that the male of the species has survived all these millennia. I wonder how many of you guys got picked off by saber-toothed tigers because you were too busy thinking about banging some female back at the cave."

"Probably more of us than we'd care to admit. But look at the bright side: That never-ending sex drive means there're always plenty of us clueless dudes around, so it all equals out."

Morgan rolled her eyes. "You familiar with the Rule of Stupid?"

"Yeah. Don't go to stupid places with stupid people and do stupid things."

"There you go. Follow those rules tonight and we'll be fine."

"Never worked that way for me."

It was pushing two in the morning, but the streets were still active. The weather had remained clear and hot, typical for a Louisiana September. Alex and Morgan headed down St. Ann Street along a collection of nightclubs. Le Purgatoire was nearby.

After Alex's come-on at the apartment, which had bounced

off her like a tennis ball against concrete, Morgan had grown quiet. Zeroed in on the mission, at the exclusion of everything else.

For some reason, that bugged him.

Challenges were his thing. He'd always pushed himself to excel—in college, at the DEA. It was in his bones. Right now, those bones wanted Morgan enough that he was willing to play the game.

She completed the call and returned the phone to her purse.

"The Russian stiff in the warehouse was Dimitri Golov. He got out of Angola two months ago."

"Huh. I couldn't remember his name," Alex said, shaking his head. "Grigori didn't recruit him for his team. I know that much."

"So how did that sales pitch work?"

"It was pretty straightforward. When a new inmate arrived, and Grigori found him of interest, he'd have one of his people chat with the newbie. Tell him how things worked *inside*, and that he had two options: get on board, or face prison without someone watching his back. For whatever reason, Golov didn't sign on the dotted line."

"But then he goes back to work for Grigori's uncle, with no hard feelings on either side?"

Alex huffed. "That's what confuses me. Of course, he did end up a corpse, so who knows."

Morgan paused, searching the street in front of them as if looking for someone. "I'm going to get bumped by a young Black guy in the next block or so. Don't go all he-man on him, okay?"

But why . . . "The hand-off?" he asked quietly.

"Yup. We keep the locations of our safe houses as secret as possible, even from those who aren't working full time for the organization."

"Don't worry, I'll stay mellow, as long as he doesn't cop a feel. I got first dibs on that."

Morgan didn't reply, pursing her lips as they continued down the street. As promised, a block later a man holding a plastic cup of beer lurched into her. Alex made sure to appear surprised, but it wasn't hard; the scene looked perfectly normal, down to the guy's confusion and stumbled apology. To his credit, he hadn't spilled a drop of the brew.

"No problem," Morgan said. "No harm done."

"Nice legs, baby," the guy said, winking. Then he was headed south toward the river, his gait telling any onlookers that he'd had more alcohol than was wise.

"He's good," Alex said as they continued down the street.

"Ben's our general New Orleans gofer. He was raised in the projects in Chicago and came here before Katrina. He knows this place better than anyone."

"If you hadn't told me what was going down, I'd have just figured he was a drunk."

"He's one helluva pickpocket. Even better, he knows how to handle himself if a cop gets too nosy."

Alex found himself wondering what other talents Veritas's people possessed. How many of them were there? Given Crispin Wilder's alleged net worth, it was probably a lot.

"Club's just up ahead. I think the best thing to do is split up and work the crowd. See if anyone knew dear dead Dimitri," she advised.

"What, no dancing cheek to cheek?" he asked, hip-checking her.

"Hey. Behave yourself. Maybe one dance. If you find out something worthwhile."

"You're offering a reward if I'm a good boy?" he said, not sure if he should be amused or annoyed. "Be still my heart."

She ignored his jesting. "Are you going to be okay in there? It's going to be packed."

Reality returned, causing Alex to take a deep breath. "I'll just have to be. Too much is at stake for me to back out now."

To his surprise, Morgan placed a kiss on his cheek. "Good hunting, Mr. White Knight."

"Be careful, Valkyrie," he replied.

Le Purgatoire was classic New Orleans, though more understated than many places, despite the neon lights. From Morgan's previous experience, the clientele varied by the time of day: heterosexual couples in the early evening, gay and lesbian couples by midnight. By now, it'd be mostly brave tourists and the folks who didn't color within any of the gender lines.

Which she'd failed to mention to Alex.

She couldn't stop the grin, knowing it was petty of her, but this was payback for him making her so uneasy, making her think things could be different than they were. He'd proved to be a master at that. Not all that unease was just on her part. She'd seen the frank desire in his eyes earlier this evening. She knew the surly ex-con was still there, just beneath the surface, but now she was seeing hints of the DEA agent he'd once been. Two sides of the same coin, both of which she found far too attractive.

Focus. It appeared she needed that as much as he did.

Like most NOLA bars, Le Purgatoire's front double doors were open, and the music and air conditioning sought the street like an addict does another high. As she made her way inside, she found that the place was busy, but not as packed as some nights. Probably because it wasn't the weekend.

Back when she was younger, this kind of meat market had held a certain fascination, but not now. Not when she knew the bad stuff that could go down in places like this. How easy it was for predators to use this as their hunting ground.

The anger rolled through her in the span of a heartbeat. Memories of *that* night in a different bar, one just a few streets away from this one. The handsome guy who'd lied from the moment they'd met. How smooth he'd been. The dancing. The emotional manipulation. The drink that he'd insisted she consume, the one that held the drug. If her friends hadn't been watching over her, it would have ended in rape, or worse. All because one man didn't understand that women weren't his personal playthings.

That hellish experience had been the catalyst that sent her

to law school, and then to work for the FBI. The cops had never arrested the man who'd drugged her—he'd crawled back into the woodwork. Nevertheless, she was paying it forward in her own way. Because there were still bastards out there who thought that anyone was theirs for the taking. For some of them, the younger the victim, the better.

"Hey, pretty dress," a guy said.

Morgan blew out a stream of air and conjured up a smile. "Thank you."

"Can I buy you a drink?"

"No, I'm good," she said. "You come here often?"

He shook his head. "First time. I'm in town for a software convention."

Which was code for: "What happens in New Orleans stays in New Orleans. You game, baby?"

Time to shut this down, since he wasn't a regular patron and most likely wouldn't know Dimitri.

"I'm a local," she said. "I'm a reporter doing a story on convention tourists and prostitution. Maybe you'd be willing to tell me some stories."

The guy paled, then shook his head. "Ah, no. Sorry, gotta go."

Morgan kept the smile to herself as she headed for the bar. Sometimes it was just so easy. It took a bit before the bartender could get to her.

"A beer, please. And open it in front of me, please."

The girl raised an eyebrow, then nodded her understanding. "No problem."

The beer was delivered as requested, and Morgan made sure to include an extra tip for the service. Not all bartenders took that request well.

As she turned around, she found herself hemmed in by two men, both of them probably in their forties. For a moment, she thought it was going to be awkward, but then she realized they were checking each other out.

Perfect.

Morgan scooted off to allow them to become better

acquainted. She scoped out the dance floor. Couples of all descriptions were moving to the music, some male, some female, some indeterminate. New Orleans didn't play favorites; whatever you wanted, it was happy to supply it.

She finally spied Alex, and as she'd predicted, he was attracting a lot of attention with his broad shoulders, his tan. Morgan sighed. With a body like that, they'd have to be stone-cold dead not to notice him. He flirted in response to the female attention, but she could see the tension in the way he held himself. The crowd was getting to him.

"Hang in there, guy," she muttered.

He was chatting up a young, busty blonde. If she was a regular, maybe she'd know Dimitri. They laughed together, and she pulled him onto the dance floor, sending all the right signals. As they danced, Morgan kept her focus on Alex, how he managed to make almost everything seem like foreplay. When he caught her checking him out, he winked and pulled his partner closer, grinding against her.

Damn you. He was just doing that to push her buttons. Morgan took a long chug of the beer to cool down.

Meanwhile, that load of coke was being divided up for distribution on the city streets. If it was laced with strychnine, the bodies would start piling up.

That morbid thought pushed Morgan into action, and she worked her way around the bar, listening in on conversations. Some were in other languages, but none in Russian. She flirted with some of the guys and carefully posed some open-ended questions. None of them knew Dimitri. Finally, she hit pay dirt with a middle-aged woman nursing a pink daiquiri.

"Yes, I know him," the lady replied. "He's okay. Never hassles me when it comes time to pay."

Morgan took another look at the woman. She was trying for twenty, when she was a lot closer to mid-forties. Her makeup and clothes—what there were of the latter—spoke of desperation and too many years walking the street. She'd probably been pretty when she was younger, but those years were rapidly fading in the rearview mirror.

"I'm hoping to find him," Morgan said. "Dimitri said he knew someone who could get me a job."

The woman raised an eyebrow. "Not likely. Last time I saw him, he was drunk off his ass, and that's saying a lot for a Russian. Something to do with boss problems."

"Did he hang with anyone else here?" Morgan asked, putting a hint of urgency in her voice. "Maybe they'd know what he was talking about."

"Only the redhead. She's Russian too. But you don't want to mess with her. She's nasty. Cut you just for the fun of it." The woman glanced around, fear in her eyes now. "People who work for her go missing."

Now we're getting somewhere. "What's her name, so I can steer clear of her?"

"Anya. That's all I know. All I want to know. She's nothing but trouble. If Dimitri was afraid of her . . . "

The prostitute shook her head and walked away, her radar quickly narrowing in on a couple of guys with name badges. Conventioneers. Always easy pickings.

"Anya," Morgan murmured. *Oh God, it couldn't be.*

Alex reined in his frustration. The blonde he'd danced with hadn't been helpful. She'd had a fight with her boyfriend and was looking to pick someone up for a revenge screw. He'd quickly backed off and continued to make the rounds. The only good thing had been the look on Morgan's face when he'd been dancing. The barely concealed jealousy. At least he was finally making progress on that front.

The crowd was pressing in on him now, and he needed to escape. He glanced around the bar but couldn't see Morgan. He was aiming for the front door when a redhead stepped in front of him. She smiled up at him with perfect teeth, then ran a finger under his collar as if they were intimately acquainted.

"Hello," she said.

Her accent was Russian and her dress very short, making her legs seem impossibly long. Her eyes were dark and shiny, her lips bright red, and her auburn hair fell below her shoulders in thick waves. He swore she looked familiar in some way.

"Hi there," he said. "Maybe you could help me. I'm looking for a friend of mine. His name's Dimitri."

The woman cocked her head. "There are many of that name. What does he look like?"

Alex described him, at least the way he remembered him from prison. His most recent encounter with the man wouldn't make for good bar conversation.

"Ah, Dimitri Golov. Yes. That one I know."

"Oh, good. Is he here tonight? I haven't seen him."

"No, he is not here," she said, pouting.

"He told me to check this place out. I'm liking it so far."

The redhead leaned closer now, touching his cheek. "The evening is looking much, much better now."

He felt his blood warming. "What's your name?"

"Anya. And yours?"

"Michael." It wasn't a lie—that was his middle name.

"What do you do, Michael?"

"I sell . . . pharmaceuticals."

Her whole demeanor changed. "Like Dimitri, then?"

"Yes. Like Dimitri," he said, hopeful. *Come on, baby, take the bait.* Maybe this way, he'd have a chance to make a significant contribution to the investigation.

Anya leaned even closer, her strange perfume filling his nose, confusing his brain. "Do you want to *dance* with me, Michael?"

The word took on whole new shades of meaning when it came out of those lips, and he hardened under her scorching gaze. Who said he couldn't score tonight? He'd even stuck a couple condoms in his back pocket just in case. As long as he got the information Veritas needed, what would be the harm? He was getting there with Morgan, but this one would be one wild ride. That way, when his partner did come around, he wouldn't be so damned desperate. He'd be the one in control.

A twitch across his shoulders reminded him that, somewhere, Morgan was probably watching him. That made him smile. Jealousy often brought a reluctant woman to her knees. Literally.

"Yes, I'd really like to dance with you," he said. It'd be hot and fast with no strings attached. Sometimes that was the best kind of sex.

"Then we are going to be very happy together," Anya said, taking his hand and leading him toward the back of the club. "And after that, we can talk about Dimitri. I know many things about him."

Better and better.

"You should wear a dress like that more often," a man said.

Morgan smiled at the newcomer. "Good evening, Sam. What brings you to this side of hell?"

He moved closer to her, so no one could overhear them. "Our boss wanted you to have some backup tonight. He's feeling edgy."

"Crispin? Edgy?"

"I'm hearing he's not a happy camper, because the Russian in the warehouse was his man inside Buryshkin's organization. Now we have no one."

"What?" That, she hadn't known. "Damn, that's not good news."

"No, it's not. Anything new here?"

"Sort of. I spoke with a woman who knew Dimitri, and I mean in the Biblical way. She said he was having 'boss problems.' And she knows Anya."

Sam stilled. "Would that be the Anya everyone warned me about?"

"Given the description, I'd say yes." Morgan tipped up onto her toes to try to find Alex, then lowered back down when she couldn't. "I wonder where Parkin is."

"Probably getting his dick adjusted. That's the first thing I'd be doing after all those years in stir."

She searched the crowd for Alex again, but with no success. Was he buried inside some girl in a storage closet somewhere?

Damn you, Parkin, you better not go there.

Where the hell had that come from? Why would she care?

If he scored, he'd stop trying to sweet-talk her into bed. A happy ending for everyone. Somehow that just didn't sit right.

"Morgan?" Sam nudged her.

"Huh? Sorry. What did you say?"

"I was saying not to worry. Parkin can handle himself. His time in prison made him tough."

"Maybe. Ask around, see if anyone saw where he went and who he's with."

"Another beer while I'm making the rounds?" Sam asked, indicating her nearly empty bottle.

"No, one is plenty."

He set off on his mission, while Morgan fidgeted. Parkin had too many enemies who wanted him dead. What better way to distract him than with a willing girl and a promise of a good time?

Anya took him outside the bar into a quaint courtyard lit with flaming torchieres set at intervals along the back wall. They weren't alone; a couple occupied a far corner, but they were oblivious to the rest of the world. Then she led him to a darkened spot and shoved him back against the building's brickwork.

"I'll take that dance now," she said.

Here? Well, it *was* New Orleans.

Alex didn't normally mind women who took charge—some of his best experiences had been that way—but his nerves were taut. It was risky being on his own with someone he didn't know. Still, why would one of Buryshkin's people try to hurt him? He was on the Russian's payroll.

"So what do you have in mind?" he asked, watching her closely in the dim light. There seemed to be a bewitching fire in those dark eyes now.

Anya stepped up, took his face in her hands, and kissed him. The kiss wasn't like he'd expected; it was one of domination more than discovery. That knowledge lit him up like a firecracker, and his groin responded enthusiastically. He was vaguely aware of the other couple leaving the courtyard, finished with their business. The door to the bar closed behind them.

"Do you know what I like most?" Anya murmured.

Alex shook his head, hoping it didn't have anything to do with whips and chains.

"I'll show you."

She trailed her tongue around his chin, then down onto his neck. It was as arousing as all hell. She gripped the sides of his face and lightly nipped him with her teeth.

"Do you like that?"

"Yeah, I do."

"Then maybe you'll like this even better," she said.

The grip grew tighter, and right before Alex was going to pull away, she bit him, digging her teeth into his neck.

With a yelp, Alex jerked back, feeling his flesh give way.

"What the hell?" he said, touching the spot and coming away with blood on his fingers. The skin felt ragged to the touch and stung like fury. "Are you fucking crazy?"

He could see blood on her lips. *His* blood. This one was into pain.

Anya went all innocent. "You said you would like it. You lied. So many of them do."

Bitch. All thoughts of fucking her vanished.

Alex forcibly wrestled his anger down. If this viper knew anything about Dimitri, he had to play along. Which was proving difficult, as he felt blood running down his neck, under his collar.

"Dimitri said you liked it rough," he said.

"He could not handle me. He could not handle a lot of things. What about you, Michael? Are you eager to taste what I can give you?" she said, running a talon-like nail down his chest, then south of his waist.

He caught her hand before it reached home.

"Here's the deal: We talk first, then maybe we'll get to the pain part. But you have to make it worth my while."

Her eyes flattened, becoming cold and calculating. If the throbbing wound on his neck hadn't told him she was dangerous, those eyes confirmed it.

Why the hell am I out here with this crazy?

"You think you dictate to me," she said, waving a finger in front of his face as if he were a naughty child. "You have picked the wrong side. You are dead and do not know it."

Side? "Just tell me about Dimitri, and I won't have your ass arrested for assault. Because believe me, I'm just about to—"

"*Zatknis!*" she shouted. She continued to swear at him in Russian, her eyes glowing black pits. He saw only madness now, and a cold sweat bathed him.

On instinct, Alex grabbed her arm as it moved toward him. She struggled, but he slapped her wrist down on his knee. An open switchblade hit the ground at his feet

He kicked it away. "What the hell is wrong with you?"

She snarled and was about to leap at him, but Alex was through the back door and into the crowd before she had a chance to stop him. Or retrieve her knife. He scooped up a few napkins from a table and pressed them against his neck to try to stop the bleeding. What if she had HIV or something?

As he headed for the front entrance, Alex shot a look over his shoulder, but the she-devil wasn't following him. The old Parkin Luck wasn't working any longer—the first woman he'd gotten close to banging had turned out to be a total psycho. Even worse, he'd gotten no useful information on Dimitri, and if he hadn't been paying attention, she would have stabbed him just for fun.

Jesus.

"You're sure?" Morgan asked, pacing outside the bar now.

Sam nodded. "He went off with a redhead. The guy said he saw them going out the rear door."

"Dammit. Either he's playing us for suckers, or he's in trouble. Go around the back and see if you can find out what's going on with them. I'll stay here in case he comes this way."

Sam headed around the side of the building as Morgan stared at the flow of people in and out of the club.

"Where are you?"

Alex found Morgan pacing outside the club, her expression lethal. The instant she saw him, she dialed Sam.

"He's here. Yeah, okay. Thanks for your help tonight. I'll talk to you later." She stuffed her phone in her purse, then got in his face. "Where the hell have you been?"

"What?" Alex said, still trying to wrap his mind around what had just happened.

"You heard me."

A little of the fog cleared. "I've been doing what you expected me to do. Asking questions. Why are you so damned mad?"

"You were with a redhead, right?"

He nodded. "Yeah, so?"

"Giving her your A game, were you?" she said.

"You're jealous."

Morgan set off down the street, moving at a fast pace, like she wanted to put miles between them. It took Alex half a block to catch up to her.

He caught her by the arm. "What the hell is up with you?"

She spun around to face him, and for a moment he thought she was going to sock him in the jaw. "Don't play innocent," she spat.

"I'm not getting the issue here. I chatted up a couple people and thought I'd found someone who had some information on Dimitri, but the cost for that information was far too high."

Morgan shook her head. "You knew who the hell that redhead was, and that's why you took off with her. Was it good for you? Did she scream your name when you got her off?"

"What? No. We didn't get it on. Whoever that woman was, she's batshit crazy."

His companion hesitated. "You didn't recognize her?"

"No. She said her name was Anya. I've never met her before."

"Think about it," she said.

"Think about what?"

"Russian accent? Named Anya? Would have been about

sixteen when you went to prison?"

The name clicked into place as a chill swept through his bones. "Oh, God."

Anya Vladimirovna Buryshkin.

The Russian's only child.

"That bitch!" he shouted. That outburst earned them a few startled looks from passersby. Alex's stomach lurched, and he swallowed to keep from vomiting. He'd been a total fool.

Morgan stared for a moment, then touched his arm. "You really didn't know who she was?"

"No," he insisted. "I'd never met her. I saw a picture of her once, but she was just a kid and had brown hair. If I had known . . . Oh, God."

Morgan reached toward the makeshift compress on his neck. "What happened?"

He pulled away the napkins, and the blood began to run again.

"The bitch bit me," he said, quieter now.

"What?"

Morgan dug in her purse and gave him a stack of tissues. When he pushed them up against the wound, the throbbing pain grew worse.

"You're lucky she didn't cut out your liver," she said, her voice hardened steel now. "Anya's known to do that every now and then."

"She would have if I hadn't stopped her," he murmured.

Suddenly, being on the street made him feel too vulnerable.

"Let's get out of here," he said. "I need a damned shower."

Chapter Fourteen

Morgan's worry increased with each step away from the bar. Alex had gone from scowling and furious to haunted. His shoulders were hunched, and he wouldn't meet her gaze. Any questions she posed were ignored.

To ensure that they weren't being followed, she kept a close watch as they took a circuitous route back to the apartment. Once inside, instead of heading directly to the shower, Alex sat on the couch, his head in one hand while the other kept pressure on the wound.

"If you let me look at it, I'll see if it needs stitches."

He slowly raised his head and removed the tissues. Morgan couldn't help but wince. The bite was irregular and deeper on one end. It'd taken a lot to do that much damage.

"It's bad, isn't it?" he asked, his voice barely audible.

"Not as bad as it could have been. The issue is whether it'll get infected. And here I thought Anne Rice was just bullshitting us about vampires in New Orleans."

Her joke totally failed.

Morgan fetched the first aid kit from the bathroom and laid it out on the coffee table. "I'll clean it now, then after you shower, I'll bandage it."

He shook his head, not looking at her.

"Alex? Come on, it'll be okay," she said, confused by his reaction.

"You don't understand," he said, his voice cracking. "She knew."

"Knew what?" Morgan asked, sitting down next to him.

His tortured brown eyes rose to meet hers. "You saw it in

the prison report. The fight, the one that damned near killed me."

What did that have to do with what happened tonight?

"Tell me what this is all about," she said, giving his arm a gentle squeeze.

He stared at nothing for a long time, and Morgan made herself wait him out.

"When I was attacked," he began, "two of the guys held me down while the third . . . When he was pulling down my pants, he told me what they were going to do to me. How I was going to like it." Alex gulped air like he was reliving the assault.

"And then he . . . bit me right on the neck, like I was some dog's bitch. Showing me I was his for the taking. It took twenty-five stitches to get it closed."

Morgan's stomach rolled over. "Jesus." She'd known about the injury, but not how it'd been delivered. It explained the wicked, curved scar.

"When it happened tonight, I was too busy trying to get away from her to realize why she'd done it. Anya *knew* what had gone down in Angola. She was showing me that I'm just as weak, just as vulnerable out here as I was in there. That she was going to make me her bitch."

Morgan took a deep breath, ensuring that her voice didn't reflect her murderous fury. She'd channel that rage later, when she had her hands around Anya's neck.

"But you showed her you weren't vulnerable. You were just surprised. Next time, you won't be. That's what's important."

He didn't seem to believe her.

"Let's get you into the shower. You'll feel better. Feel less . . . "

"Violated?" he said.

The hell this man has been through.

His solemn brown eyes studied her. "The Russians will try to use me to assassinate your boss. You know that, right?"

"Then God help you. Because the last guy who tried to assassinate Crispin wasn't successful."

"You kill him?" Alex asked.

The question caught her off guard in its boldness. "Neil did. I would have, if it had come down to that," she admitted.

"Which means that you would do the same to me, if needed," he said, his voice hollow.

"Not if I can help it, Alex," she said, caught by the thought that she might have to choose between her boss and this man. A day or so ago, it would have been an easy choice—she owed Crispin everything—but now . . .

Disturbed by what that might mean, she shifted gears. "Come on, let's get you cleaned up and into bed."

Despite all her soothing words, his eyes remained haunted. Anya's brutality, her coldly calculated mind-rape, had shaken him to the core.

You're dead, bitch. You just don't know it yet.

There was a moment in the shower, as the water rushed across his neck and caused the pain to increase fivefold, that Alex nearly wept. He'd done so only a few times in his life: at his dad's funeral, after his conviction, and after that fight in prison, while recovering in the infirmary. Each time, he'd made sure no one saw the tears.

Was this another one of Buryshkin's games, sending his violent offspring after Alex to reinforce that he was just a pawn, one that could be crushed at will? Or was there something else going on that neither he nor Morgan was aware of?

A light tap came on the bathroom door. Not surprising, given how long he'd been in the shower trying to pull his head together.

"You okay?" Morgan called out.

He couldn't hide in here forever. "Yeah. I'll be out soon."

He dried off and wrapped the towel around his hips. Any other time, he would have done it to entice Morgan one step closer to his bed. Not tonight. He found her waiting for him, bandages and ointment on the nightstand. Her eyes flickered to the towel, then away.

"Sit here," she said, patting the side of the bed.

He did as she asked, then closed his eyes while she cleaned the wound and gently placed the Steri-Strips, one by one. Her hands were warm and caring.

"One edge is really rough, but I think it'll heal smooth if the strips hold. If not, we can get you to a doc for a few sutures."

"Doesn't matter," he said.

"Yes, it does," she said firmly. "There's no way we're letting this bitch win."

It appeared that he wasn't alone on this journey. "How'd you get so tough after what happened to you?"

"I realized I had two choices: Let that man ruin the rest of my life, or fight back. It was hell. It took me a long time before I could go back into a bar again, and they still make me uncomfortable. For a while, I was convinced every guy was a monster. Now I'm better at sorting out the evil ones from the regular folks."

"So all guys who hit on you are monsters?" he asked, wanting to know if he fell into that category with her.

"No. It's the ones who tell me I have no choice in the matter that are the problem." She looked over at him and her expression softened. "Just because you want to get me into bed doesn't make you a monster. You're a lone wolf being reintroduced into the pack. You'll find your place again, and then no one will jack with you because you'll rip them apart."

"You sound so sure."

Morgan nodded. "I have good instincts. You're a threat to the Russians, or they wouldn't be effing with you like this."

"I'm not used to having people in my corner."

"You work for Veritas now. We're different."

"I also work for the Russians," he reminded her.

"Not for too much longer." Morgan delicately taped a bandage over the wound. "Too tight?"

"No, it's good. Thank you."

"Allergic to any antibiotics or pain meds?" When he shook

his head, she handed him two different pills, along with a cup of water. He swallowed them, feeling the discomfort as they went down, while Morgan tidied up.

She hesitated in the doorway. "I can stay until you fall asleep. Just for moral support, you know. No threat to your manhood at all."

He was touched by her offer. "I'd rather you be lying next to me tonight."

"Alex—" she began.

"I wasn't . . . Never mind. Good night, Morgan. And thank you for taking care of me."

As she closed the door behind her, Alex stripped off the towel and crawled into bed, hands behind his head to better stare at the ceiling. He found himself replaying what had happened tonight, right up to nearly being stabbed. Doing the "what ifs," because it was the best way to generate guilt. It was his own damned fault. He knew better than to go off alone with a Russian in this town. Once again, his dick had been doing the thinking for him.

There was a tap at the door and it opened slowly. Morgan crossed to the other side of the bed, where she placed her gun and cell phone on the nightstand. She was wearing a long T-shirt, one that hit mid-thigh.

As she pulled back the covers on her side, she hesitated. "I'm here for support, not for sex," she said, but he heard the nervousness in her voice. Like she wasn't completely sure of this herself.

"All right. I am not wearing anything, though."

"It's not the first time I've slept next to a naked man."

Morgan slid into bed next to him and moved over until she could lay her head on his shoulder. She gingerly placed her arm across his lower chest.

"Is this okay?" she asked.

"Yeah, it's good. Why are you doing this?" he asked, his voice near a whisper.

It took a while for her to answer, like she was having difficulty finding the proper words.

"After I was nearly raped, I couldn't trust any man at that point, even those I knew really well. And asking a girlfriend to curl up with me would have been awkward. So I slept alone. I lay there staring at the shadows night after night, replaying it over and over. I was too much in my own head."

"Doing the 'what ifs'?"

"Exactly."

Alex felt the need to change the subject, for both of them. "How did you get the nickname Valkyrie?"

Morgan shifted, looking up at him, her fingers featherlight on his chest.

"In Norse mythology, a valkyrie chooses who lives and dies in battle, then carries her chosen heroes to Valhalla so they can prepare for Ragnarök. The end of the world." She laid her head back down, her sandalwood scent surrounding him, comforting him.

"So now I'm a chosen hero?"

She chuckled. "You're getting there."

"You know, I swore I'd never hurt a woman. But after tonight, I'd love nothing more than to break Anya Buryshkin into pieces."

Morgan snuggled into his chest. "Lucky for you, I never made that vow."

He looked down at her. "So . . . in battle, which is more deadly: a batshit-crazy vampire, or a valkyrie?"

"We'll be finding that out real soon," her voice chillier now.

For the first time in years, he felt safe. Unwilling to let the feeling slip out of his grasp, he closed his eyes, savoring the soft touch of Morgan's hair on his skin. Her very presence soothed away the pain, the fear, the anger. Just like a valkyrie, as a warrior's life was nearing its end.

Chapter Fifteen

September 19th
Miri's House

Miri woke from an unpleasant dream, one about dead cats and bloodstained hands that came out of the darkness to hurt her. She turned over, trying to get comfortable, but the mattress-on-the-floor thing wasn't doing its usual magic.

The window air conditioner was off at Neil's request, because he said it made it hard to hear the night noises. Whatever that meant. The ceiling fan was just moving stale air with each turn. It didn't help that her babysitter insisted she sleep fully clothed, except for her shoes. She'd gone for a tank top and shorts to take the sweating down a notch. He'd also insisted that they not be brightly colored or white, and she'd grumpily complied, wondering what kind of mind it took to think of things like that.

But the real reason she was having trouble sleeping was because the other person in the house was a male, and not her brother. A male that was as ripped and hunky as they came. A total stud. The universe was cruel. If only she'd met him at the bar, then everything would be cool. But no, he had to be *her bodyguard*. Which made him off limits, if she wanted to stay alive.

Iceman had proven to be just as advertised: short on conversation, long on vigilance. He could ghost from room to room without making a single sound, and had scared the hell out of her more than once. He ate in silence and slept sitting upright in the living room, his position precisely calculated so he could cover both the front and back doors. He was always armed, a fact she'd realized when she caught a peek of him in the bathroom after a shower, towel around his trim waist, gun within reach on the counter.

Despite all that, Neil intrigued her because he was so unlike anyone else she'd ever met. A killing machine who hadn't even told her his last name, though she'd asked. Twice.

At least he's on our side.

Miri had just closed her eyes when she heard something move outside her window. It was faint, but there. A cat, maybe. It came again, more distinct now.

She bolted out of bed, but even before she made it to the door of her room, Neil was there, alert, his presence filling the doorway, Glock in hand.

She kept her voice low. "I heard something outside. It's too big to be an animal."

"I did too. Stay put. I'll check it out. Can you shoot a gun?"

"Sure can."

He bent over and pulled his backup weapon from an ankle holster under his jeans.

"It's a SIG Sauer, so there's no safety. There's already a cartridge in chamber."

Miri took the firearm. "I'll watch your back," she said.

"When's your birthday? Month, date?"

Startled, she rattled off, "October tenth."

"Then ten ten is the password. If I give you the wrong number, it means I'm a hostage. In that case, barricade yourself in the bathroom and call 911. Even if someone threatens to shoot me, do *not* open the door. You understand?"

"Ah . . . okay. Be careful." What else could she say?

Her bodyguard gave her a stern look, as if that warning really didn't apply to him. Then he was out the back door in full stealth mode.

How do you do that?

Even better, could he teach her that skill? Miri locked up behind him and wedged a chair under the doorknob for good measure. She'd barely turned toward the bedroom when something shattered the front window and rolled inside. The stench of gasoline reached her nose the instant before flames blossomed across the old wood floor. Some sort of homemade incendiary.

"Oh my God!"

Miri pounded at the flames with a couch cushion, but it only seemed to make them spread faster. She danced back so her clothes wouldn't catch fire, then dug under the kitchen cabinet for the fire extinguisher. It had been discharged. She flung it away in disgust.

As the fire gained ground, gray-black smoke climbed upward. Ducking into the bedroom, Miri grabbed her purse, looping the strap across her body. Then pulled on her shoes. While she called 911, she looked around, trying to decide what she could save. Then she saw it: the picture of Alex and her together at the park. She was five, he sixteen. It was the only photo of them from when they were kids. Miri grabbed it and jammed it in her purse.

The 911 operator came on the line.

"My house is on fire! Someone threw something in the window. I can't put it out!"

Two distinct pops came from the backyard. Gunfire.

Holy shit. "Someone is shooting at us! You've got to send the cops!" She gave the address, just in case the operator didn't have it.

"Please stay on the line, ma'am."

"I can't. He might be hurt."

She ditched her phone inside her purse and fled to the back door. Pulling the chair out of the way, she shot a look toward the front of the house. The couch was fully engulfed, and smoke rolled across the ceiling in a thick wave.

She had no choice—she had to go outside. She'd just pulled away the chair and unlocked the door when she heard more gunfire.

"Miri!" Neil called. Then, "Ten ten!"

She threw open the door, and her bodyguard rolled inside. Before she could move to close it, he was on his feet, kicking it shut and shoving her toward the bedroom. Seconds later, the back door was riddled with bullets.

"Jesus! What the hell?" she said.

"You okay?"

"Yeah. What's going on?"

"We got three tangos. One's down, but I couldn't take the others out before they started the fire. You call 911?"

"Yes. They know we're being shot at."

"Then we hunker down as long as possible and hope the cops get here fast," he said, his eyes watering from the smoke. A line of blood ran down his arm. He led her back toward the bathroom. The fire grew faster now, fumes and smoke roiling like a black serpent.

"You need to wet some towels and—"

"The door!" she said. The one behind all of Alex's boxes that led to the other unit. "I can get us out of here."

"How?"

She didn't bother to answer, flying into her bedroom. She began tossing her brother's storage boxes out of the way, sending his clothes and possessions in all directions.

"What are you doing?" Neil asked. He had his back to her, gun pointed toward the living room, though it was unlikely their hunters would bother to come inside. All they had to do was wait for her and her body guard to choose between being roasted to death, or being cut down in a hail of bullets.

"There's a door to the other unit behind all this stuff. It isn't locked." Which was why she'd piled all the boxes in front of it.

"You never told me about that," he said sternly.

"Yeah, well, I'm telling you now."

Miri kicked the last of the boxes out of the way, Neil at her side. A fast glance toward the front room told her that the fire was about to go into a flashover: the point where the contents of the house became so hot everything inside the structure would spontaneously combust. Including them.

I'll never date a fireman again. You learned too much of the scary stuff that way.

"Me first," Neil said, slowly edging open the door with a

booted foot, his gun gripped between his two hands. His grim, soot-stained face promised swift death to anyone who got in his way. "Run silent, or they'll figure out what we're up to," he whispered. The portal pushed away debris, leading to a spongy floor, rodent skeletons, and black mold.

Miri closed the warped door behind them, hoping it would offer a brief barrier to the flames. When she turned and walked through a spider web, she clamped her lips to keep from crying out.

"Is this side the same as yours?" Neil asked.

"Probably a mirror image. I've never been over here before." The only reason she'd gotten the rent so cheap was because no one wanted to live next to a rotting hulk.

They crept through the semi-darkness, only patches of moonlight through the ruined roof lighting their way. Something crashed behind them, accompanied by a shuddering *whomp* as the fire outgrew the confines of Miri's apartment. The beams above them began to groan in protest.

"This whole thing's coming down," Miri said.

Neil paused at the front door. "I'll go straight out, you go left. Get off the porch and onto the ground as quickly as possible. If you see someone with a gun who isn't in uniform, shoot them. Can you do that?"

"I'll try."

"On three." He moved forward to the front door. "One . . . two . . . three."

Neil kicked the door and rotting plywood out of the way, then rolled out onto the porch and onto the ground, coming to his feet with a grace that defied description.

Miri didn't try that move, but sprinted out, moving left and off the porch as he'd ordered. She instinctively lowered her stance, trying to see where their assailants might be hiding. Was there one by the neighbor's car?

Her hands shook so hard, she could barely keep the gun level.

"Down!" Neil shouted, and she dove for the ground as gunshots cut the air above her. He returned fire in two quick bursts. Bullets kicked up the dirt near her. She found her target, and her shots made the guy duck behind a car. Another cried out as Neil's bullets hit home.

Sirens came to life nearby, making it sound as if all of New Orleans's finest were headed their way. Miri almost cried with relief when a police car screeched to a halt near the house. Then another came from the other direction. Cops poured out of their vehicles, taking defensive positions. Right behind them was a fire engine, emergency lights slicing through the night.

"Place your weapons on the ground! Stand up slowly with your hands behind your head!" an officer shouted.

It dawned on her that the cops presented just as much danger as the bad guys, since they had no clue who the victims were here.

"Do exactly as they say," Neil called out. "It'll be okay."

"Sure. Yeah, I can see that." Miri's heart went into overdrive, her breath coming in short gasps, eyes raining tears from the smoke.

With exaggerated slowness, her bodyguard placed his weapon on the ground, then slowly rose, hands tucked behind his head. He took two very deliberate steps away from the gun, to indicate that he was not a threat.

It was a suicide move if any of the killers had him in their sights.

"Now you! Do it!" the cop called out.

Miri mimicked Neil's movements, shaking so hard it was difficult to stand. "That good for you guys?" she called out, growing angry now. "Because it sure sucks for me."

Out of nowhere, Neil laughed, a welcome sound in the middle of all the chaos. "You got some balls, lady."

She smiled back at him, still shaking. "You too, Bullet Catcher."

The cops moved up, keeping them covered as firemen swarmed toward her house. It was obvious that there was no way to save it. At this point, they were just ensuring that none of the nearby houses were involved.

"Anyone inside?" one of them called out.

Neil shook his head. "No one else. There's a body in the backyard. Gunshot victim."

So he *had* killed one of their attackers. Miri found herself strangely not giving a damn about that. Out of prison for less than forty-eight hours, and somehow her dear brother had managed to screw up her life yet again.

But this time I can fight back.

The cops moved them out onto the street as nosy locals in their sleepwear gathered along the sidewalks, staring at the sideshow that had set up camp in their neighborhood.

Looking back at her house, Miri swore. It was fully engulfed now, a huge, glowing pyre. She was told to lean up against one of the cop cars, then patted down by a female officer.

"You got a permit for that gun?" the woman asked.

"It's in my purse." Which was currently sitting on the hood of the car.

To her right Neil was told to assume the same position, and as he did so, he said, "There's a knife in my right boot and extra ammo in my back pockets. My weapons permit is in my wallet."

As one of the uniforms patted him down, Neil looked over at her. "You okay?" he asked.

"Yeah. Here's where you say 'I told you so.' You warned me it wouldn't be safe here, that someone would come after us."

"I work within the parameters I'm given. Sometimes those parameters blow, because the person I'm guarding is too damned stubborn to listen."

She deserved that. Her insistence that they remain at the house had almost gotten them killed. "I'm sorry. I'll listen better in the future."

He studied her for a moment. "Apology accepted."

After a brief stint with the paramedics—some oxygen to help clear out their lungs, and a bandage for Neil's wound—they were stuck in the backseat of a patrol car.

Miri gazed at the inferno. "Whoever did this will come

back after us, won't they?"

"Most likely," Neil replied. "They'll have to work a lot harder next time, because we're going to disappear."

She angled her head toward the cops standing near the car. "Really? I don't think they're just going to slap our wrists."

"It'll be fine."

Miri looked at him. Neil showed no hint of emotion, no impending adrenaline crash, nothing. It was as if he were a robot in human skin.

"Are you sure you're for real? Not some full-sized G.I. Joe action figure or something?"

He stared at her like he didn't understand the question. She sighed, knowing she couldn't get under his tough exterior. At least she'd heard him laugh just once.

"Okay, Iceman, we'll do it your way this time. Just make sure I don't regret it."

Morgan's eyes fluttered open, registering the sunlight slipping around the edges of the heavy blackout curtains. Morning already. They'd only had about three hours of sleep. Alex rested on his side, his broad chest up next to her, a hand lying across her stomach. He smelled of toothpaste and the ointment she'd used on his wound.

How long had it been since she'd shared a bed with a man? *Almost five years.* All because her husband had taught her a bitter lesson about trust. And damn her, she still loved Wayne, despite that lesson. Still missed him after all these years.

Lying in bed with a male, a virile one, made her think of things she really should *not* be thinking. Her heart told her that having sex with Alex Parkin would be a massive mistake. Her body, on the other hand, whispered a different tune. It'd been too long since she'd felt a man make love to her, felt the pleasure that uninhibited sex could bring.

Morgan sighed. Any other guy, she could have ignored, but Alex was too much like her.

Damaged. Hurting. Desperate to be whole again.
Any one of those would be her Achilles' heel.

"You're doing a lot of thinking over there," Alex said, his breath lightly caressing her ear.

"How long have you been awake?"

"A while. Had to make a pit stop."

She closed her eyes, knowing she should get up, but not wanting to move.

"Morgan?"

"Hmm . . . "

"I'm going to kiss you." He wasn't seeking permission.

Alex turned her face toward him and delivered on his promise. It was a light kiss, a careful one. When she didn't protest, he began another, this one deeper, more intense, the kind she'd missed for too long. Morgan placed her hand on his shoulder as the kiss ignited a fire in both of them. Their tongues touching now, his warm palm slid under her sleep shirt, resting just below her breast.

Her mind told her this wasn't good, that this way lay heartbreak. For once, her body wasn't listening.

"Alex . . . " she murmured.

"Yeah, I feel it too, Morgan." His hand covered her breast now, rolling the nipple between his rough fingers. "God, I want you so bad. I want you fast and hard, lady, then slow. I want to take you over and over all day."

Morgan pulled him to her, feeling his sculpted body press against hers. The burning, hard length of him lay on her stomach, promising only the deepest pleasure. He moaned into her mouth, and she grew damp with anticipation. Thoughts of the mission, how wrong this would be, fell away in the face of the body-aching *need*. The need to feel alive again, to cry out as an orgasm rocketed through her. To have a man make her feel like a woman.

"Yes?" he asked, and trailed his lips down her shoulder before flicking his tongue across a nipple.

She moaned as he suckled lightly, the sensations so strong she nearly cried.

"You have to tell me, Morgan."

As her mouth moved to form an answer, to demand her right to pleasure, her phone rang. They jerked apart, blinking in surprise. Alex swore, thumping his pillow in frustration.

Morgan grabbed for the instrument of torture before it could ring again, glancing at the display. *Crispin.* It was as if he knew she was about to compromise the mission. And herself.

"Yeah, boss," she said, sitting up with her back to the smoldering male temptation next to her. Her mouth still felt swollen from the kisses, her breasts hypersensitive, her core aching with the need for release.

"Morgan. Sorry to wake you. Mixed news to report."

Crispin didn't call for the light stuff. "What's going on?"

"A couple hours ago, a three-man team tried to take out Parkin's sister. They set fire to the house to flush them out. Both Neil and the girl are okay, just a bit of smoke inhalation," Crispin said, his voice vibrating with tension.

Oh my God. Alex was going to lose it.

"It was a near thing," her boss continued, "but according to Iceman, the girl didn't freak. In fact, she impressed him, which is saying something."

Morgan raised an eyebrow in surprise; impressing Neil was a rare occurrence.

"Where are they now?"

"They've just left the police station and will be going to ground. Tell Parkin she's fine, and that once they're secure in a new location, she'll call him."

"Send my thanks to Neil, will you?"

"I will."

Morgan looked at her bedmate as he slowly sat up, the bedclothes sliding down to below his navel. She'd almost slept with this man. A man who'd nearly lost his sister, again. Alex had a frown on his face now, as if somehow he'd divined the topic of conversation.

Morgan snapped her mind back to the mission and turned her back to him again.

"The sample of coke from the warehouse was laced with

strychnine, and that's what killed the dealer and Dimitri Golov," Crispin continued. "Even worse, the dope is already hitting the streets. There were five victims overnight who tested positive for strychnine. Four are dead, one is in critical condition."

It just kept getting worse.

"I need you and Parkin to interview the families and friends, see if you can find where they were getting their dope. I'll e-mail you the list of victims," Crispin said. "One, in particular, might pose a problem for Parkin. And for you."

"Why?"

"You'll know when you see the name. Be careful, Morgan."

"I will, boss. Thanks."

She ended the call, turning toward Alex. The slow burn of lust in his eyes was gone, replaced by worry.

"Was that about Miri? Is she okay?"

"Yes. But it might not have turned out that way."

Morgan laid out everything she'd learned, from the attack to the strychnine poisonings, watching as Alex's body went rigid and his eyes grew cold.

"You sure she's okay? Your boss isn't lying, is he?"

"She's fine, Alex. Apparently she didn't lose her cool, and that made all the difference."

He pulled on his jeans, oblivious to the fact that he wasn't wearing underwear. "God, she'll hate me for this. I brought all this to her doorstep."

"In the long run, she'll understand that losing her house is nothing compared to losing her brother."

"I'm not sure if she'll buy that line." Silence fell between them as he pulled on the remainder of his clothes. Finally he paused, looking over at her now. "When things quiet down, I'd like us to pick up where we left off."

"No, I made a mistake. We . . . can't go there. I'm sorry."

Alex cocked his head. "Only your mind is telling you no. Your body wants this. There's no way you can hide that."

He was right, and that made it even worse.

"I'm not giving up, Morgan. You're a beautiful, passionate

woman, and I want to be with you. I don't give a damn who hurt you in the past. This is me. This is now. This isn't done between us."

"It has to be," she said.

"Only if you let the past win." He shut the bedroom door behind him.

If her boss hadn't called, she and Alex Parkin would be more than tangled up together. Sex changed things, changed the participants. Sleeping with Alex would be a big mistake.

But God help her, she wanted to make that mistake just one more time.

"You can come on up," Neil called out over the thrum of the boat engines.

"Be there in a sec," Miri called back.

After selecting a soda from the boat's small refrigerator, she paused to let her mind try to catch up with all that had happened in the last few hours.

Veritas clearly had some serious clout, and they'd just used it. She and Neil had been hauled to the police station—in cuffs, which had really pissed her off. The only reason she hadn't gone off on the cops was Neil. He'd just sat in the back of the cruiser and bided his time.

Once at the station, the situation changed. A lawyer from Veritas had appeared, they were both interviewed, and then they were set free. Neil had to surrender his weapons temporarily, but that was it. No jacking around, no nonsense. Miri knew that if she'd had to face that situation on her own, she'd still be sitting in a jail cell.

Before she'd entirely processed all that, she'd found herself at the docks, boarding a boat. As he'd readied the vessel for departure, Neil had insisted she remain below, at least until they were in open water. Too many prying eyes, he'd said. Given what the guy had risked for her in the last few hours, she didn't even think to argue.

Tired of inhaling the residual smoke on her skin and in her hair, she'd showered and changed into clothes she'd found in the main bedroom closet. Magically, they fit her. Someone had gone shopping, found clothes in her size, and brought them to the boat before she and Neil had even arrived.

How do these guys do that?

They'd been on the water for half an hour or so now, and as the boat picked up speed, Miri adjusted her footing. Fortunately, she'd spent a summer working as a bartender and crewmember on a tour boat, so it was just a matter of regaining her sea legs. Seasickness had never been a problem.

Though the outside looked plain and a bit worn—most likely so it wouldn't attract undue attention—the inside was tricked out. Compared to her house, this was a floating palace.

The boat was about fifty feet in length and had a shallow draft, so it could go into the bayous without scraping bottom. Besides the master bedroom, there were two bunks and a living and dining room area with a bench table, cream-colored padded chairs, and a long couch that probably turned into a bed. The kitchen came equipped with a three-burner electric range and a microwave. The pantry was full of canned goods, and the refrigerator was fully stocked. Miri had no idea how much this kind of boat would cost, but she knew she wouldn't be owning one in her lifetime.

It all came rushing back to her: She was homeless. The only things she owned were the contents of her purse and her bank account. Thank God she deposited her tips every couple of days rather than store them at the house, or she'd have lost everything. That was the only upside to living in a dangerous neighborhood: You never left anything behind that you didn't want stolen.

And then there was Mr. Toes. She'd wanted to bury him, but Neil had refused to tell her where to find the body. It had pissed her off, but then he'd said it was better she remembered her pet like he'd once been, not like he was now. That told her it was really bad.

What about Alex? Was he safe, or had hit men gone after

him too? Surely Neil would tell her. Wouldn't he?

Miri made her way topside with the soda, more surefooted than she'd expected.

"Here," she said, offering Neil the can. "If it's not what you like, there's a bunch of other choices in the refrigerator."

He popped the top and took a long swig, then set it in a cup holder.

"You find everything okay?" he asked.

"Yeah. Damned fancy boat. Yours?"

"No."

His curt reply pushed her to ask the question: "Is my brother okay? I mean, you'd tell me if anything happened to him, wouldn't you?"

Neil nodded. "Your brother's fine. Morgan will watch his six."

"Six?"

"Watch his back." He looked back to the water in front of them. "We're headed into the bayou. I'll find a place for us to anchor. I'll get a shower and then we'll sleep—in shifts, so one of us can keep watch."

He was always "on mission," no time for idle conversation.

"Are you like this when you go grocery shopping?"

"What?"

"So damned serious. I mean, if you smiled, would the world end?"

Neil shot her a sidelong glance. "Probably." He pulled a black lanyard with a key attached to it from around his neck and handed it to her. "You can shoot, but do you know one gun from another?"

Though the question irritated her, she nodded. So much for getting this guy to act like a normal human. "I had a boss who worked part time at a gun range. He'd take me there every now and then. I'm a pretty decent shot."

"Good. There's an armory cupboard below deck, near the head. Bring me the Glock 21 and an extra magazine. It's the .45 caliber. Pick whichever firearm you like and carry it with you at all times."

"Can I talk to my brother first?"

He frowned, as if not liking the delay, but handed over his phone. She couldn't help but notice the dried blood on his T-shirt and felt guilty that she'd already had a shower. He'd washed some of the soot off in the police station restroom, but if you looked closely, you could still see evidence of the fire.

"Use the number for Morgan," he ordered. "It's a scrambled phone, so they can't track us. Just to be safe, don't mention you're on a boat or where we're headed."

"Sure. Whatever you want. But you have to tell me your last name."

A gruff headshake. "This isn't a damned date. Make your call. I want a shower sometime today."

When he abruptly slowed the boat, minimizing the engine noise, Miri grabbed onto a railing to steady herself. Glowering at him, she mumbled a swear word and retreated to a deck chair.

"You might be awesomely badass, but you still have a huge rod up your butt, dude," she said, figuring he couldn't hear her over the engine noise.

"No, I don't," he called out. "But I do read lips."

For an instant, she swore she saw a hint of a smile, then it was gone.

"You read lips," she said flatly.

Of course you do.

She'd just pulled into a parking spot in the hospital lot when her phone rang.

"Morgan," she said. Then she smiled and pointed at the phone. "It's your sister." She returned to the call. "I hear you were kickass this morning." Her smile grew. "Mr. Action Figure? I hope you didn't call him that. Oh, good. It's more what Neil doesn't say that counts." A pause. "Yeah, he's here. Hold on." Morgan offered Alex the phone. "This call, you'll like."

"Miri? God, are you okay?"

"What kind of hell have you unleashed on us?" she demanded.

Alex grimaced. "The worst kind."

She seemed to hear the agony behind the words, and her tone softened. "What about you?"

His hand went to the bandage before he could stop himself. It was becoming a habit, one he'd have to break. "It's been a little rough here, but nothing like what you guys went through. I'm sorry about the house, Miri."

"So am I. Not the actual place. It was a total dump. But I'd made it mine, you know?"

"Yeah, I understand. Once this is over, we'll find you a place of your own."

"What, you're not going to camp on my couch, vet my boyfriends?"

"Not unless you want me to."

There was a short silence, and in the background he could hear a faint engine noise, but he couldn't place it. A boat motor, perhaps?

"I'll be good and stay hidden until you get this settled," she said. "But remember, do not get yourself dead. You hear me?"

"I hear you, Monkey. Trust whatever Iceman tells you." His eyes went toward Morgan. "These Veritas guys are legit. They'll keep you safe."

"They better. Now go kick some Russian ass, brother. I'm just going to chill for a while."

"You always were a slacker."

"Jerk!" she said, then laughed. "Love you, Alex."

"Love you too, Miri."

He handed the phone back to Morgan. "She's doing good. Sounds stronger somehow."

"Neil can have that effect on people."

As they crossed to the hospital entrance, he asked, "Can you tell me where she is?"

"I'm not exactly sure myself, but I will say they're in the best place for an ex-Navy SEAL to protect her."

Alex's mind brought up a memory.

"I had a buddy in college named Avi. When he became a SEAL, he told me all about the hellish training they went through, how eighty to ninety percent of the '*tadpoles*' washed out."

"Then you know what they're like."

"Yeah. He said that SEALs are deadly anywhere, but you get them on or in the water and they're invincible. Of course, with Avi about every other word was fuck, but I got the message."

Morgan's smile bloomed, which told him he'd just hit gold. His dear sister was out of the city, on a boat with a former special-ops dude who would blow the world apart to keep her safe.

Alex sobered. "Thank you. Tell your boss that, will you?"

Morgan nodded as they walked through the double doors that led to the hospital lobby.

"We must be getting close to something or Miri's house would still be standing," he added.

"Or maybe her brother has a crap-ton of enemies who'd love nothing more than to let him know how much they hate him."

"Shit. Yeah. Maybe that too."

"Don't worry. We'll get it done."

"God, I hope so," he murmured. "If for nothing more than to give my sister back her life."

Morgan didn't bother to stop at the front desk; she knew exactly what room the judge's daughter was in. The instant she'd seen the man's name on the list Crispin had provided, she should have backed off. Let someone else conduct the interview. Still, Crispin had a reason for Parkin and her being here, and she'd just have to trust him.

It all came down to whether Judge Redburn remembered her as Wayne Clifton's wife. Alex didn't know that he and her dead husband had a history, one that she wasn't proud of. One that might actually make him walk away from this mission, no matter how great Neil was at watching over his sister.

"Who are we talking to?" Alex asked, matching her pace down the hospital corridor.

"The father of the only victim who survived. She's a student at Tulane University. I'm hoping he can give us some background so we have a place to start."

As they drew close to the room, Morgan caught Alex's arm and they halted. "There's something you need to know. The man we're meeting is the judge who sentenced you to prison."

Alex's eyes went wide, almost as if she'd slapped him. "Redburn?"

She nodded.

"Why the hell didn't you tell me before we got here?"

"Because I need you to keep that anger on a leash. The man might know something that could help us nail Buryshkin. What happened all those years ago is not important at the moment."

"The hell it isn't. Redburn had to suspect that my defense lawyer was throwing the case, and he never stepped in."

Unfortunately, Alex wasn't exaggerating. His defense attorney—Morgan's husband—had been under orders to ensure that his client went to prison, because Wayne had possessed secrets of his own. Secrets that Buryshkin had threatened to reveal. Secrets that would have destroyed her husband's career. So instead, he'd destroyed Alex's.

Alex didn't know she'd been Wayne's wife; she'd kept her maiden name. Now, with one wrong word from Redburn, the truth would be out, and the rapport they'd built would go down in flames.

Which is why I can never sleep with you.

"Why your attorney blew the case is a subject for another time," she said.

"You know who set me up, don't you?" Alex asked, barely keeping his voice low enough for a passing nurse not to hear him.

"We have our suspicions. We'll know for sure the moment Buryshkin is in custody."

He looked away, angry, then back at her. "Then let's get

this done."

Morgan took the last few steps to the room, steeled herself, then knocked and stepped inside. It was as bad as she'd suspected—though the heart monitor was beeping rapidly, a pale young woman lay on the bed, looking as if death was only inches from claiming her. At least Sarah Redburn was still alive. The others had never had a chance.

An older woman, probably her mother, was bent over the girl, crying. Her father, a stern figure on the other side of the bed, was trying to hold it together. It was a damned poor time to intrude, but Morgan had no choice.

"Judge Redburn?" she said, then introduced herself.

The man gave a nod to his wife and joined Morgan and Alex in the hallway.

"Wilder said you'd be wanting to talk to me," he said. He was in his mid-fifties, heavy at the waist, with graying hair and piercing eyes. The last time she'd seen him was at some legal-beagle holiday party, and he'd been telling off-color jokes to one of his clerks. Now he was bordering on tears.

Before she could reply, he frowned at her. "Do I know you? We've met before, I think."

She ignored the question, hoping he wouldn't make the connection to Wayne. "How is your daughter doing?"

"They've sedated her. It's the best way, so the poison doesn't . . . We just have to wait now."

"I'm sorry, Judge Redburn, but we need to ask you questions regarding your daughter's activities, so we can try to track down where she got the cocaine."

"Of course. I'll do anything I can to—" Then he saw Alex. It took a few seconds for the ex-con's face to register. "What the hell is *he* doing here?"

Alex squared up like he was eager for a fight.

"Let's take this to the waiting room. We need privacy." Redburn didn't budge, his face growing crimson. "Please, not out here. You wouldn't want to disturb your wife."

That was the lever it took to move him, and the judge stalked down the corridor.

Morgan caught Alex's arm before he'd taken two steps. "Keep it cool. We need his help."

"You saw him. He thinks I had something to do with this."

"No, he doesn't. He's just upset about his kid, so cut him some slack," she said.

"He didn't cut me any."

"This isn't just about you, Parkin. Not this time."

When the three of them entered the waiting room, the lone occupant, an elderly male, looked up. He took in the vibes, then rose and headed for the door, making an excuse that he needed coffee. Morgan wished she could join him.

She pulled the door partially closed to give them some privacy.

"They let you out already?" Redburn demanded.

"I did my full sentence, *Your Honor*. I'm all 'rehabilitated,'" Alex said. "You'd be surprised what I learned in there, thanks to you."

The judge fluffed up. "Explain to me why Wilder would work with someone who betrayed his badge and his fellow DEA agents?"

Alex took a step toward the man, his fists clenched at his sides. "After you tell me why a judge let the defense attorney make mistake after mistake and didn't question his competency."

This was going to come to blows if she didn't step in.

Morgan put her hands to her mouth and issued a shrill whistle, placing her body between the two irate males.

"Okay, time-out. You guys can sort this out later." She turned to the judge. "We're here to find out who did this to your daughter. Besides her, we have four other victims, *all* dead. Parkin's on board because he knows how drugs flow through this city. You have no say in whether he works for us or not, Your Honor." She shot a glance over to her companion. "Jesus, Alex. His daughter almost died. How would you feel if it was Miri in that bed?"

Alex looked away, his mouth in a thin line and the vein on his neck pounding. "I'll do what I need to do."

"Okay, good. Judge?"

The man nodded reluctantly. "What do you need to know?"

"Has your daughter used drugs in the past?"

Redburn slumped into a chair, the fury gone. "No. And I'm not some clueless parent—I know the signs. I see them every day in my courtroom."

"Is she in a dorm on campus, or does she have her own place?"

"Sarah has an apartment over in the Garden District. She rooms with a nurse named Laura Powers. Thank God, too, because Laura knew something was wrong and called 911. If she hadn't, Sarah would be . . . dead now."

"Does your daughter have a boyfriend?"

"Yes, a new guy. She wouldn't bring him home, which told me he probably wasn't on the level."

"I can't imagine bringing my dates home if my dad was a judge," she said, smiling gently.

Redburn nodded. "I love my daughter and"—he looked at Alex—"and I would do anything to keep her safe."

Morgan angled her head toward Alex. "Sounds like you and your sister."

"Yeah. Same thing."

Redburn's expression changed. "How is she? Your sister. I remember her from the courtroom."

"She's good. She found a way to live without her brother all these years."

Morgan cut in again. "Would your wife know anything about your daughter's boyfriend?"

The judge shook his head. "No, I'm afraid not. Sarah is an intensely private individual, and she doesn't share much with her parents."

"Like most kids that age."

Alex stirred. "Where does Sarah hang out? Any particular bars?"

"Are you saying my daughter's a tramp?" Redburn demanded.

"No, I'm saying she might have told her friends more than

she did you," Alex replied.

"I don't know. You'll have to ask Laura."

After Redburn gave them his daughter's address, he brushed past Alex, then paused at the door. "I wouldn't trust this man if I were you, Ms. Blake. His defense attorney learned that lesson the hard way. It cost Wayne Clifton his life."

No, it didn't. Wayne was his own worst enemy.

Morgan released a long sigh of relief once the judge was gone.

"He's right, you know," Alex said. "My so-called defense attorney killed himself right after I nearly died in prison. I'd always hoped the guilt made him put that gun in his mouth and pull the trigger."

Morgan jolted at the cold anger behind his words, at the memories that surfaced in her mind. The clotted blood, the smell of death. The fact that she'd never had a chance to apologize.

"He did feel guilty," she said. Wayne had said as much in his suicide note. "But he left behind a wife who loved him."

"Yeah, and I left my *life* behind. So which is worse?"

She eyed him. "It all depends on who you ask."

Chapter Sixteen

Sarah Redburn lived a few blocks from the Starbucks on Magazine Street in the Garden District, the old-money part of New Orleans. Morgan had insisted they stop for coffee and something to eat before they interviewed Sarah's roommate. Alex had not objected.

Across from him, Morgan demolished a generous slice of iced lemon cake, as if she hadn't eaten all day. A heavily doctored cup of coffee sat nearby. She'd yet to say anything other than placing the order, which made him feel like even more of a jerk. Especially given how things had been between them this morning.

He shifted in his seat, the part of him that had a one-track mind recalling her soft skin, her firm breasts, how ready she had been for him. Everything had changed between them at the hospital. Now Alex sipped his coffee, watching her skillfully avoid conversation through food. He had no idea how to take it all back, how to regain the camaraderie they'd once shared.

I was a bastard.

It hadn't been right for him to spew all that venom about his attorney at her. It wasn't her fault; she hadn't even known the man. And she was right, Clifton had had a wife, one who had no doubt been devastated by his death. To rejoice in the man's suicide was just cruel.

At the time, Alex had been too upset to realize that there was more going on than just an incompetent attorney. Years of thinking through every minute detail of the trial had revealed the truth: someone, probably Buryshkin, must have pulled Clifton's strings to get Alex put away.

To keep from making things worse between him and Morgan, Alex stared out the window instead. The Garden District was upscale, with expensive homes and fancy restaurants, the kind of area where you settled down and raised your kids. He wasn't likely to remarry, not after his first marriage's spectacular failure. He'd been a sucker, like most guys, buying into the whole happily-ever-after bullshit they sold you along with the diamond engagement ring.

All those years in the joint had changed him on a fundamental level. The old Alex was dead, and he didn't like the new one very much.

"You're looking really serious. What are you thinking about?" Morgan asked.

Her question jarred him; he hadn't expected her to reinitiate conversation. He answered without thinking.

"That I'm more like Buryshkin or his thugs than like the rest of these people."

"Why?"

He gestured to the street outside. "Tell me what you see."

Morgan checked out the scene, then turned back to him. "Big houses, lawns so perfect they look artificial. The people seem pretty happy. Why?"

"The houses and the people? They scream 'opportunity' to me."

"I don't understand," she replied, looking puzzled.

"When I was with the DEA, my boss told me I had to think like a criminal. It was always hard for me."

"Because you're not a predator."

"I am now. I lived with them, ate with them, showered with them. Day after day, I hung with car thieves, robbers, rapists, pedophiles, and murderers."

"The prison university," she said.

Alex lowered his voice. "If I need to steal a ride and it's a Dodge, Chrysler, or Jeep, I can jack it in fifteen seconds or less. A screwdriver in the ignition and I'm gone. I know how to kill people without making a sound."

He stared into his coffee cup, watching the dark liquid

move with the slight vibration of the table.

"I can scope out women who are the best targets, and I know exactly when to strike, when they're at their most vulnerable. I know how to case houses and pull off second-story work without setting off an alarm." He snorted. "They say prison is all about rehabilitation. It's just teaching you opportunities you never saw before."

On the sidewalk, a young woman walked by, pushing a stroller with a sleeping toddler inside. She was pretty—but right now any female from age eighteen on up to fifty looked nice. Still, his libido wasn't kicking in, not when there was a child involved. Nevertheless, she would serve as an example of his twisted mindset.

"See the lady with the kid? The instant she turns her back to put the child in the car, she's at risk. You put a knife at her throat, threaten the baby, and she'll do anything you tell her because she would die protecting that child."

"Obviously."

"You're not seeing it, are you?" he said.

"No, I get it. You internalized the evil that surrounded you every minute you were in jail," she said.

Alex's eyes slowly rose, expecting to see condemnation, maybe even pity. There was none.

"I hate who I've become," he admitted.

"You can't hunt a shark if you don't know its ways," she said. "Your years in prison taught you skills that other law enforcement folks don't have."

He held his breath, wishing it were that simple.

"Take that knowledge and use it to keep the predators from harming people like that mom and her kid," Morgan said. "That's the best we can do."

"Is that what you do?"

"As much as I can. You can take it even further."

"What if I tip over the edge, become like those guys in prison? It'd be so easy."

"You're not made that way. Your heart is too good."

He threw up his hands. "See? I already have you fooled.

That's the first step of any predator—gaining the victim's trust."

Morgan frowned at him. "I stopped being a victim years ago. Not all of us are that easily fooled, Parkin."

Alex gulped the remaining coffee and rose from his chair, wondering why the hell he'd even told her all that. "You ready?"

She gathered up her trash and deposited it in a nearby bin. "We are not done with this conversation, Alex."

"Yeah, we are. There's nothing more to say," he said, falling in step with her as she headed for the front door.

"You think you're the only one who walks that line?" she asked.

"No, but I'm the only one I worry about."

Sarah's apartment was located in a carriage house behind one of the district's old mansions. The small building was inviting, done up in yellow and white, with colorful flowers sitting in terra cotta pots on the porch.

"This is nice," Alex said as they headed for the front door. "I could live here, though it is a bit overdone."

"I could too. It's just the right size," Morgan said. She angled a thumb over her shoulder toward the big house behind them. "As compared to that one."

"I figured you for a mansion type of girl."

"When I was younger maybe, but not now."

"I like smaller places. My buddy has a camp on the bayou. I used to go there pretty often, especially when Alicia and I were fighting. It helped clear my head."

"You two were having trouble even before the arrest?"

"Yeah. She didn't like me being undercover, home only now and then. It was rough on her. Of course, I didn't figure she would screw my partner."

"Your ex had lousy taste. A choice between you and Simms? Give me a break."

Alex's smile told her he appreciated the compliment. Given where his mind had been at the coffee shop, she was pleased to see him shaking off the gloom.

He's wrong. He's not a predator. Never will be.

His words about her husband had been cruel, but after her initial shock, she'd come to accept that he had a right to be bitter. Six years of his life had been lost because of Wayne. If it'd been her in prison, she wouldn't have forgiven him either.

Morgan knocked on the door, and it opened a short time later to reveal a woman with red-rimmed eyes. Her hair was mousy brown, up in a bun, and she appeared to be on the verge of more tears. Morgan introduced herself and Alex, explaining that they were investigating Sarah's poisoning.

The woman nodded. "Her father called, said you'd want to see me. Come on in."

The house proved just as enchanting on the inside. The wood floors were old, but in good shape, and the walls were painted a warm green. Carefully selected pictures hung here and there.

Laura led them into a kitchen with granite countertops and white cupboards, a line of collector plates hanging above them. It felt like a home. She gestured for them to sit at a butcher-block table. Morgan pulled out a chair and settled in. Alex chose to lean against the counter.

Laura reached for the kettle, then hesitated. "Tea or coffee?"

"Nothing for us, thank you," Morgan said.

Laura filled the kettle. "Sarah and I met at a concert a year or so ago. We hit it off, so we decided to room together. She's really sweet. A bit bullied by her dad, but she's got a good heart. Her only fault is that she's naïve, too trusting."

Alex cleared his throat. "I know it's hard, but please tell us what happened this morning."

The woman nodded. "I'd just gotten home from work—I work at Ochsner's ICU, so sometimes my hours are weird. Sarah's boyfriend brought her in the front door and dumped her on the floor. Said she was sick. Then he took off, just left her there. I swear he'd have done the same thing if I hadn't been home. Just left her there to die."

"What is her boyfriend's name?" Morgan asked.

"Casey Calloway. He's a total prick," Laura said, her eyes sparking now. "But Sarah never saw that in him. He messed with her head all the time, and she believed whatever he told her."

"How long had she been dating him?" Morgan asked.

"A couple months. I was hoping she'd dump him. He made me nervous, you know? Just something about him felt wrong."

Laura pulled a cup out of a cupboard and added a tea bag. Alex shot Morgan a look, clearly eager to get on with it, but she shook her head. Sometimes it was best not to push too hard.

"Sarah was having trouble breathing, her heart rate was sky high, and her muscles were cramping. There was some white powder under her nose, so I figured it was cocaine. I called 911, because she doesn't do drugs. At least, she never had before."

"When did you find out she was poisoned?"

Laura paled. "At the hospital. They'd seen another case like her earlier in the evening, and they said it was strychnine." Her eyes filled with tears. "Why the hell would he do that to her?"

"You sure this Casey guy was the source of the dope?" Alex asked.

"Who else? I mean, he was always pushing her to do stuff she wasn't comfortable with."

Laura jumped when the teakettle began to whistle, then looked embarrassed.

"Hey, it's okay. I'd be freaked too if my roommate was that ill," Morgan said.

"It was so . . . " she trailed off, then spent the next minute or so making the tea. A calming ritual, apparently.

"Where can we find this guy?" Alex asked. Morgan knew he was pissed and wanted some face time with old Casey. She was right there with him.

"He lives near the university. Has his own place. The

address would be up in Sarah's room."

They followed Laura up the stairs and into a bedroom with an abundance of pink and rose-patterned fabrics.

"She's a girly girl," Laura explained, tears threatening again. "It's why we get along so well—I'm a tomboy. We balance each other out." She searched through Sarah's iPhone, while Morgan took a visual tour of the room.

"Here it is," Laura said, handing over the phone.

Morgan gave Alex a look, hoping he knew what she wanted him to do.

"You know, I think I *would* like some tea," he said. "If you don't mind."

"Ah, sure. No problem," Laura replied.

"I'll be right down as soon as I put this in my phone," Morgan said.

When Laura and Alex returned downstairs, Morgan smiled to herself. It was as if she and Alex had been partners for years, they read each other so easily. After making note of the address, she hunted through Sarah's phone for more information.

Casey's only form of communication was texting. His last one was just before three a.m., when he asked Sarah to meet him. Said he had something special for her, and this time she couldn't back out. That it was going to be great fun, and she didn't want to disappoint him. Not like the last time.

"You slimy bastard."

Why would he supply coke to a judge's daughter? That seemed guaranteed to buy you serious jail time. Had he known the stuff was tainted, or was that just bad luck?

Morgan laid the girl's phone back on the desk and did a fast troll through the closet and drawers. All she learned was that Sarah was a fan of shoes, lacy white underwear, and was a 32B.

By the time she reached the kitchen, her partner and their hostess were sitting at the table, talking quietly. Alex had a way about him that put women at ease. Though he'd claim it was pure predator, she knew it was the caring side of him, the part of him he thought he'd lost in prison.

He took a long sip of tea and set the cup down. "Anyone else you can think of who might want to hurt Sarah?"

"No, not really. She was doing well in school and had lots of friends. It was just Casey who frightened me."

Alex looked up at Morgan, and she gave a quick nod.

"Then we won't take up any more of your time. Thank you for your help, and for the tea."

Laura nodded numbly. "I'm going to get some sleep, then head back to the hospital. I'm just afraid they'll call and . . . she'll be . . . "

Alex took her hand and gave it a squeeze. "You gave her the best shot at survival. Don't count her out of the game just yet."

The tears flowed now. "Thank you."

As they walked back to the car, Alex swore. "I want that asshole in pieces. I want to hear him beg for his life."

"As much as I'd love that, you don't need the assault charge."

He sighed in understanding. "Anything worthwhile on her phone?"

"No. Calloway texted her, asking her to meet him. It'll be hell proving this guy gave her the dope, no matter how much we push him," Morgan said as they reached the car.

Alex gave her a feral grin. "It all depends on how you ask the questions."

Calloway's house stood back from the others on the block, with nothing special that called attention to it in any way. A blue Chevy sedan sat in the driveway in front of the garage. As Alex walked by it, he touched the hood.

"It's cold. Bet he's been inside ever since he ditched his dying girlfriend."

Morgan gave him a searching look. "If you do go medieval on this bastard, leave enough for the cops to haul to jail, okay?"

Alex smiled. "I'm really getting to like you, lady. You know that?"

"I figured as much after this morning."

"No, *that* was about sex. *This* is a statement of respect."

"You can't respect a woman when you have sex with her?" she shot back.

Alex counted himself lucky that they reached the house at that point. He knew conversational quicksand when he accidentally stepped in it. In lieu of answering, he pounded on the door. No reply.

He pounded again. "Calloway? We need to talk to you!"

He was about to batter the door a third time when it swung open, revealing a young man with short, curly blond hair, a scraggly goatee, and dark circles under his eyes.

Grieving for his girlfriend? *Like hell.*

"You Calloway?" Alex already knew the answer, because he'd seen a picture of Sarah and this loser on her desk.

The man gave them the once-over and shook his head. "No, he's out. Headed for the airport. Going to Europe, I think."

Alex grabbed the fool's collar and shoved him back into the house.

"What the hell are you doing?" Calloway demanded.

Morgan closed the door behind them as Alex maneuvered him down the hall and into what appeared to be the front room. It made a city landfill seem pristine, what with the half-empty pizza boxes and beer bottles on the coffee table, and the cigarette butts and burned-out reefer stubs in the overflowing ashtrays.

Morgan kicked a crumpled McDonald's bag out of the way. "Could you be any more of a slob? No, don't answer that. I don't want to know."

"Who the hell are you guys?"

"The kind of people who really don't like you," Alex said, shoving Calloway so hard he landed on the couch. Then he stood over him, crossing his arms over his chest and putting on his "I really want to tear you a new one" expression. Just another thing he'd mastered in Angola.

"We're here about the girl," he said.

Calloway's eyes narrowed. "You're with them, right?"

Them?

"Yeah, we are," Morgan said, sharing a look with Alex.

"But how do I know you're working for the Russians? You could be cops or something."

"*Vy na samom dele obshchaya chlen, ne tak li?*" Alex said. *You really are a total dick, aren't you?*

"What does that mean?" Calloway asked, frowning.

"It means I speak Russian."

"Oh, okay." The man seemed to relax, as if that was proof enough. "I got the pictures just like you asked. They're on my phone." He waved toward a smartphone resting on the cluttered coffee table. "Go ahead, check them out."

Blackmail?

Pictures of a judge's daughter snorting coke would be a potent weapon, a clever way to buy Redburn's judicial opinions on key cases, especially if Vladimir Buryshkin ever came to trial. All it would take was ensuring that the Russian's case ended up on the judge's docket.

"But you screwed up," Alex said, wanting to keep this guy talking. "The girl is in the hospital."

Calloway shrugged like it was no big deal. "I don't know what happened. Sarah was just supposed to get high, nothing more. My debt's all clear, right? That's what the big Russian dude said. I get you the photos, I'm golden."

Morgan picked up the phone and accessed the pictures. Then she slowly walked behind the couch, out of Calloway's line of sight. He whirled around to look at her.

"These are good," she said. "You got copies of these photos stored away somewhere?"

Calloway shook his head. "You think maybe I should?"

Morgan's eyes met Alex's and she raised an eyebrow. "It'd be horrible if anything happened to them."

The loser nodded. "Okay."

"Which Russian did you talk to?" Alex asked. "Vasily or Dimitri? We work with so many of them."

Calloway returned his attention to him. "It was the guy with the broken nose. Boris K-something. Ka . . . misky? I joked about the bandage, and he slapped the shit out of me. How was I supposed to know? You know, it was weird. He didn't sound Russian at all."

Well, hell.

It appeared that Miri didn't have a stalker problem—her attacker at the bar had been one of Buryshkin's people after all. Alex shot a quick glance at Morgan, and she nodded her understanding. From the focused look on her face, and her quick tapping on the phone's screen, he suspected she was deleting each of the incriminating photos.

If he could ever fall in love with a woman again, she'd be the one.

He refocused on the loser, leaning down to hold Calloway's attention. "The coke was laced with strychnine. If the judge's daughter dies, guess who he's going to be gunning for?"

Calloway's eyes went as big as dinner plates. "I didn't know! They just said to buy some blow and get pictures when she snorted it. How was I supposed to know the stuff was bad?"

"Where'd you get it?" Morgan asked, moving back around the couch.

"From some guy on the street."

"Name?"

The man shrugged his shoulders. Alex yanked him off the couch, sank a fist into his gut, and then dropped him back on the couch. Calloway bent over coughing, a step away from throwing up. As he struggled for air, Morgan set his phone back on the coffee table.

All gone? Alex mouthed. She nodded.

"Where's the rest of the coke?" he asked.

"There isn't any," Casey wheezed, still clutching his stomach. "I didn't have that much money, so I only bought enough for her."

"What a truly thoughtful boyfriend you are," Morgan said.

The conversation had run its course, and despite Alex's

sincere desire to beat the hell out of this little prick, Calloway wasn't worth the jail time.

Morgan read his thoughts. She picked up a fast food napkin and scribbled something on it, then tossed the napkin onto the loser's lap.

"That's the local DEA phone number. Ask for Special Agent Fredd. She'll want to hear what you have to say."

Calloway's expression shifted to terrified. "Wait, you said you worked for the Russians. You lied to me!" Then his future dawned on him. "They'll kill me if they know I've talked to you."

"Call the feds or update your will, because the photos are history now," Morgan said, her voice cold. "It's your choice. We don't give a damn either way."

"What?" Calloway cried out.

As Alex shut the front door behind them, they could hear him storming around the house, spewing obscenities, none of them the least bit inventive.

"What does it say about America's educational system that he can't even use the F-word properly?" Alex asked. Morgan chuckled. He grabbed her arm, pulled her back toward him, and planted a kiss on her lips.

"What was that for?" she asked.

"For saving Sarah's future."

She rewarded him with a shy smile. "Score one for us. Now that we're done with this scum, we need to talk to the other victims' families."

Which was the last thing he wanted to do. "I'd rather check with some of my sources, see if they've heard anything about where the dope is stored."

Morgan hesitated, then nodded her approval. "Let's get you a rental car, then we can meet later and compare notes."

He looked back toward the house. "Buryshkin wanted that piece of shit to set up Redburn's daughter, but somehow the moron buys the Russian's poisoned cocaine. Is that rich, or what?"

"That's the truth. I'll give my contact at the DEA a heads-up on this guy. Maybe they can talk him into testifying against Buryshkin."

"*Ko-shack-ya lapa*," Alex murmured.

"What?"

"It's Russian for cat's paw. It's what they're doing—co-opting people. Making us their puppets."

"Except you cut your strings," she said.

"Have I? From where I stand, it looks like I'm still as much of a pawn as ever."

Morgan appeared to ponder on that as they drove away from the house.

"How long, do you think, before they make their move against Calloway?" she asked.

"I give him one day, tops. Frankly, I'm surprised he isn't dead already. They must be getting sloppy."

"Like leaving the corpses at the warehouse. Maybe Buryshkin's losing his touch."

"As long as he doesn't slip through our fingers, I'll take him, sloppy or not," Alex said.

Chapter Seventeen

Once he had wheels, a sedate, brown sedan that did nothing for his macho image, Alex made the rounds and came up empty. Hunting down some of his old confidential informants proved to be an exercise in aggravation. Three were dead, one had found Jesus and owned a used-car lot, and another refused to talk to him, unsure of where his loyalties lay.

So much for bringing anything to the table.

Recently that had begun to matter; it was no longer just a game of trying to stay ahead of the Russians. He felt needed again, and that meant everything.

He was just about to pull into traffic when his phone lit up. A number he didn't recognize.

"Hello?"

"Alex Parkin? This is Sanjay at Veritas. Morgan asked me to call you."

His heart skipped a beat. "Is she okay? Or is there something wrong with my sister?"

"Both are fine. We just verified that Miguel de Francisco, the head of Los Impíos, sent those gunmen to your sister's house. It had nothing to do with the Russians."

"Huh. What about the weapon Morgan found at my sister's place? Any connection to Los Impíos?"

"In a roundabout way. It's tied to the death of one of their dealers. The cops haven't figured out who pulled the trigger on that hit yet."

"Great. As if it isn't bad enough having Buryshkin on my ass."

"You're a very popular fellow right now. Oh, and Jesus

Martinez is no more. Apparently he had a nasty accident while showering. Our contact in Angola dropped us a call on that one."

Mikhail had been right: Alex's assailant's days had been numbered.

"Thanks. I'm glad to hear that. No one will miss the little prick."

"Morgan said to keep an eye out. She's worried the gang might make another run at you, since your sister is safely tucked away. We've notified Iceman, as well."

"Good. I appreciate that."

"Happy to help out. Call if you need anything."

Alex stared at the phone after the call ended. Apparently he'd moved a little higher up on the "we trust you" scale, because now they were directly sharing intel. Which brought him right back to Morgan. The more he saw her in action, the more he respected her. She was smart, savvy, and sexier than hell. God, he had it bad. No matter how he tried to focus on other things, she was always on his mind, playing hell with the bulge behind his zipper.

While he thought through Sanjay's news, Alex drove to his friend's tattoo parlor. It was a long shot that Tucker James would know something, but you never learned anything if you didn't ask. Once again, he found himself in the Garden District, a sign that Tucker knew his market: hipsters eager to get inked.

Their unlikely friendship had begun when the artist had identified a dead drug dealer by his distinctive tats. Out of all his friends, Tucker had never backed away when Alex went upstate for a fiver. He'd even sent Alex money from time to time, because Alex's own aunt and uncle sure as hell hadn't.

Now he found himself hesitating at the shop's entrance. Would he still be welcome?

"Only one way to find out," he muttered, pushing open the door.

A guy sat behind the counter reading a thick book about economics, his brown hair closely cropped and his arms covered in intricate ink. Alex didn't recognize him, but it was a good bet that the help had changed over the years.

"Hi. Can I help you?" he asked.

"Yeah. I'd like to talk to Tucker. Is he here?"

"Should be back in about ten minutes or so. Can you wait?"

"Sure. I'll just park it over here," Alex said, gesturing toward a line of chairs near the door.

While he waited, he examined the interior of the shop, which was essentially one big room. A couple of artists were inking away, one doing a delicate angel on a young lady's arm and another working the outline of a dragon into a guy's muscled back. That tattoo was huge, and Alex wondered how long it would take to finish.

He'd never had the guts to get inked before he went into prison, so he expected Tucker to give him grief about the one on his thigh, if his friend ever saw it. The phoenix had been a lesson in teeth-gritting pain, begun a couple months before he got out. He'd been lucky it hadn't become infected, given the unsanitary way it'd been created.

The buzz of tattoo machines kept him company while he checked his messages; nothing from Morgan yet. He didn't envy her—it was a special kind of hell interviewing people who'd just lost family members.

When the back door shut and a man walked into the shop, toting two fast-food bags, Alex couldn't help but smile. Tucker James was one of a kind, a big dude with a solid, muscled body, the kind of guy you wanted watching your back in a fight. His totally bald head, moustache, and goatee, along with neck and full-sleeve tattoos, always made people judge him on the far end of the badass scale. He had to be a drug dealer, or belong to a biker gang. What else would a guy like that be?

Alex hadn't been any different. He'd taken one look at Tucker and figured he had a rap sheet as long as the Mississippi River. When he'd started in on him, trying to rattle the man, Tucker had given him a long look, as if trying to decide how best to break Alex in half.

"You done running your mouth?" he'd asked. "Because I don't do drugs, and last time I checked, I'm here to help you folks. So drop the bullshit, and let's get this done."

Alex had apologized, which wasn't his usual style. To his credit, Tucker had graciously accepted the apology, and they'd moved forward. In truth, the man was a gentle and well-mannered soul, unless you threatened his family or friends. Then the grizzly bear came out, and there wasn't a place on this earth you could hide.

The instant Tucker saw Alex, a huge smile bloomed. He placed the food bags on a table and strode toward him, beaming the entire way.

"About damned time, Parkin," he said, and they fist-bumped. Then Alex found himself in a stout bear hug, followed by a couple bone-rattling thumps on his back.

"You look good, dude," his friend said, studying him. "You've bulked up. Lifting weights?"

"Yeah. I worked at The Farm. Not much else to do inside."

Tucker nodded. "I'm really glad to see you. I was hoping you'd stop by." He looked over his shoulder at the front desk. "I've fed my people. I don't have another appointment for a couple of hours. Let's get a drink. I know it's early, but we need to catch up."

"I'd like that." More than he would ever admit.

They went to one of their favorite spots, the Roosevelt Bar on University Place, picking a table in the back. The place was empty, just having opened for the day. The strange, blue lighting always reminded Alex of a jazz club, though there was no music to be found. Tucker opted for whisky, and Alex went for bottled beer because the bar didn't serve anything on tap.

"I owe you," he said. "You stayed in touch. Almost no one else did."

"Least I could do. Your sister okay? I tried to check in with her while you were inside, but Miri told me to back off. She's a special kind of independent, if you know what I mean."

"Yeah. I know." Before he could stop himself, Alex unloaded about her current situation, the attempted kidnapping and the foiled Los Impíos hit.

Tucker's large fingers tightened on his glass. "Jesus. She

okay?"

"Yeah. She's healing, and she's got someone badass watching her back now."

"Not you?"

"Only because I got something else going on." Alex looked around the bar, pleased to see they were still the only two drinkers at this point. Too early for the regular drunks, apparently.

He laid out the whole tale, beginning with meeting Morgan on a backwoods Louisiana highway. How he'd signed on with both Buryshkin and Veritas, and was now walking a fine line that would probably lead to a slab at the local morgue.

Tucker cracked a smile. "Same shit, different day, right?"

Alex laughed. "Yeah." Then he told Tucker about the poisoned dope and how he had to find the shipment or more people were going to die.

His friend let out a long sigh, shaking his head. "I was hoping things would be good for you from now on."

"Not until I get this damned Russian monkey off my back."

Tucker took another belt of whiskey. "I know I'm going to regret this, but how can I help?"

"I don't want you involved, at least not directly. These people are evil. They'll kill you just for fun."

"Figured that out all by myself. What do you need?"

"If you hear any rumor of where that load might be hidden, or someone who wants to talk to me about it, let me know." He slid his phone across with his number displayed. "Call me anytime, but do not put yourself at risk. I don't have that many friends in my world, and I don't want to lose you. You mean too much to me."

Tucker frowned a warning. "Hey, you start singing 'Kumbaya,' I'm out of here."

Alex laughed, remembering how much he liked this guy.

"No chance." He noticed his friend's whiskey was empty. "Another?"

"Yeah. More Macallan 12 works for me."

By the time Alex returned to the table, his phone was back

by his nearly empty beer and there was a note scribbled on a cocktail napkin just underneath the bottle. It had a name and a phone number. He scooped it up and dropped it in a pocket without a word.

He gave a nod of appreciation. "Sometimes you scare the living hell out of me, dude."

Tucker gave him a toothy grin. "It's all in who insists on running their mouth while I'm doing their ink. They always think I'm not paying attention." He raised his glass. *"L'chaim!"*

"To life!" They tapped drinks.

Alex settled back as his friend told him what he'd missed over the last six years. In truth, he already knew what he'd missed the most: the opportunity to have a normal life, to spend time with his sister and good friends like Tucker.

The further he waded into this mission, the more his enemies were trying to take that happiness away from him.

This time, I'm not going down easy.

After they returned to the shop, Alex made his way to the rental car. Stuck under the windshield was a note with a phone number. Glancing around didn't reveal anyone watching him, but now his hackles were up. He dialed and a voice he recognized answered.

"Ah, there you are, Sasha Parkin," Vasily said. "I was hoping you would call."

"Hard to ignore the note on my car. What do you want?"

"I am glad you had the time to talk to your old friend, Mr. James. Friendships are important."

You SOB. He hated that he'd put Tucker in danger. "What do you want?" Alex repeated.

"We want you to pay very close attention to the security detail around Mr. Wilder. How many people guard him at any given moment, what sort of weapons they carry."

"I haven't met the guy yet."

"Oh, in time you will. When you know the details, call me

for further orders."

"And if I refuse to do this?"

"Then we will have to pay a visit to your sister in the safe house on Canal Street."

Canal Street? Vasily was wrong. Very wrong.

Alex went for outrage so as not to tip his hand. "How the hell did you find that out?"

"We have our sources."

Which are lying to you. Now that was interesting.

"You touch her, and I'll take you out."

"As long as you do as we ask, all will be well."

He frowned. "Then you need to do something for me. The hit on my sister's house the other night? It was courtesy of Los Impíos. Get them off my ass so I can do my job."

Silence.

"If I'm dead, you don't get Wilder."

"We will see what we can do."

Alex found himself sweating in the hot sun, a slight tremor in the hand holding the phone. He'd just sent one major drug organization after another. If this went wrong, it could be a bloodbath.

The other victims' families had ranged from so distraught that they could hardly speak, to a mother who went off on Morgan and threatened to break open her skull. None of them had a clue where the victims had obtained their drugs, though one had thought it had something to do with a bar in the French Quarter. Morgan was willing to bet it was Le Purgatoire.

As she sat in her car, her text to Alex unanswered, her worry level edged up a notch. When she called him, he answered on the first ring.

"Hey. How's it going?" he said, sounding downright cheery.

"Zip. Big fat zero. Except the woman who threatened to mate my head with her cast-iron frying pan because I dared suggest her son was doing drugs. The fact that he's a coked-up corpse notwithstanding."

"I love those kinds of folks. I once had a lady insist the needle in her husband's arm was for his diabetes. Refused to accept that he'd just mainlined himself into a coffin."

"Ignorance is bliss. How about you?" she asked.

"I have a lead. A lady named Natalya, and—"

"Natalya? What does she look like?"

"Don't know. Haven't met her yet. I only have her name and phone number. My . . . source suggested I talk to her. Not sure if it'll pan out."

"If it's the woman I know, she's five-six, streaked blond hair, has a thick Russian accent and an ornate cross tattoo on her right wrist."

"The tattoo sounds right. Is she a prostitute?"

"Yup. Been in the U.S. for about a year. Her pimp isn't one of Buryshkin's boys. If it's the right girl, tell her Valkyrie sent you."

"I can do that."

"If her pimp is with her, back off. Anton is a mean SOB. He'll just take it out on her."

"Got it. Where are you headed?"

"I need to check in with Crispin, give him a full report." She paused. "I'll need to tell him about Anya and what she did to you last night, but I won't mention why it bothered you so much."

There was a short silence. "Thank you, I appreciate that."

"How's about we meet at Calloway's place at about five? We'll work him over again, now that he's had a chance to think about his future."

"Good idea."

"Oh, by the way, Natalya's a very smooth operator. If you're not careful, you'll find yourself with your pants down around your ankles right before your wallet goes missing."

"Thanks for the warning. I learned my lesson with Anya. I'll only drop my pants for you, lady."

She laughed. "Nice one."

"Did it work?"

"No. Bye, Alex. Stay safe."

Morgan ended the call, then tapped the phone against her chin. She found herself enjoying their banter more and more. He was funny, and he had a nimble mind to go with that rock-hard body.

His wife was an idiot to leave him behind.

Alex rendezvoused with Natalya on Bourbon Street, just down from one of the strip joints. She was as Morgan had described her, though he noted that his partner had failed to mention that the woman was sex on two legs. Certainly not a back-alley twenty-dollar hooker.

"You Parkin?" Natalya asked, her accent rich and layered with smoky promise.

"Yes. Let's walk, okay? It's too noisy around here."

As they roamed south, toward the river, Alex marveled at how she could keep her balance on the uneven New Orleans streets in four-inch heels.

"Valkyrie said to say hi."

Natalya gave him a suspicious frown. "You know her well?"

He nodded. More than most, he suspected.

"Valkyrie is good person, though she has never sent man to me before." She smiled. "You know deal, right?"

"Refresh me," he replied.

"If you are cop—"

"I'm an ex-con. The cops won't have anything to do with me."

Natalya laughed, throaty and full. "The deal is two yards." The slang sounded funny with her accent.

"Two hundred dollars. What do I get for that?"

"Anything you want," she purred. "All night is three times that."

I am in the wrong damned business.

"How's about seventy-five for some information? No sex

needed."

"Two hundred. Sex first, then I talk," she replied. "I rarely have men fine as you. I would hate to miss opportunity."

Alex took the compliment and let it slide. "Seventy-five just for talk. I need information."

Natalya frowned. "You are gay?"

He shook his head.

They'd reached the river now, and chose a bench that looked out on the water. From behind them there came the excited shouts of children playing in front of the cathedral. The sun and the heat felt different here, not like when he was working on the prison farm.

"Tell me what you need," Natalya said after refreshing her lipstick. The red on her lips matched the color of her nails. A quick glance at her open-toed heels proved it was a consistent theme. His groin stirred.

To counteract the sensual image of the lady sitting next to him, Alex pulled up the memory of the dead men in the warehouse. It did the trick instantly.

Keeping his voice lowered, he explained what he needed to know—where the dope was—and how it was already killing people. But even before he finished, Natalya shook her head.

"Buryshkin is bad man. I will not help you. His people will hurt me."

"Even if I offer you enough money to leave New Orleans and start over where he can't find you?"

He had no idea if he could do that, but suspected that Veritas would make good if it led to Buryshkin's stash and his eventual arrest. If they refused to cover it, he had cash of his own. He'd cheerfully hand all of it over to Natalya just to find the dope.

She lit a cigarette, going through the motions carefully, giving herself time to think. "Perhaps we can come to an arrangement. But no one must know. Anton would cut my throat."

"I hear he's a mean bastard."

She nodded. "When we are no longer useful to him, we

just disappear. Right now I am . . . how you say it . . . at top of game? That will not last."

"I understand." Alex leaned over and placed a kiss on her cheek as he pressed the seventy-five bucks into her hand. "If anyone asks, this money was for services rendered."

"We have deal. I will call you if I hear anything." Natalya ran a long fingernail down the side of his face, stopping just above the bandage. "How did this happen?"

"Anya Buryshkin took an interest in me."

Natalya lurched back in shock. "*Dorogoy Bog!*" she said.

She was up, staring at him in horror as if he'd suddenly developed leprosy. A flood of Russian came his way, so fast it was hard for him to decipher more than a few words.

After a frantic look around, she hissed in English, "We have no deal. She has marked you. You already dead, you know? Anya will kill you and anyone near you. I will not be one of those."

"But—"

Natalya grabbed his hand and slapped the money into his palm. "Never speak to me again."

She spat on the ground in front of him, then stomped away, casting nervous glances over her shoulder every few steps.

What the hell?

The whore was more frightened of the Russian's daughter, than of Buryshkin himself.

Chapter Eighteen

"Where are you, Parkin?" Morgan murmured, drumming her fingers on the steering wheel in irritation. He'd said he would meet her at Calloway's house at five, but he was a no-show. When she'd sent him a text, he hadn't answered.

Natalya. All tall and blond, her clothes designed to showcase her shapely legs, her large breasts. Had she managed to talk the horny ex-con into a quickie in exchange for information? Were her blood-red nails currently scoring their way down Alex's sweaty back in some sleazy French Quarter hotel room?

Morgan groaned. Why would she care if he got laid, even if it was with the Russian bombshell? But she did, and that made no sense. Her feelings for Alex should be no different than what she felt for Lars or Neil, or even her boss. None of them got her thinking about sex.

"Why him?" She shook her head. "Doesn't matter, I'm not going there." They'd finish the mission and part company. She'd move on.

Morgan took a quick look in her side mirror. *Speak of the devil.*

Alex was on the sidewalk headed in her direction, which made her wonder where he'd parked his car.

She exited her vehicle as he drew closer. "You're late," she snapped. "Quickie run a little long?"

Amusement danced in his eyes. "Yeah, I opted for the full Platinum Package, which included a deluxe wash, a wax, and an oil change. She even rotated my tires, no extra charge."

His humor pricked at her. "You actually screwed her?"

"Why would you care?"

She noted that he hadn't denied it. "I don't care."

"Then why did you ask?"

Damn. "What did she tell you?"

"Later. I want to think it through before I give you and Crispin a report. Let's just say it got really interesting."

Morgan eyed him, trying to figure out his game. "Where's your car?"

"One street over. Figured we should have another way to get out of here if anything goes wrong."

"You think something will?"

"Call it a sixth sense," he replied.

Like before, Alex hammered on the front door. Unlike the last time, it swung open the instant his fist touched it.

"Uh oh," he said. He stepped across the threshold and sniffed. "We got fresh blood. A lot of it."

Morgan excavated a pair of nitrile gloves from her purse and handed them over.

"We've already left prints here."

"No need to add any more."

The living room was still a pit, but now it had one other feature: Calloway, tied to a straight-backed chair, his head flopped back, eyes wide. Blood fanned out around his feet like a crimson Christmas tree skirt.

Alex made sure to keep his shoes out of the gore as he did a slow three-sixty around the corpse. It took a while for him to register what he was seeing. Someone had sliced off the man's genitals and stuffed them in his mouth.

"Oh hell," he said, swallowing heavily, his gorge rising.

"Is that what I think it is?" Morgan asked.

"Yes. That sound you just heard was me whimpering in sympathy. Poor bastard."

Morgan issued a low whistle. "Russians? Or do you think the judge went lethal on this guy?"

"My guess is one of Buryshkin's thugs. Redburn would have just shot his ass, not made him choke to death on his own dick."

She knelt and picked up something from near the corpse with a discarded napkin. She held up a business card, one from Le Purgatoire. "Look, it's our favorite bar."

He snorted. "That's kinda obvious, isn't it? I mean, it's not coated in blood, so someone dropped it after they snuffed the guy."

Morgan flipped it over, then cursed.

"What?"

She turned it around so he could see it. "Look familiar?"

It was Alex's turn to swear. His sister's address was penciled on the back.

"The killer dropped it?"

"Maybe. Or it was left just to point toward you." She crumpled up the card. "A neighbor across the street saw us enter the place, so we'll have to call the cops. No way we can disappear this time."

Before he could argue, she made her way down the hallway. A short time later, the toilet flushed. When she returned, the card wasn't in her hand.

"Tampering with evidence in a murder investigation?" he said. *Again.*

"Keeping the police headed in the proper direction. Count yourself lucky you didn't see the bathroom. I may have to scrub my eyeballs with bleach to get rid of that horror."

"Some guy is cut into pieces, and you're commenting on the condition of his can?"

"Black humor," she said, taking one last look at the corpse. "It's either that, or I start heaving."

"I'm right there with you."

After calling the cops, they waited by her car as she informed Crispin of the latest development. She put the phone on speaker so Alex could hear the conversation.

"We'll have a lawyer waiting for you at the police station," the boss informed him, his words clipped. "We'll get you two out, but it'll take a while. Dammit, this whole thing is off the rails."

Morgan winced, no doubt taking it as a rebuke. "Sir, maybe someone else should be lead on this mission."

Alex shook his head the moment the words cleared her mouth. "I disagree," he cut in. "Morgan's been doing everything I would have done. Checking sources, interviewing witnesses. We've just got too many scared people, and no one is willing to risk getting what Calloway got."

Crispin didn't hesitate. "I agree. We need to find someone who isn't afraid of the Russians."

Maybe God and his archangels?

"Call me when you're free from the cops," their boss said. "We'll meet here and discuss strategy."

Somewhere, Alex could hear the Russians applauding this decision. Now he would get a chance to scope out Wilder's security arrangements, even if he'd had no plans to do so.

"When we meet up, I have a theory I'd like to run past you," Alex said.

"I look forward to hearing it."

Two cop cars pulled up, one from each direction.

"The uniforms are here," Morgan reported.

"We'll talk later," Crispin replied, ending the call.

"Showtime," Alex said, straightening up. "Don't let them rattle you."

"Funny, I was going to say the same thing to you."

Alex managed to keep his cool—then he was informed that, as an ex-con, he would have to remain in custody until the cops got everything ironed out to their satisfaction. When he protested, he was told to shut up and deal with it. Instead of being tossed in with other recent detainees—that he could have handled—he was rewarded with a cell of his very own. As if they knew that it would conjure up his demons. And it had.

He paced back and forth, though his jailers would see that on the security cameras and know they were getting to him.

His mind reeled, verging on the edge of panic. What if Veritas couldn't get him out of here? What if there was more planted evidence at the crime scene, something he and Morgan had overlooked? He could end up back in Angola for life, or for a date with the needle.

Alex stopped in the middle of the cell, pissed that they'd been able to rattle him so easily. He was tougher than this, wasn't he? Morgan sure as hell wouldn't be freaking out. She'd be demanding to be set free. Just the thought of her brought a smile to his face and heat to his loins. Yeah, he wasn't going back to prison. Not today, not ever. Not with her on his side.

"Parkin?" a voice called out.

He stepped away from the cell door out of habit. "Yeah?"

The door unlocked, and to his relief, he was escorted through a series of halls to an interview room. His initial freak-out behind him, he dug deep to find the steel that had helped him survive for all those brutal years. As his panic receded, he adopted a bored expression and waited. And waited. When the door opened and Dennis, his ex-partner, entered, he forced himself to remain calm, not to turn his hands into fists.

Keep it cool. Don't throttle the asshole. Not yet.

"Hey, there you are." Alex gestured across the table. "Pull up a chair. Sorry I don't have any coffee. These guys aren't doing their jobs right."

Dennis remained standing, as if he was afraid to sit across from him. "That's one hell of a grin you've got on your face for being under suspicion for murder."

"I'm grinning because I didn't kill that assclown, though I'm pleased someone did."

Dennis ground his teeth. "That assclown was my CI."

Alex hadn't expected that. "Well, he stiffed the Russians, and that almost always gets you dead. Except for you. You seem to have all the luck. How is that?"

"He didn't work for Buryshkin," Simms replied, avoiding the bait. "He was giving me the names of dealers who work on campus."

"He also had a side deal going on, one that involved a

loan that was going to be paid off if he took pictures of Judge Redburn's daughter doing a line of coke. You know anything about that?"

"What?" Simms blurted.

"Judge Redburn. You should remember him from my trial." Alex let that sink in. "The plan went south when Calloway gave the girl some bad dope and she nearly died. You know, from that load of coke cut with strychnine that the Russians are spreading all over the city?"

His ex-partner had gone pale, his mouth hanging open.

"Since Calloway screwed the pooch, Buryshkin sent whoever is doing their wet work to tidy up the problem. I'm betting it's a big guy with a busted nose named Boris. The one who beat the hell out of my sister when he tried to kidnap her. Did you hear about that?"

Simms shook his head, reeling like a prizefighter who'd taken too many hits to the head. "When did that happen?"

"The night before you showed up at Miri's house without the warrant."

"Shit. I didn't know. Is she going to be okay?"

Alex hadn't expected compassion from this bastard, but there it was. At least when it came to Miri.

"She's okay. She got lucky—someone stepped in and saved her. If you find Boris, send him my way. We have unfinished business."

"Why would I see this guy?"

Alex smirked. "Don't play stupid. There are only a few people who could have planted the drugs in my house—one of them was you."

"Or you could have been skimming off the busts all along."

"You know I was too straight-arrow for that crap. You saw Calloway's place, right?"

"Yeah. It was a goddamn butcher shop."

Alex leaned his elbows on the interview table, working hard to keep his tone conversational. "I bet you're thinking, 'How long before they do that to me?' Because that's where my head would be if I were you."

Simms opened his mouth, then closed it.

"As much as I hate to say it, we're on the same page, Dennis. We're both dead men walking, at least if the Russians win this round. Me? I've got plans that don't involve a grave. How about you?"

Before his ex-partner could respond, the door to the interview room opened.

"You done?" a gangly detective asked.

"Yeah, we're finished," Dennis said, then made himself scarce.

Alex smiled to himself as he settled back in his chair. He'd planted a seed in Dennis's brain. Maybe it would take root.

A young man in a tailored suit entered the room right after the detective. He gave Alex a reassuring nod; his lawyer had arrived.

Round Two was about to begin.

Bring it on.

Veritas's lawyer had earned his retainer, ensuring that Alex and Morgan were released at the same time, though apparently she hadn't rated a cell like him. Now, as they exited the hotel elevator on the way to her boss's suite, he caught her up on his "chat" with Dennis Simms.

"I had a 'come to Jesus' moment with him," Alex said. "Don't know if it did any good, but it spooked the hell out of him."

Morgan's pace faltered. "Why mess with him?"

"Because it felt good, and he's a weak link we might be able to exploit." He looked over at her. "He set me up, didn't he?"

"It looks that way, but we have no direct proof."

It was then that he noticed how her eyes lacked their usual sparkle and her skin was paler than usual. "You look exhausted."

"Not sleeping well." She cut him a sharp look. "Please

don't tell me you can fix that with a little sex."

"Okay, but it wouldn't be a 'little' sex. Not if I'm involved."

"You got it on with Natalya. You should be in good shape."

He shook his head, catching her arm. "I told you, I'll only drop my pants for you."

She huffed. "You're just being silly now."

"No, I know what I want, and it's you, Morgan. No one else is going to do it for me."

"Why me?" she sputtered.

"Because you're a beautiful, fiery, and intelligent woman. I've had the other kind. Oh God, have I. It's fun while you're at it, but it feels like nothing when you're done." He leaned closer. "You know we'd be good together, or you wouldn't be checking me out whenever you think I'm not watching."

"Once," she said. "Okay, maybe twice. You've got a nice ass."

He laughed. "No. It's like . . . every. Damned. Time."

He saw the faint crimson on Morgan's cheeks as she pulled away and hurried down the hall to the suite, no doubt trying to escape the truth. After a quick knock, the door opened, and she slipped inside. Words were exchanged and Lars stuck his head out. He smiled when he saw Alex.

"I wondered who set Valkyrie's tail on fire," he said. "I should have known it was you."

When Alex joined him at the door, the man didn't let him enter.

"You need to be patted down. No offense, but you're new to the team."

And I work for the Russians. "Don't blame you. But if you take the touching too far, we'll have words, okay?"

"Fair enough."

Alex leaned against the wall as Lars efficiently patted him down, being thorough, but not a jerk.

"He's clear," the man announced, and then gestured for Alex to enter the suite.

Crispin Wilder, the man Alex now thought of as The Boss,

sat in a chair near the fireplace, a cup of tea at his elbow. In a dark navy shirt and slacks, he looked like a cross between a modern-day pirate and Victorian-era duke. His eyes said he'd seen some bad shit and done his fair share of it in return.

"Mr. Parkin, it's a pleasure to finally meet you," Crispin said, rising and shaking hands, his grip firm and steady.

Alex hadn't expected the warm reception. "Just Alex works. Thank you for keeping my sister safe."

"Our pleasure. Call me Crispin."

Alex hesitated, then moved to the desk where he scribbled out a question on one of the hotel notepads. Holding it up, he waited until Crispin had read it. A nod returned, indicating the room had been swept for electronic bugs recently.

Alex crumped the note and jammed it in his pocket.

"Good, because what I'm about to say the Russians don't need to hear. Morgan told you I accepted their offer?"

"She did, and I understand why," Crispin replied. "It's my hope that we can free you of that obligation in the near future."

"Mine as well." Alex took a deep breath. "You should also know that they asked me to scout your security arrangements. Don't know if they're just being nosy, or if they're planning a hit."

Crispin didn't bat an eye. "They've tried it only once before, and it went badly for them. Still, I appreciate your candor."

"My contact, a guy named Vasily, claims to know where Miri is. The site he mentioned wasn't right. Whatever smoke and mirrors you folks are using, it's working."

"That was Sanjay's doing," Lars said. "He's really good at that kind of thing."

"Damned good, if he's fooled Buryshkin's people." Only now did Alex settle into a chair. "So what's the latest?" he asked.

"The death toll keeps climbing," Crispin said. "Given the size of the load, not all of it seems to be poisoned, or we'd have even more corpses lining the streets. You said you had a theory about all this?"

"I believe we're after the wrong Buryshkin," Alex said flatly.

"What?" Morgan said. "You never mentioned this to me."

"I was still working it out in my head."

"Why do you think that's the case?" Crispin asked.

"I talked to a prostitute named Natalya. She was totally down with supplying me information about where that shipment might be, until she found out that Anya Buryshkin was the one who did this to me," he said, pointing at the bandage on his neck. "She backed off so hard, she left skid marks on the pavement."

"Anya's known to be kinda crazy," Lars said from his place by the door.

"It was more than that. Natalya willingly bailed on the deal of a lifetime, one that would have netted her a nice chunk of money and a new home in another city."

"You offered her all that without talking to me first?" Morgan asked, clearly irritated.

"I didn't have time to run it past you," Alex replied sharply.

"Exactly what I would have done," their boss interjected, letting Morgan know that he was taking Alex's side on this.

Morgan pursed her lips, then gave a curt nod.

"Anya calling the shots? Makes more sense than anything else," Lars said.

"It's possible," Crispin said, then took a sip of his tea. "Buryshkin's tactics do seem to have changed recently. More erratic, for one."

"He's not on the ball, leaving those bodies in the warehouse," Morgan added. "Allowing poisoned coke to make it to the streets, when the DEA would track it right back to him? Just doesn't feel right."

"You think there's been a coup?" Crispin asked.

"Or maybe the old bastard is getting senile, losing his marbles," Lars said.

"One way to find out," Alex said. "Grigori will know what's going on. I'd like to ask him to help us find the shipment."

"Pit one Russian against the other?" Crispin said. "Interesting ploy, especially since he has always been loyal to his uncle."

"Maybe, but I got the sense that his loyalty was wearing thin over the last year or so. It wasn't anything he said, but some comments made between him and my cellmate. Something to do about someone within the organization."

"Anya?" Morgan asked.

"No. A man. He was never mentioned by name."

"You think Grigori will talk to you?" Lars asked.

Alex shrugged. "Consider it a test. If he refuses to help me, that means his uncle is still in charge."

"It might work. Let me see if I can arrange it." As Crispin walked into another room, he punched in a number on his cell phone, then closed the door behind him, making Alex wonder how many bigwigs he had on his contact list.

Morgan took that opportunity to walk to one of the windows, looking out. She seemed withdrawn. Perhaps she was still angry with him for taking the initiative, and that meant he'd have to smooth her feathers later.

He turned his attention back to Lars. "Have you heard from Iceman recently?"

"About an hour ago. Everything is kosher on their end. Sounds like your sister is doing fine and needling the hell out of him."

Alex grinned. "That's Miri, all right."

A knock came at the door, along with the mangled words, "Room service."

"It's legit. We ordered food," Lars said, though he was still on alert.

Alex was closest to the door, so he opened it to reveal a beefy guy pushing a portable serving cart topped with covered dishes.

"Room service," he repeated.

The guy's uniform didn't fit, meant for a smaller man. But of most interest was the nude tape across his nose.

Alex's instincts took over. "*Ey, mudak.*" *Hey, asshole.*

The guy started in surprise, then dug under a pile of linen napkins. Alex grabbed a metal entrée cover off the cart and slammed it into the man's face, aiming right at the recently broken nose. As he pushed the cart out of the way, the attacker reeled back. Furious Russian erupted just before Alex's foot connected with his groin.

"*Eto dlya moyey sestry, svoloch*," Alex said. *That's for my sister, you bastard.*

The man went down to his knees, clutching his family jewels, the gun no longer in his hand. Alex kicked it away. Lars supplied a zip tie from somewhere, and he secured the Russian's hands behind his back, then shoved him all the way to the floor. A deep, pained groan made him smile.

"Nice takedown," Morgan said. He looked up to find her returning her gun to her purse. Crispin was in the room as well, his weapon still out.

"Is this the guy from the bar?" Alex asked.

She nodded. "Hi, Boris. Long time no see."

The man swore in Russian, bleeding into the carpet.

"What did he say?" she asked.

"Something to do with you and farm animals."

She rolled her eyes.

He patted the guy down, found a knife in an ankle sheath, and removed it using one of the linen napkins. "Knife's got dried blood on it. I'm guessing it's probably Calloway's."

Lars picked up the gun with another one of the napkins, setting it aside.

"I'm surprised they would make a move on me again. I thought they'd learned their lesson the last time." Crispin shook his head. "Lars, please call the cops. They need to find out what this fellow did with the person who was supposed to deliver our food. Hopefully he's not dead."

"Ask for Detective Meyers," Morgan added. "He handled Miri's case."

With a nod, Lars stepped away, initiating the process.

She frowned down at the man. "He doesn't have a Russian accent, but he understood you just fine. Second generation?"

"Probably." Alex knelt near Boris, watching as the blood poured out of the man's nose. He wished he could do worse. Instead, he decided to run a bluff.

"Anya's going to cut your throat for this, you know?"

The man's eyes widened, and he began to tremble. It was as if he'd seen his own death in all its brutality.

"Damn," Morgan replied. "He's totally afraid of her."

"Cops are on the way," Lars reported.

Alex had an idea. "Ah, can I talk to you two in the other room?" he said, indicating Morgan and her boss.

"As you wish," Crispin replied. He looked at Lars. "You good?"

"Yup. I'll keep an eye on him."

After they left the room, Crispin closed the door behind them. "So what didn't you want our prisoner to hear?"

Alex pulled out his phone. "I'd like to use old Boris as a teaching moment, because I'm willing to bet money that Buryshkin didn't send him to kill you. Or me."

"How do you plan to find that out?"

"I'll call my Russian contact. You can listen in. It might be very enlightening." And a way to ensure that Veritas knew he was completely on their team.

"Just be careful not to tip your hand."

"Wouldn't think of it." Alex pushed his contact's number, and Vasily answered after a few rings.

"Sasha. What is the news?"

"The news is that your man Boris just tried to put a bullet in my brain."

Vasily hesitated. "I do not understand."

"Let me lay it out for you. I was in the *same hotel room* as Veritas's boss, and your man shows up and tries to kill me. I'm sure that when he was done, he'd have gone after Wilder, too."

Silence.

"Come to find out, he's the same asshole who beat up my sister." Alex paused for effect. "I thought we had a deal, Vasily. Instead, I start working for you people, and you try to kill me. What the fuck is going on?"

A sharp intake of breath came down the line. "There has been a . . . mistake," Vasily said coolly. "A very big one."

"Really? You're saying your boss didn't try to off me?"

"Mr. Buryshkin did not order this hit, nor the attack on your sister."

That caused Crispin to smile.

"So who the hell did?" Alex demanded.

"That is not your concern. Good day, Mr. Parkin."

The call was abruptly cut off. Alex whistled, shaking his head.

"How do you know he's not lying?" Morgan asked.

"There would be no point," Crispin said, rubbing his chin. Then he smiled. "That was very clever, turning it back on them. Well done."

"Thank you," Alex said. It *had* been clever, and right now he was feeling damned pleased with himself. "It seems we have two enemies, Buryshkin and his wacko daughter."

"But why would she try to kill you?" Morgan asked.

"No clue. Why work against her own father?"

"According to the late Mr. Golov," their boss said, "Anya hates Grigori, partly because he's homosexual, but mainly because her father adores him. Buryshkin treats him like a son. Anya won't tolerate that."

"Then why did he allow Grigori to go to prison?"

"Grigori insisted on taking the fall for the young man who visits him every month."

Alex conjured up the name. "Ruslan?"

"Yes. Grigori claimed that Mr. Kuznetsov would never survive prison."

"He was probably right." Now it all made sense.

"Are they lovers? Ruslan and Grigori?" Morgan asked.

"That's the rumor," Crispin replied.

"As Anya sees it," Morgan said to Alex. "You're one of Grigori's people, so you're an enemy. Especially since you didn't go for her sick game at the bar."

Crispin sighed. "I think, in light of this knowledge—and since Los Impíos also has you on *their* hit list—you two need to get out of town, at least overnight. That'll give me time to try to level the playing field, so you can find those drugs."

Alex nodded his agreement. "I might have a place we can go, if a friend of mine is okay with us using it. It's in Plaquemines Parish, out in the middle of nowhere."

"Good. Go there, keep your head down. No doubt, your contact will let you know when Buryshkin feels he has things under control."

"There's no way he's going to take down his own daughter," Morgan warned.

"It all depends on who is more important: her or Grigori," Alex said.

"I wouldn't want to be the one making that decision," Morgan replied.

"Do not underestimate Anya Buryshkin," Crispin added. "She's a wild card. She isn't rational, and that makes her more dangerous than her father."

"Do you think he knows that?" Alex asked.

"We'll find out soon enough. Just make sure you two are not included in the body count when the dust settles."

Chapter Nineteen

Morgan put on her shoulder harness and holstered her gun. Purses were great, but it took too long to reach her weapon, and she needed to cut her reaction time. If Alex hadn't been on the ball at the hotel, they all might have died.

Her phone rang. "Lars? What's up?"

"Your buddy Boris is dead. He was taken down in a drive-by shooting as the police were escorting him out of the hotel."

"Any of the cops hurt?"

"No. They got lucky. It was two dudes on a motorcycle. They were gone even before the smoke cleared."

"Smooth. We're headed out of here in a bit."

"Good. Stay in touch, Valkyrie."

She ended the call to find Alex watching her intently, and caught him up on the latest.

"They move fast," he said. "I figured they'd get him eventually, but even before he reached the police station?" Alex sighed. "I know my call to Vasily got him killed. A sick fucker like that? That's karma in action."

She grinned. "Good, it's not only me, then."

He handed over a navy backpack, inside of which was his change of clothes. Morgan layered in a pair of jeans, a pair of shorts, a T-shirt, and some carefully concealed underwear so he wouldn't rib her about it.

It didn't work. "No lace thongs?" he joked.

"Only if you're wearing them," she countered. "They've got some really sexy guy ones, you know."

That caught him off guard. "I draw the line at that."

"Figured."

As they headed down the back stairs, Morgan cursed herself. Now, all she could think about was Alex in a thong. And nothing else.

He followed her down the steps and to the rear of the building, trading texts with someone. At her puzzled expression, he said, "Letting Miri know the good news about our dead buddy Boris."

"How'd she take it?" Morgan asked, pushing open the door to a narrow garage.

"As she put it, 'And there was much rejoicing.'"

Morgan chuckled. "I wish he'd stayed alive. Maybe he would have rolled over for us."

"Not likely. The Russians take loyalty damned seriously. You saw him—he was almost pissing himself when I mentioned Anya."

"She does that to people."

"You sound like you know her personally," he replied.

"I've seen the kind of hell she leaves in her wake."

When they entered the garage, Alex looked around, surprised there was no car. Then his eyes lit on a sleek, black motorcycle. Leather jackets and helmets hung on pegs above it.

"Sweet!" he said, moving up to check out the bike.

"You been on one before?"

"Hell yes. I used to own one." He grinned at her. "I didn't know you were a biker chick. Damn, woman. That's *hot*."

Morgan rolled her eyes. "The jackets are Kevlar lined, and the helmets have an intercom system. Watch our backs, okay?"

"You got it. Why the bike rather than a car?"

"Because we'll have more options if we have to go off-road."

It made good sense, and not for the first time, he wished he was armed. It wasn't fair that she had to keep him safe all the time. Not that he hadn't done a damned fine job at the hotel.

Alex touched her arm, and when she turned toward him, gear in hand, he swooped in and stole a kiss.

"What was that for?"

"For taking me on a ride, baby," he said, winking.

With a tortured groan, Morgan tossed a helmet at him.

A few minutes later, they were rolling along Highway 46 through Faubourg Marigny. Alex looked over his shoulder, searching for any black sedans or motorcycles, but didn't see one. They kept along the highway, skirting along the edge of the Lower Ninth Ward. He remembered the television coverage during Hurricane Katrina, the locals' belief that the levees had been bombed to save the French Quarter, pouring the floodwaters into this area. No matter how those barriers had been breached, the water had ended up here and people had died.

Now the area was a mix of run-down houses, some new ones, and vacant lots where homes had been washed away. People loitered on the streets. The state's unemployment rate sucked, so when there were no jobs, folks talked about how bad life was and sometimes figured out illegal ways to make it better for themselves.

That could be me. If Veritas hadn't offered him help, he would be trying to find a job and probably failing at it. Then what? Stay at home and drink beer? Or use those skills he'd picked up in Angola to feed his sister and keep a roof over their heads?

One thing he'd learned in prison: there was a very fine line between the law-abiding and the criminals. Often, that moral line was keeping your family fed and sheltered.

As they drove past the Chalmette National Cemetery, Alex marveled at how easily Morgan handled the bike. It seemed second nature to her. He hadn't lied—he'd always had a weakness for women on motorcycles. He closed his eyes and savored the thrum of the engine beneath him. Maybe once he and Miri got settled, he'd save up and buy one. If Morgan and he were still friends after this was over, they could go out on the road together. Tour around a bit, go camping. Make love under the stars.

"You okay back there?" she asked, her voice coming through the speaker in his helmet.

"I'm fine," he said. *Getting better every minute.* Nothing quite like being up close and tight with a pretty lady.

"You like to go camping?" he asked, knowing she'd wonder why he'd asked that out of the blue.

"Yeah, I do. I like being away from the city."

Even better.

He tightened his arms around her waist, enjoying the feel of leaning against her as she took a curve. It took all his control not to let his hands roam. It would be stupid to mess with her concentration, even though that was exactly what he wanted to do. Yeah, he definitely wanted to unzip her jacket, run his hands underneath her shirt, touch her firm breasts.

He shifted on the seat, uncomfortable from the increasing pressure down south.

"Chill out, Parkin," she said. Which meant that she'd felt just how turned on he'd become. Not unlikely, since his groin was plastered up against her butt.

"*Hard* to do when I'm with you, lady. Pun intended."

"Just try, okay? I don't need the distraction."

"You could just help me deal with this . . . distraction."

"Anyone following us?" she asked, her way of getting him back on track.

Alex did a quick check. "No, I think we're good." There was a dark-silver Jeep Grand Cherokee a few cars back, but that could be anyone headed to home or work.

"Let's keep it that way. Where is this place, besides out in the damned nowhere, as you put it?" Morgan asked.

"On the bayou. It's a cabin. Pretty modern. No one will know we're there."

"Got AC and hot water?"

"Sure does."

"Good. After wearing this heavy jacket, I'll need a shower."

Just like that, his male brain went into overdrive again, thinking of water running over her naked skin as she bathed. Licking the droplets off her nipples. He sighed. It was going to be a damned long night.

Alex looked over his shoulder, and this time, the Cherokee

had gained on them, having worked its way up so it was about thirty feet behind. "We've got an SUV on our tail, and he keeps moving closer to us. Might be something. Might not be. They've been with us since the Ninth Ward."

"Let's see if they're for real, or just headed to grandmother's house."

Morgan slowed, then turned down a side street. She didn't speed up, just went to the next street and turned right.

The SUV followed behind them, picking up speed now.

"They followed us."

"Buryshkin's people?" she asked.

Alex could see Mardi Gras beads hanging from the rearview mirror. That didn't strike him as a typical Russian accessory. "I don't think so. Might be Los Impíos."

"How the hell did they find us?"

"No idea."

Morgan executed another turn, more abrupt than the last, and the vehicle was right behind them.

"Yeah, we got trouble," he reported.

"Okay," she replied, not sounding particularly worried. "Hold on tight. It's going to get intense."

Just as she twisted the throttle to speed up, a tanned arm extended from the passenger window and the man opened fire. Alex instinctively hunched down as Morgan took a hard turn, and he leaned into it, hoping not to overbalance. When they came back up, the bike shot forward as it picked up speed, causing the houses and businesses to blur as they rode past.

Alex did a quick glance over his shoulder and swore. "They're still there." He gritted his teeth, hoping the next shot wasn't going to blow out the back of his skull.

"I'm just warming up."

The Cherokee kept on their tail, but was having trouble executing the sharp turns Morgan made as she led their pursuers in tight circles. When it lagged behind, she ran across an empty parking lot, down an alley, and onto Paris Road. There, she opened up the bike, flying past cars at top speed.

Alex wondered how long it would be before a cop spotted

them, which might make their pursuers back off—or they'd just ice the officer and keep coming after them.

"Let me know when you can't see them," she said in his ear.

After a gut-clenching zoom around a minivan, Morgan cut back in, the van's horn letting them know that the driver thought she was a jerk. She took the bike to its top speed, chewing up another half mile.

"Now!" he announced.

"Hold on!" He tightened his grip as Morgan rapidly decelerated. Spraying gravel, she cut right, barreling into a business parking lot. They finally came to a stop behind the building near a semi-truck.

Removing his helmet, Alex hopped off the bike. Sprinting back toward the road, he peered around the side of the business, his heart beating so hard it was difficult to catch his breath. The SUV flew past them, and he watched as it vanished in the distance.

"Yes!" he shouted. "You lost them!"

Morgan's helmet was off, and it hung on a handlebar, her hair glistening in the sun, her face as sweaty as his. He trotted back, grabbed her and spun her around. Then he kissed her.

"You are awesome!" he said, giddy. "How did you learn to ride like that?"

"Motocross. I got pretty good at it."

Alex reluctantly let her go. He unzipped his jacket and swore he felt steam rising off his skin. She did the same, and he couldn't help but notice her T-shirt molded against her breasts.

"Jesus, lady, that was *one* helluva ride," he said. He clapped a hand over his heart. "I think I'm in love. Marry me."

"Yeah, yeah." She pushed damp hair off her face. "We'll hang here for a while, then head back south. If we're lucky, they won't be waiting for us." She sucked in a deep breath. "You get a plate number?"

"No, sorry." His phone rang from deep inside a pocket. He pulled it out, not recognizing the number.

"Parkin."

"*Dobriy den,* Sasha."

Well, I'll be damned. "Good afternoon to you, Grigori. Thank you for calling me."

Morgan's eyebrow rose at the caller's identity.

"I trust you are well," the Russian said.

"Right now, yes. A few minutes ago, not so much. A couple dudes tried to kill me."

There was a lengthy pause. "That was not my uncle's doing."

"Good to hear it."

Another pause. "What is it you wish to speak to me about?" the Russian asked.

"We have a big problem. A large shipment of cocaine has arrived in the city, and some of it is cut with strychnine. The bodies are just going to keep piling up unless we locate that load and confiscate it."

"I have heard this too. Why does this concern me?"

"You're getting out of prison very soon."

"*Da.*"

"Well, the poisoned dope is killing at least ten people a day. That many dead will ensure that the feds have no choice but to carpet bomb all your uncle's businesses, taking everyone down in the process. You included, my friend, because you are his nephew. It won't matter if you're just getting out of the joint or not. You'll be collateral damage."

"Why would you care what happens to me?"

"Because you kept me alive, Grigori. You know what would have happened if you hadn't stepped in: I'd have been dead or fair game for every pervert inside those walls. You kept me safe all those years. Now I'm returning the favor, while trying to prevent more innocent people from dying." Alex sucked in a breath, feeling sweat trickle down his back. "I don't want those souls haunting me for the rest of my life, however long that might be. I don't think you do either."

He heard the scratch of whiskers as the prisoner rubbed a hand across his face. "I am not in a position to help, Sasha. I am truly sorry. I have been warned that if I become involved, someone I care about will die."

Ruslan?

Alex knew it would be demeaning to beg. "Then all I can say is watch your back, my friend. We both know Anya is cleaning house, and you're standing in her way."

There was a deeper sigh now. "Anya is insane. Anyone else's child, and she would have been sent to an asylum. Or put down like a rabid dog. Yet my uncle adores her."

"He may, but she's not going to stop until both of you are dead. Please, be careful. I count you as too much of a friend to lose you, even if we are on opposite sides of the law."

"I am honored by that, but I still cannot help you, at least not yet. Go with God, Sasha."

"And you as well, Grigori."

Alex ended the call, staring into the distance, then shook his head.

"At least you tried," Morgan said, lightly touching his sleeve.

He shrugged, then tucked the phone away. "We best get on the road so we're at the camp before dark."

Morgan gave a pensive nod, put her gear back on, and climbed back on the bike, deep in thought. He joined her, all thoughts of bantering with her gone now. Not with the resignation he'd heard in Grigori's voice.

At that moment a Russian proverb came to mind, one Mikhail had taught him.

Eto surovoy zimy, kogda odin volk s'yedayet druguyu.
It's a hard winter when one wolf eats another.

Alex hadn't lied when he'd said the camp was in the back end of nowhere. A rough, shell-covered road, about a half-mile long, led to the structure from the main road. Morgan didn't know this part of rural Louisiana that well, but she guessed they were somewhere near Bayou Lery, which was south of the lake of the same name.

From the outside, the camp looked ramshackle, a victim of one too many tropical storms. As Alex retrieved the key from under a rotten log near the porch, she rolled the motorbike out of sight from the driveway. Not that she expected to have any company—there'd been no sign of anyone following them since they'd ditched the SUV.

Alex's friendship with Grigori Danshov should have troubled her, but it didn't. Grigori wasn't like his uncle; he'd always worked on the periphery of Buryshkin's crime empire, and had been sent to prison only because of a money-laundering scheme gone bad.

It was Alex's admission that he owed his life to Grigori that had touched her. It was never easy for a guy to say things like that, especially to another man.

"Got the key," he said, holding it up. "Damned weird place to hide it, but I guess most people won't go digging around in the mud for it."

Morgan followed him up onto the porch and waited as he opened the door and deactivated the alarm.

"He's changed some things," Alex observed, turning on lights as he moved through the camp. "It's even nicer now." He flicked on the window air conditioner to suck up some of the mustiness, and the thing rattled to life.

Morgan found she liked the place. The décor was masculine, in browns and blacks. A small television sat in the corner, opposite a long sofa. A table and a pair of chairs sat under a louvered window near a galley kitchen. In the rear of the camp was a bathroom and a bedroom with a queen bed. Just perfect for a single guy or a couple.

Couple?

She looked back at the sofa and realized it wasn't a sleeper.

Alex noticed. "Don't freak. I'm not going to ravage you. Actually, I was rather hoping it'd be the other way around."

Morgan turned to find him close, so close that she could smell his scent, an earthy, masculine one that called to the woman deep within her. It reminded her of how long it'd been since she'd been in a man's arms as he made love to her.

"We're safe here," Alex said, gently touching her cheek. "The closest house is a quarter mile away. You can scream my name as much as you want, and no one but me will hear."

She swallowed, her mouth suddenly dry. The question in his eyes was as stark as the need raging through her body.

"You sure?"

He nodded. "But I warn you, the first time is going to be hot and furious. No way can I go slow. After that . . . "

Without thinking, she reached out to touch the tape on his bandage, where it had peeled up on one edge. He caught her hand. Kissed it like it was pure gold.

I want this. I want him, mission be damned.

He must have seen the look in her eyes. His lips tipped up into a masculine grin. "Game on?"

"Game on."

Rational thought vanished. They stumbled back against the nearest wall, him up against her, the heat rising from their bodies.

"You're all I want," he rasped, his voice husky with need.

"Prove it."

Alex's eyes widened at the challenge, and then his lips were on hers. His tongue ran over her lips, urging them to part, and then it sought entrance. His hands roamed, as if they couldn't decide where to start first.

When Alex finally pulled back, he lightly tugged on her lip with his teeth. Morgan couldn't stop the moan as his hand found its way under her damp T-shirt. He stripped off the garment and tossed it aside, then hooked his thumbs under the straps of her bra and flipped them off her shoulders, pulling the cups down.

"You are so beautiful," he murmured as he palmed her right breast, rolling the nipple between his fingers.

Morgan sent her own hands on a safari, tracing the taut skin under his shirt, then sliding down the back of his jeans. She carefully dug her nails into his firm butt, and now it was his turn to groan.

"Damn, lady." Alex pulled her hands free and trapped them

above her on the wall with one of his. His feral gaze made her body respond, and she tried to twist out of his hold, eager for more than he was offering.

"Too slow," she said.

"We'll get there. Just let me play. Right now, you're mine. All mine."

He placed his lips on her right nipple and lightly tugged on it with his teeth.

"Alex . . ."

When he finished with the one nipple, he favored the other, and she found herself falling into sensations she'd long believed forgotten. After his hand deftly unbuttoned the top of her jeans, he pushed them down. When he set her hands free, she shucked them off, after kicking off her shoes. Her bra went next, landing somewhere near the couch.

She stood before him wearing only her panties.

He slid a hand in the top of them, caressing her flat stomach. "Red lace. And a thong too. God, woman, you are killing me."

"Strip for me," she urged.

He gave her a bad-boy smile and pulled off the T-shirt, revealing those gorgeous six-pack abs. Then his shoes and jeans were off, leaving her to study the man and his pair of briefs. She ran a finger down the impressive bulge.

"I might be able to do something about that."

Then she fell on her knees in front of him and smiled.

Alex sucked in a sharp breath, sweat beading on his forehead. God, he wanted her, but not like this. At least not the first time. This had to be for both of them.

"No, not that way," he said, taking hold of her hands and easing her to her feet. He kissed her, long and deep, and then they were stumbling across the room, finally landing on the couch with her underneath him.

He reached down and pulled off her panties, then began to stroke her nub. She immediately arched into him, seeking more.

"You want me," he said. "Say it."

She moaned.

"Say it!"

"I . . . want . . . you."

"About damned time." Alex trailed kisses down to the closest breast and feasted on it as he eased two fingers inside her. She moved against his hand, wet and eager.

"Go on, Morgan, fly. Just fly," he said.

As her body shook beneath him, her cries signaled that she'd found her wings and taken to the sky. When she regained her ability to breathe, he found her watching him, eyes sparkling.

"That's the first of many," he said, smiling. Then he remembered the condoms in his wallet, the ones he'd "borrowed" from the safe house. "Ah, hold on, I'll be right back."

She caught hold of him. "I'm covered."

"Then I'm about to go to heaven. You be sure to come with me, baby."

He began to enter her, inch by magnificent inch.

When he was fully seated deep inside her, Morgan refused to make it easy on him, tightening and releasing those glorious muscles around his length.

"Oh, God, that feels good," she said, clutching his hips, pulling him in deeper.

"You're killing me," he said, panting. Alex clenched his teeth and began to move, slowly at first.

Their eyes met as his rhythm increased.

"I want to hear you scream my name. Can you do that?"

Her ability to speak was gone, and all she could do was nod. He touched her face, kissing her deeply, then took her arms and pinned them over her head again, trapping them with one of his own. She wrapped her legs around him now, pulling him deeper inside. His control vanished as his thrusts grew deeper, more intense. Then he arched forward, seeking that spot that would drive her over the edge.

The world blew apart in brilliant colors as Morgan cried out, shaking her head back and forth, deep inside her own orgasm. With a final bellow, Alex came long and hard, emptying himself inside her.

Alex let go of her hands and sank down onto her sweat-dampened body. She was panting, trying to catch her breath, still pulsing around him.

"Jesus God," he moaned. He took her mouth with his, sucking and tasting and claiming. Then he leaned back, his arms shaking and sweat rolling down his face.

"Did you call my name like you were supposed to?" he asked.

"I can't remember," she said. "But that's only two orgasms, Parkin. You owe me a lot more," she huffed, still trying to catch her breath.

He broke out in a laugh, one that came from deep in his belly. She joined him, her eyes shining, face full of joy. This was the real Morgan, the one she kept hidden away. And he'd revealed her to the world.

She reached up and gently wiped sweat off his cheek. In that simple gesture, he knew that if this had been any other time, any other situation, he might well have fallen in love with this woman.

"Shower?" she asked. "We're pretty sweaty."

He grinned. "Sure. I happen to know that this shower is big enough for two. You still game?"

A wicked smile played across her face. "Of course."

The shower ended much like the time on the couch. Then they were on the bed. In no time, he had her moaning, crying out, begging.

"Come for me, baby. Come hard. Do it!" he called out.

She threw her head back and let go, screaming his name as his own orgasm flung him off the cliff once again.

His woman was on fire. He felt like a god.

His woman . . . That made him pause as he rolled on his back. Since when had he started thinking she was only his? Because that kind of thinking had gotten him trapped once before. He didn't dare go that way again.

Or did he?

Morgan laid her head on his sweaty chest. "We need another shower," she said.

"Ah, let's . . . give it a while. I . . . need to . . . recharge."

Morgan laughed, rising on an elbow. "Really? *Now* you're tired? What happened to the horny ex-con routine?"

"Going from nothing to flat-out is tiring, woman."

She slumped back down onto his chest. "That's the truth." She yawned, then rolled on her back. "Why'd you wait for me when you had girls throwing themselves at you?"

He looked at her. "You like chocolate, right?" She nodded. "Okay, let's say that your doctor tells you that you can't have chocolate for six years. So you don't. Not one damned bite. But when that ends, the first piece you eat, would you go for some cheap store brand, or find the most exquisite, expensive kind there is?"

She blinked at him. "I'd go for the fancy stuff."

"Exactly. I could have had a couple of girls at the bar, or Natalya. Even Anya, if I were into pain. Problem was, none of them were you."

She gave him a half frown. "It's more than that. You couldn't resist a challenge. I told you 'no,' so you were eager to prove me wrong."

She'd read him right. "Partly. Mostly it was because you are a beautiful, desirable woman who I knew would rock my world."

Morgan seemed surprised at that. "And did I?"

"Oh hell yes. Rocked it like a nine-point-eight earthquake."

She shifted, uncomfortable now. "We should talk about the situation."

For an instant, he thought she meant the situation between them, but then he knew she was stepping back from what had just happened. Probably getting too intense. Still, while they'd been going at it, people were dying from the poisoned dope. They did need to get back to business.

"I know Crispin wants us out of sight, but I want to go back into the city tomorrow," he said. "I have a couple more informants I can try. We can make another run at Natalya. Maybe you could persuade her to help us."

"Not likely. She's as tough as an old boot." Morgan rose and went hunting for her cell phone. Since she was still naked, he found himself enjoying the view. Her butt was just as fine nude as in a tight pair of jeans.

You have no idea how beautiful you are, do you?

Morgan sat on the side of the bed. "Lars texted. He says that your sister remains safely tucked away." She set the phone aside. "I need a shower. Alone this time."

Alex smiled to himself, knowing that she was just working things out in her head. He already knew where they'd be once she returned to him. No way either of them were going to pass on that kind of pleasure, not with people looking to put them in their graves tomorrow.

Chapter Twenty

September 20th
Plaquemines Parish

Morgan noticed that something had changed with Alex when she joined him after her second shower. Something about the way he moved. He was in his jeans, no shirt, white scars showing clearly against his tanned skin. He seemed at ease, not as wary as before.

She'd done that to him, brought him one step further away from the hell of prison. In return, he'd done things to her that she'd never expected. Sex with Wayne had been good, and she'd had orgasms, but she'd never lost control, not once. With Alex, she had found herself cutting loose, feeling wild. Feeling true to herself. How he'd done it, she had no idea. She only knew that she wanted to feel that way again.

He pointed at a first aid kit on the counter next to a can of soup. "Will you bandage me up?"

Morgan nodded. She delicately removed the Steri-Strips, then replaced them with new ones. "It's healing well. I don't think you need the bandage now. Probably best for it to get some air."

"Thank you. For . . . everything."

She looked up at him, then placed her hand on his warm cheek, feeling beard stubble under her fingers.

Oh hell, just kiss him.

She did, taking her time, savoring the scent of his clean hair, the strength of his muscles, the growing arousal in his jeans.

"Sex or food?" he whispered.

She didn't hesitate. "Sex."

He grinned. "I knew that once I got you going, you'd be insatiable."

The kiss he got in return did nothing to deny that claim.

As their breathing returned to normal and the sweat cooled on their bodies, Morgan placed her head on Alex's shoulder. The scent of sex mingled with the smell of soap. He shifted to be closer to her, craving the feel of her skin next to his. No matter how much he'd like to reassure himself that Morgan wasn't getting to him, it would be a lie. He wasn't exactly sure when she'd first slipped under his defenses, but this lady was more than just a one-night stand. Every time they joined, the connection grew stronger, knitting them together in ways he could not fathom.

Not possible.

He was just grateful to finally get laid, that "any old port in a storm" thing. Nothing to do with her at all, no matter what he'd told her. He wasn't a one-woman guy anymore, not after Alicia. Not after the woman who had promised to be with him "until death do us part" warmed the sheets with his partner and walked away within a week of Alex's arrest.

"Hmm . . . that was good," Morgan said.

"How long had it been for you?" he asked, tracing a fingertip across a breast, enjoying how the nipple peaked at his touch.

"Almost five years."

"Damn. No wonder you were hotter than the center of the sun."

He expected a smile at the compliment, but it didn't come. Instead he saw a frown forming, which was odd.

"You must have loved your husband a great deal to turn into a nun."

She went stiff in his arms, as if a steel curtain had suddenly descended between them. Then she was up, her bare back to him, the sheet tucked up against her chest. In his experience, women he'd just bedded didn't shut him out. If anything, they were resting up for another round. Eager, even.

All because he'd mentioned her husband.

"Did he hurt you?" he asked, quieter now.

Morgan took a deep breath, and he couldn't help but notice the increasing tightness across her shoulders.

"Come on, this is me," he said. "I've told you things I've never told anyone else."

When Alex sat up and touched her back, intending to massage away that tension, she flinched.

"Okay, what is going on? We just had a really good time, and now you're freezing me out. What did I do wrong?"

Morgan looked over her shoulder at him, her face bleak. Then she was off the bed, pulling on her clothes and shoes, her hands shaking the entire time. Like she was getting ready to run.

"Hey, talk to me."

She paused in the doorway, her back to him, hugging herself. This wasn't the Morgan he knew. Growing increasingly worried, Alex pulled on his own clothes. When she heard his zipper go up, she turned. Her eyes were glistening now, her face pale.

"It was wrong to sleep with you."

"Why?" he said, tugging down his T-shirt.

"We . . . It was wrong because . . . I should have told you first."

"Told me what? Why are you so spooked? All I did was mention your husband."

Morgan shook her head as if resigned to her fate. "You're going to hate me."

He stepped closer. "Not going to happen."

She moved into the living room and slumped onto the couch. As he followed her, his mind raced. What had her so scared?

Morgan looked up at him now. "My husband was an attorney, one of the best. He was really good at getting acquittals. But . . . " She took an uneven breath. "He had a secret. He liked prostitutes, the young ones, between the ages of sixteen and eighteen."

"That had to have been rough for you."

She gave a sad nod. "Yeah, well apparently paying for sex was a big turn-on for him. He claimed that he always made sure the girls were of legal age, but how the hell would he know for sure?"

He wouldn't. The prostitutes would lie because it was all about making money.

"He finally admitted that he was being blackmailed for his . . . activities, and if he didn't do what he was told, his career was history."

"Damn," Alex muttered. "You had no idea?"

"None. I was working a major case—a high-profile juvenile kidnapping. We got the girl back safe, and I was so jazzed. I came home, and there he was . . . like the bottom had fallen out of his world. He told me what he'd done, how he'd had no choice."

Morgan swiped away tears, and his heart ached to see her this upset. Alex noted that she'd never mentioned the man's first name.

"I said I never wanted to see him again, and I left him there . . . " A sob broke free. "I left him alone. I didn't stay with him, didn't keep him from . . . "

Alex sat next to her now, taking hold of a chilly, shaking hand. "Go on."

"My husband canceled his appointments for the next day, then put a gun to his head. One shot, in the temple. He died in our bed."

Alex jolted. "Jesus."

"I came back in the morning to pack my stuff and . . . "

"You found him," he murmured, knowing exactly what the scene would have looked like.

Morgan's tears welled, but she waved him off when he moved to take her in his arms. If anything, she put more space between them.

"Look, I don't want to be an ass here," he said, "and I'm

very sorry for your loss, but what does this have to do with us?"

Her chin wobbled. "I didn't expect you and me to be so good together . . . I just thought it'd be fun, and now . . . " She blinked away the tears. "I can't hide this anymore, Alex. Not after . . . "

"You're not making much sense, honey."

Morgan straightened up now, her tear-filled eyes meeting his. "The last case my husband worked on was a twenty-six-year-old DEA agent who had been accused of skimming drugs off the top of his busts. They arrested him because they found cocaine in his home."

Alex's heart skipped a few beats. His defense lawyer had killed himself a few months after the trial. "Wayne Clifton was your husband?"

"Yes," she said, nodding. "I kept my maiden name—that's why you didn't know. Until your case came along, Wayne had a great track record. He was brilliant." Morgan gave a pained smile. "Flawed, but brilliant. It was the flaw that got him hooked in Buryshkin's claws."

"Son of a bitch!" Alex surged off the couch. "Your husband fucked me over?"

"Yes," she said. "His orders were to ensure that you went to jail, or the videos of him with the prostitutes would be sent to his boss and the New Orleans's television stations."

This was why his lawyer had been such a disaster: Wayne had purposely sabotaged his case. Before Alex knew he was moving, he'd pinned her against the back of the sofa.

"Your goddamn husband ruined my life! Ruined my sister's life. And you didn't think to tell me you were married to the bastard?" he said, shaking her.

Morgan's breath came in panicked gasps now, her eyes wide. He saw fear and . . . resignation. As if anything he did to her now was what she deserved. That surrender turned his gut to ice. He pulled himself away from her.

"Why the hell didn't you tell me this right off?" he demanded. "Were you too busy eyeing my package?"

"I wasn't the only one doing the eyeing, buddy. Besides, if I'd told you this up front, you would have walked. We needed you."

"Damn right, you do, but you've been lying to me all along."

"No, I just didn't tell you the whole story."

"Jesus," he said, swiping a hand through his hair in agitation. "At least when Anya hurt me, she did it right up front, didn't stab me in the back."

"She's no saint, Alex," Morgan said. "Who the hell do you think was the first girl to seduce my husband?"

He blinked. "What?"

"Anya went after Wayne on her daddy's orders. She was barely sixteen, and she picked him up at a bar. Wayne paid her a hundred for a couple hours. Then she set him up with her 'friend,' a girl named Ina who was fifteen. Anya made sure they were videotaped, and from that point on, Wayne was Buryshkin's puppet."

"You're lying." *Just like my ex-wife. You just twist the truth to suit you.* "Dammit, you should have kept him home, off the fucking streets, and—"

Defiance flamed in Morgan's eyes. "Don't you think I've spent the last six years trying to figure out how I could have missed the signs? I was a damned FBI agent. I should have seen what he was doing."

"No way you're getting any pity from me, lady. While I was trying not to get raped, you sailed on through your life. It worked great for you that he died. You were free and clear."

Before he could stop it, her hand slapped him hard on the face. "You bastard! You think you're the only one who has suffered? I lost my job at the FBI because of what Wayne did."

His cheek stinging, he backed away from her. "How the hell would they know?"

"Buryshkin made me a job offer. If I worked for him, all evidence of Wayne's activities would disappear. I told him to screw himself and reported the offer to the FBI. Buryshkin made sure one of the videos landed on my superior's desk. My boss didn't want an investigation, so I was gone."

The Russian never stopped destroying people's lives.

To see her like this, weeping over a dead man, made Alex pause. Her tears were genuine. He'd been in the law-enforcement business long enough to know.

"Why did you tell me now?" *Why jeopardize the mission?*

Morgan's head rose, her hair falling around her face. Her eyes were red, swollen, full of tears. "Because . . . what happened between us wasn't . . . what I expected. It was more, and I can't hide the truth anymore. It hurts too much."

"Shit," he muttered. He was headed for the front door before he took his next breath.

"Alex?" she asked, her voice a mix of fear and hope. "I can't fix it. I cannot wave a magic wand and give you back those six years."

Hell, that's what he wanted, the chance to go back and make it right for all of them. Make it so when he first met Morgan, she'd have no reason to hide things from him. No reason to be like every other woman.

But that was all a dream.

Alex grabbed his shoes and was out the door and off the porch before he realized it was night and that he didn't have a flashlight. He stood still for a time, letting his eyes adjust. A faint light came from the east, a sign of the coming dawn. He'd spent the night having sex with the woman whose husband had betrayed him.

With a curse, he pulled on his shoes and set off down the driveway, not really caring where he was headed, as long as it was nowhere near Morgan Blake.

Morgan curled up on the couch and wept as hard as she had the day she'd found Wayne's body. It was all gone now, all the beauty she and Alex had shared, all the loving. She'd felt something for him, something more than she thought possible, and she'd thought he felt something for her. It was why she'd finally told him the truth. This was what happened when you mixed sex with a mission: people got hurt. She'd been a fool to think her life could be like other people's. That she might find a man who could love her.

She'd placed the mission ahead of everything, all about the revenge, a chance to bring Buryshkin to his knees. The opportunity to destroy his life, like he had hers. In the end, she'd manipulated Alex just like their enemy.

Only now did she know the truth: she loved Alex Parkin. The mouthy, arrogant ex-con had stolen her heart, and she'd had no way to stop it.

When the tears finally ran out, Morgan blew her nose, laced up her shoes, and went out the back door. She headed for the water, her Maglite lighting up the path, as gators bellowed in the distance. She'd done the same thing after Wayne's death, gone to water to find solace. It hadn't worked then, and she knew it wouldn't work now.

Sitting on the dock, ignoring the mosquitoes, she found herself remembering the pleasure, the joy of making love to Alex. The shining moments that sent light into her darkened soul. Now it was all gone.

They'd finish this mission, and if it looked as if he was staying in New Orleans, she'd move out of the city. Maybe to another country.

But in her heart she knew the distance wouldn't matter, because every night, as she curled herself around a pillow, a sad substitute for a man's body, she would remember Alex Parkin for all that he was. And for all that she'd lost.

She was Wayne's wife.

Alex remembered how his defender had consistently let him down, made one dumb move after another as if he'd been a rank amateur. Alex had wanted to hire another lawyer, but Alicia had tied up all their money, so he'd been stuck with Wayne. In fact, she'd been the one to recommend him. Was she somehow tied to Buryshkin?

He stomped down the shell driveway, fury boiling off him in waves.

"I'm fucking your old lady, you bastard. How about that?"

The moment he said it, Alex felt disgusted, nauseated. It wasn't like that with Morgan. It hadn't been after that first time, not for either one of them. Though it had clearly hurt her, she'd revealed the truth about her husband, and it had ripped her up in the process.

He could still feel her moving underneath him, responding to his touch, his thrusts, and hear her crying out his name when she came. How she'd touched his face, cared about each of his scars. Wanted to know how they'd happened.

She was the man's wife.

"Dammit to hell," he said.

He hadn't ever wanted to feel this way again, not after what Alicia had done to him. Was it stupid for him to hope that someday he'd find a woman who wouldn't hurt him? One who would love him and never leave him behind? Was Morgan that woman?

No. She left her husband alone when he needed her the most. *She'll do the same to me.*

His self-righteousness whirled around and kicked him in the balls. After he'd found out about his wife and Dennis's affair, he'd shouted down the roof, called her a whore, and then bailed on her. The only difference was that Alicia hadn't put a gun to her temple and pulled the trigger.

As he looked back, he realized that he'd contributed to the death of their marriage just as much as she had. He'd loved the thrill of being undercover, even if it took him away from Alicia for months on end. He'd just expected that she'd be there when he returned, the princess awaiting the conquering hero. Reality wasn't like that. He'd mortally wounded their marriage, and she'd been the one to put it out of its misery.

His anger burned away, Alex slowed his pace now, increasingly mindful that it would do him no damned good to steamroll over a gator, because the prehistoric creatures always won. They'd had eons to learn how to be badass.

By the time he'd made it to the main road, his skin dripped with sweat. Curiously, the mosquitoes weren't bothering him, but he suspected that wouldn't last long. Now what? Walk to the next town and catch a cab . . . where? Or return and face Morgan? Try to work it out between them.

He just couldn't go there, at least not yet. She'd reopened wounds from Alicia that he'd long thought healed. Now they were fresh, bleeding and aching with each pound of his heart. With an oath, Alex turned and headed back to the camp. He'd finish the mission and move on. Chalk this whole thing up to stupidity.

With each step closer to the camp, he thought of his life, how badly he'd screwed up. How his arrogance at the DEA hadn't made him any friends, and his workaholic drive had ruined his marriage. His life could have been so different if he'd only taken the time to think things through, recognize that some things were more important than others.

Like the love of a good woman.

To his right came the throaty bellow of a gator. Another one answered from deeper in the bayou. Nature didn't care about his problems. It just went on taking each day as it came.

When Alex reached the porch, he hesitated. This was going to be ugly, but they had no choice but to get through it, even after some of the vicious things he'd said to her. Things he regretted now.

"Morgan?" he called out.

As he opened the camp door, he found her sitting on the couch, her eyes filled with warning. She wasn't alone. Three men were with her, all armed. The Russians had found them.

Chapter Twenty-One

To Morgan's relief, their captors hadn't put a bullet in their skulls and dumped them in the water. Instead, they were herded into the back of a black sedan, which had arrived shortly after she'd been taken prisoner. A man named Vasily sat up front with the driver, while two other goons followed them in another car.

Morgan had been so caught up in her own misery, she hadn't seen them coming. She'd heard something on the water, and then there was a boat, men, and guns. Then this smiling Russian who'd insisted that he just *had* to talk to Mr. Parkin.

On the other side of the backseat, Alex stirred. "How'd you find us?" he asked.

"It was very simple," Vasily said, looking over the seat at him. "You don't have that many friends you trust, so we checked into Mr. James and found he owns a cabin. We had someone watching it from the water, and when the lights went on tonight, we knew it was probably you."

It was a smart move, and one Morgan hadn't anticipated. From the deep frown on his face, Alex wasn't happy about it either.

"There better be a damned good reason you've outed me in front of *her*," he said, angling a thumb toward Morgan. "Because now Veritas is going to be gunning for my ass."

"Perhaps yes, perhaps no." The Russian looked at Morgan. "Mr. Buryshkin wishes to see both of you. Consider it breakfast, for two."

Breakfast?

Morgan looked out the side window. She'd been disarmed

and they'd both been relieved of their phones. There was nothing to do but wait and hope this day was survivable.

She looked at Alex, but he stared at nothing.

I didn't keep you safe. And I hurt you.

Both regrets carried equal weight.

The car abruptly swung off the highway onto a side road and wound its way through some of the most magnificent old trees Alex had ever seen, each draped in Spanish moss. The driveway circled in front of a large plantation house. As they exited the car, he studied the structure.

"This is new. He didn't have this when I went into prison."

"Built it a couple years back," Morgan said, her eyes still red from crying.

He'd done that to her, and right now, it made him feel guilty. He wished he could talk to her about what had happened between them, but it was best that the Russians didn't know. Though they might be able to figure it out, what with the rumpled sheets on the bed.

Knowing he needed to have his head in the game, he switched his attention to the scene around them. The house, set far back from the main highway to avoid prying eyes, appeared to have two points of access: the driveway and the bayou beyond. The place was well secured, with video cameras and guards, all toting AK-47s.

Alex wasn't sure what a Russian crime lord's dwelling should be like, but this one channeled the Old South like *Gone with the Wind,* shady backroom politics, and collard greens. Apparently modeled after one of the grand plantations of the mid-eighteen hundreds, it was done up in a pale yellow and teal color scheme, with twin stairways that led to a grand entrance on the second floor.

Whoever had installed the gingerbread work and the iron railings had gone overboard, in Alex's opinion, but the final result spoke of money and power. It also spoke of Buryshkin's cunning, how he'd utilized classic Louisiana architecture to signal to his visitors that he was lord and master of this place.

A young man walked toward them from the house, tall and blond, with the grace of a dancer. He wore a tailored, dark-brown suit that said he'd be better suited to a boardroom than working for a notorious mobster.

"Good day, Mr. Parkin, Ms. Blake. I am Ruslan Kuznetsov."

Morgan's eyebrow rose as she made the connection.

"Good morning, Ruslan," Alex said politely. "Grigori sends his best."

"Thank you. We are all very eager to see him free again."

Some more than others.

"You are invited to breakfast," the man said, gesturing toward the house.

Alex looked at Morgan. "Hospitality. It's a Russian thing. Usually it's offered right before they kill you."

"It's the little touches that make life worth living," Ruslan said, apparently not offended by his comment.

Alex laughed. He could see why Grigori cared for this guy.

As they ascended the stairs to the house's second floor, Alex took a casual look over his shoulder, cataloguing the guards' positions. To get out of here, they'd need weapons. Given the number of guards, obtaining one wouldn't be a problem. Getting to the car alive was another matter.

Still, sometimes fate worked in your favor, which was why he'd made note that their driver had placed the car keys in his left pants pocket, and the man had a knife stuck in a sheath under his right trouser leg.

Above them, a set of French doors swung open, and the supreme boss of this swampy kingdom strode out to greet his "guests." The mobster was in his late sixties, stocky, with silver hair and thick jowls.

Buryshkin had begun his life as a soldier, then worked for the KGB in various countries, including what used to be East Germany. There he'd spent time with another equally ruthless man, one with the same first name: Vladimir Putin, Russia's current president.

Buryshkin had quit the KGB right before its failed coup

against Mikhail Gorbachev and started a small import/export business. It proved a savvy move, and Alex had always wondered if Buryshkin had been warned about the plot ahead of time. The man's many connections, both inside his own country and throughout the world, paved the way for him to assume control of this part of the U.S. for the Russian mafia.

"Welcome, Mr. Parkin. Or should I call you Sasha?" the man asked, offering his hand.

"Parkin will do," Alex replied. They shook hands like civilized people, a micro-thin polite veneer that could vanish in a second.

Buryshkin's grip was strong, but not overdone. This man was sure of who he was, what he could do, and whom he could intimidate. He wore a light-brown short-sleeved shirt and dark-brown slacks. Blackwork tattoos were visible on his arms, the kind the Russian mobsters liked so much.

"Ms. Blake," Buryshkin said, offering his hand to her as well.

Keep it cool, lady. Pissing off their host would only get them dead that much quicker. Buryshkin had to have a reason to be this social, so it was best to play it out to the end.

For a second, Alex thought Morgan was going to spit in his face, and given how the Russian had ruined her life, he wouldn't have been surprised.

To his relief, she shook the man's hand. "Mr. Buryshkin."

"I have long regretted that you did not come to work for me," the mobster said amiably, waving them across the balcony that ran along the outside of the building. "I was dismayed to learn that you went to work for Wilder instead."

"I wasn't dismayed at all," she replied.

Buryshkin laughed, clearly not upset by her response. "Wilder chose well. You have done right by him." After a look at Alex, he added, "Come, we must talk about the future, and how you will repay your debt to me."

Morgan gave Alex a puzzled look, and all he could do was shrug in reply.

They followed their host to the rear of the house, where

the view from the balcony was impressive, to the expansive lawn and the bayou beyond. A pair of white ibis waded near the shore, in search of small fish. A well-maintained dock jutted into the water, three boats tied to it. Armed guards patrolled the water's edge as well.

Set near the balcony railing was a white-linen-draped table with three place settings. A low floral arrangement of water lilies sat in the very middle. The china was expensive, the crystal equally so. It paid to be a crook.

Alex hadn't missed the admiring gaze the Russian had given Morgan, so he pulled out a chair for her, which earned him an amused look from their host.

"A gentleman. That is rare nowadays," Buryshkin said.

"I only do it when I'm in the presence of a lady," Alex responded.

He felt Morgan tense, but ignored it. Besides being polite, Alex used the gesture as a distraction, allowing him to size up the guards around them. There were two on each side of the table—armed, if the bulges under their suit coats meant anything. Ruslan hung in the background, like an executive assistant awaiting orders.

"There is coffee or tea, if you wish," Buryshkin said, gesturing expansively.

"Thank you," Alex replied. He poured himself coffee as Morgan made herself a cup of tea. He knew she was doing the same thing as him: calculating their odds of survival and arriving at the same dismal conclusion.

"I heard about the attempt on your life the other day at the hotel. I am pleased you were able to stop the assailant," Buryshkin said.

Here we go.

"The assassin was Boris Kaminsky," Alex said.

"Ah, yes. I also hear he suffered an *accident* on the way to the police station. Does that news trouble you, Parkin?"

"No," Alex said. "Not after what he did to my sister."

Buryshkin nodded. "As I thought. Do you have any notion of who he was working for?"

"We thought it was you," Morgan said, dropping a teaspoon of honey in her tea.

Jesus. Was she trying to get them killed even quicker?

"*Nyet*," the man replied, shaking his head. "I am *not* a fool. I tried to have your boss killed once, and failed. I learned that he is a *very* dangerous man to cross."

The Russian feared Crispin? *Well, hell.*

"Yet you told Vasily to have me scout Wilder's security arrangements."

"A wise man always knows his enemies," Buryshkin replied.

Before Alex could follow up, two uniformed maids bearing serving trays appeared, and breakfast was laid before them in all its glory. If he was going to die, it might as well be on a full stomach.

Over the next few minutes, plates were loaded with food and they savored the meal.

"This sausage is very good," Morgan said, sounding surprisingly pleasant. "Do you have it specially made?"

"Yes, I do," Buryshkin said, clearly pleased at the praise.

It was like having breakfast in Wonderland, except the March Hare was a Russian mobster and Alice was fighting not to slit his throat. Alex kept waiting for the Mad Hatter to show up.

Speaking of which . . .

"Will your daughter be joining us?" he asked, his voice as smooth as the honey on the table.

The Russian's face went unreadable. "Anya is not here at the moment."

"Ah, I see. I met her recently in the city. She gave me this," he said, pointing toward the healing wound on his neck. "Can't say I appreciated it."

Buryshkin shrugged. "She has, how do you say it? Issues?"

Morgan choked and then took a hasty sip of her tea. "A few, maybe."

Time to get down to it.

"So, this is very kind of you," Alex said, gesturing at the

meal. "But why are we here? Or at least, why is Morgan here? I can understand you wanting to talk to me."

"He has told you of our agreement, then?" Buryshkin asked Morgan.

"We figured you'd try something like that." She gave Alex a tight smile. "If he betrays us, he's dead."

That sounded a little too honest.

Buryshkin smiled. "You are a she-wolf. I think that is why I respect you."

"If you respected me that much, you wouldn't have had your daughter sleep with my husband."

What are you doing?

"It was purely a business arrangement," Buryshkin replied. "Such things happen."

"A mere business arrangement that ended with him committing suicide and costing me my job at the FBI. Can't say I'll ever forgive you for that."

"I would be troubled if you did."

"Okay, now that we've established all that," Alex said, cutting in, "Really, why are we here?"

Buryshkin wiped his lips with a napkin. "I wished to ask about my nephew, Grigori. I am concerned about him."

"He looked well when I left prison."

"Since then, there have been rumors that his life is in danger. I am trying to learn who would dare do such a thing."

Alex saw Morgan tense, and he feared she was about to tell Buryshkin exactly who might be doing such a thing. His mind scrambled for a safe way through this minefield.

"I have some thoughts on that. Perhaps we could institute a . . . trade?"

"It could be said that you already owe me your life."

"Possibly, except you were the reason I ended up in prison in the first place."

"Ah, yes. Your partner, Mr. Simms. He did only as I asked."

So it was Dennis. Somehow his gut had always known that.

"Did you tell him to sleep with my wife?"

"No, that was of his own volition," Buryshkin replied,

pushing away his empty plate. "What is this trade you propose?"

"You have a new load of cocaine in the city, some of which is poisoned. It's killing people, and that makes the DEA go ballistic. You don't need that kind of heat."

Buryshkin leaned back in his chair, frowning. "You are saying the load is poisoned. How?"

He doesn't know.

"Strychnine. We've got bodies stacking up in the morgue, and a near miss with a judge's daughter. This is only going to escalate, and you'll find the feds on your doorstep, taking your operation apart brick by brick. It'd be best if you ditched the shipment before that happens."

Buryshkin's right eyelid twitched. He was gripping one of the knives tightly in his hand. As if realizing what he was doing, he set it down. After a quick look at Ruslan, he eyed Alex.

"I am not pleased to hear about the strychnine, but sometimes that happens. Yet you are suggesting that I should give up a product worth many millions of dollars, in trade for information?" he asked, his tone less social now.

"Yes."

"Not possible."

"How about some middle ground: You test the coke and get rid of the stuff that is cut with strychnine. The rest, well . . . you use as you see fit," Alex said.

"No!" Morgan snapped. "That stuff can't get to the streets."

"It's already there, and it'll keep being sold if we don't come to an arrangement," Alex said. "At least this way we can keep more people from being poisoned."

"I can't agree to this," she said.

"You don't have to. This is my deal, not yours."

"If I agree to do this, what will you give me in return?" Buryshkin asked.

"I'll bring you whoever plans to kill your nephew and is trying to destroy your operation," Alex said.

Morgan's mouth dropped open.

"You think you know who this is?" Buryshkin asked.

He really doesn't see it. He's totally blind when it comes to his daughter. Grigori had said as much.

"I believe I do. I need to verify some things first. I don't want to accuse an innocent person."

"If you are not able to find this person?" the mobster asked.

"No harm, no foul, as we say here in the States," Alex replied. "You still have the coke."

From his position nearby, Ruslan appeared shell-shocked. Had he not known about the threat to Grigori's life? Or if he had, maybe he'd been wise enough not to suggest that this man's daughter was trying to destroy them all.

Buryshkin thought about Alex's offer while he drank another cup of coffee. To Alex's left, Morgan sat ramrod straight in her chair.

"You're insane," she whispered.

"Maybe."

The Russian roused from his thoughts. "We have a deal," he said. "You give me a name, I will ensure the product that reaches the streets is not poisoned. At least, no more than usual. But I want absolute proof of the traitor's actions."

"Alex," Morgan said, "Crispin will never go for this."

"Then we won't tell him, will we?"

"You know it doesn't work that way."

He ignored her, turning back to Buryshkin. "I'll make sure you have proof. You promise the person I give you will never hurt anyone again?"

"*Da.*" He extended his broad hand across the table. "We have a deal?"

Somewhere in hell, the devil was smiling.

"Yes, we have a deal." Alex shook the man's hand.

"God," Morgan moaned. "This won't work."

"Yes, it will." *Because we have no other choice now.*

Right before they left, Alex had a private conversation with Buryshkin, out of Morgan's hearing, conducted with their backs to her.

Ruslan kept looking at them, then at her, his brow furrowed. "Is your Mr. Parkin usually so reckless?"

"Yeah, he can be that way. This is a crazy deal," she said.

"Yes, however, Mr. Buryshkin loves his nephew very much."

But does he love his daughter more?

After Alex executed another handshake with the Russian crime boss, they were escorted to the car.

"What the hell was that all about?" she demanded.

"Just firming up the details of our agreement."

How could he even think about allowing that much dope to hit the market, even if it was *just* cocaine? It made her wonder where Alex's loyalties lay. Had this all been a clever ruse? Had he been playing both her and Veritas all along? No way in hell was Buryshkin going to buy that his sweet, demented little daughter was gutting his empire, one operative at a time.

It fell to Vasily and the driver to escort them away from the house, except this time they didn't warrant a second escort car.

When they reached the highway, Morgan leaned closer to Alex. "Do you have a freakin' death wish?"

"No. I don't owe Buryshkin a thing, but I do owe a friend in prison. If it gets the bad dope off the streets, win-win."

Not if you die, you moron.

Morgan understood loyalty—she was that way with Crispin. She would do anything to save his life, because, in his own way, he'd saved hers. But to make such a deal with the Russian . . .

She closed her eyes, desperately looking for some reason this might actually work.

"We'll get it done," Alex said. Then he leaned back and closed his eyes. One of the Russians was on the phone, talking to someone in a clipped tone. Once the call ended, he said something to the driver, who shot a quick glance over the seats at them. Then they began to talk to one another in a lowered tone.

Morgan's skin twitched. Something felt wrong. "Alex?"

"Just stay cool, no matter what happens," he said.

They headed north and half an hour later, they turned onto a side road, one that led toward the water. When the car stopped, men approached from both sides. Morgan was hauled out at gunpoint, as well as Alex. Something had changed between Buryshkin's place and here. Had the crime boss decided to renege on their deal?

Alex's expression remained neutral as he studied an approaching figure: the one woman Morgan would gladly kill if she ever had a chance.

"Anya!" Alex called out. "Long time no see. How goes it?" *He knew she was going to be here.*

Had that been what the Russians were talking about on the drive over? But why would Buryshkin send them here? *Maybe he didn't.* That would mean that this woman had her own people buried inside his organization. That made sense. Though Anya was reportedly crazy, she was cunning. Perhaps even more cunning than her dear old dad.

Morgan had only seen her once before—she'd had the balls to come to Wayne's graveside service—but hadn't known who Anya was until later. Schooled in both Moscow and Paris, she'd been married, and was now a widow. Rumor had it that she'd killed her husband, and Daddy had hushed it all up. That was all Veritas knew, other than the fact that more than one person claimed she was a psychopath.

Anya walked up to Vasily and spoke with him briefly, keeping her voice low. Her eyes flicked to Alex, then Morgan.

"Thank you. I have no further need of your services," she said.

Vasily returned to the car, and as the driver began to back up, Anya gestured to one of her men. He took a position in front of the vehicle, raised his AK-47, and sprayed it with gunfire before the two occupants could react. Morgan looked away, her heart lurching.

Once the gunfire ceased and the stench of fresh blood rose, Alex sighed. "So how are you going to spin that with your father? He's going to know that you killed them."

"No, he will believe that it was Veritas's doing. I will make sure of that."

She wants a war between Crispin and her old man.

It was a slick move; Veritas would destroy Buryshkin's organization, while she set up her own little mob. But in the long run, it wouldn't work even if Alex had to kill this bitch himself.

I could save Wilder the trouble.

"Why Vasily? What'd he do to piss you off?" Alex asked.

"He was thinking of double-crossing me. Now he won't."

Morgan turned her back on the bullet-ridden car as Buryshkin's daughter circled her like a shark.

"You are the lawyer's wife," Anya said. "The one who could not keep him in her bed." She ran a hand down Morgan's cheek, letting her nails dig into the flesh. "Your husband, he did not have that problem with me. He begged to fuck me."

Morgan didn't hesitate, her fist landing a vicious blow to the woman's chin. Anya collapsed to the ground, blood running down her face. As she struggled to her feet, she screamed in Russian. Curiously, none of Anya's men had stepped in to help her.

They hate her as much as I do.

"Oh, you shouldn't have done that," Alex said, shaking his head. "But damn, that was sweet."

It was, even if it got her dead.

Anya pulled a switchblade and waved it in front of Morgan. "I will cut out your heart."

"And that's supposed to frighten me?" Morgan asked. Because it didn't. Anya's madness was a weakness, and she was eager to exploit it.

Alex stepped in between them.

"Get out of the way!" the crazy woman snarled.

"Really? A cat fight?" He looked at Anya, jutting a thumb toward Morgan. "Why mess with her? She's a waste of time. I would think you'd be too busy trying to have Grigori killed."

Anya's fury faded just as quickly as it had appeared. "Don't worry. He will be dead soon, as well as his . . . lover." She spat at the thought. "You sided with him. That was a mistake."

"I sided with whoever would keep me alive in prison. That happened to be Grigori. I didn't see your ass offering to help me."

"Get out of my way, Alex. This bitch is mine," Morgan demanded, shoving him.

"Not this time, babe," he said, keeping his back to her. *You arrogant bastard.*

His distraction had worked: The woman had zeroed in on him now, as if Morgan didn't exist. She cursed him out, but neither of them paid her any attention.

"My father is a fool. He has no notion of what I have done," Anya explained.

"Like poisoning the cocaine and killing Dimitri?" Alex asked.

"*Da.* We only poison some of the packages, just enough. My father will be blamed. And Dimitri? He was working for Wilder," she said, turning her predatory eyes on Morgan now. "He deserved to die."

"That's why you left his body in the warehouse? So the blame would fall on your father?" Alex asked.

"Of course," she said, folding the switchblade and tucking it away.

"You sent Boris after my sister. Had him kill her cat."

"You needed to be sent a message, and he wanted her as his whore. So I let him have her. She was not giving him proper respect, so he killed something she loved. Why not? She is of no concern."

Alex growled under his breath.

"Except I got in the way," Morgan said.

Anya looked past Alex to her. "That was my mistake. I should have sent two men, not just one. Then you would have died when they were through with you and the girl."

Morgan buried the shiver. "Why do you hate Grigori so much?"

"He is *pee-da-rahss.*" Anya spat again, as if being homosexual was a sickness. Then she smiled, and a feral light came to her eyes. When she issued a series of orders in

Russian, Alex tensed.

"I want their deaths on video. Every minute. Every scream. That way, I can enjoy it whenever I am bored."

She walked up to him now, pushing at his chest with a finger. "You thought to betray me to my father. You do not understand—he is dead man walking. Now so are you."

She whirled away. "Get them out of here. The alligators need feeding."

"Anya," Alex said, "you don't want to do this."

"Do what you wish to either of them." Her eyes tracked back to Morgan. "*Anything* . . . you wish. Make sure I get the video." She smiled now. "I will send a copy to Wilder. Perhaps even put it on the internet for all to see. People pay for those kind of things, you know? You could be making me money for years after you are dead."

Anya's laugh engulfed them now, a brittle sound that reminded Morgan of expensive glass shattering on tile. The sound of a broken mind that no longer harbored any sanity.

God help us.

Chapter Twenty-Two

There were three guards on the boat as it headed into the bayou for what promised to be a one-way trip, at least for Alex and Morgan. One of the Russians was drinking, and of course, it wasn't tea. He had a video camera set up on a tripod, but had yet to begin recording. The quality of that video wasn't going to be Academy Award worthy, but Alex doubted that the goon's crazy boss would care. The thought that Crispin or his sister would ever see this snuff film made him sick.

The trio talked back and forth about what they intended to do to both of them, especially Morgan. After some knife work on Alex, he was going overboard first, so they wouldn't have to worry about him interfering with their plans for his companion. From the worry on her face, she'd guessed most of the conversation as well, though she did not speak the language. The seething fire in her eyes was reserved for him.

They sat huddled on the deck, backs against the starboard side of the boat.

"Sorry," he murmured, hoping she could hear him over the boat's engine and that the others could not.

"For selling us out to Buryshkin?"

He knew she'd be furious, but still, her words felt like acid dripping on his skin.

"I didn't sell your people out to Buryshkin. And I'm sorry for what I said at the camp."

"Save it. You can plead your case to the devil. My bet is that you'll be meeting up with him soon enough."

The Russians were sharing jokes and the bottle. With their attention diverted, now was the time.

"I was wrong to put the blame on you. The problem was between Wayne and me. I said things I never should have said. I am truly sorry."

No reply.

He'd tried. "My phone recorded what Anya said about her father and Grigori. I'd hoped to send the recording to Buryshkin and let her own words hang her, rather than us, but it's unlikely they're going to let me do that."

Morgan turned away, her cheeks red again. "I believed in you. I"—she lowered her voice—"slept with you. How the hell can I trust you now?"

"You have to. I'll do everything I can to keep you safe, but this isn't looking good."

Her eyes met his now. "Yeah, I don't need to speak Russian to know what they've got in mind."

"Then we need to make sure they don't get a chance to hurt you. When it's time, I'll ask for one last kiss. Be sure to go along with it so I can get my phone to you."

Their phones had been returned to them when they left Buryshkin's and his was in the front pocket of his jeans. There was no way he could pull it out now, or they'd know something was up. Frankly, he'd been surprised they'd been allowed to keep them. Yet another indication that Anya wasn't as smart as her father.

"You know there's no way they're leaving me alive after they're done with me," Morgan said. "I'll be over the side of the boat, just like you."

"You have to stay alive. I'm going to try to give you a chance to survive. Take it, no matter what happens to me, okay?"

Morgan grimaced, then looked away. "Alex . . . " She blinked away tears. "I . . . "

His attention went back to the men and what they were saying. He couldn't catch all of it, not with the engine's drone, but one of them was bitching about how, once they were done with this, he still had to ferry a load of coke to New Orleans tonight. Which meant Veritas had been wrong: The shipment wasn't hidden in the city. Alex quietly relayed what he'd learned to Morgan. She frowned, but nodded.

"Hey!" he called out. "Got anything to drink on this garbage scow?"

One of the Russians laughed, the one not drinking. The other two didn't seem to understand, which led Alex to believe they didn't speak English. The guy piloting the boat gestured for his buddy, who ignored Alex. Instead he staggered over to Morgan and offered her the bottle.

She eyed him, then took it. A swift swig, and it came back to him. Alex waited for her to react, but she didn't. Like she drank straight vodka every day.

Okay, then. His respect for her edged up another notch.

The tipsy Russian accepted the bottle, then gestured for Morgan to come to him. As she rose to her feet, the man leered, his eyes raking down her body. Alex's blood began to boil.

Fortunately, she didn't understand the names he was calling her, or she would have ripped off his balls. As she leaned into the guy, letting him grope her, no doubt trying to find just the right moment to cripple him, the boat's motor cut out.

"*My zdes,*" the pilot said. *We are here.*

Morgan's guard grabbed her arm and pulled her out of the way. She looked at Alex, panicked.

Let her get out of this alive and unhurt. That's all I ask.

The pilot gestured to him, like he was supposed to be a good little boy and let them kill him without a fight.

"Ah, no. I don't think so. Not my kind of thing. I'm allergic to drowning."

The guy laughed, then pulled a gun. "You first!" he ordered, gesturing toward the rear of the boat. The third Russian stood watch, hands on his hips.

Alex rose slowly, buying time. "Can't I give the ice babe a kiss goodbye?" he asked.

When that was translated, it provoked laughter, and he was shoved toward Morgan. He pulled her out of her guard's grip, then he kissed her like it would be the last one they ever shared. His blood sang, bringing back vivid memories of their only night together. How that might be all they'd ever have.

"Stay alive, no matter what," he whispered in her ear as he pushed his phone into her front jeans pocket. "I'm sorry we didn't have more time. You are the most amazing woman I have ever met."

As her eyes widened, Alex pushed her away.

"No, still cold as a dead fish," he announced, playing to his audience. "I'd just toss her overboard. You'll be wasting your time."

More laughter, along with crude suggestions of how to warm her up. Using their distraction as a weakness, Alex dove at the closest guard, ramming him to the deck. His element of surprise ended quickly as the other guard waded in. They battered at him until he fell to his knees. Swearing, the pilot of the boat encased him in a heavy log chain, winding it around him like a spider would to secure a helpless fly. Alex struggled, but had no leverage.

When he looked up, blinking, he found Morgan on her knees as well, a gun aimed at the back of her head. Her eyes were wild with fear and a trickle blood ran down the side of her face. She'd fought and lost as well.

Alex opened his mouth to say something, anything, but a blow silenced him. He tried to fight, but his movements were uncoordinated with the heavy chain, his balance off. He felt his legs bump the side of the boat.

The second guard was in his face now, waving a knife. It appeared they were going to carve on him, then toss him overboard. The pilot bellowed something, and abruptly, the man backed off, sheathing the blade. Instead he headed for the video camera. The time had come, and Alex looked into Morgan's deep, green eyes one last time.

"Wish I'd met you years before," he said. Then he rammed into the pilot, managing to get his hand around the man's throat, and they toppled overboard.

"Alex!"

As he sank into the murky water with his captor, he thought of Morgan and prayed that he'd given her a fighting chance. It was his final gesture to a woman he could have loved if given more time.

Even before the beefier of the two guards shouted for help to rescue their friend, Morgan was on her feet. She rammed her elbow into her captor's breastbone. As he reeled back, she brought his arm down on her leg, snapping the wrist, the gun dropping as he shrieked in agony. Still, he came back at her with a knife from his boot. Waving it around, he cursed her in his own language, but he was at a disadvantage because she'd broken his dominant hand.

Morgan skittered backward, grabbed the gun, then put two slugs in the center of his chest. The man stared at her in stark surprise. He stumbled a few steps, then slumped against the side of the boat, blood covering his shirt.

"You're outta here," she said, kicking him overboard, generating a huge splash.

She'd barely turned when the man who'd been manning the video camera tackled her, and she went down hard. As he clawed for the weapon, she kneed him in the chin. Two shots echoed in the midmorning air, and the final Russian sank onto the deck, dead.

Her head dizzy from the blow it'd taken, Morgan forced herself to her feet. "Alex." She sprinted to the rear of the boat. The chain that was imprisoning him was attached to a cleat on the stern. Apparently they used it over and over, victim after victim.

Maybe he still had a chance.

Setting the gun aside, Morgan tugged on the chain, but it didn't move. She tried again, but realized the metal was too wet for her to get a good grip. She stripped off her T-shirt, wrapped it around the chain, and this time she was able to pull it up a few links.

Putting every bit of strength she had into the effort, she kept hauling away, praying as each link dug into the gunwale. Some distance away from the boat, a face surfaced, the pilot who'd gone overboard with Alex. He splashed frantically, trying to swim to safety. Suddenly he disappeared underwater, and when he came back up, his voice erupted in a bloodcurdling scream.

An alligator surfaced next to him, its muzzle bloody.

"Oh Jesus, no!" Morgan kept hauling, her muscles burning and shaking. "Come on, Alex! Help me!"

A patch of brown hair appeared on the surface. She kept pulling, her hands cramping, bloodstained now. Finally his face appeared, then his shoulders. As she grabbed onto his shoulders and pulled him up, her back convulsing, she feared she was too late.

Finally, both of them flopped onto the deck in a tangle of chains. Her hands were numb, but she climbed to her knees and rolled him over to his side.

He was unresponsive, even as she shook him. Rolling him back over, Morgan whacked him hard in the center of the back. She repeated it, crying now. "Come on, damn you, don't give up!"

The third blow caused a thick cough, and then Alex gasped for air. He spewed water onto the deck. Then, finally, he opened his eyes.

"Oh God, yes!" she said.

Her joy was cut short by a scream.

"Don't let him—" Alex began, but was cut off by a bout of coughing.

Morgan understood. She picked up the gun and walked to the back of the boat where the Russian flailed in the water, begging God for mercy as two alligators fought over him.

A single bullet in the forehead ended his torment.

Alex heard the shot, then no more screams. For a time, he'd thought those screams were coming from him, but that couldn't be right. He'd been under the water for so long, even felt one of the gators bump him, no doubt trying to figure out if he was food. Instead it had gone after the other man, the one who had panicked and was not covered in chains. But there wasn't only one of the beasts down there. In time, one of the others would have come for him.

Now he lay shaking on the deck, still trussed in chains. The fact that he was alive meant Morgan had overpowered two burly Russians and saved his stupid ass.

A damned miracle.

She knelt next to him in a black bra and jeans, stripping off the chains, loop by loop. Once they were gone, she smiled down at him, tears of relief in her eyes.

"Hey. Look at you. You're still alive."

"Yeah. Go me!" he said, then coughed again. His mouth tasted like the bayou, a mix of dirty water, fish crap, and whatever else. He'd be lucky not to die from some hideous disease.

Using herself as a brace, she helped him sit up against the side of the boat. A rough blanket went around him, and despite the fact that it was hotter than hell, it felt good. Then she was back with a bottle of water. It proved impossible for her to open, so she put her T-shirt around the cap and twisted it. When she held out the bottle to him, he saw blood on her hands. Her blood.

A swig of the water helped him wash out his mouth, and he spat it to the side. Then he took a long drink, savoring every swallow. When he was done, he gestured for her to spread her hands. Over her protests, he washed away the blood and found cuts and blisters forming. It had to hurt like hell.

"Jesus, Morgan, what happened?" he asked.

"The chain," she said. "It kept slipping." And ripping her skin, link by link. "My T-shirt saved your life."

No, you did. "Thank . . . you . . . " he whispered.

She left him alone for a time, and he took cautious breaths, which determined that his ribs were not broken, probably just bruised. There was no reason for him to still be alive, other than Morgan being too stubborn to let him go to his grave.

She settled next to him now, another bottle of water in hand. He took it from her and opened it, then handed it back over. Her smile told him he appreciated the gesture.

"No boat keys. I'm guessing they're in some gator's belly by now," she reported.

"My phone?"

She tugged it out of her jeans and waggled it at him. He closed his eyes and listened as she called Sanjay and was patched into Crispin. Her voice was in control, not a hint of the panic he'd heard as he struggled to take that first breath only a few minutes ago.

"Thanks. I'll tell him." She ended the call and set the phone next to her. "They're sending Neil to get us. He's out here somewhere. They'll use the phone's GPS to geo-locate our boat."

"Miri still with him?" She nodded. "My sister is going to"—he coughed—"lose it when she sees us."

"Probably." She laid her head on his shoulder and wrapped her arms around him. "Thank you for not dying."

He had no proper reply. She could have let him drown, let him be torn apart and stuffed in some gator's larder. It'd be an easy tale to spin to her boss—sorry, couldn't save the ex-con. Shit happens.

But she hadn't. Morgan had risked her life, cut up her hands pulling him to safety. He could hear her now, whispering over and over that it would be okay. Trying to convince herself as much as him.

Looking back at his life, frame by frame, woman by woman, he'd never expected to find one like this. What he felt for her—was that love? He didn't know. He swore he'd forgotten what that word meant.

But now as she held him as close as her own skin, and he began to wonder if that was what fate had in store for him. For them. Because he knew, no matter what it took, he would never let anyone hurt her.

Not even himself.

Chapter Twenty-Three

Once he'd rested, Alex insisted on typing out the e-mail to Vladimir Buryshkin. He forwarded the audio recording of the man's daughter telling Alex how she had poisoned the coke and planned to kill Grigori. How she was going to get revenge against the father she hated.

"Take that, asshole," he murmured. "You harbor a snake, you get bit."

"Buryshkin won't believe it. He'll come after you instead," Morgan said, standing now.

"Probably, but I kept my part of the bargain. Now it's all on his head."

"I shut off the video camera and erased the footage. I really wanted to send it to Anya, just to piss her off."

He laughed. "I can get behind that."

The thrum of a boat engine had her picking up the gun.

"Trouble?" Alex asked.

Morgan squinted into the distance. "No. Our ride's here." Then she looked down at her bra, and sighed.

"Here. Can't have you flashing Iceman," he said, cautiously stripping off his T-shirt in pained motions. As she pulled it on, she noticed the red marks on his chest, deep ruts and bruises from the chain's links.

Her stomach damn near emptied itself.

Alex was checking them out as well. "Like I said, my sister is really going to freak."

"You want your shirt back?"

"No. I want you covered. No guy sees you in your bra but me."

She knelt next to him. "That's pretty Neanderthal, Parkin."

He grinned. "That's how I roll." His hand touched her cheek. "Can we start over? Before what I said at the camp?"

"I'm not sure."

"I was an asshole. I took all my anger out on you, and that wasn't right."

"But you *were* right in some ways. I didn't tell you about who I was right up front, and Wayne wasn't there for you when you needed him the most."

"Neither was my wife, so there was a lot of that going around. None of that was your fault. Promise we'll talk, once this is all over?"

Morgan gave him a tentative nod, then went to welcome their rescuers. She knew she looked pretty scary, with bruises on her arms, her hair in a tangle. She tried to push it out of her face and failed. Her back felt like it had been ripped apart and glued back together wrong. A visit to a chiropractor was in her future, along with some strong drugs. She could only imagine what Alex felt like.

The yacht was within a few feet of their boat when Miri went sailing over the side and onto the deck with an ease that said she'd spent time on the water.

"Alex?" she cried out, and took off toward her brother. As she flew by, Morgan noticed that she'd found a way to comb her hair to hide her injury. In fact, she looked good. Certainly better than her sibling at the moment.

Morgan found herself staring up at Iceman. Knowing Neil never missed anything, she figured he'd already noted that the shirt she was wearing was too big to be hers, that she held her hands by her side as if they hurt, and that there was a large patch of dried blood on the deck near where she stood.

"Bad?" he asked.

She nodded. "Nearly lost him," she said, keeping her voice low.

"You hurt?"

"Yeah. My head, hands, and back. Alex might have a cracked rib and water aspiration, I can't tell."

Neil looked at the brother-sister reunion with a concerned expression. Miri was crying while giving Alex hell for being injured.

"You and she doing okay?" Morgan asked.

"Yeah. She's damned tough."

Again, high praise. "Careful, she'll get under that thick skin of yours."

Neil shook his head, as if that were impossible, then tied off the boats so they wouldn't drift apart. He landed lightly on the smaller boat's deck, then noticed the video camera and tripod.

"Anya wanted a memento of the event," Morgan said.

Neil's eyes went stone cold. "So she's as fucked up as they say?"

"Worse."

With a nod, he headed for the wheelhouse.

"What are you looking for?" she asked.

"Charts. Anything that our boss might find of interest."

Leave it to an ex-SEAL to think of those kinds of things.

A short time later, Alex was on Veritas's boat, making his way through the kitchen toward the master bedroom. His sister was by his side, Morgan following behind.

"I need a shower," he said. "I smell like hell."

"No worse than normal," Miri said, joking.

"A shower, some sleep, then food. In that order," he said, his tone telling Morgan that he wasn't going to be deterred.

"You're not steady on your feet yet. You'll faint and bash your head," Miri warned.

"I'm taking a shower. You can stand in there and watch me get clean, or back off."

"Naked brother bits are not something I want to see," she replied, shaking her head. "Get some sleep and then maybe—"

"Morgan?" Alex called out.

She knew what he wanted, and that it would out their relationship to the others.

She sighed. "Okay, I'll make sure you don't kill yourself in the shower."

Miri slowly turned toward her, eyes widening as it dawned

on her what that meant.

"Yes, we're sleeping together," Alex said. "Which means she can keep an eye on my bits so you don't have to."

Miri colored. "Ah . . . okay, that's good." She stepped back as Morgan took over her duties.

"Thanks, Monkey," Alex said solemnly.

She shook her head at him again, dropped a kiss on his cheek, and left them behind.

Alex looked at Morgan now. "Sorry about that. I should have asked if you were okay with that announcement."

"You want a shower, and we're both adults. No big deal."

"Will it get you in trouble with your boss?"

"No. Neil won't say a word to him. Come on, let's get you cleaned up."

The shower didn't last long because Alex'd faded fast, just as his sister had predicted. While he washed, she cleaned her hands in the bathroom sink, letting the sound of the running water muffle her curses as she scrubbed the rust and crap out of the wounds. He wanted to dress them, but she refused, insisting that Neil would take care of her.

"It's more important that you get some rest." Nearly dying was a tiring business. She knew that from experience.

Morgan replaced the strips on his neck and put some ointment on the places on his chest where the chain had abraded the skin. Others needed a bandage. All the while, he fussed about her injured hands and whether she should get a tetanus shot. She reassured him that she was up to date on her vaccinations, but he continued to worry.

He kept mumbling until his eyes closed and his breath leveled out. She smoothed back his hair and then kissed him gently. But for sheer luck, she'd almost lost him today.

Alex woke when Morgan slid into bed next to him. He was pleased to see that her hands were properly bandaged. She'd showered, and smelled of soap and shampoo. Now, after a nap, his body told him it wanted to know hers a lot better.

Situation normal.

Other than the fact that he'd damned near drowned and his ribs ached like he'd been worked over by a methed-up biker gang.

"Are you having any problems breathing?" she asked.

"Nope, I'm okay."

"Let me know if you do. You inhaled some water, and that's not good."

"I'll be okay." He traced her lips with his finger. "Are we better now? The two of us?"

She looked away for a moment. "I . . . understand why you were so angry."

"Being angry is one thing. Being an asshole? Not good. I am truly sorry."

Morgan nodded in reply. Then her eyes met his, and he saw the spark in them.

She must have read his mind. "No make-up sex. Not now. You need to sleep."

Alex wanted to argue, but she was right. He was exhausted. "Rain check?" he murmured.

"A rain check is a possibility. Now sleep, Parkin."

Alex nestled her against his body, smelling the scent of clean hair, the scent that was this woman. She was alive, and that meant everything.

Morgan woke about an hour later, feeling better. Part of it was the anti-inflammatory drugs she'd taken, which had reduced her aches a notch. Most of it was that Alex was still alive.

She'd forgiven him. It was hard not to, his apology was so sincere. Lord knew he had enough to be angry about. But if they stayed together as a couple, then what? Her job took her all over the world. Alex wouldn't want to go very far from his sister, at least not until Miri was settled in a new place.

Complications. Those were always the bane of any new relationship. In this case, those complications might shut it down even before it gained any traction.

Quietly, Morgan rose and dressed, aware that the boat was stationary now. Neil had said he'd move it to a new location, away from the Russian's boat. It was only a matter of time before someone checked on why the three goons hadn't returned to home base.

Shutting the bedroom door behind her, she found Miri in the kitchen, making sandwiches. On the deck above them, Neil was doing his watchdog thing. Morgan wondered if the man ever slept.

"Is Alex up yet?" Miri asked.

"No. Still sleeping," Morgan said. That earned her a sidelong glance. "Go on. You can ask about anything you want."

Miri paused in her sandwich assembly. "You're actually shagging my brother?"

Rather than be offended, Morgan grinned, liking her for the "what you see is what you get" attitude. "Yes, I am."

Miri cocked her head in thought. "He's a good guy, but he can be an ass with women he's just screwing for fun. Maybe he'll act different with you."

"He will, or we're history."

Alex's sister smirked. "Oh yeah, he's in trouble now. The man has finally met his match. I am so gonna love this."

Morgan joined in the food-making process, smearing butter on slices of bread and then handing them over, trying not to mess up her bandages.

"You're not like his ex. Alicia was all about herself," Miri said. "Someone who's just in it for themselves wouldn't have come after that perv in the alley. She would have gone back into the bar because it wasn't her fight. You got involved. You got hurt because of me."

Morgan's jaw ached at the memory. The bruise was

slowly turning dark green now and looked pretty ugly without makeup. "I need to have Iceman teach me a few more self-defense moves, like for guys who are *way* bigger than me."

At the mention of the former SEAL, Miri waggled her eyebrows. She checked to make sure the man in question was out of earshot, and then whispered, "He's *totally* hot. Watching him do his one-arm planks just about killed me. This hiding-out gig hasn't been that hard at all, at least when I'm not worrying about Alex."

The sound of feet on the stairs made them snap apart like guilty schoolgirls.

"We need to talk," Neil called down the stairs.

"Okay," Morgan said, knowing that tone meant business.

She and Miri joined him up top. "Any sign of the Russians?"

"No, but there are more boats going by us now. Most of them have one occupant. I've been tracking their transit times, and they're gone for about an hour or so, then they're back. Not nearly enough time to fish."

Morgan's body reminded her that tangling with two big Russian dudes wasn't for wimps. "Unless they're like me," she said, gingerly sinking into a chair. "I can't handle drowning worms for more than about ten minutes."

Neil handed over a pad of paper that sat on a table near the binoculars. Her eyes skimmed down the page and found that he'd listed what looked to be boat registration numbers, the times he'd seen them going out and coming back, and descriptions of the occupants. He'd kept his head in the game.

Unlike me. Her mind kept straying to the guy asleep downstairs.

"Sanjay's checking on the reg numbers to see if they have anything in common," Neil explained. "Something doesn't feel right. It was why I brought the boat back to this location."

"Your gut is rarely wrong," Morgan said, one of the reasons she liked working with him. His instincts had saved her butt more than once.

"Are they like those guys from this morning?" Miri asked.

"No. Sanjay checked out their boat registration numbers and those losers were locals. The Coast Guard has had run-ins with them, since they like to screw with other boaters, at least if they think there's a chance they won't get their asses beaten."

All heads turned as Alex came onto the deck, dressed in a pair of sweatpants and a loose T-shirt. His feet were bare, and he seemed more alert now.

"How's the breathing?" Neil asked.

"Pretty good. Why is everyone worried about that?"

"Secondary drowning. You think you're golden, until you're not. If not treated quickly, you'll die. I lost a buddy that way. Fine, then gone."

"Hell," Alex replied. "No, I'm sore, but okay. If there's any change, I'll let you know immediately." He looked out on the water. "You guys had trouble this morning?"

"Just some morons who didn't understand that 'no, I don't want to party with you' meant just that," Miri replied. "Fortunately, they understood a shotgun up the nose."

Neil wasn't a shotgun type of dude, which meant that Alex's sister must have been the one so armed. Morgan flicked a glance at Iceman. His expression remained neutral, though there was something almost like pride in his gaze.

Was there something cooking between Alex's sis and her bodyguard?

"Glad you guys handled it," Alex said. He leveraged himself into one of the deck chairs. His movements spoke of sincere discomfort, and Morgan made a note to slip him some pain meds later. "Did I hear you say something about more boat traffic?"

Neil nodded. "It happened yesterday afternoon as well. I didn't think much of it, but today I decided to track it because I saw some of the same people. I'm not sure what it means."

"I think I do. One of the Russians taking us out for a swim bitched about how he still had to make a coke run into the city tonight. My guess is that we've been looking for the dope in the wrong places. I think it's out here." He paused to let that sink in, adjusting himself in his chair.

Morgan shot a questioning look at Neil, who shrugged in response.

"If the dope *is* out here," Alex continued, "they're bringing in small loads, a bit at a time. They could hide it in a bait cooler, and no one would be the wiser. Since it's a big shipment, it's either in kilo or pound bricks. That means they need an assembly line to cut, weigh, and bag the stuff before it's ferried into the city."

"Explains why we couldn't find the dope in New Orleans," Morgan said.

"Exactly. So you know," he said, looking at Neil now. "I had a deal in place with old Vlad, but it's pretty much toast now."

"Deal?" Iceman asked, frowning.

Morgan leaned back in the chair, closing her eyes and letting her mind drift while Alex explained the arrangement he'd made. The one that still pissed her off.

"That sounds like something Wilder would do," Neil replied. "Worth the risk, though."

She ground her teeth. Allowing any of that cocaine to reach the streets was unthinkable to her. People like Alex and her boss didn't work in absolutes. They often chose "this is as good as we can get." It bugged her, mostly because it was a real-world solution, while often hers were more like a fairy tale.

Before she could weigh in, Neil's phone rang. He stood and walked away, his back to them out of habit. He promptly returned and consulted the list, making little marks next to a few of the boats' numbers.

"All the same corporation?" He sounded pleased. Anyone else would have smiled at having his instincts validated. Neil took his gut for granted, just like breathing.

There was a short conversation, and the call ended.

He looked up. "Four boats on the list were out for much longer, most likely fishing, and were registered to individual owners. Six out of the ten boats are owned by the same company, and they were the ones that returned within an hour. As was the boat with the dead Russians."

"Which company owns them?" Morgan asked.

"New Doma Enterprises. They also have warehouses in New Orleans, including the one where you found the bodies."

Alex smiled. "We got him! *Doma* is Russian for home. New Home Enterprises."

"If the dope is out here, how do we find it?" Miri asked, gesturing toward the water. "There are so many places it could be hidden."

"Actually, the couriers helped us out there," Alex said. "Take the transit times of those six boats, divide the total in half, add about five minutes for loading, another five minutes for bullshitting back and forth, and that will narrow the area down considerably." Neil was nodding even before Alex finished. "You got a chart of this part of the bayou, Iceman?"

The man's mouth thinned, as if Alex had just insulted him, and he headed into the wheelhouse to retrieve one.

"If we call the DEA into this and we're wrong, there will be hell to pay," Morgan warned.

"Sometimes you just need to unzip your fly and pray to God everyone applauds the view," Alex said. "In short, you gotta take risks."

Miri snickered. "You go, bro."

"Don't encourage him," Morgan said. "He's insufferable enough as it is."

"Don't I know it," his sister replied.

He raised an eyebrow. "Runs in the family."

That earned him a middle finger from his sibling.

Once Neil had the map, they retreated to a pop-up table on the deck. As Miri brought up plates loaded with sandwiches and Morgan delivered bowls full of tomato soup, the guys worked out travel distances and times, based on the size of the boat motors. By the time they'd all chowed down, they'd come up with two possible locations for a floating drugstore.

"I'm thinking here is where we need to check first," Neil said, pointing at the map. "That's *not* where I'd locate the boat, but then, these guys aren't special-forces trained."

"Reverse psychology, huh?" Alex said.

"Most times, your enemy is not as smart as you are."

"What if they're at a camp instead?" Miri asked, pouring more cola into her glass.

"Might be, but I'm willing to bet it's on a boat," Alex said. "One that can move fast in case the Coast Guard or the DEA comes after it."

"Or one that isn't that fast, but can easily be destroyed," Neil added.

Alex blinked. "Good point. I hadn't thought of that."

"So what keeps these guys from just taking off once you find them?" Miri asked.

"Boats aren't a problem," Neil said, rising from the table. "They're vulnerable to all sorts of malfunctions. I'll rig something up." He vanished to the front of their boat. As Morgan finished off her lunch, strange sounds began, like Neil was hauling something around.

"What's he doing?" Miri asked.

"Going full-metal SEAL. It's a sight to see," she replied.

"Meaning?"

"Meaning he's getting the inflatable Zodiac ready so he can do some recon work. He'll probably rig up a few C-4 charges to disable the Russian's boats."

"C-4?" Alex said, nearly choking on his drink. "He has explosives on *this* boat?"

"Sure. Iceman never leaves home without them, or his tactical knife. It'd be like me going out without my lipstick or my gun."

He blinked in astonishment, sharing a look of surprise with his sister.

Morgan laughed. "Welcome to the big leagues, dude," she said, patting his shoulder. "Do your best to keep up."

Chapter Twenty-Four

The plan was surprisingly straightforward: Alex and Neil would take the Zodiac farther into the bayou in hopes of scouting the position of the "mothership," as they'd taken to calling it. Once they had an idea of where to set up surveillance, Morgan and Miri would position the bigger boat to keep an eye on incoming traffic. That way, if trouble showed up, they could give the guys a warning.

The part of the plan that Alex didn't like was leaving Morgan and Miri on their own. It was completely irrational. Morgan had saved his life multiple times by now, and more important, had proved she could watch out for his sister. Still, they were the two women he cared most about in this world and he couldn't stop worrying.

After an hour of preparation, he and Neil were dressed like fishermen, rods and a bait box in plain sight as they headed toward their destination. Under a tarp was his companion's scuba equipment and weapons, along with the explosives. Apparently the reconnoitering would involve underwater work as well.

Alex's mind circled back to the women. "I don't like leaving them alone," he said, just like he'd said at least two times before.

"Morgan's lethal, and your sister can get seriously hardass if she needs to be. She proved that this morning."

"What happened with those guys?" Alex asked.

"It was four dudes in a couple Jon boats. They saw your sister first, alone, so they made for us like we were a cold beer in a hot desert. I suggested Miri go below. She did, and she returned with a pump-action shotgun and a box of cartridges."

"Damn."

"Yeah. One of the boats went to the port side, the other to starboard. Classic boarding maneuver," Neil said, steering them around a floating log. "Miri was on port. The guy got his hands on the gunwale and found himself facing a shotgun. She'd racked the slide before he tried to climb in, and the tango backed off real quick. Especially after she told him she was going to take his fucking head off if he tried to get on board."

Alex laughed. "You know, I was so worried about that girl all those years, and she's . . . awesome. Better than I hoped."

"She's tough. She must have gone through some bad shit to get that way, though."

That made Alex sober. "She did, but she never told me about any of it, even when I asked. Miri ran away for a while, lived on the streets. Had to have been hell for her."

"Your family didn't take care of her?" Neil asked, his voice hard now.

"My sister and my ex-wife hated each other, so Miri went to live with our mom's sister and her husband. They couldn't deal with her. She took off twice, I think. Scared the hell out of me, because there was nothing I could do to help her," Alex said.

"Now you can," Neil said. "That's all that matters."

Alex sucked in a deep breath, ignoring the ache in his chest. "Yeah, that's all that matters."

He turned his attention back to the bayou around them. When he and Morgan were headed toward their graves this morning, there was nothing pretty about the place. Now that it wasn't trying to kill him, he rather liked what he saw.

Gray-green Spanish moss draped from the trees and was reflected in the placid water. Occasionally, a dock would jut out, leading to a run-down camp. One constant was the gators, either sunning themselves on the bank or gliding through the water.

"Damned things," Alex said, remembering all too well his too-close encounter with the prehistoric beasts.

"Just efficient hunters," Neil replied.

"Like you?" he asked, before he had the good sense to edit his mouth.

The man didn't appear offended. "Exactly like me."

"What made you become a SEAL?"

"Because I wanted to make things right in a world that's so messed up, it can't help itself."

Alex nodded. "Same with me. I had a friend who was one of you guys. Avi told me a couple of totally wacky stories, the only missions he could actually talk about."

"Avi Brinkman?"

"Yeah. You know him?"

"I met him a few years back. He's one tough SOB. I never could drink the bastard under the table."

"Tell me about it. I lost that bet. Cost me a hundred bucks."

They shared Avi stories for a time, and he actually saw Neil smile. Well, at least what passed for a smile when it came to Iceman.

"What are our chances of bringing Buryshkin down?" Alex asked.

"Not great. He's got the kind of clout that makes evidence and witnesses disappear forever. It's happened before."

"Just my kind of odds."

"Hooyah!"

The stakes kept rising for him, his sister, and for Veritas. They had to secure the drugs and ensure that Buryshkin and his daughter went to jail for life. Anything less was unacceptable.

They settled the Zodiac in a cove near the shore, as if it was their fishing spot for the day, just two guys drowning worms.

"What do you think?" Neil asked, passing the binoculars to Alex. "The boat's not designed to move fast in case of trouble, but it's big enough to house a drug operation."

Alex studied the houseboat in the distance, the kind used for party trips into the bayou. People milled around inside it, but beyond that, he couldn't see much detail. What made it different were the four smaller boats tied around it. One was just pulling away, headed back the way they'd come.

"Is that one of the boats you were tracking?" Alex asked. Neil nodded. "Okay, then. Can we get any closer?"

His companion shook his head. "*We* can't, but I can." He dug under the tarp and began preparing the scuba gear.

"I don't want to diss your SEAL rep here, but there are things in this water that would consider you a very tasty meal. I speak from experience on this."

Neil shrugged. "Business as usual. Sharks or gators. Something always wants to eat you," he replied, not sounding the least bit concerned.

"How do you handle them?"

A knife came out of a nylon sheath. Avi had one just like it, a custom-made Winkler blade, eight and a half inches long and wicked sharp.

"Okay, that oughta do it," Alex said. "I'll just stay here and count mosquitoes, how's that?"

For a second, his companion seemed amused. "You any good at climbing trees?"

"Usually. The ribs are a little sore, but I can probably get it done."

Neil pointed toward the shore. "Pick a tree and get up high. That way, you'll be out of sight, and you can give me a bird's-eye view of what's going down on the water."

It was a sound idea. "Consider it done."

"While you're getting into position, I'll check out the main boat and make sure it's what we think it is."

"Tempting though it is, don't blow anything up."

Neil kept checking valves and other pieces of the gear. Alex had no idea what he was doing; scuba diving had never interested him.

"I'll be sure to leave enough of the boat intact so the feds can swoop in and play cops and robbers."

There was more than a note of derision in that last sentence.

"If anything looks strange, I'll let you know," Alex said.

"Thanks. Have Miri move the boat here," Neil said, swiveling around to point to a section on a folded map. "That way, if anyone does get past us, they'll take care of them."

Which was the last thing Alex wanted them to do, but he had no choice. He wasn't in charge of this mission now, and he had to trust that Neil knew what he was doing.

"If I didn't say it already, thanks for saving my sister's life."

The man issued a curt nod. "Thank you for giving Morgan a fighting chance. She told me what went down this morning, how you took one of the tangos over the side with you."

"It was the best I could do. Luckily, it worked."

Neil sent his gaze in the direction of the houseboat. A few minutes later, he went over the side of the boat backward, with nary a splash.

Just like a damned shark.

Alex shivered at the lethality involved in that kind of stealth. Once again, he thanked God that Iceman was on their side.

Climbing a suitable tree proved to be a giant pain in the ass, especially with how sore and stiff he was after his morning date with the chains and water. Alex settled on a thick branch, allowed himself a well-earned groan, then hefted the binoculars to check for any sign of his cohort in the water. And came up with zip. Neil had already warned him about that, but Alex hadn't believed him. Now he did.

"Freaking ninja frogman," he muttered, but it was in awe. His radio's earbud crackled in his ear, and he pushed it in for better reception.

"It's the mothership," Neil confirmed. "About to dive again and rig the propeller."

"Roger. I'll let the damsels know."

Alex switched channels and reported to Morgan. She was in charge of contacting Crispin, who would in turn contact the DEA and get the whole shooting match going. But how long would it take for their team to arrive?

Another of the smaller boats departed with a single occupant. Unless you were looking for the bigger vessel, tucked back in this remote cove, you'd never realize that a drug-running operation was right under your nose. Alex adjusted himself on the branch, trying to ignore the mosquitoes and the occasional larger bug that skittered across his hand or leg. As he turned his head, something caught his attention. A large snake slitheres its way down the tree toward him.

Ah shit.

It was black and shiny and seemed huge from his position. As a Texan, Alex knew a venomous snake when he saw one, but he didn't know Louisiana's killers that well. It wasn't a cottonmouth, but that didn't matter—it was a snake and headed right for him. His hand dipped to the knife in the sheath at his waist, the one Neil had given him from the boat's armory.

Now that the thing was closer, he was relieved to see that it had none of the characteristics of a pit viper. In fact, it looked like a black rat snake, which could bite you if you messed with it, but wasn't poisonous.

The thing veered its way toward another branch and then downward, as if Alex didn't exist. He let out a puff of air, sweat dripping off his forehead, and the reptile continued to the ground, then headed off, doing whatever its snaky brain told it to do.

He leaned his forehead against the tree bark, trying to slow his heart rate. After a few moments, he began his vigil again, keeping an eye on the mothership while searching, in vain, for any sight of Neil. If he encountered one more snake, he was totally going to lose it.

He'd dived under worse conditions, but bayous and swamps weren't Neil's favorite locations. The visibility ranged from two to six feet, and was only made worse by the churning of one of the smaller boat's propeller as it departed—not to mention the constant threat of alligators and venomous snakes.

He'd completed a thorough recon, beginning with the small boats, attaching a tracker to each one. Then he'd moved on to the houseboat. It took a bit of time to rig up the explosive to its propeller—not enough to destroy the ship, but enough to keep it from moving. Once that was done, he was golden.

Still, something held him in place. A fellow SEAL had called it a sixth sense. He just called it "this shit doesn't feel right." If he were a paranoid Russian mafia boss, he'd make sure there was a way to destroy the incriminating evidence, and his employees, if needed. No evidence, no witnesses, no problem.

Moving forward, Neil inspected the bottom of the houseboat, foot by foot. He wasn't surprised when he found two explosives attached to the keel, C-4, just like he had used on the propeller. These bombs were overly large and crude, not done by a pro. Probably rigged by some fool who'd learned his skills on the internet. Neil disassembled both of them, letting the explosive material drift to the bottom of the bayou.

After another check to ensure he hadn't missed anything, he headed back toward the Zodiac. As he swam, he found himself thinking about those men who'd swarmed around the yacht that morning. How they'd have been an excellent distraction if someone wanted to attach a bomb to the hull.

Hell.

He swam faster now, skillfully avoiding debris in the water. He'd lost his own sister—no way was he going to allow Alex to lose his.

Using Neil's directions, Morgan had steered their boat to exactly the right spot. As Alex's sister lowered the anchor, Morgan's cell phone rang.

"It's Crispin. The special delivery you requested should be arriving in twenty-five minutes."

"That was quick," she said. Then she realized why. "You told them about this before we'd confirmed it was the right ship."

"I took a gamble. Both the DEA and the Coast Guard will be hitting the ship hard. Pass that on to the others, will you? I don't want them in the way."

"We will. Thanks."

There was a brief hesitation. "Glad you're still with us, Valkyrie. And thank you for rescuing Parkin. He has his uses."

She grinned, thinking of a couple uses that she knew Crispin wasn't considering.

"That he does."

Neil pulled himself onto shore with little effort. After stripping off his facemask and tank, he waited as Alex shimmied down the tree.

"The cavalry should be here in twenty, both DEA and Coast Guard," Alex told him.

Neil nodded. "Need your radio," he said.

Alex handed it over, wondering what was bothering him. Neil walked out of hearing range, which struck him as odd. When he returned, Alex took back the communication device.

"So what's up?"

"There were explosives attached to the bottom of the mothership. It got me thinking about something. Morgan's checking our boat for me."

"You think . . . oh hell," Alex said, looking back across the water, as if he could see her and the yacht. "We need to get over there, now."

"If there's a problem, she'll take care of it. She knows how to deal with explosives."

"She's not you," Alex insisted.

"No, she's not, but I trained her, so that's as good as it gets. Chill out. It'll be fine."

Despite Neil's reassurance, the next ten minutes were the longest of Alex's life as they waited for Morgan to report back in. One mistake, and he'd lose not only his sister, but the woman he cared about. Maybe had even grown to love.

While Alex worried, they'd returned to the Zodiac and moved to a new position, closer to the houseboat now to keep watch for the DEA. He couldn't pace, so he tied and untied knots with a piece of rope. Neil watched him, solemn, not showing his concern in any way other than through his eyes.

"Iceman?" Morgan's voice crackled through the radio.

Neil picked it up. "Go ahead."

"All clear. No problems above or below."

"Roger that."

Alex growled. Then it dawned on him what *below* meant. "She went into the water alone? With the gators?"

His companion set the radio aside, scowling. "She didn't earn the nickname Valkyrie just because we thought it was cute. If you want a future with her, you damned well better get that through your head now. You treat her like a fragile flower, and she's going to ditch your ass, pronto."

Alex's glare bounced right off him. "You so sure of that?"

"Yes, I am," Neil said through clenched teeth. "Don't be stupid. She's worth it, man." It was the most emotion Alex had seen out of him so far. Which meant that he was probably right.

He sighed. "Thanks. I'll . . . yeah."

Did he have a future with Morgan? Was it possible? Was that what he wanted?

Yeah, maybe he did.

A shout went up from the houseboat. Neil hefted the binoculars. "Looks like someone has decided we're a problem."

Three smaller boats revved up, turned, and headed straight for them.

"Bluff it out or take off?"

Shots strafed the water, which answered the question.

"Go!" Neil shouted, digging under the tarp for a weapon. "Get us to Morgan."

Alex started the motor and made a sharp turn. While bullets pinged around them, he gunned the motor and Neil returned fire.

Skimming over the water, Alex kept his head down, keeping an eye out for anything that might flip the boat. He picked up the radio and keyed it. It was time to let the women know that things had just gone to hell and that they were bringing that hell to their doorstep.

Chapter Twenty-Five

Morgan sat up at the sound of gunshots echoing across the water.

"DEA?" Miri asked.

"No. They would have gone by us to get to the houseboat. I'm guessing the guys are in trouble. Get the anchor up."

As Miri hurried to comply, the portable radio squawked.

"We're coming in hot!" Alex shouted, no doubt his code for "the shit has hit the fan."

"Roger. We'll be ready," Morgan said. She sprinted to the arms cupboard and pulled out a rifle, extra ammunition, and two more sidearms.

By the time she was back on deck, the anchor was stowed.

"Can you shoot a rifle?" she asked. Miri nodded, taking it and the box of ammunition. "You set up on starboard. Neil will dock on port. Alex can't use a gun, so he'll take us out of here once they're on board."

"You sure this isn't DEA we'll be shooting at?"

"They're not here yet, so this has to be the Russians. If you have to kill someone, do it, because they sure as hell won't hesitate to do the same to us."

Miri nodded grimly, pushed a piece of furniture out of the way, and set up a shooting location. Morgan started the engine, leaving it in neutral. She raced to the port side, dropped a ladder, and then returned to join Miri. Raising the binoculars, she spied the Zodiac flying across the water, bouncing at top speed. Alex was at the helm, leaving Neil to fire at their pursuers. She counted three boats in their wake.

Morgan called Sanjay to report the situation.

"I'll pass that on to the DEA and the Coast Guard," Sanjay said. "You guys going to be okay?"

"We'll find out soon enough," she replied. She stashed the phone back in her jeans.

She glanced down to find that Miri was shaking. Morgan put her hand on the girl's shoulder, and she jumped.

"Hey, it'll be good. Don't worry."

"I know that tone. Alex uses it when things are really bad," Miri replied.

No fooling you. "There're four of us. We're armed, and the moment the guys are in the boat, we're out of here. Just shoot anyone who gets too close, okay?"

Miri nodded. She sighted down the rifle and waited, trying to calm her breathing.

Just like Neil would.

The Zodiac raced toward them so fast, it seemed impossible that it would avoid a collision. When it got within thirty feet, it abruptly slowed and swung around the back of the bigger boat. As soon as they were close enough, Neil and Alex would board, pulling their gear in with them.

Morgan ignored the pair, returning fire on the other boats as they closed in. Bullets pinged into the superstructure. Miri fired repeatedly, and at least one of her shots took a man over the side of one of the boats.

"Go!" Neil shouted as he joined Miri at the rail. "Head for open water!"

The engines revved, and then the boat turned in a wide arc, the smaller ones right behind. When Morgan shot a quick glance over her shoulder, Alex winked at her from his place at the wheel.

Morgan turned her attention back to the men trying to kill them, and tried picking them off, one by one. It proved hard, given how much the boats were bouncing on the water. Iceman had a sniper rifle now, aiming carefully, almost always deadly for whichever target he sighted. Miri was kneeling next to him, just as focused.

Despite their efforts, all three of the boats closed in, moving faster than theirs; one aft, one port, one starboard, hoping to catch them in the crossfire. Morgan sprinted to port, and as she reached the railing, a bullet buzzed by her head. She ducked down.

"Hold on!" Alex shouted. A moment later, their boat swung out, smashing into that craft. Within a heartbeat, the crushed boat and its occupants vanished into the deep water.

One down.

Neil raised his rifle, sighted, then squeezed the trigger. And missed. That was the problem with a speeding boat—there was no stability. He sighted again, and his bullet hit its mark, dropping one of the shooters.

A helicopter came out of nowhere, and for an instant, Morgan feared it belonged to Buryshkin. At least until bullets came raining down on the two smaller boats. Within moments, they swiveled around and headed back toward the mainland.

She waved her hands at the chopper pilot. The man waved back and then turned the bird to chase down the two boats.

"Miri?" Neil called out. There was blood on her arm.

He set down his sniper rifle and took hers from stiff hands. The boat slowed beneath them. "How bad is it?" he asked.

Miri frowned at the wound. "Not bad," she reported.

Then she fainted into his arms.

The sight of his sister falling into Neil's arms, blood coming from somewhere, nearly destroyed Alex.

"Go on. I got it," Morgan said, sliding in next to him to take control of the boat, though her bandaged hands would take the brunt of that effort.

He skidded across the deck and landed next to Miri on his knees.

"It's not bad," Neil said, examining the wound. "Most of it is just the shock of being hit. If you're not used to it, it can easily take you out."

He looked up at the man, then back down at his baby sister.

"She's okay, Alex," Neil insisted. "I know it's hard to see, but she's good. And a pretty damned good shot, too. Miri would make a great sniper."

Alex was shaking his head before he'd finished. "Not my sister. Don't even mention it to her. Because she's just stubborn enough to give it a try."

Neil lifted her up in his arms and carried her to the bench seat, where he gently laid her out, then headed off to retrieve the first aid kit.

"She okay?" Morgan called out. Alex nodded. It was then that he noticed she had blood on her arm as well. Both his women had been hurt.

He slumped into a deck chair, shaking as hard as if it were twenty degrees below zero.

They're alive.

But what about the next time?

When the invitation from Special Agent Fredd came an hour later via Morgan's phone, Alex thought he'd misunderstood the message.

"She wants *me* on the mothership?" he asked.

"That's what she said," Morgan replied.

His distrust rocketed into the stratosphere. "Why?"

"To celebrate the drug bust. Why else?"

Why else, indeed? He looked at his sister, who made a shooing motion with her uninjured arm.

"Go on. You deserve the glory, bro."

His eyes then moved to Neil, who made the same motion.

"Looks like I'm going," Alex said.

The houseboat had a lot in common with an overcrowded beehive: too many worker bees. But now the worker bees wore DEA vests and toted serious firearms. Once Alex and Morgan received clearance to board, she brought the Zodiac close to the houseboat and tied it off.

He was all too aware of the eyes staring at them, some of which were hostile. He'd worked with several of these agents, and they knew he'd been in prison.

Screw it. His sister and Morgan had been wounded during this operation. He needed to see whether it was worth all the agony.

Alex was met by Senior Special Agent Fredd, a no-nonsense Black woman who was renowned for running a very tight ship, no pun intended. Alex had worked with her a couple times and had always been impressed. Given the scowls from some of the other agents, she'd pissed them off by inviting him on board. Fredd clearly didn't give a damn.

"Parkin. Good to see you. You're looking good," she said, eyeing him. "Keeping fit, I see."

"It's that new prison workout. It's all the rage," he said.

Her mouth quirked into a wry smile. "Mouthy as always. Glad to see that's still there. Come on, take a look at the haul. I swear to God, y'all just got me a promotion."

Ignoring the stares of the other agents, Alex and Morgan followed Fredd into the main room, such as it was. The usual houseboat amenities were gone, except for a sink and two rows of tables were lined up down the middle. One side held stacks and stacks of cocaine, all in one-pound bricks, the tables sagging with the combined weight.

Alex walked the entire length, doing a quick calculation.

"Ninety pounds?" he asked.

"Eighty-one now. About three to four million dollars' worth of blow. A very sweet haul," Fredd replied, smiling.

Alex walked to the other table to examine where the dope would have been cut with various substances, then bagged and weighed. "Any of this strychnine?"

"It's possible. I'm guessing it's diluted with talcum powder, probably fifty-fifty, so the folks doing the packing had no clue it's poison. Still enough to kill anyone who uses the dope."

"Anya has her own people within her daddy's organization, so it would be easy to do."

"Just as long as we can tie this shipment to him, we're good," she replied.

"What the hell is Parkin doing here?" an agent demanded,

stepping into the room.

Alex recognized him immediately—Weston had been one of his rivals in the agency.

Fredd shot the man the evil eye. "He's here because he helped us find the load, so be nice and thank the man."

"I'm not thanking some goddamn drug-dealing felon," Weston argued.

With that, the feel-good vibes were history. Alex would never be able to outrun his past.

"Time to go," Morgan said quietly.

"Yeah, looks like it."

By the time he and Morgan were in the Zodiac, headed back to join the others, Alex felt the need to hit someone. One of the sneering DEA assholes would do just fine.

"They don't care that we damned near died helping them get this load off the streets. I'll always be a felon to them. Just scum. A loser," he said. He hadn't expected a brass band, but at least a "thanks, dude." Only Fredd had appeared to understand.

"The truth will come out. Hang in there. We'll find a way."

"So what if it does? They won't believe it. Dammit, I want my reputation back."

"Probably not a realistic objective," she cautioned. "It's time to build a new life. This time, you set the rules, not them."

Even as he raised his head to answer, he saw the question in her eyes. Would that new life include her?

While the DEA put everything in motion for Buryshkin's arrest, Morgan and the others spent the night on the water, savoring the peace of the bayou. It was a way to decompress, unwind, and talk through the mission. Morgan had done that countless times at the FBI, as had Neil with his SEAL buddies, and Alex at the DEA. Miri was the only one who didn't have that kind of background, but it didn't seem to bother her.

Over hamburgers and beers, Neil related what he'd found under the mothership and admitted to having been investigated by a gator who had wisely backed off. Miri joked that he should have brought her the hide, that she'd love a pair of alligator shoes.

"Good thing you found the explosives. Agent Fredd said that one of the Russians did try to blow the boat, and that he was very puzzled when things didn't go boom," Morgan added.

She was next to Alex on one of the bench seats, a beer in hand. It felt good not to have to hide their relationship. He must have felt the same, as every now and then he leaned in and nuzzled her neck.

Miri noticed. "You keep it up, you're out of here. I'm a young and impressionable person. I shouldn't be forced to watch rampant displays of affection between my own brother and his girlfriend."

A low snicker came from Neil.

"What?" she demanded, frowning at him.

"Impressionable? You? You'd make a Marine blush, the way you swear."

Her frown grew deeper. "You weren't supposed to hear me."

"I hear everything."

"Yeah, I noticed."

Neil had a beer in hand as well and looked more relaxed than Morgan had ever seen him. Miri sat near him, but not so near as to tip her hand. Still, from the glances she sent his way, Morgan could see that Alex's sister had it bad.

Sorry, honey. He's not going there.

She suspected that Neil had his share of one-night stands, but even those he didn't talk about, his personal life one big black hole. Which was a pity, because he and Miri would do well together. She was strong enough to stand up to him. Most women didn't know how to approach a man like that.

"Why don't you ladies take the big bed tonight? Iceman and I will take the bunks," Alex suggested.

Morgan gave him a side-eye. It was an odd remark, and for an instant, it made her wonder if he was backing away from her. Had he decided that, since they'd nearly completed the mission, their time together was through?

Or maybe he wanted to talk to Neil without them present.

As if he'd heard her worries, Alex leaned closer and whispered, "Nothing to do with us. Just want you guys to sleep well."

Miri took his offer at face value, and after a big yawn, went downstairs first. Realizing that this was a battle she couldn't win, Morgan gave in and headed for bed. Behind her, she heard Alex rise from his chair, proving her instincts were correct.

Her guy was definitely up to something.

Chapter Twenty-Six

Once the ladies had left the deck, Alex moved closer to Neil, who didn't seem surprised by the gesture.

"Now that they're gone, what is it you want to talk to me about?" Neil asked.

Alex shook his head. "Little gets past you, does it?"

"I can be as oblivious as the next guy, but not right now. You didn't pass up on an opportunity to share a bed with Morgan just to hang with me."

He laughed. "How's about I get you another beer and then we talk?"

His companion nodded, so he returned with two bottles. Neil took one and leaned back in his chair. He wasn't in special-ops mode at the moment, so he almost seemed like a regular guy spending time with a buddy. Alex owed this man so much, and he didn't have that many friends at the moment. He'd like to add Iceman to that very short list.

"This isn't over yet," Alex said. "We might have gotten this load of dope off the streets, but the Buryshkins are going to be gunning for me because of it. They'll go after the people I care about."

"Crispin is aware that you and your sister are even bigger targets now. Morgan, as well," Neil said, then took a sip of beer.

"Exactly. So . . . is your boss going to stay in this for the long haul, or do I need to make other plans to keep them safe? Because I'm real familiar with being screwed over."

His companion pierced him with a glare. "We don't do that kind of shit. Why do you think I joined up with Veritas? It's the closest I could find to the SEAL code of honor in the real world. They don't leave anyone behind. *Ever.* Bailing on you and your sister would be doing just that."

A body-weight of worry fell from Alex's shoulders. "I'm not used to that kind of backup."

"Well, now you will be."

Alex drank his beer in silence, listening to the water lap against the boat, studying the lights of one of the huge oil rigs in the distance.

"If I'm Buryshkin, there are two ways I could go," Neil began. "I either neutralize my daughter to reinforce to my crew that I'm top dog, or I go after the people who ruined my delusions in regard to that daughter. Which do you think he'll do?"

"Plan B. Go after us. It'll hurt his ego too much to admit that Anya has been outmaneuvering him." Then he remembered what day it was. "Unless . . ."

"Go on," Neil said, stretching out his long legs.

Alex stared up at the stars, thinking it through. "His favorite nephew will get out of prison this morning. Plan C might be pitting Anya and Grigori against each other and letting the biggest bastard win."

"Which one do you think will come out alive?"

"Anya," Alex said. "She has no morals, she's a pathological liar, and she'll kill you without thinking twice. Grigori is . . . he's a scholar born into a family of crooks. He ruled his crew in prison with an iron fist, but I could tell it wasn't second nature. He had to work at it every moment of the day."

"Is there a rivalry between Buryshkin's daughter and nephew?"

"A one-sided rivalry. Grigori doesn't really want to have anything to do with the family business, but Anya doesn't believe that. She only sees him as a threat."

His bottle empty, Neil set it at his feet. "Based on that, my guess is that something will go down in the next few days."

Alex rose, stretching, feeling the pull on his ribs and the sharp sting of pain that move brought. "I agree. How long are we staying out here?"

"Until Crispin says we can come back to land. I'll move the boat in a bit, shift our position into the Gulf in case someone noticed where we dropped anchor."

"You want me to take watch sometime overnight?"

"Sounds good. Come up on deck around two."

He dropped his empty bottle in the sink and headed toward the bathroom. As he passed the bunks, he noticed that his sister was asleep on one, and he smiled. She'd done that on purpose. Now he had no choice but to join Morgan in that big bed.

I owe you, Monkey.

After Alex locked the bedroom door behind him, he set his phone to vibrate at a little before two a.m., visited the head, then crawled into bed against a warm, soft woman. *His* woman, if he was brave enough to admit that.

"You better be my white knight, or I'm going to have a problem explaining why Iceman is sharing my bed," she said, muzzy.

"Right guy. Right woman," he said, and kissed her.

When the kiss ended, Morgan snuggled up against him, but he noted that she made no attempt to seduce him. That wasn't surprising; they were both exhausted, and right now, curling up with her was nearly all he needed.

Before he'd married Alicia, he'd been all about as many sexual romps as he could score. One night with a woman, maybe two—that was plenty. He was easily bored. Though sex was still high on his list of must-haves, being here with Morgan, lying next to her, held a deeper satisfaction.

I love her.

He knew it as surely as he knew the sun would rise over the water in the morning. Felt it deep in his bones and his very soul. He loved her, and there was nothing he could do to stop it.

Hell.

Should he tell her? Or would it spook her to find out an ex-con was head over heels for her? Make her take off even before he'd finished telling her? The sound of her soft breathing told him she'd fallen back asleep. So instead of revealing the truth and risk learning she didn't feel the same for him, he kissed her cheek gently and settled in next to her.

As he dozed off, he thought through the events of the day, one horror after another. Through it all, she'd been there for him, sharing his humor, caring for him, keeping him alive. In Alex's mind, that was exactly what love was all about.

September 21st
Gulf of Mexico

Alex sat in the deck chair, a blanket over him to ward off the chill. He'd relieved Neil at the appropriate time and had watched the man slip into the bunk and fall into a dead sleep almost instantly. Across from Neil, Miri was still asleep, her bandaged arm lying outside the covers. It'd been a helluva run.

It was near nine a.m. when a call came through on Neil's phone. He was up and on the deck before it had even rung twice.

"Iceman," he said. He listened for a time, gave Alex a look, and then swore. "Hold on."

"What's up?"

"The war has begun: Someone tried to kill Grigori Danshov this morning as he was leaving prison. Fortunately, he survived."

"And Ruslan?" Because it would have been his lover who picked him up.

"Wounded, but expected to live."

"Thank God."

"That's not all," Neil continued. "There's a hostage situation at Buryshkin's place. The Russian demands you join him, or he'll kill that hostage."

"Who have they got?" Alex asked. Because pretty much everyone he cared about was right here.

"Dennis Simms."

His mouth fell open, then closed with a click. "What the

hell? Why would Buryshkin think I'd waste my time saving that bastard's ass?"

Neil didn't reply.

"Is that the boss?" Alex asked, furious now. Neil nodded and handed him the phone. "Wilder? Explain to me why I give a damn if Dennis Simms dies. You know, the man who fucked my wife and set me up for a coke bust?"

"Because there's more to it than that," Crispin replied.

"Like what?" Alex asked. As he turned to pace in the opposite direction, he realized that both Morgan and his sister were on deck now, watching him with concerned expressions.

"It'll take too much time to explain, but Simms is as much a victim in this as you and Morgan are."

"I'm not buying it. Why would I bother saving him?"

"Because you have a conscience. Neither Anya nor her father have any idea what that entails."

A conscience.

"You can walk away and let his death be on your soul for the rest of your life. Or you can go in and make the best deal you can to save him."

There it was, the difference between him and the Russians. Alex had a conscience. If it had been Grigori as the hostage, there would have been no question. The test of his honor was Dennis.

He sank into one of the deck chairs, his eyes meeting Miri's.

She shook her head. "Don't you dare."

Morgan remained silent, though he knew she was thinking the same thing.

Dammit to hell.

He turned away, looking out at the water. "Tell the Russian I'm in. But I want a guarantee that Simms comes out of there alive."

"No, Alex," Morgan whispered from behind him.

"How soon can you be there?" his boss asked.

At that question, Alex handed the phone to Neil to make the arrangements.

"Ninety minutes to the closest dock," the man said. "I'll let you know when we're fifteen out." He ended the call and headed for the wheelhouse.

As Alex moved toward the stairs, his sister stepped in front of him.

"Why? He's not worth it," she said.

"No, he's not, but it doesn't work that way. Wilder is right: I can't judge one person's value over another's, or I'm as bad as Buryshkin."

"You just can't stop being the hero, can you?" she said, her eyes filling with tears.

"It's not about being a hero," Morgan said quietly. "It's about being a human being. Your brother can't back away. It's not how he works."

He paused in front of her now, then leaned close so only she could hear him.

"I need to be with you. Alone. Because . . . "

This might be the last time.

Morgan understood, and after a look at Neil, she led him down the stairs and to the bedroom. As the lock clicked behind her, she began pulling the drapes over the small windows.

"You're crazy to go in there alone," she said, her voice shaking.

"It's gotta be done," he replied, toeing off his shoes. "I didn't get this far to have some damned Russian put me in my grave."

Her task finished, she stepped in front of him. "If I ask you not to go—"

"I have to, Morgan. I hate Simms, but Neil said it: Never leave a man behind." *Even one you hate.*

She lowered her head, as if acknowledging that there were no words that could convince him not to throw his life away.

"I love you," he said. Her eyes rose in shock. "Yeah, color me surprised. Smoking-hot lady tries to pick me up on some Louisiana back road, and I"—he shook his head—"I get steamrolled. You're . . . everything to me, Morgan. You're my oxygen, the blood flowing through my veins. You're my future.

My hope."

Her eyes blurred in tears. "Great timing. Tell a girl you're in love with her right before you go to—"

"Rescue a hostage. That's what I'm doing."

She took his head in her hands and kissed him, long, deep, her tongue playing against his. His arms wove around her, pulling her up against his body.

"I need you so badly," he said. "Now more than ever." He swallowed hard. "We don't have that much time. But after this is over, I'll give you anything you want. Anytime you want."

"You promise to be around to do that?"

"Yes. I promise. It may not be easy, but—"

Morgan stopped his rambling with a kiss that stole his breath and made him grow harder.

"You might have to help out. I'm not one hundred percent," he said, though he was loath to admit it.

She urged him back on the edge of the bed. Then after he undressed, she stripped off her clothes in a few economical motions. Alex stared at her, worshipping every curve, every mole, even every bruise. Morgan Blake's body wasn't perfect, but that didn't matter to him. She was his. As she turned, he saw the stippling of a healed wound on her flank. Somehow, he'd never seen that before.

"What happened to you?" he asked, pointing.

"I was shot during a rescue attempt."

Closing his eyes, he willed away the images of her bleeding, how serious that wound had been. How she could have died, and he never would have met her.

He jerked in surprise when she touched his face. "Lie back."

He did as she asked, wondering what she had in mind. Then he found out. She crawled in bed with him, then slowly flicked her tongue over first his right nipple, then his left, giving each a little tug with her teeth. His body responded eagerly. Then she was there, touching his erection with her soft fingers, stroking him. Her tongue swirled around the tip, making his hips rise off the bed.

"Oh, Morgan."

She took him inside her mouth, and then it was all sensation. How she worked him, how he felt himself building toward the edge.

"Come here. I can't take much more of this," he said, then gritted his teeth to keep from losing it.

"Patience," she said, ceasing her attentions. Then, just as he was regaining his control, she was back. Twice, she ran him right up to the brink, so close he could almost feel himself exploding, and then she stopped.

"God, you're killing me," he said, his voice husky with desire.

"Just wait," she whispered, and then she positioned her legs on either side of him. Her bright-green eyes smiled down at him. When she leaned closer, he brought a breast to his mouth, returning the favor, kissing, kneading, and sucking it until she moaned.

"Take me," he said. "Make me yours." She slowly sank down, and he groaned in sweet agony. "Move, will you?"

"I don't think so," she said, but he felt her tightening and releasing her inner muscles. "I like to watch you suffer."

"Morgan . . ."

She must have heard his desperation, and she set up a rhythm, moving up and down on him. He grabbed her hips and arched into her. Morgan's head flew back, like a goddess sharing her power with her lover, stiffening as her release roared through her body.

Her cry of pleasure was lost in the burr of the engines.

Alex let himself be carried over, falling into pleasure so intense, he thought he'd die. Shaking, crying out, he came within her, branding her, claiming her as his. When it was over, Morgan curled up on his chest, her thighs on either side of him. He still rested inside of her. He wanted to remain there forever.

"Damn you," she said when her head rose, her hair flowing around that beautiful face. "I swore I'd never trust another man, and then there you were."

"Your fault. You ignored the road signs that say not to stop for hitchhikers."

"So that's why they were there," she said, shifting her hips.

His body responded, not ready to end this lovemaking session. Not wanting it to ever end.

"I want you again," he said.

"I'm yours, for as long as we've got."

Morgan felt him harden inside of her, felt that strength touching her core. Once again she made love to him. His fingers touched where they were joined, stroking her, bringing her closer to orgasm.

"Come for me, baby. Just for me."

As if he'd broken something loose inside her, she did come, hard and long. It felt like the orgasm would never end. When he joined her, their cries mingled together.

As the pleasure ebbed, she curled up next to him. He stroked her hair. She wanted this every morning, every evening. It was time to admit that.

"I love you, Alex."

He blinked open his eyes, startled. "Really?"

"Color me just as confused as you about this."

"Well, I'll be damned. The Parkin Luck has returned."

"Let's hope it hangs in there for a bit longer."

Chapter Twenty-Seven

When Alex stepped off the boat, he turned to help his sister down onto the dock. He didn't need to—she was quite capable of that—but he wanted to touch her, to reassure her. He needed Miri to know that he wasn't being suicidal.

"Monkey . . . "

"Listen, bro, I get that you have to do this and all, but dying on me now is a bad plan. Who knows what stupid stuff I might do if I'm on my own," she said, glaring up at him. "I might join a biker gang or—"

He hugged her tight, feeling her shivering in his arms. "Or you might do really cool stuff, because that's the kind of woman you are."

"You come back to me. Don't you leave me now. I couldn't handle it," she said, tears wetting his collar.

"I'll try not to. I have too much to live for now."

Lars and a sedan awaited them. Iceman asked about a sniper rifle and got a nod in return.

"In the trunk," Lars said. "Just like you specified."

"Thanks, man," Neil said, taking the car keys. "Let Sanjay know the boat's got some holes in it. I sent him the coordinates for the Zodiac already so it can be retrieved."

"You're hard on stuff, my friend," Lars said.

Neil slapped him on the back. "Tell me about it."

He slid into the driver's seat. Miri joined him on the passenger side, not a word said between them. So much for Alex's hope that his sister would stay away from whatever was going down at Buryshkin's house. He didn't bother to try to change her mind because stubbornness ran in their blood.

He joined Morgan in the backseat, taking hold of her hand. There was no need for talk; everything that needed to be said had passed between them when they'd been one.

The trip to Buryshkin's house went too fast, and too slow. Alex wanted more time with Morgan and his sister. He wanted this over. When they turned into the driveway that led to the house, they were stopped by a quartet of grim-faced DEA agents. Once they were cleared, Neil took them up the drive to a cluster of official vehicles located about two hundred yards away from the grand front balcony.

Agent Fredd was having a terse argument with Agent Weston; Alex could tell she was barely holding back her temper. Seeing him and Morgan, she waved them over.

"I don't trust this bastard," Weston said, jerking his thumb toward Alex. "He has no reason to be here."

"But I *am* here, so let's get this done."

"Why? I heard he was screwing your wife."

"Old news, dude," Alex said. "I got my own lady now, so I don't care." He winked over at Morgan, and she returned it, her way of telling him he'd come a long way since the day she'd first met him on that highway.

Agent Fredd pushed a number and handed over the phone. "They're using the hostage as the go-between."

"Jolly," Alex said.

"About damned time you got here," Dennis said, his voice more highly pitched than usual. "Buryshkin is getting antsy. You get your ass in here, or they're going to put a bullet in my head."

"Tell the old fart to take a chill pill," Alex replied. "I'm coming in, and I'm unarmed. If he doesn't want this house burned down around his ass, tell him not to be stupid."

He ended the call before Dennis could answer, and handed off the phone. "How many guards are inside the house?" he asked.

"None," Fredd replied.

"What?" Morgan blurted.

"None alive, at least. There are a few bodies outside, but

we're only picking up three heat signatures inside, probably Dennis and the Buryshkins." Fredd sighed. "This whole thing feels hinky."

"You think?" Morgan said. "Buryshkin never does anything without a full contingent of bodyguards."

"Which means it might not be him in control of the situation," Alex said. "This feels more like Anya's doing than his."

"How did they get ahold of Simms?" Morgan asked.

"I have no idea. We weren't going to execute the Buryshkin's warrant until this afternoon. And no, Dennis did not know about that," Fredd added.

"He found out somehow," Alex said. "So, did he come out here to tell his boss, or did they just snag him off the street?"

"Why the hell would he tell the Russian?" Weston demanded.

"Because he's the one who planted the coke to send me to prison."

"That's—"

"The truth," Morgan said. "Buryshkin told us himself."

"You're shitting me," the agent replied. Weston and Dennis had been pretty tight at one time, but the man's surprise looked genuine. Maybe he was still his own man.

"Frankly, if he comes out of there in a body bag, I'm not going to weep," Alex said, "but if I can get all three of them out of there alive, that'd be better. Then I can enjoy the Buryshkins spending the rest of their lives in prison."

"Good luck with that," Fredd said. "For the record, I never believed you were dirty."

Alex smiled at her, then eyeballed Agent Weston. "Thanks. At least there's one of you."

In the end, he refused the offer of a tactical vest. No real point. All it would take was a head shot and he'd be worm food. As Alex moved past the line of DEA vehicles, heading toward the house, Morgan caught his arm.

Not caring that they had an audience, she pulled him close and gave him a kiss. There were wolf whistles and hoots, but they ignored them. When it ended, Alex touched her face with reverence. How quickly he'd come to love this woman.

"If things go bad, please take care of my sister. That's all I ask."

"Crispin promised he would," Morgan said. "I'll be coming with you."

"What? The hell you are."

"You think I'm going to stay out here, wondering what they're doing to you, if you're wounded or dead? Not happening. This thing between us isn't just one way. I'm there with you, or you're not going."

"Morgan, please don't—"

"Alex, *this* is the way it's going to be. If you don't like it, after this is over you go your own way. But right now, I'm at your side."

He stared at her, astounded. "Jesus, you are hardheaded."

She grinned at him.

"I love you," he added.

"And I love you," she replied. "Now let's go bag ourselves some big, bad Russians so we can get back to the important stuff."

He laughed, and they set off, walking toward the house at an even pace, as if this were a date. She squeezed his hand, and he returned the gesture.

More time. We just need more time together.

When they reached the stairs, they climbed up to the second level. At the double doors that led into the house, Morgan turned back toward the cars, the agents, and the guns.

"Lovely view," she said. A second later, a buzz came from her pocket—Neil letting her know he was in place at the rear of the house, sniper rifle in hand.

"We're coming in," Alex shouted, then turned the doorknob and pushed open the twin doors.

The interior of the house felt sticky as if the central air conditioning had been off for a while. Three ceiling fans moved the humidity as best as they could. The foyer was empty except for a giant urn of flowers set on a pedestal and the body of a guard, his blood drying on the wooden floor. Curiously, the color matched a few of the roses in the bouquet.

"Think there's been a coup?" Morgan asked.

"Real possible. But of the two, I'd rather deal with Buryshkin than his crazy-ass daughter," Alex replied, keeping his voice low.

"Amen to that."

The door at the end of the foyer was open. Alex led the way, his gut tight and his nerves strung out, his heart pounding so hard he could barely hear himself think. He entered the main room first, Morgan right behind. His eyes bounced over the occupants: Buryshkin, his daughter, Dennis. His brain did the math, and it didn't add up.

"You're freaking kidding me," he said, shaking his head.

Dennis Simms wasn't the hostage, he was the one with the gun. A few feet away, Anya and her father were on the couch, secured in zip ties, their feet bound. She had a gag in place, her eyes furious over the obstruction. Buryshkin's mood was hard to read, but there was both anger and resignation in his cold eyes.

"What the hell is this?" Morgan demanded, looking back and forth between the Russians and their captor.

Simms frowned at her. "Why'd you bring her along, Parkin? Are you an idiot?"

Alex grumbled under his breath. "She insisted. Arguing with a woman is a lot like arguing with a solar flare. It's a waste of time and always gets you roasted."

Morgan shot his ex-partner a glower. "I don't get it. Why claim to be a hostage?"

"To see what he'd do," Dennis replied, the gun pointed at Alex now. "You surprised me. I didn't figure you'd come in here to save my ass."

"I surprised myself," he replied. "So what's the deal, Dennis?"

"This is suicide," Buryshkin cut in. "I warned you what would happen if either of you crossed me."

"Yeah, yeah, I know," Dennis replied. "You're going to kill

me. You know, I don't fucking care anymore."

His face was covered in beads of sweat, probably because he was wearing one of the DEA windbreakers, had it zipped up in a room that had passed ninety degrees a few hours ago.

What's up with that? Alex's ex-partner appeared heavier than the last time he'd seen him, but he might be wearing a flak vest under the jacket. He took note of the man's gray complexion, the haunted expression in his eyes.

He's gone over the edge.

"So walk me through this, because I'm sure as hell confused," Alex said.

Dennis looked at him with a shuttered expression. "You're not as arrogant as you used to be. You never would have admitted that you didn't understand something when you were at the agency." He shifted positions, careful to keep his distance from them. "Smartass Alex Parkin, always right, always there for the glory."

"I'll admit to being a prick, but not to the glory."

His ex-partner shrugged. "That's how I saw it."

"Doesn't mean it was right. You still haven't told me what's up here."

"These people—and I use that term very loosely— destroyed both of our lives." Dennis gestured toward Morgan. "Hers, too. Yeah, I knew they had your husband by the balls. I saw the video of him and that girl."

Morgan colored. "So let's take them in. They'll go down for life."

Dennis shook his head. "Not good enough. I want payback. I figured you'd be good with that, old buddy."

"Me? I want to see these assholes serve time." He looked over at Buryshkin now. "Of course, with Mikhail watching your back, you'll probably serve the full term. He's very good at keeping people alive. I owe him. You, on the other hand, will come to hate that because it means every fucking day you're still breathing and behind bars."

"It will not happen," the Russian said, shaking his head.

"Yeah, it will." He turned his attention back to his ex-partner. "Why'd you screw my wife, Dennis?"

"I'm sorry about that," he said. "It just sorta happened. She's . . . a beautiful woman. I wish we could have stayed together. I really liked her a lot."

It appeared that Dennis had cared more for Alicia than he'd realized.

"It's because of her you're here. Once the coke was confiscated, that bitch," Simms said, angling his head toward Anya, "wanted me to kidnap Alicia. She figured that would flush you out."

It would have. Even if he didn't love her anymore. "So how did you get the better of them?"

"I had some good luck." Dennis unzipped his coat with his free hand. The reason he looked heavier became apparent: He was wearing a suicide vest.

"Jesus Christ, are you nuts?" Alex said.

"Probably. You'd be surprised what a little outfit like this and a Taser can accomplish. Especially when I got here and found out that Anya's guards had killed her daddy's. Then it was just a matter of mopping up."

Anya finally maneuvered her gag down, and outraged Russian spilled out.

"Pipe down, will you?" Alex said.

She shouted a single sentence at him.

"No!" he shouted. "*Y nikogda ne budet lapu kto-nibud koshku snova.*"

I will never be anyone's cat's paw again.

Anya spat at him. "You are no better than my father." Buryshkin glowered at her now. "He refused to let me marry the man I loved, but I did anyway. Then he had Pietr killed."

"*Ne pravda,*" her father said, shaking his head. "Not true."

"I heard you killed him," Morgan said to Anya, moving closer. "That you butchered him like a pig because he dared look at another woman."

"You lie!" the woman shouted. "I will kill all of you. And your sister, Parkin, she will be a whore in a seraglio."

Alex shook his head. "You had your crack at Miri. You

were playing all of us. You knew I was working with your
father, but you kept screwing with us. Had us confused for a
time, but then we got it." He smiled at them both. "All I want
to see is your perp walk and the expressions on your faces
when you're sentenced to life in prison."

"It will not happen," Buryshkin repeated. "I own too many
judges in this state."

"You see why I like my solution better?" Dennis said.
"They'll get off. They'll decide she's a nutcase and bang her
up in an asylum for a couple of years, and then she'll be out
to raise hell again. Him? I doubt he'll even see the inside of a
prison cell."

Anya's bizarre smile grew wider.

"Look, let's call the bomb squad and get that thing off
you," Alex offered. "You can testify against them. It'll work
this time."

"No. You see, I've been a flunky for these assholes for
seven long years, and today I'm handing in my resignation."

The man's emotionless response told Alex that his ex-
partner wasn't expecting to come out of this alive.

"No need to go that far," he said. "You'll get the credit for
the bust."

"Not what I'm after. All I want is a chance to make it
right," Dennis replied solemnly.

"So how do we resolve this?" Morgan asked, her voice
calm, though Alex could see the tension running through her
body.

Dennis shook his head. "We don't. I'd be sent to prison
with them." He looked over at Alex now. "I'm not like you. I'd
die there. I don't have the balls to tough it out."

"How'd they get their hooks in you?" Alex asked.

"My sister. Yeah, strange, isn't it? You'd do anything for
yours, and I gave up everything for mine. Even though they
paid her medical bills, Theresa still died from the brain tumor.
By then, these bastards had me by the balls, and I'll never be
free."

He pulled a small plastic bag from under his jacket and

tossed it to Morgan. "That's a key to a safe deposit box at the Bank of New Orleans on Magazine Street. It's in my name. You'll find photos, documents, audio tapes, everything from the last seven years. It should be enough to clear your name and for the DEA to clean house. I'm not the only dirty one they've got on their payroll."

Alex's mouth fell open. "Why are you doing this?"

"Because one of us should walk away from this mess in good shape. And it's not going to be me."

That sounded too final.

Dennis held up a cell phone. "The vest is rigged to blow when this rings. Nothing can stop it once I push the number."

"Come on, we can work this out. They're not worth it," Alex said, taking a step closer.

"I will give you money, anything you want," Buryshkin said, his eyes wide and sweat rolling down his face now. "What do you want? Name it. I will give it to you."

"All I want is revenge," Dennis said. He gave a sad grin. "No money involved."

Anya began to cackle. "See, old man, see what it is like to skate the edge of death? Is it not glorious?"

"Laugh all you want, you crazy bitch. You're dying too," Dennis said.

"Go on! Do it!" she said, still laughing. "You are too weak."

Alex dove at him, but Dennis had already pressed the call button.

"Get out of here," he ordered. "Or you'll end up in hell with the rest of us." Alex staggered back in shock. "Go!"

Morgan grabbed Alex's arm and dragged him toward the double doors. His survival instincts kicked in, and they ran toward the entrance.

Behind them, Anya began to sing an old Russian lullaby, caught deep within her own madness. Her father's pleas grew louder now, his voice cracking in desperation. "You cannot do this! You are insane!"

Dennis's resigned laughter followed them out the front

door. They pounded down the stairs, taking them two at a time, then sprinted across the open ground. Alex's lungs and ribs protested, but still he pressed on.

They'd made it only fifty feet or so before an explosion rocked the earth underneath them. As they fell, he covered her body with his. The concussive force of the blast roared over them, raining down pieces of timber, glass, and roofing. Underneath him, Morgan cried out. He felt something heavy hit his legs. At first, there was nothing, as if they'd been sheared off. Then the pain bitch-slapped him into oblivion.

Chapter Twenty-Eight

The low murmur of voices, accompanied by the beep-beep of a heart monitor, called Alex back from the darkness. As his mind began sweeping out the cobwebs, he parsed the sounds. The first voice, he knew as well as his own.

Miri. His sister was safe. Then he heard *her* voice and knew his prayers had been answered.

"Mmmm . . . " he managed, unable to form Morgan's name on his lips.

When his eyes opened, Alex found two faces within his field of vision: his sister's and his lover's. Both wore an exhausted "thank God he's alive" expression.

"Hey, look, he's awake," Miri said, a smile busting out. "I told you he wasn't going to give up."

Morgan blinked away tears. "What is it with you, Parkin? First you nearly drown. Then you get blown up. You got a damned death wish or something?"

"I'm a damned white knight, don't you know?" he said. Then coughed hard, which proved not to be a smart idea. Sharper points of pain came from his right leg and thigh. Given all the debris the explosion had generated, he was lucky he hadn't been staked to the ground like a vampire.

"So what's the damage?"

Morgan leaned back, somber now. "Your right leg got speared by a piece of wood. It was a mess, but they got it cleaned up, and so far there's been no infection, which is pretty amazing, since we were both covered in a lumberyard."

"And you?"

"A mild concussion and some cuts and bruises. Nothing big."

Like hell. Anything that harmed this woman was huge in his eyes.

"They kept you under to let you rest. They wanted to ensure that you weren't suffering from any side effects from your near drowning."

He remembered waking up every now and then, ever so briefly, but then he'd go down again. Considering all they'd been through, they'd both been more than lucky.

Miri gave him a kiss on the forehead. "I love you, bro," she said, her eyes brighter now. "Glad to see you're back among us." She studied the pair of them. "I'm . . . going to get . . . something to drink. I'll be back."

Then it was just the two of them.

"Not subtle at all," he mumbled.

"She gets that from her big brother."

"Dennis and the Buryshkins are dead?" he asked.

"Yes," Morgan replied. "Forensics found some body parts, and they're still figuring out who those belong to."

"So one of them could still be alive," Alex said. Like crazy Anya. Because those kinds of people seemed to have nine lives.

"No one came out of the back of the building. Neil made sure of it."

Then it was over, and Dennis was really gone.

"Damn," Alex muttered.

Now he understood what Crispin had meant when he said Alex didn't know the whole story. Apparently Veritas's head honcho had suspected that Dennis had his own reasons for working with the Buryshkins.

A sister. Alex had made a deal with those bastards for the same reason: keeping Miri alive. He'd just had a stronger team on his side.

"I want to know when Dennis's funeral is. I need to be

there. And Alicia should know too. Whether she attends is her decision."

"I'll find out for you," Morgan said. "The district attorney and one of the bigwigs from the DEA opened the safe-deposit box yesterday. Lars was there too, just to make sure everyone was being above board. They're still going through all the evidence. Initial word is that there's enough to get your conviction overturned."

To his embarrassment, his eyes clouded over. What could he say? There was no way he could repay Dennis now. "He shouldn't have done that."

"He ran out of hope. We all do sometimes."

"Not all of us. I had someone who gave a damn."

"It went both ways." Morgan gently kissed his lips. "Parkin?"

"Yes?"

"You ever do something that insane again, I will kill you myself."

Alex grinned. "I'll try to rein in my superhero tendencies just for you."

Tears glistened, then her arms went around him, tight and warm and full of love. When she began to sob, his tears joined hers.

✦ ❖ ✦

September 29th
Hotel St. Sebastian

Still using a cane, his injured leg aching, Alex made the slow journey to see Crispin Wilder. When invitation had been issued, he knew it would be unwise to refuse it. He owed this guy everything.

His brain was still buzzing from the call he'd received from a DEA hotshot in Washington just that morning. The man had offered him a half-assed apology, during which Alex had resisted the desire to tell the jerk to go screw himself.

Instead, he'd suggested that the agency should do a better job of policing their own. No surprise, the call had ended shortly after that. Clearly the people at the top didn't care what he thought, just as long as he didn't file a lawsuit against their sorry asses.

He tapped on the door to Crispin's hotel suite, the same one as before. Apparently the management didn't have a problem with assassination attempts when the man paying the bills was rich and well mannered. After the locks were disengaged, the door opened to reveal Wilder himself. He held a 9mm down by his side.

"Alex, thank you for coming," Crispin said, beckoning him into the room. It was only the two of them today, which told Alex this was something different than just a "thanks for all your help" sort of chat.

Once the door was secured, Crispin set the gun aside and gestured toward a pair of chairs. "Let's sit by the window. More light there. I need to get away from the work to let my head clear."

A quick glance at the suite's dining room table revealed that work—a laptop computer and a legal notepad filled with notes. From what Morgan had told Alex, her boss always had a full background study completed on every potential mission. Veritas couldn't take them all on, so Crispin chose the ones he felt had the best chance of success. When he was conflicted, he asked the other members of Veritas's board to weigh in. Exactly who those folks were was strictly "need to know." Even Morgan wasn't privy to the names.

They settled in the chairs near the window.

"Aren't you worried your enemies will come after you again, since they obviously know you're staying here?" Alex asked.

"Predictability is an issue for me. I love this hotel, so my enemies know I stay here. I'll have to change it around next time, or life will be boring."

"And if they manage to take you out?"

"There is always someone waiting in the wings to take my

place," Crispin replied.

"The king is dead, long live the king?"

"Just like that, but with less pomp and circumstance."

It was an interesting notion. "Is that why you gave up gunrunning? Changing it up?" When Crispin didn't immediately reply, Alex realized he might have overstepped. "If that's a sensitive subject, I apologize. Truth is, I'm curious, because it'll give me an idea of why you're heading Veritas. You have to admit, it's a big leap from one job to the other."

Crispin rose and poured himself two fingers of a dark amber Scotch. He raised the bottle and gave Alex a questioning look.

"Yes, thanks, but half that. I'm a lightweight now."

Crispin returned with the glasses, took his seat, and crossed his legs. His shoes were neatly polished, but it looked as though they weren't new. More like a comfortable pair he was loath to part with.

Another curious facet of this most curious man.

"Your question is one I don't usually answer. But in this case we share something in common, the fact that I started over and you will need to do the same." Crispin sipped the liquor, then leaned back in the chair.

"It is easy for one man . . . or woman . . . to say his actions have little consequence in this world, because it gives them a convenient out. But it's not true. It doesn't matter if you work at a 7-Eleven or if you're an arms merchant, you make an impact on society. Admittedly, the latter more than the former, but we all contribute either by enforcing the rules of that society, or by breaking the bonds that hold us together as humans."

"So you were a very substantial chaos generator?"

Crispin shook his head. "I was Death's very gifted apprentice, minus the robe and scythe. I cannot possibly guess how many people died because of my activities."

Alex tilted his head. "It could be argued that someone else would have done the same job with similar effect. You were fulfilling a need, hideous though it was. Not that I'm condoning it, mind you."

"No, but another wouldn't have been as efficient. I was particularly adept at my trade," Crispin said, his voice full of bitterness. "Now, I'm adept at balancing the scales, making those who hurt others pay the price, if possible."

"Then you're still Death's apprentice, in a different way."

Crispin pondered that. "Yes, I guess I am," he replied, smiling slightly. "I'd like you to work for us, Alex. Though you don't think you have skills, you do. You speak passable Russian, you know the drug trade, you think like a criminal. And—this is the most important part—you have a conscience."

"Let me guess—if I hadn't gone in to rescue Dennis, we wouldn't be having this conversation."

"Exactly. The world needs more honorable people, like you and Iceman and Valkyrie. If you had walked away from that hostage situation, I would have known that you put your pride above the life of another. Even the life of a man who betrayed you for his own personal reasons."

"His sister." Crispin nodded. "Did you know Dennis had double-crossed the Buryshkins when Morgan and I went into the house?"

"No, I did not. I expected the problem to be Anya. Dimitri warned us she was growing increasingly unstable."

"I'm guessing that after I talked to Dennis at the police station, he decided to break free of the Russians. I had no idea he'd been keeping my 'get out of jail free' records for years."

"That's my assumption as well. What do you think will happen now that Vladimir Buryshkin is out of the way?"

Alex took a long sip of his Scotch, letting it burn its way down to his belly. "It's going to go to hell. I doubt that Grigori will take his uncle's position—it's not his goal in life—and with Anya gone, there will be a substantial power vacuum."

"I agree. New Orleans will suffer through a change of gang leadership, at least in the drug and prostitution trades."

"Los Impíos will try to gain more ground," Alex said. "They'll claim the city as theirs, even if it isn't. Unless they've changed since I was in prison, they're more likely to war among themselves than execute a full takeover. It's going to be ugly for a while."

"Again, I agree. There's already been a change in leadership just in the last couple of days. Miguel de Francisco, the one who sent his men to burn out your sister, is dead. His cousin, Arnaldo, has taken over for the time being. The word we received is that you and Miri are no longer targets."

"Because . . . ?"

"Arnaldo is too busy fighting his own battles to mess with you. Also, he was warned that if they made any further attempts on either of you they would answer to Veritas."

Well, hell.

"He agreed to that ultimatum?"

"He did. He is infinitely smarter than his predecessor." Crispin sighed. "Unfortunately, the power vacuum is going to be felt on the streets. That's the downside of removing a strongman or a dictator. Post-Saddam Hussein Iraq is a good example. He kept the factions in check through a particularly brutal regime, but removing him upset the balance of power. We're still paying for that mistake. Hopefully, we won't have that degree of carnage here."

That comment could only lead to one question. "Did you ever meet him? Hussein?"

Crispin didn't reply, which was an answer of its own.

Alex shifted gears. "So what's your sales pitch?"

"Before I get to that, we owe you something." He walked to the table, retrieved a large manila envelope, and handed it to him. As Crispin settled into his chair, Alex turned the envelope over in his hands. Only his name was on the front.

"What's this?"

"Our agreement was to supply you with all the information we had compiled as to who set you up and how you might go about clearing your name. Events have overrun what's in that report, though some of it might still prove useful when you return to court."

He nodded. "Dennis did our work for us."

"In many ways, yes. Once his sister became gravely ill,

Buryshkin swooped in. The Russian was an expert at exploiting any personal weakness."

"Thank you, anyway. You honored everything you said you'd do for me and my sister. I'm not used to that kind of backup."

"Well, you will be if you join us. We work across the globe, sometimes with the blessing of a country's government, sometimes without their knowledge, or occasionally as their enemies. Our name says it all: truth. We reveal it whenever and wherever we can. We make a small difference, here and there, but at least we are trying."

"Did Veritas exist before you came on board?"

"Yes, on a smaller scale, with limited funds. They made me a job offer, once upon a time."

"You're kidding me," Alex said, stunned.

"No. I was recruited, just as I am trying to recruit you. The first time they made contact, I told them I'd kill them all if they didn't back off. Then . . . things changed," he said, his eyes sadder now. "The second time, I accepted their offer."

"Well, I'll be damned." Alex knew better than to ask what had pushed this man to make that decision.

Crispin set his now-empty glass aside. "The salary is excellent, and the medical and dental have to be, given what you'll face. It's a dangerous commitment that means you might come back in a box, if there's enough left of you to bury. We fight hard. Sometimes we win, sometimes we die."

"That's a helluva sales pitch. What about Morgan? Would I work with her?"

A knowing smile came his way. "What is your status with her?"

Alex weighed his answer. "We've got the start of something good, but need to sort things out. Trust has been an issue for both of us in the past, but it's looking promising. At least for now."

What if Crispin said they couldn't work together? Would he still want the job?

"If she is agreeable to partnering with you, I have no

objections to that or to you sharing a personal relationship. You two are a very strong team. Better than I had hoped, actually."

"Is that why you sent her after me on that stretch of Louisiana highway?"

A nod returned. "I knew you would butt heads, but you did what I'd hoped—you located the cocaine and put an end to Buryshkin's empire."

"We found the dope, but we didn't stop Buryshkin. Dennis did. He should get all the credit."

"Indeed," Crispin said, conceding the point gracefully. "Will you join us?"

Alex drank the remainder of his Scotch and set the glass on the nearby end table. "Let me do some thinking. It's a big step, and I'm not the only one involved."

"Understood. Let me know either way."

They shook hands, and as Alex opened the door to leave the suite, the man who might become his boss returned to the dining-room table, flipped a page on his legal pad, his brows furrowed in thought.

"It never ends, does it?" Alex asked.

Crispin looked up at him, shaking his head. "Evil offers us a perverse form of job security. Personally, I'd rather be unemployed."

Amen.

Chapter Twenty-Nine

October 6th
Superior Court

Alex found himself so nervous he kept fumbling with his tie. It looked like a third grader had tied it, no matter how many times he fussed with the damned thing.

"Here, let me do that," Morgan said, straightening it with her nimble fingers. She was dressed in a severe black suit, a brilliant blue silk top, and black pumps. Her "going to court" outfit, as she called it. They were headed there in a few minutes to see if there was enough evidence to overturn his conviction.

Alex was alternately confident and freaked out. Morgan had tried to calm him down, but nothing much had helped, not even the sex they'd shared in the shower this morning.

"You sure this is going to work?" he asked, probably for the tenth time.

Fortunately, she took it all in stride. "Yes, it'll be fine. Now just chill, okay?"

He sighed. The district attorney had studied the evidence gathered by his ex-partner. It'd been thorough, probably the most comprehensive case Dennis had compiled in his career, his final message from the grave. In it, he admitted to exactly what he'd done over the years, why he'd done it, and who had blackmailed him into doing it. He named names, gave dates, and said where the bodies were buried. Sometimes literally.

As Alex waited in the hallway outside the courtroom, he was relieved not to be alone today. His sister and his friend, Tucker, were present. He had no doubt there would be a tattoo

in Miri's future the way they were talking back and forth. A
short distance away, Neil stood near Alex's new boss.

Crispin gave him a nod and Alex smiled back. It had
been an easy decision to join Veritas—they never left anyone
behind. It would be good to make a difference once again.
Nearby, Senior Special Agent Fredd was texting someone, her
brow furrowed. The job never ended.

"Sasha?" a familiar voice called out. He turned to find
Grigori walking toward him. Ruslan was at his side, his left
arm in a sling.

"My dear friend," Alex said, not caring who saw him
shaking the hand of another ex-con. "Good to see you outside
the walls."

"It is good to see you as well, Sasha. I am pleased you have
survived all that my family visited upon you."

"The same could be said of you as well," Alex replied. He
looked at Ruslan. "How are you doing?"

"Better. And you?" the young man asked, gesturing toward
Alex's leg.

"It's getting there. I don't have to use the cane any longer."
He shot a look at the others, and saw Agent Fredd staring at
them.

Live with it. This man kept me alive.

"I was worried when I heard there'd been a hit on you," he
said to Grigori.

"It was a near thing, but fortunately, someone warned us
that it was going down." Grigori's eyes had drifted to Crispin at
this point. "It made all the difference."

"Dennis called Crispin, didn't he?"

"Yes. Paying off old debts is how it was explained to me."

"Mikhail, is he okay?" Alex asked. "I miss him."

"*Da,*" Grigori said. "He hopes you will visit him someday."

"I intend to, as often as I'm allowed. He kept me sane all
those years. And he taught me a lot of dirty Russian jokes."

Grigori laughed. "He will be pleased to see you." He
looked at Ruslan now. "We were worried that some may object
to us sitting in on your hearing, but I thought we should stop by

long enough to wish you good luck."

Alex felt the warmth behind the sentiment. "Thank you. I really appreciate that. Are you staying here in New Orleans or heading out somewhere new?"

"We are leaving later today. We'll be going to the Mediterranean. Certainly not to our homeland." Grigori reached over, took hold of Ruslan's hand, and squeezed it fondly. "We are not welcome there, not with Mr. Putin in power."

Ruslan muttered a swear word under his breath.

"Who knows, maybe someday he won't be," Alex said.

"All things are possible," he replied. He set his lover's hand free now. "We are headed to Malta first. I have always wanted to study the Knights Templar, and Ruslan will find much to photograph. You must come visit. Bring your lady. We'd be honored to have you stay with us."

"You're on," Morgan said as she joined them. "Thank you for the invitation."

Grigori broke out in a smile. "We shall look forward to it. Ms. Blake, it was good to finally meet you," he said, inclining his head in respect.

"Please call me Morgan. And thank you for watching over Alex all those years," she said. "He means everything to me."

Grigori smiled, then shot a quick look at Ruslan. "I know how that is."

Alex and Grigori embraced.

"*Ee-deete ce Bogom*," Alex said. *Go with God.*

"And you as well," the Russian replied.

The two men walked away, talking quietly among themselves. As they reached a set of doors, Grigori turned and waved. Morgan and Alex returned it.

"They look happy, like they belong together," Morgan observed. She turned as the courtroom door opened. "It's time. You ready?"

He took a very deep breath. "Let's do it, lady."

"No matter what, I love you," she said.

"That's all I need to know."

Morgan could feel Alex vibrating with worry as they entered the courtroom. They sat at the defense table, and she opened her file, the one she'd spent the last week memorizing just in case the district attorney or the DEA decided to be difficult.

She knew Alex probably had nothing to worry about, but she also knew that powerful people often played games with the truth to hide their own failings. Crispin had told her everything was on track, but until the judge delivered the verdict, it was all in the air.

Morgan smiled at her lover, trying to reinforce the courage he needed to face this moment. "It'll be okay," she whispered.

There was no reply, as Alex's eyes remained riveted on the door where Judge Redburn would enter. No doubt, he was flashing back to the day when he'd been found guilty.

The door opened, Alex took a quick breath, and then the clerk called for those in the courtroom to rise. The onlookers came to their feet, then returned to their seats when the judge took his chair. Redburn looked older than the last time Morgan had seen him, at the hospital. Even though his daughter was expected to recover, the shock had still taken its toll.

The judge looked down at them. "Mr. Parkin."

Alex, to his credit, kept his voice free of panic. "Good day, Your Honor."

Redburn addressed the courtroom. "The case before us today is to determine whether there is sufficient cause to overturn the conviction of Alexander Michael Parkin for possession of a Schedule Two narcotic. To that end, both this court and the district attorney's office have reviewed the new evidence." He consulted a sheet. "Mr. Douglas?"

The man rose. "Your Honor. Our office has worked in conjunction with the Drug Enforcement Administration and local law enforcement to review the documentation that was compiled by the late Special Agent Dennis Simms."

"And your conclusion?"

"We have verified every claim in this rather impressive collection of information, and we have come to the conclusion that the cocaine that resulted in Mr. Parkin's conviction was indeed planted by Agent Simms. Further documentation was provided in the form of audio recordings of conversations between Simms and Vladimir Buryshkin, also deceased, wherein the agent was ordered to frame Mr. Parkin. It appears that Mr. Parkin was close to busting a new drug-running operation that Buryshkin had established in Baton Rouge, and they wanted him out of the way."

"Does your office have any objection to vacating the conviction?"

Alex gripped the edge of the table, his hands shaking now. Douglas looked at him. "None whatsoever."

"Then it is the opinion of this court that a miscarriage of justice occurred when the jury, acting on the information they were provided, found Mr. Parkin guilty of this crime. This court vacates that verdict, rendering it null and void, thereby restoring Mr. Parkin's full rights of citizenship."

Redburn leaned forward on his elbows, looking directly at Alex now. "If you were any other man, I would caution you against feeling bitter about what has happened to you, because we both know those years in prison cannot be returned to you. However, your recent actions have shown that you have found yourself on solid ground, and I expect that your future actions will prove this court's decision to be a wise one." He banged his gavel. "Now get out of here, and go have a life."

"Yes!" Alex shouted, pumping his fist. He spun around and grabbed Morgan, squeezing her in a tight embrace.

"Plan on celebrating tonight, lady," he said in her ear. "All night long."

"You're on."

He'd barely made it outside the courtroom when he was mobbed by his sister and his friends. Tucker slapped his back hard, while Miri cried.

Thank you, Dennis. Rest in peace, guy.

Morgan noticed his expression. "Are you okay?"

"Yeah, I'm good."

"You ready to party, Parkin?" Tucker called out.

"Bring it on, dude. Bring. It. On."

Chapter Thirty

The interior of the bar was crowded and raucous, and though this was where Miri had been attacked, she had insisted that it was where they needed to go. She said it was her way of dealing with the memories.

The Veritas crew commandeered a table in the back corner, away from the speakers and the band. The first round of drinks came courtesy of Crispin, and it went on from there. There were jokes, dancing, and then more drinking. It was like a family celebration.

He trusted these people, and they trusted him. It was more than he'd ever expected just out of prison: a good job, good friends, and a woman to love. Whenever he thought about it, his chest tightened and his eyes grew misty.

He was on his second beer and eyeing Morgan, who had stripped off her fancy suit jacket, the fine silk of her blouse caressing her breasts. The sight made him wonder how soon he could spirit her away to begin that night of one-on-one celebration. Because now, he was truly free.

She must have caught the "I want you" glint in his eyes, as she leaned over and whispered, "Meet me in the supply closet in five, okay? It's near the restrooms."

"Ah. Okay."

He had no idea what she had in mind, but watched as she made her way through the other patrons, toward the ladies' room, her shirt moving across her butt in a way that made other guys check her out. One whistled.

Too late. She's mine.

Tucker moved over next to him. "Fine lady you got there.

Pretty, smart, and tough. That's a helluva combo."

"She's a keeper." Alex thought for a moment. "You any good at adding ink to prison tattoos?"

His friend raised an eyebrow. "You got one?"

"Yeah. A blackwork phoenix on my leg. It just doesn't match my life any longer. Needs some color, you know?"

Tucker's eyes followed his, settling on Morgan as she disappeared down the hallway.

"Understood. What colors are you thinking?"

Alex already had that worked out. "Red for passion, yellow for the sun, blue for the water, and green for . . . my Morgan's eyes."

"Stick a fork in you, you are so done, my friend," Tucker said, laughing. "Just call and make an appointment. It's on the house."

"Damn, you're gonna make me wail like a baby if you keep that crap up."

"You are such a wuss," Tucker said, grinning. "Good to have you home, my friend."

"Good to have a life again."

A couple of minutes later, Alex followed in Morgan's wake, skirting around his sister, who was dancing with Sam. She was laughing and having fun, though the guy was probably at least a decade older than her.

Out of the corner of his eye, Alex caught a glimpse of Neil who watched her with more interest than was required, now that the threat was gone. Alex paused by him for a second, feeling the need to play Cupid.

"You know, you could ask her to dance, and I wouldn't rip your heart out for it."

Neil looked up, then shook his head. "Best not to."

"Your choice. Great girl. I know she can hold her own with you."

The barest hint of a smile came to Neil's lips. "No doubt about that. That's why it's not a good idea."

"Your loss."

After a quick trip to the men's room, Alex located the

supply closet. Hoping no one saw him, he ducked inside. The light was on, and at the back of the small space was Morgan, her silk blouse partially unbuttoned to reveal her glorious cleavage.

"Lock the door," she said, her voice husky and full of promise.

He fumbled behind him to see if there was a lock. To his surprise, there was a slide bar, and he pushed it across. There were fresh wood shavings where the lock had been installed, which made him wonder if Morgan had had something to do with it.

She beckoned to him with her finger. As he walked toward her, his body screamed that this was *his* woman, and he wanted her *now.*

"Hi. My name is Morgan," she said in a low whisper.

"And what's a hot lady named Morgan doing in a supply closet?"

"A couple things," she said, pulling him closer so he could smell her perfume, and her desire. "First thing? I'm an idiot."

"That's kind of harsh."

"No. I'm an idiot. I spent five years blaming myself for something my husband did. I blamed him for being weak."

"And now?"

"Now I know that we're all weak in one way or another. It all depends on whether we let those mistakes destroy us, or make us stronger."

"What's the verdict?"

"That I'm stronger when I'm with you. That you make me feel alive, and I want that for as long as I can have it."

"I concur. What's the other thing? You said there were a couple."

She undid the remaining buttons on her silk shirt, revealing a black lace bra, her nipples straining against the fabric. His mouth went dry.

"I've always wanted to have scorching sex with a hot guy in a place like this. You game, Parkin?"

His mind reeled as his blood heated. What the hell had he

done to deserve such an amazingly sexy woman? "Hot, fast, and hard?"

"You got it. We can do slow, sensual, and sultry later."

"Definitely sensual and sultry later. But right now . . . "

He skimmed his hands across her breasts, rubbing hard across the beaded nipples, and then down her thighs. He pressed his burgeoning erection against the sweet spot between her thighs.

His hands reached under her skirt and only found soft skin. Her panties were gone.

"Jesus, Morgan. Do you know what you do to me?"

"I suspect I'm about to find out," she said, undoing his belt, then pulling down the zipper. The pants fell to his knees.

Pulling her up against him, he felt the warm wetness that told him she was ready for him. "You're going to kill me one of these days."

"Not yet, baby. Not yet."

She tugged down his briefs and then he was home, driving inside her with a power that he never knew he possessed. Every stroke made her moan, her nails digging through his shirt.

Her long legs lifted to wrap around his waist.

"Harder," she cried. He shifted so every stroke rubbed against just the right spot. She sucked in air, shaking in his arms, then screamed as an orgasm surged through her, the sound lost in the noise of the bar and the band.

Her muscles tightened around him, pushing him higher, then kicking him over the edge. Alex cried out her name as his release tore through him, lifting him so high he didn't know if he could ever find his way down.

Even after he stopped moving, she was still moaning, rubbing against him. He knew what she wanted, and a few more thrusts brought her another body-shaking orgasm. Finally, she slumped against him. He remained inside her, not ever wanting to leave.

"Jesus, Alex. You're going to kill me one of these days."

He laughed as his own words came back to him.

"Let's test that theory, okay? Give it a few years. Decades.

See how it goes. You game?"

Her eyes rose to his, and he could tell the instant she realized what he'd just suggested. "Decades, huh?" she asked. He nodded. "Yeah, I'm game. Because who else is going to keep you alive and happy?"

"No one, baby. No one but you."

"Then let's do it. You and me," she said, touching his face.

"I love you, Morgan. I love you so much."

"And I love you more than I ever thought possible. That frightens me. But it exhilarates me more."

He kissed her, feeling the bonds tightening between them, the ones growing stronger with each passing day.

"We better go. Someone will miss us."

"Come back here exactly a year from now?" she asked.

He laughed as they straightened their clothes. Morgan pulled her black panties out of her purse and slid them on, and he groaned at the sight.

"You got it. Every year, right here. Or the nearest bar, wherever we might be. Until, well, until we can't do it anymore."

"Like that's ever going to happen," she joked.

"Well, maybe when I'm ninety."

"They have pills for that kind of thing," she said, winking.

"God, what have I gotten myself into?"

Morgan laughed and opened the door. As they walked out, Miri strolled by them on her way to the restroom. She looked at the pair of them, taking in their "I just got laid" expressions and the open supply-closet door behind them.

She grinned. "You are so busted, bro," she said.

"I will never hear the end of this," he moaned.

"But it was worth it, right?" Morgan asked.

"With you, lady?" he said. "Always."

His sister took hold of Morgan's arm. "Walk me to the restroom, will you? We need some girl time together."

He knew in an instant that it was because of her attack, how she'd been grabbed in this very hallway. Now she was confronting those fears with typical Parkin chutzpah.

"Sure," Morgan said, understanding as well.

They slid their arms around each other's waists and walked away. Watching them, Alex knew he was truly one blessed man. He'd gotten a second chance at life.

When he returned to the bar he found more than a few envious eyes on him. Crispin raised eyebrow, but kept his expression neutral.

"Get lost, Parkin?" Lars said, grinning. Neil smirked, but held his tongue.

"Not a chance," he said, shaking his head.

I'll never be lost with Morgan at my side.

Epilogue

October 10th
New Orleans

The doorbell pulled Miri from her breakfast. Shanita looked up, but didn't move, still half-asleep. That was one of the best things about having her as a roommate now—she wasn't a morning person, so she didn't talk much.

Since Alex had gone all older brother on her and insisted Miri find a safe place to live, she'd finally allowed him to lend her enough money to move in with her friend. With her new job at a classier bar, she was on her way to paying him back for the loan. Win-win for everyone.

The lady on their doorstep wasn't someone Miri knew. Still skittish after everything that had happened the previous month, she tensed, wondering if the Russians weren't finished with her yet. Then wondering how long it would be before she'd stop worrying about that.

"Are you Miri Parkin?" the woman asked, consulting a sheet in her hand. She was middle-aged, tanned, and sounded like a two-pack-a-day smoker.

"Yes, I am," Miri said.

"Cool. I got a delivery for you." The woman gestured at the pet carrier near her feet.

Shanita shuffled up in her bathrobe, stifling a yawn behind her palm. "What's up?" she asked.

"Ah, a delivery." Miri looked down at the carrier. "What's in there?" A plaintive *meeeoow* came from inside the carrier, answering her question.

"It's a kitten," the lady said, as if that wasn't obvious now. "He's seven weeks old, and he's had all his shots. Here's his paperwork." She slapped a fat envelope into Miri's hand.

"Ah, but—"

"Must be a birthday gift," Shanita piped up.

It *was* her birthday, but . . . "I can't have a cat. Can I?"

"They're cool by me, and the landlord doesn't have a problem with them. We'll just need to pay a pet deposit."

Her friend didn't seem the least bit surprised by all this.

"You did this?" Miri asked, eyeing her. Shanita shook her head. "Alex?" Another shake of her head, but her broad smile told Miri that she knew who had.

Confused, Miri took the pet carrier, because there was no other choice. It was a kitten, for God's sake. No way could she turn one of those cuties away.

"If you need anything, just call the number in the paperwork. Congratulations!"

The pet-delivery lady left Miri standing in her own doorway, wondering what the hell had just happened. As she dream-walked her way back into the apartment, she saw a huge grin on her roommate's face.

If it wasn't her roommate or Alex . . .

Miri set the container on the counter and opened it. A small white, black, and gray kitten stuck his nose out. He had brilliant blue eyes and elegant, long, black whiskers.

"Oh my God, he's beautiful!"

"He's like your other cat," Shanita said. "He's got too many toes."

A polydactyl. Her friend waved an envelope under her nose. Miri snatched it away and tore it open. It took some time for her to decipher the unfamiliar scrawl.

Miri,
This kitten needs someone to love him.
Happy Birthday,

Neil (Iceman) MacFayden

Miri's eyes misted. Neil had remembered her birthday. Of course he had. That man never forgot anything. She scooped up the bundle of soft fur and hugged the squirming creature as if he was the last kitten in the whole world.

"You knew Neil was doing this," she accused.

"Yeah," Shanita admitted. "Your SEAL dude came by a few days ago to see if we could have a cat. He told me what he was up to, and I thought it was just so sweet."

Miri snuggled the little animal, so stunned by Neil's kindness she didn't know how to handle it. It just wasn't something she'd ever thought he'd do for her, especially since he'd avoided any contact with her since the Russian mission.

Kitten ownership responsibilities flooded her brain. "Oh, I have to get cat things and food. It all burned in the house fire."

"No worries. All that stuff is under my bed. He delivered it when you were at work. That's some hunk you got there, my friend."

I wish he was mine. But at least I have a small piece of him now.

Shanita stroked the kitten's head. "So what are you going to call this little guy?"

Miri eyed the note on the counter and smiled. "MacFayden. Mac for short."

Because Neil finally told me his last name.

"Happy birthday, girlfriend." Shanita gave her a quick hug and left her alone with their newest roommate.

"Hey, Mac," she murmured. The kitten looked up at her, batting at her hair with a paw. A throaty purr erupted, causing Miri's tears to fall. "Yeah, you need some love. We all need do."

Even those too proud to admit it.

THE END

Mission Notes

Before Veritas undertakes a mission, a comprehensive background dossier is created to get the "lay of the land". Such was the case for the Buryshkin Crime Syndicate mission, code name CAT'S PAW. Here are some interesting items from that dossier:

The Italian mafia, under the direction of Carlos Marcello (a Sicilian), ruled the streets of New Orleans from the 1940s through the early 1980s. As one confidential informant explained, business back then had strict rules of conduct, gentleman to gentlemen, despite the fact they were managing the drug, gambling and prostitution rackets. Once Marcello died, the Italian mob's control diminished, a vacuum eventually filled by others, including the Russian mafia.

Since New Orleans is a popular convention destination, prostitution is rampant, and the FBI has made arrests related to human trafficking. In 2015, after the police launched an undercover investigation code named Operation Trick or Treat, five French Quarter adult clubs lost their alcohol and tobacco licenses because of prostitution, lewd activities and illegal drug sales.

An informant revealed that when prostitutes were no longer of value to their bosses, some would be taken into the Gulf of Mexico, just into international waters, and thrown overboard, weighted down by chains. Louisiana's coastal waters, swamps and bayous have long served as a convenient dumping ground for corpses.

Cocaine is frequently diluted with everyday substances such as talcum powder or milk sugar to stretch the yield. In 2011, the DEA found that over seventy percent of street cocaine was cut with levamisole, a drug used to kill parasites in humans and livestock. Levamisole has a number of side effects, including plummeting white blood cell counts. It also increases the "high" which is why it is a popular additive.

After review of the background dossier, it was verified the Buryshkin Crime Syndicate presented a significant danger, and not only in terms of their drug and prostitution rings. Certain internal sources warned of a power struggle within the organization, one that might herald a city-wide mafia war.

Based on the information gathered, the mission was approved and Morgan Blake (aka Valkyrie) was assigned to lead it.

About the Author

Jana Oliver never planned to become an author. In fact, she told her sixth grade teacher she wanted to be an international spy, which sounded very cool at the time.

That so didn't happen.

After pursuing various careers (registered nurse, disc jockey, travel agent, copywriter) someone flipped a switch in her brain and stories began to pour out. There were so many stories she decided to write them down and publish them. Then someone else published them, in the U.S. and then all over the world.

She's still surprised by all that.

A few years down the line Jana's an international bestselling author with over twenty books to her credit, and has won over a dozen major writing awards, including the Maggie Award of Excellence, the Daphne du Maurier, National Readers Choice and the Prism Award.

Nowadays she can be found writing her tales in Portugal when not sharing time with her very patient husband and their cranky (ghost) Feline Overlord, Ms. Dali.

www.JanaOliver.com

Also by Jana Oliver

DEMON TRAPPERS® SERIES
Forsaken (formerly The Demon Trapper's Daughter)
Forbidden (formerly Soul Thief)
Forgiven
Foretold
Grave Matters
Mind Games
Valiant Light
Lost Souls
Bitter Magic

TIME ROVERS® SERIES
Sojourn
Virtual Evil
Madman's Dance

VERITAS SERIES
Cat's Paw
Killing Game
Broken Dreams

DRAGONFIRE SERIES
The Circle of the Swan
The Healer's Path
The Summoning Stone
The Lore of Dragons

STANDALONE NOVELS & NON-FICTION
Briar Rose
Dead Easy
Tangled Souls
Socially Engaged: The Author's Guide to Social Media
(co-authored with Tyra Burton)